Lethal Abscission

Gerald Brent Fitzpatrick

This story and characters contained within are fictitious. While certain institutions, agencies or other entities are mentioned, the characters are all fictitious.

ISBN: 978-1-0688942-1-3

FOR JENNIFER

Every person along my path in life has contributed to this publication. Thank you.

Original cover art created by Kaitlyn Goetz.

Abscission: The act of cutting off or separating a part of the original; sudden termination.

1
JUNE 2002

This is for clarity, not vanity.

I suppose it all started June 13. Doesn't have a ring to it, or the fullness of a particular day that makes it one that a person would remember. Doesn't have the connotations of December 7, or November 3, or September 11. It doesn't even have the joy of December 25 attached to it. No, June 13 just doesn't seem like a date that was the beginning of anything but a long hot summer.

In 2002 it was just a day.

In early June, El Nino seemed to have finally made its presence known on the prairies. Winter was so long and cold, many thought that maybe the masses had stopped using hair spray to try to make a hole in the ozone layer of the atmosphere. But the summer proved everyone wrong. Late December to early February, according to Environment Canada, was a record breaker. We went 38 consecutive days without climbing above minus 15 Celsius. Not once. We went below minus 15 a lot. Minus 40 seemed well within reach nearly every day. That was a temperature I remember from my youth, not something that anyone in this part of the world would know anything about. Winters in Poland were the stuff of legends.

Of course, all of that was before we saw the effects of global warming. El Nino, El Nina, and their little brother El Drought-O. It was hard to put a finger on it, but the world had become obsessed with their impacts on us all, even though for most of us, the whole thing just wasn't all that important. Maybe one day it would, but not that day in June of 2002.

Looking back, Kenny really didn't look all that bad a few days before, on June 9. Well, he didn't look too bad, considering what he had been through. There isn't one human being, after being tied to a colostomy bag for the better part of three years, who would see the joy of everyday existence. Somehow Kenny had seen the joy of living, eventually, after being given half a year to live. However, he managed a wee bit longer than that, giving the finger to the experts and living nearly four more years. The bag that hung from the wheelchair had gone full circle in Kenny's perspective. Initially, it had been a ball and chain, the 'thing' that tied him to his wheelchair and to the place we called home. Well, we called it home, but none of us felt at home. It was the 'thing' that forced him from his own home and into this particular residence. Kenny never considered it, and many would agree, it wasn't their home. It was a rest stop.

The bag passed through other stages of uselessness. From being the brunt of a joke, to rejection, to frustration, and finally full circle to acceptance. By the time he reluctantly came to accept the fact that he would have one of these bags tied to him for the rest of his life, other medical setbacks laid a course for his body. The bag seemed to be the least of his troubles.

All those troubles hit home on June 13, when Kenny Hildebrand died. Well, I assume it was the 13th. I had left him laughing just before midnight that evening and when I checked on him the next morning, he was gone. At least his last night wasn't spent alone, in a room surrounded by beeping monitors, and the coughing, moaning and crying of strangers that surround us every day.

To this day, it brings me some solace that the last person to see him, left him smiling.

Sure, he smiled when his family came to see him. Those were short visits twice a year, more out of obligation than any real desire to connect. But for those who knew him, who cared enough to really know who Kenny was, we could see through the thin cardboard smile. There was no doubt the smiles were pasted on, like the, 'Hi, I'm Jinny and I'm a Volunteer' buttons the Women's Auxiliary wear. His smile was an obligation, there because they expected it, not because they earned it. It was pasted on his face and no more. It was a tolerant smile, putting on the show, until they finally left him, his heart monitor, the bag and, most importantly, his money alone.

So, Kenny smiled in a far off, Sound-of-Music, everything-is-rosy sort of way. He watched the heart monitor while they blathered on about their lives, their struggles, their financial crises. They watched the monitor as well, knowing the longer the monitor indicated his ticker was doing what it was supposed to, the longer the wait until the cash was in their bank accounts. So, they were all watching the little green line blipping its way across the screen. Them hoping the noise would stop, and he urging it silently to push along strong. He liked to see the little blip that was his heart beating strong. But like all things in this place, his heart finally broke. I'm sure when his family got the call that Kenny had died, somewhere on the vast web of phone lines, a faint sound could be heard.

"Cha-ching."

Yup, ol' Kenny hung in there, happy to be alive those last few months. Deliriously happy to be tied to a cold steel bed in a single room on the fourth floor of this shithole. Yup, just how happy could he be? Really, really fucking excited. Yes sir.

I always dropped in to see him in the evening, once that old nurse's aide finally got the hint and slinked away into the bowels of the building — her soft, squeaking shoes, not heard again pounding down the polished hallways from one room to the other. Once she was off the floor, the patients had found it took nearly an act of God to bring her or anyone else back to the rooms on the fourth. Sure, there were rules about the minimum number of staff that should be on any given floor at all times. I'm sure every person in the building would know those rules, chapter and verse. But the staff also knew that re-runs of The Dukes of Hazzard were on TNN in the basement cafeteria every single night. So, Kenny and I knew we had some time between their last walkabout until they made the rounds just before their shifts would end at midnight. The two of us had enjoyed those moments alone on the darkened fourth floor of the place we loosely called home. It gave us a chance to talk, to reminisce, to tell lies about the lives we had led.

Heavy accent on the 'had led' part of that sentence.

Towards the end, Kenny couldn't get up from the bed ... hell, he couldn't piss without someone holding

Mr. Limpy over a bowl or making sure it was jammed in the right tube. His bowels were on the downside of fully functional as well. They worked just fine, depending on your definition of fine. If it means they passed shit until they were done, then waited, like some coiled up shit machine, until the next batch came smooshing through with absolutely no control, then yes, they worked just peachy.

I often looked at Kenny as he talked, knowing that I was looking at my future self. The way things were going, I knew at some point in the future, I would be that frail, veiny guy laying in a bed hooked up on both ends waiting the long wait. Wasn't something I was looking forward to in any way, shape or form, but accepted it.

Kenny and I had a running bet on the length of time it took for pork chops and corn to end up in the crapper after making its way through his faulty digestive tract. Lucky bastard usually got it right. Of course, it's his shit machine that the bet was always on. Maybe that was giving him a bit of an edge? I often wondered if the old bastard was bullshitting the fact he had no control over his bowels, just so he could win the loonie pots. Ah, who the hell knows? Right now, it doesn't seem all that important. But if that guy did have some control ... nah. At least it gave us something to talk about other than that fucking '65 Pontiac Lemans he "owned from new and should never have gotten rid of." Blah, blah, blah. I could recite the whole monologue, start to finish, from memory because I've heard it so many times.

But telling the story made Kenny smile, so it wasn't such a bad thing. So, I sat through it time and time again. I just wish occasionally that there was another car he bought in a different year that changed the story up. Just once in a while a new car to hear about. Maybe a '67 'Vette. That would be okay. Hell, I'd even take a piece of shit Polara. That wouldn't be too much to ask, would it? Just once in a while, a story about getting laid by his secretary in a '68 Dodge Polara? Nah. Never happen, the story would always center around the Pontiac, with its silver exterior, turquoise interior and polished silver sport hub caps. Custom ordered from the factory, and according to Kenny, cost more than he made in two years at the Studebaker dealership. Uh-huh.

Oh yeah, I should mention that Kenny and I had a very open and honest relationship. Not much escaped our little talks, embellishments, bullshit sessions or whatever you would want to call them. Not much was considered too secret to talk about, to share between the two of us. No, not much at all. It really was all we had left of the lives we had led.

There are some things though, that a friendship shouldn't bear. Kenny had his secrets I'm sure, because I certainly did. He didn't need to know everything about me. In fact, I am pretty sure he wouldn't want to know everything about my life. There was a lot in my past that no person on this planet was ever going to know. So, maybe it wasn't all that open and honest. But we did share a friendship, which was pretty important in that place.

I heard about Dorothy McNeil and the '65 Pontiac Lemans. She was Kenny's secretary while he worked at the Studebaker dealership in town. Cute little redhead, with a whipping ass, big boobs and loose morals. Dot, as he called her, loved the horizontal polka in the back seat of that fucking Lemans. At least he said so.

"Best car I ever owned," he would always end the

story with. It was the signal that other topics of conversation were now allowed. It was the firm period on that topic.

Personally, I think that Pontiac never made it out of his own back yard. But I would never have told Kenny that. He was a friend. He was a good friend. Truth be told he was the only actual friend I ever had. Ever. In thinking about it now, I suppose in the fullest sense of the word, my ability to actually have a friend was nearly impossible. I knew what they were, pretended a lot of folks over the years were friends, but knew it was just camouflage. They were brought into my sphere as an accessory for an outfit that was worn shortly, then tossed aside. But Kenny remained the longest of any.

So yeah, considering all he went through, he looked pretty good. Still had that little smile. It was the kind of smile that gave you the impression that he knew something he shouldn't. The 'I know, and you know, but I'm not telling' look. Somehow, for that small moment, his mouth appeared to be two decades younger. Considering he was 82 when he passed, that's saying something. Again, I felt a certain amount of satisfaction knowing that his family never really got to see that unique, pure smile. That one was reserved for us and our conversations. So yeah, it was worth it to hear the stories over and over again, the same punchlines, the same damn car. All for that smile.

His blue veined hands laced together on his chest, skin as thin as rice paper with sparkling blue eyes beneath his taped eyelids, Kenny looked just fine. I ambled up to see him as I got to the church. It was good to see him lying on something other than that steel monstrosity of a bed they brought in for him. I half expected to see the heart monitor attached to the lid, a steady green line streaking its way across its width, with a large '0' indicating that his heart had finally said enough is enough. That large '0' telling his family that yes, the flood gates to the bank accounts were finally open and it was time to party.

He looked good, even though Kenny's hair was parted the wrong way, and the colour of his skin was off just a little, like an old sepia-coloured photograph. The funeral director naturally assumed the bleached-out tones of the picture, which must have been taken in 1966, were in fact what he looked like last Thursday. I suppose pictures taken while he could still do his own hair, or even make it to the shitter on time, weren't the full, happy perspective they were looking for. You can be sure that the makeup artists didn't want you to look as you were the last few days leading up to your death, so an old picture would suffice.

But all in all, Kenny looked pretty good.

The service went well. I guess. I didn't really listen because most of it I had heard before. Maybe not the exact same, but close enough that I could let my mind wander a little. Counting Kenny, this was the thirteenth funeral I had been to since I moved into Pinetree. Thirteen lives gone. Stamped out in a sterile environment of patient care. More than that had died in the four years I have lived here, but I didn't know them. I had come to the funerals of 13 of my casual acquaintances.

So yes, I had heard of his unending devotion to church and family, the years in the Elks, the Legion, or the Masonic Lodge, or whatever group had corralled him. I had heard of his three children, one now dead, two others scattered from one end of the country to the other. His son, wife and grandchild were in attendance. Well, at least 50 per cent of the family had made the trip.

The service though wasn't without humour. A comment by the priest about Kenny's eternal love and devotion to his wife, Edith, had brought a barely contained lurch of laughter out of my throat. My chuckle earned a couple of well-placed "Shush" in my direction. After all, this was a solemn occasion, not to be sullied with humour in any way. Only tears of sadness and loss were welcomed in this hallowed place. No tears of laughter. Nope, just not acceptable.

Except now.

Eternal love and devotion? What planet was this guy on? According to Kenny, his wife wasn't the warmest bowl of chili in the neighbourhood. Years married to man who didn't advance out of the Studebaker accounting department had turned her bitter and dark. Kenny was the first to admit he just loved his job. It paid well, had Dot at his beck and call, and allowed him to keep her in the fashion she really enjoyed.

Edith — Christ, even the name is enough to evoke swimming images of a wicked witch. She was originally from the lower mainland in British Columbia. He had met her at a dance in Vancouver, where he was working for some dealership or other. It was lust at first sight. Kenny said, "That was the last time I ever let my little head do the thinking for the big one buddy." He would smile and add, "no brains that little guy, but lots of gusto." We would both laugh at that.

Kenny figured she always wanted to move back to British Columbia, not happy with the long, cold winters in Manitoba. Each year she had to plug in the car, Pontiac or Studebaker, was another year of resentment against him for dragging her east to the prairies. It didn't matter that Kenny loved it here, she was infected with hate for the place. That hatred pulled their relationship apart, in all aspects, part of which drove Kenny to Dot and the back seat of the Lemans in the first place.

So, when Kenny turned 82 last year, Mrs. Olson from 3C came in and did Kenny a favour. She had her teeth pulled way back in 1955 as was the fashion of the time. She also suffered from a progressively bad case of Parkinson's which made her handwriting basically illegible. But that disability helped significantly in other areas. Or so I've been told. So, after that warm July evening there were no more complaints out of Kenny about never getting laid. He was leaning back in his bed the next morning when I came in, his left arm tucked neatly behind his head, and a far away glassy look in his eyes. If he could have smoked, there would have been a Royal Albert hanging from his lips. Kenny looked very pleased with himself.

Mrs. Olson even left a birthday card on the table. "Happy Birthday Ken, all my love, Connie." At least that is what the two of us figured it said. But really you couldn't tell what was written in the card, it looked more like a Spirograph came off the wheels. But it made us laugh even harder as we made up the words that she 'probably' had said. Or maybe not.

No, there was no more talk about sex after that birthday. That topic moved into the realm of things he and I never talked about again. Thankfully. Too bad he had died a month short of his next birthday. Just 32 days more and Mrs. Olson would have left another birthday card for my friend. God really does move in mysterious ways.

I heard Connie had already bought the card.

Kenny's family sat in the front row, looking properly bereaved in their dark clothing, flaccid makeup, and pasted down hair styles. It was half of a pew of bland, grey tourists who had picked the wrong spot to rest and relax. It was announced at the beginning of the service that the daughter and her family who lived in Toronto couldn't make it. You know...life.

Watching the son in attendance was interesting though. From my vantage point three rows back and to his right, I could see his eyes darting from the open casket to the gold watch on his arm. I know it was gold, because that same watch had sat in his father's room on the credenza for as long as I've known him. A retirement gift from the dealership he ended his career at. Probably not real gold but had to be worth something for the kid to hang onto it. From what Kenny told me, his kids didn't hang on to anything of value. Rather, they hungrily appreciated it for what it could bring them in the way of money. Cash for his kids made the world go around. The watch, at least for the boy was representative of all the money waiting for him in some far away bank account. It didn't really matter as a watch. I guessed how well it kept time wasn't an issue for him either. I suppose it mattered a little so he could make sure he got to the pawn shop before it closed. The watch definitely wouldn't be making the trip all the way across town to have it appraised at the antique shop. Nope, straight to the pawn shop at the end of the block.

As the service dragged on, the son's eye movements sped up, alternating quickly between the two icons of his father: the body and the watch. It must have been a terrible position to have been in. He was forced to go through this one-hour-long piece of hell, in order to get the tens of thousands of dollars tucked away in safe keeping for him and his sister. The boy must have been thinking it was cruel to make a person go through all of that formality and was probably a little jealous and pissed off that he hadn't thought of a way out of the funeral trip. I'll bet he thought they should hand out the money first, then hold the funeral. At least that way you can decide if it's worth attending or not. From the look on his son's face, and that of his wife, no amount of money could have been worth the time in the church.

Kenny's funeral was worth going to for me because he was my friend. All I was going to get out of it, was the memories he and I made together. Unlike the other 13 services I had attended, this one meant something more than just a day out. It meant my only friend in the world had gone and I would miss him.

Once Kenny was in the ground, we all went back to the church, and into the basement for the lunch. I meandered my way over to the family's table with my hands full of dainties and a Styrofoam cup of coffee, to perform the obligatory function of wishing them all the best in this terrible time of loss. They were silent, not even talking with each other as I walked up. I sat down the dainties and coffee with a single motion and stuck my hand in the direction of the bewildered son, Josh.

"My name is Ivan McDonald. I live in the same home as your father did. Sorry about your loss, Josh," I said, as I pumped his hand hard. "Kenny was a good man. We are all going to miss him."

As I spoke, Josh lowered his eyes to the table that the kitchen staff had filled to overflowing with little 'bite-wiches', coffee and tea in actual china and other better-looking morsels than I normally got at Pinetree.

"Thanks Ivan. Dad talked a lot about you." He shifted his gaze across the sea of food and grey hair to the priest who had ingratiated himself to their table and was filling his porcelain plate with as much food as it could hold. Both Josh and I watched, as the man said a silent prayer over the food, then dived in. "Uh, Ivan?" Josh said hesitantly.

I looked up at him with wide eyes that said "Uh-huh."

"Do you know how long family members are supposed to stay at these things?" He shifted his whole body away from the priest, steering me away from my coffee cup and dainties. He obviously didn't want the man of the cloth to hear what he was saying, yet I knew from the way he had held himself at the service he really didn't give a shit. "I mean, we have buried dad and all. We don't really have to stay do we?"

I just stared at him. I probably looked like an idiot, eyes wide open and my mouth hanging slack. What did the doctor say during his regular weekly rounds? Oh yeah, "Looked like that medication was finally kicking in."

"I, uh..." I didn't have a clue what to say to this moron. What could you say? He had to be shitting me. 'How soon until they can leave?' No way! The guy they just dropped into the ground brought this ungrateful asshole into the world. Paid for those stained, greasy teeth and the education he vaguely received. The man they put into the ground, not an hour ago, helped to raise him, took him on family holidays to the mountains or fishing, played baseball with him and paid for a Christmas tree full of presents.

The guy he was referring to, was his dad and he wants to know how soon to get out of Dodge.

"It's just that our son is getting a little anxious, you

know how teenagers are."

I was about to tell him that I never really got around to have any children, when he took a breath and kept on talking.

"The service was great, and the lawyers are going to look after everything for us on this end, so there really isn't much for us to do here." He didn't have to tell me that meant sending the cheque for all the money that was left over after the funeral expenses were paid. "But we have a long flight ahead of us. And then it's back home and to the world."

It was all such bullshit.

Where we were standing was an easy 20-minute drive to the airport and the flight would be no more than three and a half hours. So, even with some airport delays because of increased security, missed connections or what have you, Josh, his wife and snot-nosed rug-rat would be back home in four and a half hours. Back home in time to catch a re-run of Friends or Seinfeld. Ready to 'face the world.' Whatever the fuck that meant I didn't have a clue. But he soon made it abundantly clear.

"I mean, sorry, but you old people don't really have a clue about what is going on out there, do you? No offence." I held up my hands in defence to show that I took none — but really, I did. I really took offence. He was implying that once you hit the magic age of retirement, they sucked out all your brains and made you eat pudding all day long, all the while laid out in a La-Z-Boy sleeping your days away. And you would smile in that chair because at least you were getting pudding.

I mean Jesus Christ. What an idiot.

Josh shook his head. "I mean, mortgage payments, kid in school and sports, wife on the booze." He dropped his eyes rapidly when he let that comment flow. I watched him quickly swivel his head to see if his wife was about to shove a plateful of dainties up his ass. But she was far too busy staring at her hands and her own watch. Josh was obviously a guy who didn't really turn on the grey cells before he opened his mouth to speak. "Well, you get the idea, right?"

"Oh, I'm with you one hundred per cent Josh." I nodded in a façade of agreement. "One hundred per cent."

I looked around the room to see more than a hundred people in the entire goddamn basement that I would rather spend time with other than this little puke. Funny thing was, the first person I saw was my proctologist and didn't really feel a great desire to slide my ass over to his table, but would still take five minutes with him over Josh. I turned back to Josh and smiled. It was my best smile. It was one I had practiced in a mirror daily since I was 16 years old. It was the only smile I had. Some people didn't like it when they saw it, because they knew it was empty -- cold. I am pretty sure he didn't like it either. For some reason I found some righteousness in my back pocket and spoke up.

"I think there are a lot of people here in this room that really liked your father, Josh. These are people that want to say hello to you. It would mean a lot to them if you stayed for a while. You can always catch a later flight or stay the night. There are a couple of hotels only a block from here."

Josh looked like I had just informed him that all of his front teeth were infected with small worms, and that the only thing we could do is pull them out, without any freezing.

"I don't think so Ivan. Uh, we have to get back, I

have important work waiting for me."

I shook my head in amazement. "I suppose you do Josh," I observed. My head was still shaking when my mouth opened again. "But right now, don't you think that these people need you, just a little more than what's waiting for you back home. Just one day, even just another hour." I couldn't believe I was almost begging him to give us a little more time. It was weird, because at the same time I was wanting to get him as far away from me as possible. I backed away from him a foot, because his ungrateful stink was overwhelming everything.

"But," he looked over at his wife who happened to be a reincarnation of Josh's mother, Edith. I guess it's true that children do psychologically marry their parents. Her gaze at the man standing next to me, tolerant and forced, told me all I needed to know. "But we have a flight booked for about an hour from now." He was still looking at her. "We, uh, I thought it wouldn't take this long. You know, the service and the burial and all." He looked at his father's watch incredulously. "I mean, it's going on two hours now. Who'd have thought it would take this long? I didn't. I don't mean any disrespect, but we have to go. Time is tight now to get on the plane, you know, because of the security."

"Josh" — I tried as diplomatically as I could — and it should be noted here, that diplomacy was never my strong suit. "You have to understand. This is important to us." I swept my hands around the room. "It's of great consequence to those people who knew and loved him, your father. This is an important time for us. It should be an important time for you too. It's a time to say goodbye to an old friend. To make new friends. To remember."

Again, I was begging this guy. Truth be told, I hated myself a little for doing that. I still do.

He looked at his wife, whose stare now entered the realm of pure, iced hatred. Somehow her makeup had blanched even more than it was at the beginning of the day. He turned back to me, and leaned forward to bring us into an intimate, personal situation. Josh took a deep breath. "Well it's important to you people, because you're old, and it's all you've got!" He stopped for a moment, perhaps, I thought, to apologize for what he just said, once again speaking without thinking. But he seemed to be just catching his breath. "I mean shit, what else do you have Ivan? Bingo. Fish Fridays? What the fuck do you have? You're old!"

Now as you may have gleaned already, I'm not one to go short on the foul language. But there is a rule about respecting your elders that I kind of hold on to. It's entrenched into society, or at least I thought it was. I mean, I won't even say the big word to Harry Carpenter in 2H, and hell, he's only 91. I respect Harry, I respect the extra years he has on me. I don't cross that line -- ever. And that little shit Josh didn't just cross the line but leapt over it. And he dared to cross it at his father's funeral.

"What the fuck do I have?" I spat back at him. Something in his lifeless brown eyes told me that my little retort caught him completely off guard. Pushing my advantage, I took a step forward, forcing him back towards his wife with just my index finger poking almost through his fatty chest. When he bumped into the table, edging it back a couple of inches and making all the silverware tinkle, I reached down and picked up my coffee, dainties and anger and turned away. One or two people gave me some space as I walked down the aisle. They were looking at me, then Josh, then down to their toes. I suppose they heard my little outburst. I didn't have to look at the priest to know he was mentally jotting down my name on his 'home visit' list for this week. I was sure he was thinking that the illness of aging had finally caught up with that heathen Ivan McDonald. Time to slip in the 'God forgives all' shit and collect some of my money so I can be rest assured of a spot in heaven.

I smiled as I rushed towards my seat, "Just let him try and save my soul," I thought as I finally got to where my coat was hanging over the back of the plywood seatback. "I don't think that guy has the time to mess with my soul," I snickered. "But let him bring it on."

"What was that, Ivan?" Mary asked.

I hesitated for a moment, not really sure if I said what I was thinking out loud. But I must have. "Nothing Mary, just a little pissed about that kid of Kenny's." I made the standard imitating face, "How long is long enough before I can get out of here, back to civilization, collect my inheritance, and forget there ever was a Pinetree Retirement Center." Mary laughed at the line. "What an idiot."

"How many times have we heard that before, Ivan? Five?" she wondered, "Ten?"

"More than I care to remember. What ever happened to respect your elders?"

Mary squeezed my arm. "They respect you about as much as you respected yours. It's just that you mouthed off to them in private, behind closed doors. They don't have any of that tact Ivan. It seems today, any place is a good place to show disrespect."

"I suppose you are right," I thought as I popped the first of the small cookies in my mouth. "It just pisses me off. Kenny was a good guy." I stared down at my hands, suddenly missing my friend very much. "It's his day today."

I stared back at the family through the sea of bobbing heads, laughter, unsolicited burps and slurping of tea. They were all now staring at their watches intently, ignoring everyone around them. I figured they were calculating that if they left right now how many martinis could they get in at the airport bar before they were on the big eagle out of here.

"But that kid was such an asshole," I said with an exaggerated stage whisper. Mary laughed into her napkin, glancing quickly around the table to make sure no one else had heard, especially Connie Olson, who was one of the biggest blabbermouths ever. I looked down the table and saw Bernie talking to a bunch of other ladies, her mouth just bobbing along like the batteries were just topped up.

"I wonder if she kisses her mother with that mouth?" I asked as I thought of the smile on my friend's face after his 82nd birthday gift. Quite a way to make a mark.

"Sorry Ivan, what was that?"

"It's okay, I was just talking out of place," I patted her hand as I spoke.

Mary leaned into my shoulder and spoke in a whisper, "Not you Ivan McDonald. You never speak out of turn, do you?"

I leaned back into her. "Not today, Mary." We both laughed and it felt good to put to bed a little of the emotions that seemed to be filling up my head. The headache that was threatening to bounce into my head seemed to back off a little as we laughed at the table, sharing jokes and memories with our neighbours. I told a couple of off-colour jokes to the assembled folks. Most people appreciated them except for the

Carnegies, who were sitting directly opposite us at the long paper-topped table. They attended the late afternoon church services every Sunday at Pinetree's little in-house chapel. They religiously gave away fifty dollars to the member of the clergy each and every week to ensure their place of honour. Of the 20 or so people at the table, only those two thought the jokes were totally off base. But Kenny would have liked them, so I didn't give a shit what they thought in their little pious world. The jokes were for Kenny and for my head space anyway. A pair of noble causes if I ever heard of them.

In about ten minutes, Josh, his wife and kid looked around once more, checked their damn watches in unison, stood up and started making preparations to head for the door. However, as they rose, a sudden flood of action filled the room. The seniors in attendance pushed their chairs back in a wild chorus of squeals as the metal legs were drawn across the forty-year-old linoleum. People started to shove the last morsels of food in their mouths quickly, and line up at the only exit door from the basement, blocking the bereaved family's path to freedom. They were bombarded with handshakes and folks saying, "I'm sorry." As Mary and I chatted, it was satisfying to see the heartful outpouring of grief and caring directed towards that bozo and his off-lings. I could see their eyes darting down the line that nearly snaked around the room, all those people wanting their ten seconds with the three of them.

The wife's face was frozen in an evil, wicked smile. His was less harsh, but no less hateful. The boy just melted away from the hands that were reaching out to ruffle his hair or just to talk. It must have been torture for him, the little anti-social worm. After a few minutes, he looked at his watch, his mom followed his eyes towards the small face on his wrist, made an even more sour look and both of them seemed to deflate visibly. Then they looked at Josh, still trapped by well-wishing hands and blue hair. I am pretty sure if they could have figured it out, they would have left him there, surrounded by all this heartfelt sadness.

"Missed your plane, you miserable little fuck." I nodded my head and smiled as Josh looked unhappily in my direction. "Yeah you, fuck you," I made the words large with my mouth so he could figure out what I was saying.

My elbow nudged into Mary's arm, "Come on Mary, let's go up and say goodbye to the bereaved."

Mary looked up at the long line of people. Now almost as many were waiting in the impromptu reception line as were sitting. Each was talking animatedly to their neighbour, waiting for the family to work their way down to them. More of the attendees were crowding into the line to make sure they got to meet them. A couple of the heavyweight eaters took some small sandwiches with them on paper plates or napkins to snack on while they waited. It was a good thing they did that, I thought, otherwise they might waste away during the ten minutes they had to stand up.

"Are you sure Ivan? There's a long lineup of people. We might be there a while."

"That's okay," I said, pulling her chair out for her, "we've got all day." I grabbed her elbow and led her towards the reception line, whispering into her ear, "And all night, too my darling."

Mary nudged back into me, her hand gently whisking past my thigh, "You are a wicked man, Ivan McDonald." She smiled and nodded to a lady who pushed her chair out in front of us and started to apologize. “I like it, a lot. But you are wicked just the same.”

“It’s a dirty job ma’am, but I am good at it. Unless of course you have an objection?”

“Uh-huh,” she replied, as we started to slowly edge our way to the line. “Objections? Would they do any good Ivan? Or would your silver tongue just override any possible roadblocks I put up?”

My hand accidently brushed against her breast. “If you say no ma’am, that is as far as anything will go. You have my word as a member of the honourary society of senior citizens.”

“Your word?”

“My word. Good as gold.”

“So, your word that you didn’t mean to rub against me just there, is good. You didn’t purposely try to touch me?”

My smile was barely contained. “I can’t believe you’d think I would do something that forward and, in a church, yet. That hurts me, Mary. That hurts me that you would think that of me.”

Mary pushed her upper torso against me, and once again her breast and my arm brushed delicately. “Uh-huh,” was her response, but the smile told the entire story.

It was 20 minutes of nice-nice with the fruitcake couple next to us, before we finally could smell the evil of her royal bitchness getting close to us. Josh’s wife’s demeanour showed me that her temper was nearly on the edge of violence. The ice-cold smile was set with a quicklime of pure venom. She darted her hand into the next person’s without even looking up to see who it was. She simply didn’t care. A one-second flash of skin to skin and then she withdrew her hand, crossing both into the safety beneath her armpits. Safe for a moment from liver spots, clinking jewelry and good intentions.

Josh wasn't much better. No eye contact, a millisecond of time tolerating a handshake with the thick line of well-wishers and a quick peek at the watch. It was actually, quite impressive, the personal discipline it took to shake a hand, and in a smooth, almost imperceptible move, check his watch and let out a frustrated breath of air. You wouldn't have noticed it, unless you looked for it. To the casual observer, each check of his watch would seem like the first. Not the one hundred and third. But no one noticed, as they were focused on that moment of time with the Hildebrand family. They talked about Kenny and their individual remembrances of him. With that small physical intimacy with the family, they shared a private moment that was repeated through every person in the lineup.

Though my date and I were ten feet away, I was sure I heard Tom Murphy tell Josh the Lemans story. I'm sure it was the cleaned up, family rated version. Well, it may have been cleaned up. Murphy has early-stage Alzheimer's and sometimes forgets he is in mixed company. It can be a little funny, the things that he will spurt out. It's a little scary, too, to be honest. I tried to think quickly of the stories I had told with Murphy in attendance. I knew some things wouldn't have been talked about, but I just wasn't 100-per-cent sure of what I did say to him. Murphy used to be an ordained Protestant minister which meant the off-coloured flavour of stories were even funnier when he told them. The disease rotted away his ability to see good and bad, tactful and rude.

Or maybe he just doesn't give a shit because he's

pissed off that he has Alzheimer's. He knows he has it and can't do a damn thing about it, so what the hell. Either way it was a fifty-fifty shot that the story came out without the secretary.

Well maybe sixty-forty; judging by the look that Josh gave him. Yup, that deer in the headlights look. Murphy told him about the secretary. The dirty minister was laughing his brains out at the story and Josh just stared in disbelief.

I looked at the son, standing awkward and still. "See what you would have missed if you'd left early. Ya little shit."

"Pardon," asked Mary.

"Sorry Mary, no nothing. Just thinking out loud." I pulled her a little closer. "Sorry."

"Nothing to apologize for." Mary suppressed a laugh, and leaned into my shoulder, close to my ear. "But every time I hear that story about the Lemans and the secretary," she giggled, looking at Murphy who was still laughing. "It's hysterical. Especially to hear a man of the cloth tell it."

I was genuinely surprised. "You know that story?"

"Sure, who doesn't?" She laughed again.

"Who told you?"

"It was Agnes Pierson in 4D. Must have been, I don't know, a year and a half ago. We were doing Christmas crafts in the sitting room." She giggled again. I love her laugh. "Dorothy Maitland laughed so hard, her tea came out of her nose. Now that was funny."

"You guys told that story while you were making Christmas decorations?"

"Yes." She looked up at me. "Why?"

"Christmas decorations? Isn't that a sacrilege or something?" I couldn't believe it. "I mean aren't you guys going to hell for that?"

"What century are you in Ivan?" Mary pushed me a little towards the grieving family. I hadn't noticed the line had shuffled a couple of steps. "Going to hell. What about all the stories you and Kenny used to tell one another. I mean, if going to hell were on the agenda, you two are halfway...." She looked up at me with big wide eyes, and a mouth, curled open in horror. Her hands immediately covered her lips and her eyes darted around her. "I can't believe I said that."

"It's okay."

"No, I can't believe I said that..." she held up her hands to make the point, "…here. Now."

"It's okay. He's not going to hell honey." I leaned into her, "It was all bullshit. You know, stories told between guys who have nothing better to do than change history to reflect what we didn't get around to doing." Then I remembered. "How the hell did you guys know about those stories anyway? Were you eavesdropping? Was Agnes?"

"Doors are open Ivan. You know that. That old lady across the hall can't sleep more than an hour at a go. She sat up and listened." She giggled for a moment in remembrance. "Thank God Mrs. Pierson doesn't have Alzheimer's. In fact, she has quite a good memory for details."

I looked up at the ceiling, rolling my eyes. Quickly tallying how much damage this revelation would do to me. "Oh God. She heard?"

"Pretty much everything, I guess. I mean, thank goodness you two repeated yourselves so often it gave her an opportunity to memorize them."

"Oh, my God." My mind was still grappling with this revelation when I sensed we were at the end of the wait. I didn't see them; I just knew they were there.

Finally, it was our turn. I took Josh's wet limp hand in mine and squeezed hard. I may be a little older than he is — OK, a lot older — but still have a working man's handshake. I was taught to shake another man's hand with exuberance. But for the snot-nosed rug rat, I turned up the steam, just a little. The increased pressure caused both his eyes to pop open like an overheated beer can. He looked hard into my eyes, almost pleading for me to stop. Something primitive, almost guttural came out of his mouth, but nothing I could really understand. So, I held on.

I pulled him forcibly closer to me. Our eyes were less than a foot apart. Small beads of sweat started to form on his forehead and nose. I tried my best Clint Eastwood stone-faced impersonation. "What I have in my life, you piece of shit, is a lot more than you will ever have." I pulled him really close. I could smell the cheap aftershave he had put on this morning and the armpit smell overrode the deodorant he had applied at the same time. Hoarsely, I whispered, "Fuck you Josh." My head motioned to his fish-cold wife. "And fuck your lovely wife as well."

He was shocked at the words, but still managed to spit back, "You old prick," he started, as he tried to loosen his hand from mine. "You fucking asshole. Let go." He wrung it like he was snapping a towel, but still I hung on. "Let go ... Karina, he won't let go of me." His eyes pleaded at his wife, who was still not sure if there was anything she should or could do. "Karina?"

"Just let the old man hang on to your hand for a minute darling. Maybe it gives him a dirty thrill." And she smiled. That was all she could do, make a belittling comment. It was enough, though. My hand instantly relaxed its grip, and he pulled his back, rubbing it with his left hand. He was still moving away from me, though his time was now divided between the three of us: his wife, his watch, and me.

And that was that.

It was then, that very moment, June 20, a week after my friend Kenny died alone in that cold room, that the whole course of the remainder of my life was decided. It was the first time in many, many years of living on this earth that I can honestly say that one moment defined it all. But standing there in that church basement, surrounded by all of those people, looking at the family of my friend who just didn't give a shit, it happened. The arrival of the 'it' wasn't with a lightning bolt. It wasn't anything that grand or jarring. It just swept over me, completely, welcoming. A warm blanket of purpose.

I watched Josh and his lovely wife Karina pushing their son out the door, towards the rented car, to the airport and back to their lives.

Around me, people were saying words like:

"Rude."

"Seemed a bit off."

"No time for us."

"Dickhead." That, I think came from Tom Murphy, our retired Protestant minister. Actually, I'm pretty sure it was from him. It seemed an appropriate thing at the time.

My head slowly nodded up and down, as the crowd started to head back to their tables with their coffee and dainties. More words came to me from the people milling around, "No use letting all that good food go to waste."

"Hell of a lot better than that stuff at Pinetree."

"Could use a little more tea."

"Tea, shit! Where the rum?" That was Murphy

again.

I kept on nodding. A kaleidoscope of action rolling around in my head. Mary was still at my side and looking up at me. "Ivan, are you okay?" I said I was just thinking. "Well, why don't you think about getting me home?"

"Sure sweetheart, let's go." Looking around the room, my arm went around her waist, "I think the entertainment here is about done anyhow. You want any more food before we slip away? I hear the party could be heating up. Murphy is looking for some rum."

"Nah," she said, "let's just leave."

"Okay." I slipped down the line of people, haphazardly strewn chairs and half empty cups of tea to our spot, grabbed my jacket, along with Mary's sweater and her purse.

As I worked my way back to her, little things started to make themselves known to me. I briefly looked down at my right hand and noticed the small tremors that had arrived with my 65th birthday had taken their leave. My hand was steady as a rock. Not many rocks I knew of had thin blue veins and liver spots, but steady it was. The stairs didn't seem to be the huge insurmountable wall they were coming down earlier today. I didn't need the handrail at all. I was managing to have a conversation with Mary, and still, at the same time, rolling over everything in my head. It had been years since that sort of organizational capability had visited me. It was welcome. It was exhilarating.

There was purpose. Definition.

I smiled again. That was most assuredly the moment.

Mary hummed a tune from our ancient past as we

walked to the exit arm in arm. It seemed appropriate at the time, so I joined in. I don't much believe in all that psychic stuff. It has to be proven for me to see it and buy into it. But that song, at that moment was pure coincidence. It was magic. Or maybe some kind of precognition. Or maybe it was more. Who knows?

As I walked out of the church, I didn't have a hot clue how I was going to go about it, I didn't even know what kind of obstacles were in my way. But, I knew I had to kill those fucking people. Kill them dead. All of them.

I had stopped killing people when I turned 65. It was getting too complicated, too risky. It was kind of a birthday present to myself. But I had missed it. Missed the act, the discipline of it. Missed the release. Perhaps then, I owed Josh, Karina and their spawn a small bit of thanks for bringing me back.

On second thought, fuck 'em.

My grin broadened into a full smile.

Mary and I started to sing out loud as we approached my blue K-car. I opened the passenger door for her, and let her in, still singing with gusto. Mary popped the power door locks and I slipped in behind the wheel of the car and started it up. As we waited for the air conditioning to kick into high gear and take the thick edge off the June afternoon, we started singing the Bobby Darin arrangement, from the top.

I am not sure how the mystic lines of the world sometimes work, but the two of us singing Mack the Knife seemed somehow prophetic.

For Josh and his family, it wasn't going to be a good prophecy.

2
JUNE 2002

Mary and I spent the rest of the afternoon, doing what people our age should be doing when we are out on a date.

We stopped off at Ol' Ice Cream Shop and proceeded to add a little more fat to our already heavily clogged arteries. There is nothing like an ice-cream cone to take a hateful edge off an afternoon. Then we walked through the park, ice cream melting over our hands. It was a good thing I grabbed a mitt-full of napkins on the way out of the store because by the time we were done, most of them were crumbled, sticky and headed for the garbage can. I do like my bubble-gum ice cream on a warm summer day. It's one of the few pleasures I allow myself these days. I so craved the rush of sugar after the funeral. I needed to have my head fully charged and in high gear. The thought of killing that particular group of people made my head spin with excitement and anticipation. It was almost too much to hold in. But I really didn't think Mary would approve of such evil thoughts. Truth be told, I knew most people on the planet wouldn't get it or condone it. But over the years other peoples' thoughts really hadn't played a big part in my life or chosen career. I did my thing without permission or guilt. And I was good at it.

As Mary talked, I nodded my head in agreement, throwing the odd comment back towards her, just to show there was some semblance of attention being paid to her. She talked about the troubles we had at the home when Kenny died. How terrible it was, that the moment his body was out the door, the room was cleaned up, stem to stern, and another man, a stranger from the local hospital, was moved in to Kenny's spot. The gargantuan steel bed had been replaced with one of the regular types with the hard plastic mattress.

I knew what Mary was talking about.

It seemed like just a few moments had passed since the time Kenny made his last trip out of his room and down to the elevators and the waiting hearse tucked quietly at the back door. Now the belongings of another man were carried back in from the same door, up in the elevator to the same room. All nice and neat. Mary and I had stood at the end of the hall, away from the elevators and watched as our friend was taken from his room. A small surge of sadness overcame me, when his feet emerged first, covered in that damn grey blanket. The Body Blanket as we called it was the last thing a resident was wrapped in at Pinetree. It was grey, and seemed to be fuzzy, almost cuddly and warm. At the same time, it was reviled, shunned. The only way any of the residents would ever touch it would be when we had no way of objecting to its proximity. For those of us here, it was the final indignation. The end.

Kenny's possessions went down the hall packed in a box that was set on a small flat trolley. Duct tape was holding the seams together of the old potato chip box. I guess that was a thousand and two uses for duct tape which now included holding the miniscule piece of a man's life together all in one compact container. It made me pause, thinking how small an entire life could be compressed when need be. When you moved into this place, you didn't need a truck to bring your possessions. No kitchen knickknacks or bedroom furniture was needed. Just the clothes on your back, a change or two, some of the most important mementos of your life and that is it.

Like his family at the funeral, the treatment of Kenny's possessions could be summed up in a single word: impersonal. It was just stuff now that he was gone. Actually, if you had asked the staff beforehand, they would have told you it was only stuff then too. They didn't see the value, the history that was tied up in the few things he was allowed to keep. Kenny's son saw the value, but it wasn't intrinsic or personal. It was financial that moved his world.

Josh had such a hard-on for us senior citizens that it was almost unfathomable. Didn't he know that all seniors are lovable wonderful people? We're grandparents for God's sake. At least some people are. How could he not love a grandma or grandpa for that matter? But the venom spat at us during the service and reception was obvious. Tangible. Hateful.

Where would such a strong emotional reaction come from? Maybe he had an old aunt, smelling like lavender and washed in hair dye that forced a kiss on him at Christmas. Maybe at some point in his past, an old man had walked up to him, pulled open his trench coat and shown him his wang.

Who knew?

But more importantly, who cared? While we drove to the park in silence, I thought maybe Josh was afraid of becoming his old man. Afraid of skin that wasn't drum tight, bowels that perhaps weren't at their best. Perhaps the reduction of hair on his head while it grew unchecked out of his ears and nose caused him concern. He did have a little paunch, so the expansion of the waist probably wasn't a concern. But who knew? His reaction to us, to the friends of his father, wasn't just about the service or about his dad. It was a unilateral contempt for anything older than he was.

Like the hippy era of the Sixties and Seventies, their battle cry had now been somewhat perverted by Josh who never lived through that time: 'Never trust anyone over 70.' I suppose as that generation hits the 70 mark that will change again. Soon there won't be anyone left alive on the planet to trust.

Before the funeral I dropped in to see the new guy just to say hello. New, if you could call him that. He looked like death was already lining him up for a personal visit. Mary asked about him while we were driving, I told her I thought his name was Gary something or other. I told her not to put the funeral dress away. It won't be long in the closet.

Mary shook her head. "It was amazing you know, that Kenny made it what, nearly four years in that room? Tied to all that stuff?"

Nodding my head in agreement, "I think that's about right. I got to know him just after he moved in. That was about six months after I joined the little family on the fourth floor." I laughed softly, watching the kids running in the park, always under the watchful eyes of their parents. "God, he hated being tied to the machine, the heart monitor," I answered her unasked question. "He felt like it was the scoreboard of his life. You know when the tally got down to '0' it was all over. Game over. Which I guess, in a way, is the way that it really was. But he revolted against it any time he could."

It was a few months after meeting Kenny that I was introduced to Mary Carlton. Like most of the folks at Pinetree, she was alone in the world, her husband dying five years earlier. A retired teacher, Mary has a wonderful sense of humour and a brain that hadn't suffered with the degradation of time. She wasn't tall, just five feet five inches, but probably started out a couple of inches taller than that. Mary had a way about her that captivated me. Mary Carlton carried herself well. That is the best way to put it. She carried herself with confidence, knowing full well, like the rest of us, that this place was nearly the last stop. She didn't care, because she was alive now, with her friends at Pinetree. Next would be palliative care, if you made it that far.

I really enjoyed her company, and it appears she enjoyed mine as well. She was just lovely.

I popped the last of my ice-cream cone in my mouth, and steered Mary over to a well worn, but unoccupied bench.

Mary sat beside me on the wooden slats of the bench, our hips nudging against one another. "His machine," she said, "was always breaking down, wasn't it? At least until a few months ago. I remember there were always nurses running during the day shift down to his room with those de-fibber things pushed on the cart in front of them. You'd think this place could afford better monitors, or at least pay the money to have it fixed properly."

I laughed, "Kenny's monitor was fine." I leaned over to smell her perfume and share one of my late friend's secrets. "He would just unplug a wire or two once in a while to see if the staff were on their toes."

"No!"

"Yeah. Couple of times a month at least." Both of us laughed. Mary wiped away a tear with her perpetually rolled up Kleenex from her sleeve.

"But didn't they catch on?"

"Nah, Kenny was an old guy," I said by way of explanation. "He gave the staff that big eye look when they walked in the room, you know like that guy Newman in the Mad Magazines, 'Who me?'" I shook my head at the memory of all the laughs the two of us had shared at the expense of the nursing staff. "Stupid guy just kept on doing it and they kept on running down the hall, like the Medical 500 or something." I looked at Mary who was smiling tolerantly at me. It was obvious she didn't see the humour that Kenny and I shared over the heart monitor. I shrugged my shoulders and offered the explanation, "It made us laugh Mary. You can't blame us for having a laugh. And in that place any time we could laugh was a good time." I reached over and held her hand, "Like now. They can't take this away from us. This moment."

"It's not such a bad place Ivan. The rooms are clean, the staff, by and large, are okay. They aren't Florence Nightingales or anything, but they're okay. And the food is..." she stopped talking, and looked at me, a slight upturn on her lips. "Well, you know, the food is crap."

We both leaned back in laughter.

"Total crap," I added.

"Biggest pile of crap I have ever tasted in my life." She blurted out another chortle, then snorted, which made us laugh even harder. After a time, the joke faded and we sat quietly, hand in hand looking at the families opening up their picnic baskets and coolers. She looked over at me and said, "It's been a long time since I did that."

"What, laugh? You've laughed."

"No, not just laugh. But laugh hard enough that I," she looked down at her knees, "you know."

I nodded in agreement and gave her hand a little squeeze. "I know. Since you did your Porky Pig impersonation." And we both descended once again to the pleasure palace of laughter. I snorted a couple of times, and we continued on the laughter train. "Let's go and get some supper Mary."

She looked at the watch hanging limply on her wrist and said, "It's nearly seven Ivan. We have been sitting here for over an hour." She smiled at me and nodded slightly. "I feel bad. We missed our daily serving of supper crap."

"True," I said. "But we did have our daily quota of breakfast crap and there was the lunch crap. Although we did miss our brunchy serving of crap today."

Mary smiled again. It was something I liked to see. "I forgot about the lunch crap." She made a sour face, "thanks for reminding me."

"It's my job. I like my job." I looked at her. "So do I take you home, and we have a re-heated serving of crap, or do you want to go out and get some real food?"

"Let's go out. We'll have a double helping of crap tomorrow to make up for tonight's real food. Right?"

"Right you are."

I stood up, turned around, and held out my arm for Mary to take. She grabbed on, and the two of us helped her get up. I knew since the hip replacement she was a little slow in getting up off the furniture. But she did love to walk. It took us nearly half an hour to walk the half block back to the parking lot and the car. We stopped and watched the families laughing and playing. Little children, their knees stained green, rolling in the grass, with moms and dads running after them with baby wipes.

No one cried.

I noticed that. Not one child in that park and there must have been a hundred. Not one was crying. They all laughed, played, pushed, fell, yelled and ran. But no one cried. It was wonderful. With all the action going on in front of us, there didn't seem to be any noise.

Not irritating city sounds, like sirens, horns, or people yelling in hatred and anger at one another. Just fun sounds, no doubt as loud in decibels, but way off the bottom of the irritating scale. It didn't hurt the ears to hear the din of the park. It was a happy, content sound.

It sounded like life.

As I watched all of the happy families, I realized I was going to be taking the life of a mother and father, and a son. Looking at the eyes of the parents in the park had shown me one thing. They were very happy with life. It was good to be breathing oxygen on this Thursday. It was good to be at the park, having a couple of senior citizens staring at them in their happiness. It was good.

I realized that Josh and the queen bitch Karina had never had a moment like that. They never really knew how to let themselves go. Even at the park, they would be looking for a way to corrupt it, change it away from what it was. In their eyes, you couldn't see a thirst for life or happiness. Deep in their pupils, one could only see a consumption of it.

"It's time for an end to that particular food chain."

"What did you say, Ivan?"

Oh God I was thinking out loud again. "Sorry, just wondering which food chain you and I should eat at. McDonald's, Burger King. How about Wendy's?" Mary looked up at me, not believing it for a moment. She was perceptive that way.

But what could I have said? 'Honey let's go for supper, and I'll tell you about the plans I have to kill an entire family. You don't have to worry because I am very good at it. In my estimation I am the longest running serial killer in North America. I have been mostly undetected. Mostly.'

"We don't have to eat out Ivan. We can go home."

"No. It wasn't that, Mary. I was thinking about Kenny, about his son. I was thinking about the families that are here in the park, having such a great time on a day that you and I are in such pain. I was thinking that Josh and his family are having a great time too. But they are laughing because they know in a few days they will be getting a cheque for Lord knows how much. Having a good time because Kenny died." I shook my head, clearing the image. "You know Mary, random thoughts."

The two of us stood for a time, at the point where the asphalt of the world meets the park. Not really wanting to step over the line and get back to our lives. It was like the world just stood still, letting this one small patch of multi-green colours stand on its own. Life just let whoever was inside its borders play with absolute abandonment. In the fading sun, Mary's face was radiant, more beautiful than I had ever seen her. Our fingers were intertwined, and our bodies close. I turned towards the gleaming cars in the parking lot, reluctantly pulling her away from this world, and into the harsh world of concrete, steel and noise.

"Let's go get some real food Mary. My treat."

Mary looked at me with reproach, and wagged her finger, "You bought last time Ivan. I think it's only fair that I buy once in a while. This is the new millennium after all. I do have money of my own you know."

"I know you have money, Mary. I also know that it is the new millennium. I read that somewhere. But in that same book, it didn't mention anything about courtesy being withdrawn from the world. There are some things that are important to me." We reached my old K-car. "Here let me help you." I pulled the door open and led her into the seat. She thanked me as I closed the door. When I was inside the car, I looked at her and said, “Let’s do this. What if I buy you supper, and then we go back to your room and snuggle? Just a little. Or you can buy supper, and we go back to my room and snuggle.”

“But you have a roommate Ivan.”

“Yes, I do.” I stared at her, starting the car. “I do have a roommate, and he has a bladder problem, so he never, ever sleeps. He’s up and down taking a leak all night. But it seems to me that you have a private room. Live by yourself, don’t ya? Even have a little couch, what do they call them, a lll-ooooo-vvvve seat?”

Mary wagged her finger at me again. “You are nasty, Ivan. Very nasty. Again, I like it, but it’s nasty just the same.” She looked out the window for a moment, then turned back to me, her hand reaching across the seat, “So where are we going to eat, big spender?”

“I feel like chicken and ribs. Let’s get messy.”

3
SEPTEMBER 1967

Frank Kopp hated the old tube radio in the Dodge. He absolutely hated it!

It took all day to warm up the ancient tubes, spewing out static intermixed with rasping and audibly tangled noise. Each and every time you stopped the truck, winter or summer, it didn't matter, the tubes cooled down. Then, each and every time you started up the Dodge, you had to wait for what seemed like 15 minutes while the tubes inside the radio crept their way to the maximum operating temperature and finally kicked out a few minutes of music. That was, until the next time you turned off the truck, at which point the whole cycle started once again. He hated it, plain and simple.

Kopp tried to convince his bosses that they needed a truck that had a radio that didn't require the long warmup times. They needed a truck, according to the young driver, that was made in the current year. Or in the last couple of years. They needed a truck that wasn't an antique. At the very least, he had pleaded, they needed a new radio!

The answer was always a firm no. Tradition was an important part of the dry-cleaning business, he was told. The truck with its large logo and telephone number emblazoned on the side and the old radio would stay. People knew the truck and the business.

And so, Frank Kopp had endured the slow static of the old Dodge radio. He would sit in the cab, waiting for the radio to heat up, after each delivery. He would burn their gas and take a little more of the buck and a quarter he earned an hour each day, just to show them.

And while delivering laundry around the city, you turned the truck off every time you turned a corner. His route would include between 30 and 50 stops a day. That is an awful lot of waiting for tubes to warm up, rattling through the static for the radio stations and just plain being pissed off.

Delivery in the core area was the worst. Because there were so many apartment buildings, Frank had to stop almost every block to take in somebody's dress shirts or dresses. It was always terrible. You had to pull all the crap from the back, lug it into the lobby, and push the security buzzer to let them know you were there. Then you had to climb all the stairs. The Willows was the worst. Seven floors, and no elevator.

"Who the hell would build an apartment building seven floors high in this day and age without an elevator?" Frank said as he pondered the large modern building in front of him. "Seven fucking floors. You have got to be kidding? What kind of morons are they graduating from architecture school these days. Shit," he said as he shook his head from side to side. Had he asked, the building janitor would have told Kopp there was a service elevator at the back of the building, near the furnace room. But the delivery man had never asked and always bore an attitude with him when he arrived in the building. He had walked into the lobby, looked around, then headed for the stairs. The janitor didn't tell Frank about the elevator because he wasn't too keen on children being allowed to use it. And it appeared anyone under the age of 50 was a child.

Spring and fall were the worst, because all the fur coats were either put into or taken out of storage. Minks may be cute when they are alive and running around inside a fenced compound, but bundled together in a coat, sewn together with inside matting and insulation, made the coats very heavy and awkward. And every single lady in 1967 had a fur coat. Every single one. And every one of those fur coats smelled like the lady that wore it. Many didn't smell good at all. Stale, dated perfume just didn't mix well with moth balls. It was a stink that invaded the truck, then overwhelmed the large vault they all found themselves in later that day.

In front of the Willows, Kopp sat in the cab listening to the music, that for some miraculous reason had suddenly cleared up. When the song ended, and the announcer came on spouting off about some contest, Frank took in a huge breath, flicked the key off, and exhaled as he bounded from the cab. Around the back of the aluminum skinned cube, Frank unlatched the door, and grabbed the parcels that were stacked near the door, ready for delivery. He checked each one, placed them into the crook of his arm and flung the long dresses and shirts over his shoulder.

He slammed the door shut, locking it, and looked up at the building. "Seven floors and no elevator?" He sighed again and headed for the front entrance.

Frank Kopp sidled up to the stainless-steel panel with nearly four dozen different buzzer buttons on it. Putting all the pressure he could on it, Frank managed to hook one elbow onto the button he thought was the one he wanted and pushed. Something shifted on the top of his load; he thought it was the dress for the old lady in 2C. He scrambled quickly, changing his balance to offset the imminent fall of the ladies' unmentionables. But it was too late. They fell along with a few of their sanitized friends, wrapped in paper into a crinkled pile to the floor.

Frank stood staring at the pile on the floor, and let his arms, fall to his side, contemplating the mess in the foyer. “Son of a bitch.”

“Pardon me?”

Frank literally jumped away from the mechanical voice. His heart stopped, then forced itself to restart. “Hello?” he managed.

“Is there someone there? My buzzer buzzed?”

“Mrs. Hamilton, is that you?” It was an old lady Frank had never met, but knew well.

“Yes?”

“It’s Frank Kopp, Mrs. Hamilton. From Don’s Drycleaners.”

“Yes? My buzzer buzzed, Frank.”

Frank looked up at the tiles lining the foyer. She still didn’t get it. “I know, ma’am, I buzzed you. I’ve got your laundry.”

“Is it Friday already?”

Frank took a moment, then said, “No ma’am, only Wednesday.”

“Well, I get my laundry on Friday,” said the confused voice through the metallic speaker.

This was a new wrinkle in the dance the two shared each time he brought laundry. “Well, uh. It’s ready a couple of days earlier Mrs. Hamilton.”

For a moment there was silence in the room, then her mechanical voice boomed back, “Okay come on up.” Frank stared at the slotted speaker and shook his head in amazement.

“Oooohhhkey dokey pokey,” Frank Kopp sing-songed.

Mrs. Hamilton wasn’t really the person he wanted to see, but she was always home. Always. And she always let Frank Kopp in. In the two years the young man had been on route 42, Mrs. Hamilton had never once sent anything to the laundry. But each week she let him into the building, without fail, without knowing who it was that she was letting in. Frank would walk past the security devices that each of the tenants in the Willows paid so dearly for each month. He buzzed her because her little black button with her name stenciled next to it was at the exact height of his elbow.

"They probably keep her locked in her room," Frank thought. He figured she was so scatterbrained that if she did go out, old lady Hamilton would probably get lost, never to be seen again. "Safer for everyone," Frank mused, "that she stay behind closed, and securely locked doors."

Kopp had just managed to pick everything up off the floor in the order he needed it to be when he heard a distinctive horn outside the building. Turning around, he saw the grape-coloured Ford of his buddy Eddie Moore. He loved that car. It had been painted deep Passion Purple with metalflake and was lowered four inches, barely skimming across the asphalt. Often at night he would tear down 13th Street, scraping it hard at intersections, sparks showering where he drove. It had the biggest, lowest tires Eddie could buy, gripping the road like they had double-sided tape wrapped around them. The radio was blasting something new that Frank didn't recognize. But he knew that when Eddie turned on the ignition he wouldn't have to wait until the second chorus of any song to start hearing music.

"Damn Dodge."

Frank took one of the larger bundles from his load, and jammed it into the still buzzing door, to hold it open, then moved to the big glass doors. He pushed one about halfway open, slivering his foot in the doorframe. "Hey man," Eddie called up at him from the street.

“Yoo, Eddie. What is going on?”

“What time are you off tonight, Frankie?” Frank Kopp knew that Eddie knew perfectly well what time he got off. It was all part of a time-honoured ritual the two always went through when their paths crossed. Eddie Moore was the only guy that could call Frank Kopp, Frankie, and not see five knuckles heading straight for his nose. No one but Eddie could use the nickname. Well not really no one. But his dad was dead, so maybe no one was accurate.

“Five thirty buddy.” He looked at his cheap Timex. The worn leather wrapped around his arm had started to discolour his wrist brown, the dye finding better places to stick than to the strap. “In about three hours. What are you up to tonight?”

“I think Coz and Mona and I are going to the pit, drink a few beers, have a few laughs. You in?”

The pit was the local hiding place the kids went to when they were looking for a little solitude, a little sex, or a place they could drink, throw up, and not tell anybody over 30 about it. Everyone figured their parents, and the cops knew about the pit, but they all turned a blind eye. Kids had to have somewhere to go, didn’t they? If it wasn’t at the pit, it would be in the basement of the church. Now who would want that?

“Oh yeah, I’m in. For sure man. What time?” Frank’s arms were beginning to burn with exertion, and he was thinking about letting the whole thing drop to the ground again. But Eddie churned up his mill and barked the Coker’s.

“Pick you up at eight man. Cool.” And in a burst of blue smoke, Eddie Moore flew down the street, the sound of his Ford, pounding each and every cinderblock along Eighth Street creating an oilcan of reverberation along the way. You definitely knew when Eddie was barking down the street.

The first delivery was to Mr. Crandall on the ground floor. The guy didn't like living above the ground. "No place to go if there's a fire," he had told Frank, many times.

Frank didn't mention that most of the building was brick, so probably wouldn't burn. Besides that, buildings were built so well these days, there was no chance that anything could burn. But Frank nodded his head, shoved his tip in his left front pocket, and headed for the second floor, and Mrs. Bitch-o-matic.

Her name was Mrs. Bilonavich, but the nickname seemed a better match. Actually, Frank figured it fit her to a "T." She was a bitch. And a cheap one at that. Rarely tipped.

He knocked on the door of 2C and waited.

"Who is it?"

"Mrs. ..." 'What the hell was her name?' "It's Don's Drycleaners, ma'am. Frank Kopp. Your laundry."

"Put it on the floor. I'm not decent."

"You're cheap too."

"What was that?"

"Nothing. Okay on the floor?" Frank stared at the door for a moment. Then bent over to put all the clothing on the floor.

"Don't put the dress on the bottom, it'll wrinkle. Hang it on the doorknob."

"Yes ma'am." He looked at the bill, stapled to the thin plastic covering over what he could only describe as the ugliest dress he had ever seen, and Frank had seen a few. "The total is a buck twenty-seven."

"How much?" she asked, her voice cracking and rising a half octave in surprise.

Frank sighed. Boy, was this a broken record he had

heard before. “A dollar twenty-seven ma’am.”

“For what?”

Frank already had the bill in his hand and was reading it. “Let’s see,” he started, “a dress cleaned with a small coffee stain removed from the front....”

“I didn’t do that. Someone spilled on me at a dance.”

“Yeah, whatever you say, twit.”

“What? Speak up. I can’t hear you through the door?”

Frank shook his head. “The dress, two slacks, and a blouse.”

“That’s it?”

“Yes ma’am.” But Frank checked the bill, to make sure everything that he had picked up last week, was in the paper bags on the floor. “Yes, that’s everything.”

“You mean a dollar twenty-seven for just those few things?”

‘Here it comes,’ Frank nodded to himself, resigned to the coming onslaught.

“That is highway robbery young man. There is no way I’m going to pay that amount of money for what you did. That is far too much.”

“Ma’am, that includes the credit for the order that we made a mistake on last week. So actually, it should have been a lot higher than it is right now.”

There was a slight pause. “Oh?”

“Yes ma’am, it is a lot cheaper today.”

From behind the door, there was a faint smooshing sound, like somewhat running crinoline over a tabletop. “Very well, leave the bill. I’ll collect the clothing and leave you the exact change on the ground in an envelope.”

“Okay, ma’am.” Frank stood stock still for a moment. There was one more little thing that was coming but hadn't arrived just yet.

"Oh, and leave the envelope behind, don't take it." Mrs. Bilonavich yelled at what had to be the top of her lungs. Frank smiled. He moved forward until his lips were only fractions of an inch from the door.

"Okay," he hissed in a hoarse stage whisper.

"Good," Mrs. Bilonavich said from behind the door, suitably startled by the intimacy of the word from Frank. More smooshing sounds preceded a repeat of "Good," as Kopp could hear her walking away from the door. Her housecoat lazily caressing the walls as she moved deeper into her apartment.

"God, what a bitch."

He turned away from the door and back towards the stairs. He was almost done the deliveries for the Willows.

The last stop of the Willows was on the fourth floor, 4F, and Mrs. Carrington. He always saved her for last. Mrs. Carrington was a little older than Frank; he figured she was in her mid-20s. She had the most beautiful sandy brown hair he had ever seen. No matter the style she wore, it always seemed to have been created just for her from some big Hollywood hair stylist. Up or down, her hair always looked as elegant as he had every seen.

Mrs. Carrington's eyes were brown. Dark, deep, like Hershey bar dark.

Frank knew he could go on and on about the things he liked about her. Suffice to say there was very little he didn't like about Mrs. Carrington. The name on the mailbox downstairs said, "C. & M. Carrington." Frank figured she was a little more liberated than most of the women in the building, so her name would be first on the box. But her first name, he didn't have a clue. Late at night, when lying in bed, letting his mind wander around all the problems of the world, Frank Kopp thought her name would probably be Carol. She had that look. Solid, dependable Carol. Yup, it was definitely Carol.

As he came out of the ornate stairwell, beads of sweat locking on his body, Frank's vision immediately swung to 4F. It was just a few feet from the doorway, to his left. He stopped dead in his tracks, his rough breathing the only sound in the hallway. The whole floor was quiet.

Today the door was wide open.

Though he couldn't be sure, Frank was sure everyone on this floor worked, or they were out most of the time during the day. Mrs. Carrington was the only person he ever saw on the fourth floor.

But the door was wide open. 4F was never open. No door in the Willows, no matter which number was open. Ever.

Frank Kopp took a step, then paused as he emerged from the stairwell, watching the door closely. There was no sound from inside. No little movements that indicated there was someone moving around. He let the stairwell door lock softly click shut behind him and started tentatively towards 4F.

He couldn't think of a good reason for it, but he moved the small package for Mrs. Carrington, a sweater he thought, to his left hand. He did it very slowly, trying to keep the paper from crinkling loudly in the barren, silent hallway. That shift would give free range to his stronger right arm. He had no clue why he did that. It just moved from arm to arm, very slowly and deliberately.

Frank noticed that with each step he took toward the open door, his breathing and pulse picked up a notch. He figured that by the time he reached the door, his pulse would be about three and a half thousand while his breathing would be, oh, into 'hyperventilation land'.

His senses were on high alert. He could smell what she had cooked for lunch. Fish, with fresh ground coffee. As he eased closer to the door, he could hear music faintly playing in the background. Instrumental stuff, nothing he would ever listen to.

But once he rounded the corner of the door and looked down the short 15-foot hallway into the depths of the apartment there was no way he would be able to eat or think about food for a long time. There was nothing he wanted to know, to feel, to become part of, as he stared down the hall. All his senses, his emotions were of complete revulsion.

Mrs. Carrington was there, naked to the waist. Her mint green panties were torn, and seemed to be wet, soiled. She had one sock on, a little lace topped one with pink frills on her left foot. The right foot was bare. Her hair, normally perfect to a strand, was completely messed. It was without any purpose or design.

Frank could tell that whatever had happened was not voluntary. That much was obvious. He had heard that some people like sex a little rough. But he could see that this wasn't something that anyone would want to go for. Sexual or not.

Mrs. Carrington's eyes were looking straight at him, without seeing him. There was no thought there, no recognition. Both her eyes were swollen, pink and blotchy, so Frank knew they would eventually turn black, scarred. A small bead of bright red blood was hanging from her nose, not moving, just frozen on the tip. The right side of her mouth was swelling badly. Though a few feet away, Kopp could tell it was split.

Her cheeks were red, scuffed, like they had been dragged on the carpet. Mrs. Carrington's arms were bruised and scraped. Her knuckles were red, deformed with congealing blood.

What Frank Kopp remembered and loved about Mrs. C. or M. Carrington was now gone. That aloofness, that knowledge, the beauty was dirty now, compromised. Even battered, lost, Frank couldn't help but admire the woman crumpled on the floor.

Frank stood stock still. Taking in the scene. Wanting to do something, but not sure what he could do. Or more importantly what he should do. From the carpeted floor he began quivering in his work boots. Even the change in his pocket jingled a little, like fairies dancing in a field.

"Mrs. Carrington," Frank managed to croak softly, taking a very hesitant step towards the hallway. "Uhm, Mrs. Carrington." He couldn't think of anything else to say.

Her eyes suddenly pulled into focus, right on his. The sudden, slight, hard movement caught him off guard. He took a quick step backwards, away from her.

Mrs. Carrington said, "I have to call the police."

The words didn't seem to be able to come out of her lips, purple and swollen as they were. The sentence seemed to be just a rubbery flow of sound. The words were slurred together — a mush of sound and syllables. The words were still identifiable, but you had to listen. She looked up, focusing even more clearly on the Don's delivery man. "I have to call the police," she repeated.

"I'll call, Mrs. Carrington." Frank took another deliberate step towards the woman on the carpet in the hallway. "I'll call the police for you." She seemed to follow his footsteps, gauging him carefully. As he got closer, he could see a small tear in her left eye. "Are you all right?" he asked as he knelt down beside her.

"I have to call the police, now."

"I'll call, Mrs. Carrington. Don't worry about that, I'll call. Where is your telephone?"

Mrs. Carrington stared at him for a moment, and he wasn't sure if she understood the question, or knew the answer. He figured she was in shock, so things might be a little scrambled for her. But she turned her head and gave him the answer by looking across the large living room, to a small table beside the sofa. The large black phone was resting on its side, a slight buzzing sound coming from the handset. Frank nodded his head.

"Okay. I'll call. Right away." He reached up to push a hair that was matted near her eye. But she pulled quickly back, banging her head into the wall.

"Oh," she managed, wincing at the pain.

"I'm here to help Mrs. Carrington. It's Frank from Don's Drycleaners. I'm going to get you a blanket. Then I'll call the police." He looked down at her lap, then quickly averting his eyes by staring into hers. "And I'll call for an ambulance too."

As Frank stood, Mrs. Carrington reached for his left arm. "We need a doctor too," she looked down at the man, lying with his head in her lap. "For Carl."

'Carl? *His* name is Carl? What the hell is her name? Starts with an M.' Those thoughts ran through his mind quickly, then were pushed out in a flash of horror.

Frank forced himself to look down at the other face, then caught himself quickly, looking away. What he had seen in her lap convinced him he couldn't do the pit that night. No way. Not with what was in her lap.

Carl had both of his eyes open. Like he had a

choice. His right eye was looking in the general direction of the laundry delivery man. The left though was falling away towards the green patterned carpet. It was attached to his head by a milky white strand of cartilage. The right eye wasn't focusing.

Frank Kopp lost his self-discipline, and his gaze moved from the man's eyes, down past the badly damaged cheek, the limp mouth, the scuffed chin and finally to the neck that was laid waste.

"Yes, ma'am, I'll make sure a doctor comes for ... Carl." He stood up and started for the rooms down the hall looking for a blanket, but stopped when he heard her sniff.

"Hurry."

"Okay. I'll go now, okay."

She nodded her head in agreement, shifting her vision slowly down to the head in her lap.

Kopp paused to look at the pair then sprinted to the corner of the living room and the telephone. He hung up the phone for a moment, then picked it up again listening for the loud dial tone. He called the police but felt there wouldn't be a rush on the ambulance for the husband. Mrs. Carrington though, definitely was in need of medical care.

Carl would no longer be needing a doctor.

4
JUNE 2002

It was nearly midnight when I finally got back to my room. Predictably my roommate Harry, was sound asleep as I crept in and headed for the bathroom to relieve a lot of pressure I had on my bladder and then get ready for bed. I stopped at the door to the bathroom, and listened for a moment to his rhythmic breathing, noting any change as my hands gripped the latch, twisting it and the door opened.

When completely undressed as was my habit, I brushed my teeth, washed my face and combed my hair. A quick check of my fingernails showed I hadn't picked up any barbecue sauce from the restaurant—a testament to their little wipes. But from the gurgling in my stomach, I knew that I had picked something else up. It was going to be loud, noisy and a might smelly in room 4G tonight. I knew all that grease and salad would come back to haunt me, but what the hell. You don't go out on a date with the prettiest girl in the building very often, so you may as well splurge.

I looked at my body in the mirror, another ritual with a long-forgotten rationale behind it. I checked under each arm, along my chest and stomach, under my sack and down each leg. What I was looking for I hadn't any idea. It was habit. Ingrained like a permanent fixture in my psyche. If I was being honest with myself, I did know where it came from. It was the double check that I had brought nothing home with me in the way of injuries. Something that could be linked back to my nocturnal activities.

When I turned around, I saw the small, faded scar from the 1988 operation to remove a small lump that had sprung up on my back. Other than the tiny army of neat round holes near my backbone, wounds I'd had for decades, nothing had changed. The little pattern looked larger than they actually were because of the shadows cast by the cheap light bulbs.

But for some reason, the random pattern itched. It was the first time in ages I'd even noticed them. I stared for a moment in the cold light of the bathroom, remembering the pain when I'd received them. Remembering the lessons taken from them. I tried, but the elasticity of my arms had long before given up the ability to reach them. So, I just looked at them. The itching died away, fading the longer I looked at them.

"In the back, uh." I smiled, turned to the back of the door, and grabbed my pajamas that were neatly hanging there.

Stepping back to the mirror, I looked once again at the body standing in front of it. Life had been very hard on it. Besides the scarring on the back, there was plenty inside. Cancer at age 43. Half a lung out then. That brought a long pink scar along my left side. Then another bout at 58. That pretty well finished my desire to smoke. It cost me the rest of the lung that time. The final bout was six years ago. This time melanoma. Someone had told me you don't get cancer three times. You get it twice, and then you die from it.

I had told my doctors that there would be no more heroic measures taken to save my life. I was not going to go through all that shit again. They didn't have to throw up for days on end or watch every hair fall out of every follicle on their body. An added bonus was I wouldn't have to answer all the stupid fucking questions about why my skin colour was such an interesting shade of orange when I was at the grocery store hunting. That really didn't help me in the inconspicuous department. Not at all.

The face looking back at me was happier than I had seen it in years. Despite losing Kenny, despite the falls, the sallow sockets and loose skin, this was still a very happy, contented, excited man. My eyes were clear and focused.

I looked down at my cock, hanging down the center of the gap between my flabby thighs and smiled, "At least one of us stretched a little skin tonight bubba. You lucky devil." After throwing the clothing over the toilet, I picked up the washcloth, held it under the warm water for a moment to take the chill off, then wiped myself down. I didn't want to take a shower in case it woke up the guy in the next room, so settled for the sponge bath. It felt good to get all the residue of the love making off. It felt good to be clean again. Once again, it was a habit that was long-standing and somehow important to me. The washcloth was then hidden in the garbage, underneath Kleenex and an empty tube of toothpaste.

After I was done, I looked at myself once again in the mirror. I couldn't see the eyes of the killer there, but knew somehow, he was still in there. Staring back. Hidden from view by Ivan McDonald, who was standing in the way. Ivan wasn't blocking him from staring back, just putting in the motions needed until it was time for the other to break free.

But the killer was there, waiting in the background. Planning, and plotting. The eyes were the same colour, the temperament a little more addictive and compulsive, and the physical body in a little worse shape, but he was still there. Like a lion, hidden perfectly in tall dead grass, cloaked by his natural colouring. The killer was waiting to pounce on a quietly grazing fat herd.

My head cocked from one side to the other, still looking at the person staring back in the reflective glass screwed to the wall. Inside there somewhere was the person that I needed. Somewhere within myself was the one man that could help me do the job I had tasked myself. It was just a matter of finding the key to let him out.

Somehow, I knew the key was the look Josh had given me after I taught him that senior citizens can still have a firm handshake. I could still see the hurt, the hatred, in his eyes. I felt and understood that emotion as I turned his ungrateful face over and over in my mind. It was the key that was needed to open the gate. Knowing that the man I needed to be was just inside, simmering, was enough that night. It was having all the pieces of a puzzle, counted and laid out for you on a tabletop. Knowing they were all there is enough until you are ready to take it on. To finish it.

But that night, he wasn't coming out. He was staying hidden, stashed away behind the loose skin and brittle bones of Ivan McDonald. I quickly pulled on my pajamas, housecoat and slippers, and turned off the light. Maybe tonight would be a good night, not to wake up the man. It might be better to let him sleep. Leave the lion in the grass, sniffing the air, looking for prey.

In bed, I listened to the rhythmic breathing of my roommate. He wasn't getting up to make a dash to the bathroom yet. I checked the clock, it said '12:11 AM'. I knew from his like-a-clock bladder, that just after one he would be getting up, rushing to the pooper to drain the lizard. Though I couldn't figure out what all the rush was for. From what I could hear through the ultra thin walls, there was only about a quarter of a cup that actually hit the bowl. How hard could that be to hold in? From the regularity of his bathroom runs, it was obviously pretty tough for him. Me, I could wait all night with a load large enough to put out the great Chicago fire. It was all a matter of mind over matter. I forced my mind to ignore the pain, while maintaining the muscle control needed to keep the bed from being flooded. It was a source of pride, a little of my younger self still present in my old age. The body would still react to what my mind was ordering it to do. It felt good.

The dreams didn't really hit in full that night. Mr. 'Have to empty the bladder hah hah hah', made his regular one o'clock trip to the bathroom, and flushed the toilet, waking me up. He snuck back into bed, thinking he had gotten away with it, smacked his lips and fell hard asleep once again.

Harry fell fast asleep. Right now.

He never ceased to amaze me. Harry can be sawing logs like Paul Bunyan himself, no sound on this earth that could wake him, when suddenly an internal alarm bell goes off. The bladder fills to the point of having an accident, he wakes up and is throttling off barefoot to the bathroom. He dumps his what I think is far-too-little load, and is back to bed, and BAM! He's back in the land where Marilyn Monroe is still doing whoever's left in the Kennedy clan, and the King never did leave the building. Never seen anything like it.

Harry is certainly nothing like me. It takes me hours to fall off. Then, the slightest sound of someone near the room, and I'm wide awake and on full alert. Another old habit that I would truly love to shake off. Because of it, I haven't had a full night's sleep in over 50 years. Five decades of not sleeping more than five hours a night. Each and every night. I've read somewhere that is an impossible feat. People need a certain amount of sleep in every 24-hour period so their body can re-charge, reload. I don't know anything about that, but for a longer period than any staff member in this building has been alive, I have been doing just that. I guess my body just doesn't need the down time like others do. Some would call it a gift, you know, more time to accomplish what you want in your life. I see it from the other side of the coin. It gives you more time to ponder the shortcomings of the fact that you can't fucking sleep! Pills, booze, drugs, whatever. It didn't help. I even tossed in sex once in a while for purely therapeutic reasons. Didn't work. I would sleep out cold for a couple of hours, then someone would fart near the room, and zoom, back again among the living. Truly a pain in the ass.

If someone is coming down the hallway, there is no trouble until they get within one room of ours, and then I'm awake. I would love to put some yellow tape down on the floor, like the police have. Except it would say, 'Sleep Line — Do Not Cross.' Would be very happy with that. Very happy.

By 2 AM, I knew that sleep wouldn't be heading my way that night. Over an hour of listening to Harry across the room just added to my frustration. I really wanted to shuffle across the linoleum floor and bop him in the nose. That was another weird thing about that guy. He has a really small nose. I mean a really, small one. From a distance, you would figure all the guy had on his face was a pencil drawing of the olfactory organ. I kid you not. It didn't stick out more than a half an inch from his face. We are talking really, really small. But can that guy snore! Sounds like one of the lumberman competitions from the television with all their Husqvarna chainsaws in bed next to me.

The stupid shit has actually snored so loud that he woke himself up. I had seen Harry bolt straight up in bed, eyes wide open, throw back the covers and run right to the bathroom. Probably scared the piss out of himself. It had been kind of fun to watch.

Had I known that sleeping with Mary would have been the only rest I would have gotten that night, I think there would have been a change in plans. I would have let her buy supper, so we had to come back to this room. I looked across the room at Harry, lying flat on his back, sawing away and smiled. "That would have definitely put a damper on any romantic inclinations I may have had, Harry." I threw a spare pillow at him, hitting him square in the face. "You fucking idiot, shut up!"

But Harry just turned away, tossed the pillow about halfway back towards me, and fell right back into a natural snoring rhythm. I shook my head in wonder. "You are a moron, Harry."

I tossed the blankets off, grabbed my housecoat, slipped on my slippers, and headed out of the room. I didn't really have a clear purpose as to where I was going, but just the same I seemed to know where I was headed. The nursing shortage guaranteed that I wouldn't be disturbed during my nocturnal wonderings along the darkened halls of the institution. Mary wouldn't like that word, institution. She would prefer something a little more liberal, like home for the recently retired. There are people in here that have been retired half a century. So, let's call it what it is: an institution. You can dress it up any way you want, the dressing is only in name. For people living there, they knew. It was an institution.

The nursing station, as I predicted, was lightly staffed. I checked on the phone lines, and nothing was lit. So, no one on the ward was talking on the phone. That was another pastime of the staff. Everyone was probably down in the cafeteria, playing a little gin or poker, reading the National Enquirer or the Globe or whatever was available to do during the long sprawl of the night shift.

I started back towards my room and smiled a little. I could hear Harry snoring all the way down the hall. No wonder the staff all buggered off to the basement. I stood outside Kenny's door for a while, not looking in the room with that other guy in there. I didn't feel comfortable staring at a stranger. I just stood there, letting the memories of my friend, and his irritating little shit of a son, wash over me in a dirty laundry kind of way. There was no way to escape the muddy thoughts that pounded silky smooth through my tired head. It had been years since those kinds of thoughts even visited me. The dark thoughts retired when I did. Or at least I thought they had. Sure, they popped up now and again, but nothing strong enough to force me to action. But here they were again. Old friends come back for a visit in a place where active evil just doesn't exist anymore. Here, even evil takes a holiday. In its place was meanness, the occasional outburst, and sometimes a whole lot of swearing.

Now though, standing alone in that hallway, just the re-acquaintance of those lost thoughts filled me with resolve. I found myself nodding my head slowly, with determination and promise.

"Yeah Kenny. For you." I nodded my head slowly, then turned firmly on my heel towards the stairwell. "It's what friends do for one another."

The clinical grey door wasn't locked. Thank God for fire regulations. I remember some of the buildings I used to sneak around in. Christ, you could hardly move without having to unlock one door or another. It had meant a lot better planning to move undetected and quiet once you got inside.

Now, the hardest problem for me would be to make sure I didn't have to walk past the lone security guard at the front doors. He was the only person that could let you in after regular office hours. That meant getting out wasn't a great problem; all I had to do was pop open an outside door with panic hardware and no alarm and walk through. As long as I didn't need a key, all was good getting out. The getting in was another story, but one I felt I would never have to deal with.

The stairwell to the basement was well lit. I quietly closed the door behind me, standing stock-still for a couple of minutes to listen for anyone else in the concrete chamber. I knew that all of Kenny's possessions were in the basement, down four floors. Not that there was a lot of the jumble left of his life. Once the staff had gone through it, there was probably just half a box left. What I was looking for, though, would be in there.

It wasn't all that long of a hike, but I wasn't as young as I used to be. The trip down the stairwell with the pauses at each floor to listen for any movement and to catch my breath, took about 10 minutes. I knew that once I got to the basement, the door opened onto the main hallway that ran the length of the building. The boiler and mechanical room would be to the immediate left of the doors, with the cafeteria across and to the right. The storage rooms were down the hall, the very last rooms on the left side. I really didn't think that any of the staff would bother me in the stairwell. They were all just too habitually lazy. I mean the elevator was right there. Why invest an ounce of extra effort into walking the stairs?

The basement floor finally came up to greet me and my Hush Puppy slippers. The door had a wire screened window about a foot wide and three feet tall right above the door handle. Cautiously looking across the hallway towards the cafeteria, my eyes adjusted to the lazy soft light of the hallway. The stairwell was relatively well lit, but more like the lighting they used to use in the blitz. Enough to see, but not enough to stave off the darkness. I squinted a little, waiting for my eyes to adjust to the light. I knew there would be another adjustment coming up when I went into the storage room that held all of Kenny's stuff. The room had a large, screened window as well, so I would have to work in relative darkness. Well, that is unless one of the staff had forgotten to turn the lights off. But in this day and age of cost cutting and capital punishment for such an infraction, I was almost sure the lights would be off.

The coast appeared to be clear. I slowly pushed the button on the door handle and eased it open. I stood beside the edge of the door listening hard, in case any of the staff had found a sudden need to actually do their jobs and go see if anyone had died on any of the four floors above us. But things were just about normal. As I paused at the stairwell door, I could hear the happy murmur of the staff in the kitchen at the far end of the hallway. The sounds of chatter was intermingled with the soft clinking of china and silverware. The disenfranchised sound of a television was a constant buzz in the background. They really were having the time of their lives down here.

The doorway I wanted was about 40 feet down the hall, on my left-hand side. I quickly pushed my head into the hall and took a look in the direction I wanted to go. There was no one there. Again, I really didn't think there would be, with all the happy times from the opposite end of the hallway. Taking in a deep breath, I pulled the door slowly open, and slipped into the hallway closing the door gently behind me. I was now totally exposed should one of those idiots in the cafeteria get a conscience and decide to perform their job. But there really wasn't any doubt about that happening.

Walking backwards, I started towards the storage room, keeping my eyes on the cafeteria entranceway and attuned for sounds of any randomly approaching footsteps. Every couple of paces I would turn around and check on my progress down the hallway. The grey door got larger and more imposing with every couple of steps. The first door on my right was the beauty salon. It was next door to massage therapy. Across the hallway, my fingers rubbed over the door handle of the cleaning supplies room. Even though I was across the hall and a few doors down from the mechanical room, I could feel a tingly light vibration in the handle. You certainly knew something was going on in the electrical room, even during the quiet, low power draw of the night. From behind the steel safety door, was a constant simmering buzz of white noise.

One room on my right and a couple next to me on my left were complete mysteries to me. I hadn't been in the basement very often, and when I was down here, I couldn't get into most of the rooms. They were rooms with no outside labels and no glass partitions to give you a hint of what went on inside. To the right of the door was a plastic card with numbers on it: B12. Probably small offices for one of the unusually high number of managers that seemed to permeate the entire building. It seemed to be the way the world is going. Not enough players, but a shitpile of coaches.

The final door before I reached the storage room was the laundry room. It was a room I knew was always open, though it had a large window in it that took away any ability to hide. A quick glimpse told me the lights in the room were out, so no one was toiling inside. Once again, that wasn't a big shock. More out of a sense of comfort than one of urgency, I gently pushed on the door, and was gratified to feel its heavy structure gently move smoothly and quietly under my coaxing. There was at least one place to slip into should anyone meander into the hallway. The laundry room was about two-thirds of the way down the hall; it would offer a welcome refuge if needed.

The door to the storage room had a tumbler lock which was never securely bolted shut. 'What could be of value in here?' So, it was just a matter of slipping inside. I noticed I was breathing a little heavier than I should. I suppose the excitement of all this covert work is something I hadn't experienced in quite a while. That, and the now painfully obvious loss of one lung. It was very comfortable to feel the adrenaline rush again, the pulsing of blood in my temples and my lungs screaming for more air. It was as if an old friend, long since abandoned, had snuck back into my life, bringing with him all the welcome habits of my past. Many were generated out of necessity to survive, while a few were simply out of desire. This dark friend was very welcome back in my life.

It took five minutes of standing still to allow my eyes to fully adjust to the lightless din. My breathing took nearly as long as my eyes to settle back down into a regular in and out metre. I could hear the laughter of the staff down the hall, and the clink of their china as the all-night coffee break continued.

Kenny's box was near the front of the tall featureless heavy-duty metal stand. It didn't take a lot of effort to pick up the box, the most awkward thing was its size. Mentally doing some measuring work, I figured it must have been about two feet high by 18 inches wide, with a volume of nine cubic feet. You do the math. There really wasn't enough in the potato chip box to warrant the size of container the staff put it in. Probably the only box they had on hand the day he died.

"Bastards," I muttered under my breath.

I was right. The scavengers some liked to call 'the staff' had managed to cleanse the few possessions of Kenny's in the few days since his death. I didn't think his family thought there was anything of value in the box. I assumed they had cleaned him out when he moved from the home he had raised them in and into Pinetree. All that would have made the trip would have been mementos … nothing else.

I knew most of his clothing had ended up at the Salvation Army. All of it except his underwear, that is. His most private of privates got burned in the Pinetree incinerator. But like so many of us here, once you take away the very clothes on our backs, there really isn't a lot left. Except for our dreams, our humanity. That the fuckers couldn't touch. They try, but a few of us hold on. We keep on looking for the light in each and every day, warding off the scavengers, fighting the good fight. For most of us we find it. We find the light that is our hope. The darkness, though, is everywhere. It's hard sometimes to ignore it or to keep on pushing yourself into battle. So, it's no wonder that every once in a while, another of the light seekers falls to the darkness. And it's interesting, that each and every time another of us falls prey to the easy way out, it's a truly dark day for all.

I smiled a little as I gently tore the duct tape off of Kenny's box. It was comforting to know that Kenny didn't take the easy way out. Kenny fought until the end. Tooth and nail. And from the feel of the box beneath my hands, Kenny truly gave it all, even though he didn't know it.

They were both right on top, what I was looking for. I knew the scavengers wouldn't be interested in it. What did they care about Kenny's friends and family? No, the scavengers didn't care about the people that mattered in his life.

How much was left in the chip box made it appear that neither did the family. No, they didn't take anything from it. Probably didn't think they could get more than a few cents out of what was left after they had picked through. Of course, I don't think they thought at all. They wouldn't have given a second of consideration to other members of the family, who might want what I held in my hands. They just didn't care.

I did care though. And again, I smiled. Kenny gave it all up when he died. He didn't go quietly into that good night. That I knew. He did not want to die. But the darkness got him napping, literally, and took him away despite his express wishes to stay.

Now with Kenny's address book and empty wallet in my hand, it was my pathway to see if even heartless shits like his son and family got to see that bright light. For a moment, I was drawn into memories of eyes that saw that absolute clarity, only the dying could see. It was their final moment on this earth. You can tell when the light hits them square in the retina. A look of awe, of shock and amazement that they were in this place; this tick of time when everything stops for them.

I pushed the small red and tan address book deep into the depths of my housecoat pocket, slipped the thin wallet beside it and stood up.

Damn my failing senses!

Because, had they been working at 100 per cent I would have heard the footsteps that my old ears hadn't picked up until it was nearly too late. Fifteen years ago, I would have heard them meander up and stop right outside the door. But not that night.

5
SEPTEMBER 1967

Tick Smith had always worn more than one hat. He didn't really think that it was a special ability, at least not while growing up with the responsibilities of school and his family weighing on his shoulders. When Tick was nearly a teenager, his father had died in a car accident, driving on a highway at a significantly higher than allowed speed. When the young cop came to the house to tell them what happened, he had checked his notebook and said with some finality that it was the booze that had caused the accident. His father had been drinking with friends in a bar for the better part of a day and decided that he could make the two-mile trip home safe and sound. In later years, Tick came to know it was just stupidity that killed him. The old man drank, that much was true, but anyone who would drink that much and drive, especially at the speeds his old man did, was just plain stupid.

It was a couple of months after the father's funeral, his 13th birthday, when that revelation really came home to roost for him. One of his old man's friends had given him a bottle of cheap wine as a gag gift. Said it was what his father had gotten for him when still a teenager. Tick Smith had thrown the bottle in the garbage. He hadn't even waited for the friend to leave. Courtesy was never very high on his list of priorities, especially after the old man's death. The last person Tick ever wanted to be like was his father. The old man was a labourer at the local flour mill, working at the very limit of his capabilities. He didn't seem to want to be anything more than that.

From that day Tick Smith wasn't a real fan of stupid or inconsiderate people. Actually, if the truth be told, he didn't like being around them at all. Somehow, that kind of person knew when they weren't wanted, and managed to stay well out of his way.

From the day his father was killed, Tick was forced into the 'second hat' role of man about the house. Not really fair to a child, true. But his mother was a little old-fashioned and believed there had to be a man at the helm. The structure of the family unit would fall apart if there wasn't a man running things. He became captain of the Smith ship. It was a lot of pressure on the kid who looked for relief from that pressure with friends.

He had hung out with a bad crowd at the end of high school and a group of them had terrorized an old man living down the street from him. It was just dumb kid stuff: busting up a fence, breaking windows in a garage and banging on the walls of the old house. He was easy to pick out by the senior citizen because of his height and jet back hair and was quickly brought in for questioning. The cops had given him a choice: go through the juvenile justice system or enter military service. So, while not being able to legally drink, he was legal age to kill. So, the choice was easy for Tick.

He served his country well for six years. By the age of 21, Tick had been in the army for three years. At that point in his hitch, he migrated to the military police. He found the honour of the uniform struck a strong chord with him. He liked the awesome powers the military police wielded on the base. Tick saw the fear that welded men's eyes open, when an MP asked to have a look in their footlocker. Normally you didn't find much outside of the odd bottle of booze or a well-worn girly magazine, but the fear was always there when an MP took an interest.

Tick knew it wasn't the man inside the dark uniform they feared, it was the power behind the badge that was represented by the uniform. The men in the barracks made fun of everyone. Everyone. No ethnic group, no sexual deviation, no mother or sister was safe from their stinging jokes, or sadistic comments. No one was safe except the MPs. No one talked about them and certainly no one made jokes about them to their faces. That just wouldn't end well for the soldier dumb enough to speak out loud.

Tick Smith liked the organic respect everyone had for the military police. He liked the rules they represented. He liked the hat.

When he opted out of the forces after six years, he walked straight into a patrolman's uniform with the Brandon City Police Force. He liked that hat too.

After five years on the beat, he was promoted to a detective — fairly young for the role at 29. Brandon, being a smaller city, warranted only a pair of detectives, and he was honoured to hold the hat of that relatively unique responsibility. Tick Smith bore it well. But in Brandon, the only things a detective did were investigate thefts, vandalism, maybe the odd assault, or car crash.

Now standing over the body of Carl Carrington, Tick Smith was holding his hat in his hand. After five years on the force, there had never been a cold-blooded murder. At least not like this one.

In Tick's first few days on the force, Beatrice Cooper had shot her old man dead away. One shot with a 410 shotgun straight between the eyes. He remembered watching as a rookie street cop, as then detective James Mullins looked around the house slowly, drinking in every detail. He watched as Mullins talked to the murderess, her hands shaking so badly she could barely bring a cup of tea to her mouth. He saw the pain in Mullins' eyes as she told him about the hundreds of nights in their 33-year marriage her husband had beat her with his leather belt. How his hands would pound her face so hard that her children didn't recognize her in the morning. Mullins, Tick noticed, even winced when Mrs. Cooper showed the disfigurement on her left arm where her loving husband had twisted it so hard, it tore the bone like a cardboard shipping tube.

He learned a lot that day watching that 20-year veteran. He had learned that a detective can also wear the hat of a compassionate peace officer. He had learned that you can forgive a person for simply killing to protect themself. Tick learned that day he wanted to be a detective. He wanted to wear that hat. Three years later, he had the chance, and didn't pass it up. He applied for and got the job thanks in large part to the recommendation of Detective Mullins, now appointed chief of the department. Things have a habit of always working out.

Now Tick Smith was looking down on the body of Carl Carrington and wondering what the hell had happened in the apartment he was standing in.

Someone had thrown a sheet over Carl Carrington, leaving a ghostly outline of his body with only small traces of blood near the carpeted floor where it had all seeped out of the man's body. There wasn't nearly as much blood as he had anticipated. Tick had overheard one of the white-coated attendants say he had died almost instantly. His heart just ran out of blood.

"Lucky bastard."

"Sir?"

"What?" Smith momentarily had forgotten where he was. "What was that, Russell?" he asked, turning to a young, blonde officer standing next to him.

"You said, 'Lucky Bastard', Detective." The wide-eyed look on the young patrolman's face told him he was thinking out loud.

"I was just thinking that of all the ways to go, this one isn't so bad."

"I suppose," the officer said, turning away from the body and walking away from Smith, "if you have to go." Tick watched the young officer move away. The colour of his skin had started to blanche a little away from a normal rich brown tan to a shade just a little off the grey hue of Smith's kitchen linoleum.

"Sorry Russell, I was thinking out loud."

Officer Russell Jenkins had been the first officer on the scene. 'What a scene it must have been,' Tick thought. When Jenkins walked in, he had to deal with a dead guy staring up at him, silently asking why, a very shaken up and sexually traumatized wife asking the same question and a young laundry delivery guy wondering when he could get the hell away from the dead guy, the wife, and the apartment building in general.

The dead guy would probably have been the easiest to deal with.

Smith walked toward the young officer, who was now looking out the large patio doors, making sure to miss the sheet and the body underneath. The view was probably one of the best in town. It looked over the lazy green river valley the city was built around, with a view that stretched for 20 miles either way. Smith thought you could probably see the air force base to the northwest, nearly half an hour away, when they had their runway lights going.

"I used to work over there," he said, looking to the horizon.

Jenkins looked at him and said, "Military Police?"

Smith nodded his head. "Three years here with the MPs and before that, three all over the country in the regular army." He motioned his head to the east, "I'll bet you can see the base at night from here."

"From our house," Jenkins motioned ahead of them, to the north. "We live up on the hill, you can see the runway lights reflecting in the clouds. It's kind of neat." There was a moment of silence, as both officers looked out at the city below them. "He didn't suffer any, did he? That's what you meant?"

"Yeah. That's what I meant." He looked back at the body. Beyond it the two attendants were waiting patiently, talking in hushed tones in the hallway near the door. In the opening to the hall, Smith could just make out the dark uniformed elbow of Jenkins' partner. "You okay Russell?" He made a small wave with his hand. "With all this?"

Jenkins nodded his head slowly, thinking about the answer. "I just, uh, never thought a body would look like that, you know. It's not like the training films at all." The officer reached into his tunic pocket and pulled out a package of cigarettes with matches stuck into the sleeve. He pulled out two, offering one to Tick Smith. Smith held up his hand to say no.

"I quit. Heard they were bad for you."

"Yeah right." Russell Jenkins shoved the rejected cig back into its slot, lit his, inhaling deeply. He looked back at the sheet and the body underneath it, "Not as bad as some things though."

6
JUNE 2002

The door handle turned to its full extent and allowed a small sliver of light into the room. A shoulder pushed against the frosted glass, and a small slender hand moved along the wall, until it found the light switch and flicked it on. There was no reason for any of the staff, especially in the middle of the night, to be in the storage room. That meant the scavengers were on the prowl.

'Lucky shit, at least gets to use a light,' I thought as I skittered along the wall towards the door hoping to hide behind it. 'Big brave scavenger,' I sneered. 'Little baby needs a light to see where he is going to steal. Hell, a man three times your age can do it in relative darkness.' Of course, he probably is afraid of the people he is supposed to care for. Maybe that's why the walls on each of the wards are peppered with night lights. All this time I thought it was to help us, when really, it was to keep us scary old people from slinking up on the scavengers and scaring them to death.

'Boy, how long can you live without knowing the truth about a thing,' I mused. There was a mental note made to pass along that little gem to Mary the next time I saw her.

The door swung open and from my limited vantage point I could see a slender hand holding it. His ill-kept nails just 18 inches from my head.

"Oh shit," some male voice muttered. Too little to make a positive identification, but if I were a betting man, I would have guessed it was Atkinson. He was one of the good ones I thought. No matter the task, he would help without being asked or begged for assistance. His fellow union brothers and sisters didn't like that get-up-and-get-going attitude. He didn't fit in with them and so simply put, the man wasn't liked at all.

"Ron," he yelled out. "Ron!"

From down the hall I could hear a faint grunt of a reply.

"I thought you told me you put that fucking Kenny's shit away." It was definitely Atkinson, but the acidic tone of his question was surprising to me. Maybe he wasn't such a good guy after all. Perhaps Atkinson was just one of those guys who was able to act the part enough and for so long that it became a real part of his persona.

I could understand that. I lived nearly an entire life as a fictitious person. Though he was young, the staff member had already figured out the nuances of working at Pinetree.

Again, a muted reply. Now that I was wanting to hear what they were saying, all I could pick up were phrases, small catches of a sentence. A single word here and there. From whom I assumed was Ron, came, "----- you. I ----- up that shit. ---- up and get back --." I got the message.

"Yeah, well you didn't tape up the box very fucking good you idiot. If administration checked on it, they would know someone had been taking a look." Atkinson jarred the door open, locking the closer at its widest point. The door pressed against me, preventing it from opening fully. Luckily, Atkinson was too focused on the half-opened box before him. I am sure that he probably licked his lips in anticipation of a big haul as he bent over the box, folded the flaps shut, lacing them together, and pushed it back on to the shelf. He paused for a moment, looking at the box.

You could see the indecision on his face as he wondered what treasures it would hold.

The scavenger thought he heard something, looked at the doorway, and muttered, "Ron?" After a moment or two of waiting and hearing no response, Atkinson turned his focus back to Kenny's box and made his decision. He quickly pulled the box off the shelf, opened the folded top and peered inside. A disgusted snort came from his nose, then he started to shuffle the meagre contents around looking for the lost treasure the other scavengers had missed. He must have been the third or fourth person to look through the box, so the treasures had long since been liberated.

From behind the door, I knew he could have turned around and discovered me. But two things were playing into my favour. First, I was hidden in the shadow of the door, bathing me in grey as I remained motionless and quiet. Plus, something else had caught his eye. Another box. He quickly folded the potato chip box back together and slipped it onto the shelf. Nearby, a box sat on higher shelf, with the name Greely handwritten on the side. Mrs. Greely had passed away the previous weekend. Atkinson started to move towards the small box.

'Little fuck.' Atkinson knew that Mrs. Greely's family wouldn't be in for a few days, because they were on holidays somewhere in the southwest. He walked over to the box, which was sitting under an unassuming shadow on the upper shelf and pushed it onto the floor. He slipped his hand along the tape, opening the box effortlessly. Almost like it wasn't taped at all.

'Greedy little fuck. Leave her stuff alone.' My eyes watered, and my hands quietly worked themselves together in balls of angry liver spotted skin and brittle bone. Closing my eyes, I took in a great silent breath and pushed all the black thoughts from my mind. I focused on getting the hell out of there and leaving Atkinson alone to do his worst.

I managed to slip around the jammed door while Atkinson studied the contents, loudly scuffling through the papers, boxes of mementos, photo albums and the rest of the contents of the freshly opened box. He was muttering something about, "no good shit in here," as I checked down the hall. The decision was made quickly. No thought, no second guesses. I started my quiet rush back to the stairwell and relative safety. Once again, I was lucky. No one emerged from the rooms in that long hallway and the quick march back up to my room took half the time that it had taken to get down here, even with the pauses on each landing to allow my ragged breath to catch up.

An hour later I was laying in bed, the small address book and wallet gripped tightly in my hands that were folded across my chest. The family of my friend would be there when I got to them. They weren't going anywhere. There was no panic now because I knew where they were. It was a big trip, but certainly doable.

Quiet in bed, the blankets pulled tight around me, I pushed and pulled fresh air in and out of what was left of my one good lung. I wanted to get the blackness out of my body as quietly as it had invaded. I had always been susceptible to blackness, more than any other affliction. I was always a happy victim to its presence. I welcomed it when it came to me, tasking me to do its dark bidding. Over the years as I mellowed, I learned how to excise it from me as much as possible. How to ensure it gave me plenty of room to breathe, to be able to live a normal life. But it stayed there, simmering in the background until tasked to come out again.

Darkness was a good friend for me. But it was one I invited over when I was sure I could contain the explosion. You could never afford to let it out, without some sort of chaperone, a chain of restraint.

So, in bed I laid down, staring at the ceiling inviting anger in but with a strong grip on its collar.

I was going to let it loose again, not just one day in a murky future, but within the days ahead. It was going to be fulfilling to let the monster out once again, let my body be the means to his horrid activities. In the past, I let the monster enjoy his many and varied desires. I had let that dark energy rule all of me, the very fabric of my being for so long. I discovered that it never really left me, this darkness, at any time. Once in a while, it had graciously allowed an almost normal personality to visit me for a bit. At times that lightness would be me for months. That light was such a departure, a balance for me from the anger and death. Then the darkness would come back to excise from existence any light within me. When it did come back, it was dangerous because of the free way it chose a direction and the subsequent black tasks it commanded.

Now, though, there was a direction and task to follow. It was my goal that was to be met, not at a random, opportunistic target. I wasn't going to stray from the path that had been laid out by me. Now the monster would serve me, and I would use all of its well-oiled violence to my end purpose.

Of course, I knew of Basil Rathbone, the British actor. I always enjoyed his portrayal of Sherlock Holmes in those grainy black and white movies. But I had never heard of a Rathbone Street — ever. Especially never in Kamloops. But that is where I was going to be headed very soon.

The first order of business was going to be killing Josh and his family. After that, maybe the monster would be let loose to play for a while longer.

7
JUNE 2002

A couple of days later I went shopping. I have to say that I really don't like shopping.

This wasn't something I did very often because I really don't care for it. Actually, should the truth be known, I hate shopping with a passion. It is such a waste of time. Just to go shopping at a huge store that's only purpose is to shove enough product in your face that eventually you will see something that you want, or need, or just plain have to have. What a waste of time and money.

I have reached an age where I have seen the transformation of the small 'mom and pop' operations, to the giant box stores. I like the 'mom and pops' a lot better. When you went to Grahams Mercantile, they helped you find what you need and 'shazam' you were in and out of there in less time than it takes to wait in an express checkout at Kennedy's to pay for two pairs of underwear and a Milky Way. No extra gadgets to help you around the kitchen stuffed into your plastic bag. Just bang! Get what you need and nothing more.

I don't even get the seemingly religious pull of the giant malls for my age group. Sure, they have those 'morning walkers' that chug along in endless circles around the mall concourse. That's not such a bad idea. Though the circuit would certainly get a little tiring after oh, say one trip. The same route past the same featureless mannequins, with the same overblown nipples sticking through a sheer blouse (or whatever they call it now) can get a little long in the tooth.

It's the grey haired 'sitters' as I call them that are a complete mystery to me. I just don't get them. They sit on the benches watching, well . . . whatever it is they watch, go by. No one talks to them, no one pays attention to them, except other members of the 'sitters'. What do they talk about? God only knows. They aren't pariahs, but they don't seem to fit in either. They just sit, silently, on every bench throughout the mall. Their walkers or canes are always directly in front of them, held close in a death grip to their bodies with rice paper hands, laced together with blue veins. Like a 16-year-old is going to try to grab their $50 aluminum cane. Really.

All day they sit, walk a little, maybe to the next bench, then sit some more. That's it. I just don't get it. I don't get the point. Are they so beat down by the fact they have aged and haven't managed to spend the required portion of their lives in the mall? So maybe they now have to log in a certain amount of time to make sure they have the requirements topped up before they leave, permanently? You know, Saint Peter tells them they can't get to heaven without 624 hours and 15 minutes at the mall. "Sorry, you are going down!!"

Come on.

My trip to the mall was surgical. Or at least I had a specific store in mind. I drove straight to the parking spots closest to the front doors. No need to go anywhere else in the mall. Just a quick visit to the giant glass and concrete box.

Kennedy's Department Store.

It's the everyday store for everybody with everything. Even a senior citizen bent on hunting and killing a small family can find what they need at Kennedy's. It was the logical choice to buy the supplies I needed. First off, they have everything under one roof. Literally. Plus, they are everywhere with the exact same product lines so no matter where you are, you can get what you need. And it's because of that fact that I am onto my second point.

So many people come through the store you can rest assured no one will remember some old fart buying a few non-descript supplies for a little camping trip. They do have, however, a very good in-store security system. The cardboard signs at the front doors tell us the security system is how they keep their prices so low. The system is very oppressive from a would-be thief's point of view. Multi-axis cameras strategically dotted around the store for general surveillance and then there are the floor walkers. These people are very good at not looking like security people. Except of course, if you know what to look for. You know, the sweating man in the heavy parka, walking around the store in early September. The woman with the shopping cart filled with items that are laid out just a little too neatly. They are just a little too obvious not to be floor walkers. But I wasn't worried about them. I was going to be paying for everything I placed in my little hand basket. Cash on the barrel head every time.

Now they have added the centurions standing at the exits, that beep loudly, telling you, "We 'Kennedy's staff' have forgotten to check some item in your possession through the till, please return to the store."

Kennedy's is not the place to go to borrow stuff with extreme prejudice unless you are the best at what you do. Amateurs need not apply, you will go directly to jail.

I wasn't worried about that this trip. I did, however, wear my large-brimmed wicker golf hat. It helped to keep the sun off of my ever-growing forehead and keeps the security cameras from getting a really good look at me. Besides, one bout of melanoma was enough for this guy. No need to tempt fate. Never golfed a day in my life, seems like another huge waste of time. Besides, how hard could it be, getting a little ball in a big hole, in the middle of a big over-manicured chunk of grass? Not too damn hard. But I had bought the hat a few years ago because it seemed to go with the persona I had wriggled into at the time. Eventually I got to kind of like it so kept it as a souvenir of that time in my life.

It was too bad I would have to throw it out after this trip. I really did like the hat. But there was no way something that could be identified would be found anywhere near me or the place where I live. So, the shirt, pants, shoes, everything, even the underwear and socks were going to be heading to six separate dumpsters around the city. It was the safest way. No trace evidence whatsoever. It was the discipline one had to adopt to stay invisible.

But I did like the hat.

8
JUNE 2002

"Sir, can I help you find something?"

The voice crackled like he was talking through a shitty old microphone. And the up inflection on 'something?' told me immediately that he wasn't very good or hadn't been on the job a very long time. He was still nervous about meeting people and coming up to them to give them his years of life experience in making a purchase decision. No, this one would have to wait for a few years to help me. Each person would be remembered by him because he was trying so hard.

"That's okay," I began, not even turning around. "I'm just having a look around."

When I turned towards the voice, I was surprised by the good-looking young man now looking at me with somewhat saddened blue eyes. His blonde hair was cut in the style of the day, pushed all to the right side of his head, and dyed — streaked I think they call it — with light purple. On this kid it didn't look bad. The name tag on his chest told me his name was Scott C. Sorry Scott C., not today.

"All right." He nervously looked at the wall of sporting equipment to his right. "If there is something you need just come and get me."

I smiled my disarming smile and put the impossibly small emergency blanket back on its hook. "I will, Scott."

Scott C. straightened up a long row of plastic egg holders, then headed back to the mystery place all employees go when they aren't helping senior citizen men find the supplies they needed to kill three people. I have no clue which department that would be, but he appeared to find it quickly.

What I was going to need for this job, I wasn't sure about. There was an idea in my head, but the details of it hadn't gelled just yet. I knew what I wanted to do, but how, specifically how I was going to mechanically go about the procedure of killing them, I wasn't sure. But I was pretty confident it would come to me.

It was a procedure I had used in my life many times. I suppose the roots of the methodology was my family history. On my mother's side, her father and his entire genealogy were blacksmiths. They created something out of nothing in a time when nothing was all everybody had. I remember days spent in my grandpa's blacksmith shop. The smell of the forge piercing straight through my nose and swathing me in a warmth that I still can't explain. Even at this moment, the smell of coal is enveloping me. That was more than six decades ago, and the smell still is attached to the memory.

Grandpa would need something to fix a farmer's thing-a-ma-bob. He would first look around his shop and the discard bin out the back door. This was a very exciting time for me. After a few minutes of hearing him curse, banging metal around, he would walk back in, grab his hat from its old worn hook to the right of the door, slip it quietly onto his balding head and say to me, "Looks like we are heading to the nuisance grounds."

Oh joy! The nuisance grounds, the dump, the landfill site, the first and best recycle bin.

He would walk around picking up this item or that, talking to me like I was an adult and looking for the perfect piece of garbage that would help him fix what he needed to. It was a blast. Of course, more often than not, we would bring a lot more home than we needed.

One hot summer day, I found a prosthetic left leg under a bag of National Geographic magazines. It even had the shoe attached. That was gold! Of course, my mom wouldn't let me have the leg in the house so it stayed out in the back shed.

It's the long way of doing it, but this is how I have always approached problems. I knew what I needed to do or what had to be done. I had a faint idea how I was going to go about it, and then looked for the goods that would physically allow me to pull it off. From my position, it was the logical way of going about any problem that stood in my way. And it always worked out in the end.

So, I stood in the sporting equipment aisle at Kennedy's, thinking of nothing even remotely related to a few relaxing days at the campground sitting around the smoky campfire roasting marshmallows. Roasting was on the agenda, after a fashion. In half an hour my shopping cart contained the few items I needed. It really is amazing what you can buy at Kennedy's. Equally amazing is what you can do with what you buy at Kennedy's, if you have even half a creative streak running through you. That and absolutely no conscience.

But you have to think outside the box.

If you let the dark side out to play for a bit.

9
JUNE 2002

The trip was memorable only in the fact that it was uneventful.

The most difficult part of it was getting away from the home without attracting too much unwanted attention. Boy, the questions they ask when you want to spend a couple of days away to kill some family members of a buddy in a distance province. Man, oh man!

"You want to do what, Ivan?"

"I want to take off for a couple of days." I felt a little sheepish sitting on the leather chair in front of Mrs. Keegan. "Just to get away." To be honest I really didn't have to ask permission. It wasn't the sort of place that you were admitted to. I paid to be lodged in Pinetree. I know, I know. It was me paying my own way. But still, I was the one who was contributing to their well being. And paying well I might add.

I had a very strong compulsion to reach out and grab the small brass nameplate that faced me on her cheap cluttered mahogany desk and pummel her with it. "Mrs. Joyce Keegan, Administrator." But I held back, doing my best to look hopeful and sheepish. In my world she was the top of the scavenger pile. None of us in Pinetree knew her background other than she really didn't have much hope in making this place 'The Best Place to Live,' as their brochure proudly stated. She hired people based on their ability to accept the extremely low starting wage which brought the bottom feeders to the barrel. There was no real effort made to keep a watchful eye over the staff, who were pretty well allowed to run amuck. It was inevitable that they would dip into the cookie jar that fed them. The lot of them would start out wanting to assist the seniors living in the building but ended up as scavengers.

Sitting there made me feel like I was sitting in front of a priest without the anonymity of the confessional. Perhaps a delinquent young man in the principal's office would be a better way to put it.

"I thought I would take off for a couple of days, you know, for a holiday." I tried my best to be casual about it. I really didn't want her wondering what the hell I was doing.

"Ivan," she said, as she sat back, now more amused than shocked and concerned, "you are retired dear, you don't need to take a holiday." It was the condescending tone, I suppose, that pissed me off. My blood pressure, I could feel, was edging closer and closer to causing the top of my silver haired head to blow clear through the pale white suspended ceiling tiles. As if we didn't need a holiday from this place.

"You people," I began, a little more indignantly than I intended, "you take a holiday from this place, don't you?"

"Of course, Ivan. We take holidays. We work here. We get paid to be here."

"Why shouldn't we take a holiday? There is money changing hands, it's just going the opposite direction."

"Ivan, we work. So once in a while we need a little break from the job."

"True, I'll give you that. But each night you get to go home, away from the job, away from this place. We … I … don't ever get to get away from here. We are surrounded by the same people, day after day." Again, it was a fun line of horseshit. I actually didn't mind most of the people. Well, some anyhow. Especially

Mary. She, I really liked.

"But where will you go on this ... holiday ... Ivan?" Keegan said the word "holiday" like it was dirty, something that an old man shouldn't be allowed to have. I may as well have told her the truth because she probably would have had the same incredulous look on her face.

"I'm just going to hop on a bus and go see my sister in Calgary." I held up a brochure I had picked up at the travel agency in the mall after my shopping trip to Kennedy's. "It says here," I said, pushing the brochure across the desk to her, "that I can get to Calgary if I take the express, in about 12 hours. Only a couple of stops." To help with the deception, I had gotten the travel agent to highlight a couple of bus routes for me to Calgary. Complete with prices.

Mrs. Keegan looked a little pensive. Her eyes scanned the bus brochure for some sign of a lie. "But I don't remember you having a sister in Calgary, Ivan. You didn't put that down in your application." She shook her head, still probing the photocopied bus schedule she held in her hand. "I don't know about this. I don't know if you know what you are up against in Alberta. I would be worried about you."

For a moment I was worried about the lies I had told four years ago. It was getting more and more difficult to remember the misdirection I have told people about my life. I should have thought through the need for a 'sister' in Calgary — or anywhere, for that matter. I just hoped she wouldn't care too much about it and start to check the details on that photocopy of my application that was tucked into a drawer somewhere. Most of the information was a complete fabrication, from my name on down to my late wife. No truth anywhere. It was probably the most outrageous pile of shit I had ever written down. Normally, you write lies that are a half-step off of the truth, so they are easier to remember if you are asked anything about it. But when I completed the application, I really didn't think I would need to worry about it in the future. It kind of felt like the last dishonest thing I would get to accomplish in my life. But I should have included a relative somewhere as a safety net. Damn!

Oh, how times are changing.

"Mrs. Keegan, I'm paid up until the end of next month and I've already instructed my lawyer to pay out the rest of the year. I like it here. I just want a break and a chance to see my sister." I pulled out my best puppy dog eyes. "You don't have to worry about me. I've been there before." That part was true. I spent a lovely summer there in the mid-70s. It was a growing town back then with so many new people coming in that everyone was unfamiliar with the region, their neighbours, or the rules. I had so much fun letting the blackness out to play that summer.

But now, sitting in that grey office, it was as if the sun suddenly broke through an impossible bank of black evil clouds. I had said the magic words, "coming back ... money paid up front ... more money from the Bank of Ivan, even if I'm not here." Boy, how shallow can you get? Yes, she was deeply concerned about my well-being out there in the wilds of Alberta. I was grateful she had passed by the Curious George stage of the conversation and didn't pursue the 'sister' thing any further. That family member was on a whim. Some little nuggets to keep her happy. There was no sister or any other relation in that part of the country. Actually, as far as I know, I don't have any relatives anywhere in the country, or the world.

"Well, I suppose we could let you slip away for a few days Ivan. After all, it is just to Calgary, isn't it?" She leaned back in her big leather chair, comfortable in the fact I was coming back, if not the flow of my money. "When do you leave?"

"Tomorrow," I said, standing up. "I thought I needed a little time away after Kenny died and all." I shrugged my shoulders, "You know, just a little space." Where the hell did I hear that? Oprah? Space? No idea what that means.

She nodded her head like one of those dogs you used to see in the back windows of cars bobbing down the highway. Well, you used to see them that is until someone decided having a four-pound chunk of porcelain in the back window of a car going 60 miles an hour was like have a loaded mortar round go off when the car hit something hard. Who'd a thunk that something so cute would cause a massive amount of cranial damage? Not me. I still have one in the back of my Chrysler. It is the least of my worries.

"Well, you have fun Ivan. We'll see you in a few days."

How hard was that? Not so hard.

The rest of the trip was just too easy. Free to move about with impunity, I caught a cab to the bus depot the next morning and yes, I boarded the Greyhound that was going to Calgary. However, in Calgary I was going to get off and change buses to continue on to the Thompson Country of British Columbia. Because it was a Greyhound, I didn't even have to show any identification, paid with cash and used Kenny's name when asked. He certainly wasn't going to mind. Not now or ever. It seemed kind of appropriate to use his name on this trip. But no one ever asked for identification of an old man travelling the country by bus.

There were a few moments of angst when they were checking in my oversized carry-on bag. I thought for a moment they would make me open it. The clerk looked at me awfully hard when I threw it up on the stainless-steel counter. It sounded and looked as heavy as it was. Twenty-three pounds. Maybe he was looking hard at me because this grey-haired man could wield that kind of bag around with relative ease. Oh, the joys of staying in shape.

He gave me a sly smile and pushed the bag onto the antique luggage cart that would be pushed out the massive cargo doors to the outside of the building where the buses were all angle parked, idling and waiting.

I held my finger to the side of my nose in a salute I had seen in a movie before this little shit was born and smiled.

We both laughed, me a little harder than maybe I should have, but there was a small sense of relief that the bag had made it that far. Well, maybe a very large sense of relief.

The trip was going to be 18 hours. Long enough, but it would give me time to think through all the details I needed to. Plus, at my age, sleeping is kind of an in-and-out thing. I would sleep when I could. I got lucky when I pulled the 'age thing' so was seated first. Then, I welched my way into a window seat. The privileges of being a senior. All things considered the fact I was a senior served me well on that trip.

When we finally got there, I stood up, stretched my legs and headed outside into the humid Thompson Country air of Kamloops. I breathed deeply. Mixed with the diesel fuel, the air was filled with the aroma of fruit and pine trees, fresh cut grass. As you breathed in, it held a crystal-clear sensation that can only be described as pure. Notwithstanding the diesel fuel fumes, of course. It had been a while since the symphony of smells mixed together for me.

There was a certain sense of accomplishment to be back in Kamloops. Not only just to be standing in the town but to have made it that far. Full circle. For no reason at all I stood on the ramp and smiled. My only regret was that I wouldn't be able to spend too much time in the place I used to call home. Tomorrow about the same time, I would be boarding another bus to continue my somewhat delayed trip west to Vancouver. I really did want to see the ocean again before being driven back to the prairies.

I picked up a rental car, something in the mid-size range. Kenny's driver license was still valid, so it paved the way for me. The counter clerk didn't give me a second look when I handed her cash to use for payment. It mustn't have been that unusual for a car to be paid for with cash, because she counted it out quickly, tucked the cash into a drawer then asked for my credit card. Had I been about 40 years younger, a bit taller and a lot more handsome, she may have paid attention. For me, she had nothing. I had given her a credit card that was more than a decade out of date, with a name not remotely close to the name on the driver's license. She tossed the card through the machine quickly. It would only be keyed into the system if I brought the car back with a couple of inches missing off the front end of it. Her only concern was that my credit card was legible on the carbon copy.

Through my entire life I kept a couple of 'safe' cards and ID ready for a quick getaway. Coupled with a couple of small bundles of cash, the 'personal go' kit was easy to grab, stash on your body without any unsightly bulges or bags. Literally fit in an oversize lunch bag. When I was busy in the days prior to retirement, it wasn't all that hard to do, but required discipline to maintain the cards, keep them valid and close to a zero balance. I let everything slide once I checked into Pinetree, so was thankful she didn't check the card too closely. Luckily, Kenny kept all his documentation in the little booklet and the wallet I had taken from his box at the Pinetree. His identification would be burned once I got back to Manitoba. It was a single use endeavour. I was sure his daughter in Ontario wouldn't want his licence and I knew that Josh would definitely have no need for it by the end of the day.

A couple of miles down the highway from Kamloops I stopped at a small motel. Again, Kenny wouldn't mind that I used his name on this little trip. I didn't want anything that would make folks look too closely at me or my luggage. I wanted a mom-and-pop operation that was used to people dropping in for anything from an hour to a month. With the plastic flowers strategically planted around the entrance and the "Massage Bed—Free!" sign on the stained wall behind the counter, I knew this was a 'cash is okay' kind of place. That was perfect, so I could lessen my footprint anywhere out here.

Inside the dingy room, a quick sponge bath was all I needed to refresh from the trip. The excitement and energy of the coming events overwhelmed my need to rest or relax. My body begged me to get going — begged for release. It had been edging closer and closer to this time, my mind rolling over the details and the delicious thought of the events that were going to unfold.

I took a quick sweep of the room, making sure nothing personal of mine was left in there, then spun around, headed out of the room and started on the short drive to the city. It was the discipline. No matter where you dropped down you take everything with you just in case you didn't come back. You just never knew when some little kink was going to throw a giant wrench into the best laid plans and force an immediate change in direction. Always use a single bag so it's easy to grab and to toss if needed.

There was a 7-11 just a few miles down the road from the hotel so I stopped in for a cup of coffee. Just a little pick-me-up. The neat thing about the Thompson Country is the fact that a lot of convenience stores have benches and tables under big flowery umbrellas. So, I sat, looked at the white capped mountains, with the grey hard stone beneath and rested. Not once did I look at the Ford and remember what was in the trunk. I didn't need to. Inside was a small collection of implements that I may need. Those that I didn't use would be tossed into the nearby lake or river. I would be travelling back to my meager home with no luggage save a shaving kit.

After finishing my coffee, putting the cup into the overflowing trash bin, and stretching my muscles, I headed back into the store, and the public phone. I tossed in a quarter and dialed the phone number I had memorized.

"Hullo?"

It was the boy.

"Is the lady of the house in? I have a special offer from Fuller just for her."

"She's not available right now and I really don't think ..."

"How about the man of the house?" I interrupted.

"Are you him?"

"Listen mister, we don't need any of that stuff." There was a pause, while he reflected as to what exactly I was selling. "Really and my dad is sleeping, so waking him would be a bad idea."

The phone slid quietly back into its cradle, and I stopped to pick up another cup of coffee for the drive across town. Just a small one this time. I added a couple of extra cream, so I could drink it a little faster.

The house was exactly as I had imagined it. Small, but relatively neatly kept. It was not outrageously trimmed and laid out, however, like many of the neighbours on their block. It was just a house. Maintained as required, nothing above and beyond the call. There were little signs of who lived there. The sidewalk was cracking badly, and huge chunks had been pulled out and replaced with grass. The time to repair the slab never entered the lazy shit's mind. Just cover it up and make it look nice for a little while. The paint on the door was starting to peel and then covered up with another coat right over top. It was all probably just enough to get that crazy wife off his back. If she had been my wife, part of my trip to the lovely Thompson Country would have been redundant because she would have already gone missing — permanently. But then, not everyone wears the liberal moral suit better than I do.

I smiled at the thought as I grabbed what I needed from the surprisingly large trunk of the rented car and gently closed the lid. The crepe-soled shoes didn't make a sound as I ambled up the walkway to the front door. There was no window near the door, but there was a peephole resting in the middle. I stood off to one side, my back to the door after I knocked.

When he opened the very tired, steel, painted door

and there was this grey-haired man standing there holding a very large and obviously heavy duffel bag over his left shoulder, he must have thought, 'Oh great, a bum.' It took a few moments for him to realize who was standing at the door.

But then, as the small motor in his head finally kicked in and smoke began to pour out of his ears at the effort, his eyes rolled in recognition. "What ..." was the only and last word he managed to get out.

He didn't move, didn't react at all. I suppose he would have, had he noticed the foreign, weighted object in my right hand. But I am pretty sure I wouldn't have given him time to move or pull away anyhow.

Despite my years of inactivity, the movement came easy, smoothly and with surprising vigour. Far more than I needed.

It felt so fucking good.

10
JUNE 2002

Some big time fucking avenger of the meek and weak I am. A Robin Hood for the oppressed masses. ‘Come beneath my aura of safety, my friends, no harm will come to you.’ I don’t think so. Sure, my friend Kenny gets fucked over by his own children, his own flesh and blood. Then there I go, the great white knight on the big white-maned steed to avenge his being fucked over, and.....

Christ, it pisses me off! Well, that was a bad choice of words.

I mean Jesus Christ! What kind of statement is that going to make? What are the police going to say when they arrive at Kenny’s kid’s house? Sure, they are going to be a little excited ‘cause there were three people dead in it. Well, technically two in the house and that snotty little kid in the garage ... but still there is going to be plenty of testosterone floating around that place for a good long while.

I still can’t believe it. What the hell? You can prepare yourself mentally, you can get yourself into fighting shape, you can work through all the shitty little details that go into an action like this. Then … well it just pisses me off.

The father, Josh, went out like a light. One moment he was on, opening the door, and then bang, dead. Not even enough effort expended to make me break a sweat. Just pop, down he went like the big wet pile of shit he was. It took a moment for me to check the field of view from the front step, but the overgrown lilacs prevented much in the way of a clear view of the door from the street. The front was clear. Then I stepped in, kicking his legs back inside, so I could close the door.

For a moment, I stopped and looked down at him, blood streaming from the large wound the machete inflicted on his pulpy flesh. Just too easy. I stood over him, legs on either side of his shoulders.

The machete I purchased at Kennedy's did really well. It was advertised as being able to cut through saplings up to one inch in diameter. No problem at all with a little bit of skin, tissue and most of his neck. No problem at all. I now believe the advertising I read on the packaging of the weapon. Of course, the half hour I spent with a wet stone making sure the blade was honed to perfection helped. Yup, preparation is everything.

Shhhhkkkkkk!

And out he went.

Lights out.

End of story.

For some reason, a moment in time entered my stream of consciousness. I am sure we all remember the 'Blue Light Specials' at the big box stores. However, at that moment, it was my special I thought about. "Attention Ivan shoppers, there's a head at the main doors, on sale right now, a whopping 88 per cent off. This is a blue light special for a limited time only!"

The second safety shot was vertically across his forehead, nearly from the crown of his prematurely balding head to the bridge of his nose, opened up the skull like it was a coconut dropped from the top of the Empire State Building. I was able to make that a full force, down shot, so all of my weight was firmly behind it. It might have made a noise as it connected with his head, I don't remember. But it certainly did change the man's appearance.

I paused for a moment, looking at his eyes. The left one slowly feeling the pull of gravity and slipping to his right. The right eye was buried somewhere in his eyelid. There was a small trickle of blood out of his opened mouth. However, the catastrophic impact on his neck pushed a fountain of blood from the wound onto the carpet. I took a couple of steps further into the house making sure not to get any blood on the soles of my boots.

"For being such a heartless bastard," I mused, "you sure have a shit-pile of blood."

From behind me I heard someone exhale loudly, "Holy fuck!" It was the boy. He was in the arched entrance to what I assumed was the kitchen or dining room. His face was white, drained of blood — somewhat prophetic I think — and he froze for one second, eyes wide open in shock.

Suddenly he found his muscles and bolted down the hallway away from his father and slammed through a door at its end. The whole house shimmied as the door piled into its frame. From somewhere in the bowels of the house, I heard someone yell.

"How many times do I have to tell you not to slam the goddamn doors!"

"That," I said as I moved down the hall, "sounds like your charming mother." I checked each room as I walked the 20-foot run down the hallway. No one else was in the place. As I expected. No one liked these people enough to pop over for a cup of tea.

It sounds to me, like she's a little upset about the doors. On the wall near the door, was a picture of the whole family. Kenny included. That stopped me mid-stride.

It was the four of them, sitting on a log, obviously somewhere in the mountains. For some reason, they were all smiling. Kenny had his arms wrapped around his son and daughter-in-law. The boy was standing behind, his arms on both his parents' shoulders. There was something in the smile Kenny had. It was his smile all right. But it wasn't the same as the one he had when talking about his secretary and the Pontiac. It wasn't an honest, open, "happy to be here" kind of smile. It was a smile that wanted to be let go. But it was held tight, close to his chest. It was a restrained half smile. An obligatory 'have to' smile. It struck me that it was the same smile he had when they visited him at Pinetree. Sad.

I nodded my head and continued my journey through the mahogany doorway at the end of the hallway. Its brass knob glowing in the shadowed light of the dim walkway.

The boy was hiding in the garage. As the door slid open, I could see the typical minivan sitting in the middle of its double width, completely surrounded by hundreds of boxes of what I assumed was just a massive collection of shit. Some opened, overflowing with papers, clothing, the flotsam and jetsam of life. It was much messier than their house. I suppose it all came here when its usefulness had passed inside the home. Kind of like the boy.

It took no time to track him down. The wracking sobs steered me directly to him. He was hiding in the back seat of the minivan like a little baby. He even had his seatbelt on — like he was going somewhere. Or that he was going to be made a little bit safer by the 'click to live' motion. The door of the maroon Dodge made the same Shhhhkkkkkk!! sound as the machete as it rolled open. The boy made a slight squelching noise as the door revealed his position in the back seat.

We both stopped in our tracks for a moment. I held

up the machete and made a big show of putting it on the grimy cement floor of the garage. His eyes watched the move as a moth would be attracted to a light. From the middle of my back I withdrew a large hunting knife, another great deal at Kennedy's. The blade was about six inches long, with a fake bone handle. It was a heavy weapon with a chine that was close to a quarter of an inch thick at the hilt. Experience told me it would take an incredible amount of strain before it broke.

My knife beckoned him out of the confines of the vehicle because it was a close quarter weapon. The machete needed a long swing arch to give enough energy to do the damage.

The boy shook his head out of fear, and rightly so. His eyes were still wide but glistening now with tears.

The knife was shifted to my left hand, though it was the weaker of the two because it would allow a more significant range of movement in the attack. The right hand would have struggled to gain enough momentum to deliver a fatal blow. The seat, the door and his position deep in the van all played into that quick decision.

"Sit up and take your medicine like a man," I said to him. But no, he just sat there, weeping like a woman shaking his head back and forth. "Come on," I urged, "out you come. Come on." The knife underlined my order with quick motions towards the crowded garage. He didn't even have the courtesy to look at me. He was staring straight ahead through the windshield at a wall of cardboard. There was nothing to see. His breathing was ragged, short and interspersed with sobs. He was glistening with sweat, his trendy t-shirt showing blotchy darkness at the pits and the chest. I was pretty sure it would be stained in the back as well.

"What do you want mister?" he asked slowly when his eyes finally shifted in my direction.

When I looked at him it was sad. Not sad that he was going to die. Not sad that this young life was going to end so quickly and violently. But rather, sad because he really didn't know what was about to happen. Sad because he was unaware.

Now before everyone gets all crazy here, a quick statement for clarity. The kid was in his mid-teens, not a child. He had lots of time to change the path his parents had started him on. I know, I know, he would have had a chance to change before he became an adult, to set things right. But two things were against him: first he saw my face. And secondly and by far more importantly, I just really wanted to kill the little fucker. I needed to.

End of story.

So Shhhhkkkkkk! He went out like a bed-bug on the seat of the Dodge. Shhhhkkkkkk! The second impact sliced cleanly through the seatbelt, and into his neck. The now free seatbelt made a noisy, quick retraction into the plastic of the rear window pillar.

Actually, kind of scared me a little. I *may* have jumped. A little.

The kid just slumped down, his hands at his side, teetered slightly towards the window of the van, his matted hair resting against it. I didn't waste a lot of time admiring my handiwork but did notice the large dark red stain appearing beneath him on the light beige seat material.

And again, for clarity sake, I took no pleasure in this. It was simply the thing that had to be done. The darkness demanded three, and he was number two.

Now, the woman was a different story.

I suppose looking back on it now, some of what

happened probably was my fault. I should have thought about it while I was having a coffee at 7-11, let alone the second cup on the way over. It should have at least crossed my mind. But my thoughts were in other places, in planning for contingencies. What if one ran? What if the kid answered the door? What if they started to make a lot of noise? What if the neighbours called the cops?

My mind was running at a smooth three thousand miles an hour, turning over everything. What to do? How to do it? When to do it? Yada yada yada. I mean, I had other things swirling around my old noggin' than how much coffee I had drunk. A lot more pressing things were to be considered. For example, how I was going to kill three people that afternoon. I had things to think about.

But at that moment I needed to know where mom was. I paused only a moment watching the son go dark, before I cleaned the blade of the knife on the seat of the van and slipped it back into the scabbard that was still secured at the back of my belt. I picked up the machete and turned back to the quiet house.

I have to tell you, a quiet house is really something I love. It really is. Everyone has those moments when your house is quiet. There is the soft ticking of a house just settling. The furnace or AC blowing, the movement of small items with small breezes or the home just breathing in place. But when you are in a house after killing everyone in it, the sounds are different. The house knows something bad has happened and it really does seem to hold its breath. The silence is heavier, blanketed by the weight of the bodies strewn about. I would often just sit quietly on a chair and listen as the house came to the realization that it would never be the same. Eerie, I know, but very true.

When she yelled at the son about slamming the door, I wasn't sure where the voice came from, so I knew a thorough search of the entire house was in order. I was, however, pretty sure she didn't know I was in her house. That would have caused a bit of a louder stir. Crying, slobbering, begging, screaming, that sort of thing. If she knew.

I started towards the upper floor. She wouldn't be on the main floor. That I discounted immediately. All the ruckus, quiet as I was in the killing of her husband and silent as he was in the dying, was still enough noise to have made her curious if she was anywhere near. Plus, her kid did let go with a little blue streak when he saw me standing over his dead father. Her bellow at the kid about the door sounded as if it came from deep within the house. So, she hadn't heard the boy yell, but probably felt the vibration of the door to the garage slamming shut.

After climbing the carpeted stairs, I worked my way through the messy bedrooms of the family (God, did they need a housekeeper), then the upstairs bathrooms. I checked each room methodically, the closets, under the bed, master bathroom, walk-in closet. Messy as the entire floor was, it was empty. I finally worked my way back to the main floor, finding another stairwell that led to the basement. It was opposite the second-floor stairs just off the entrance to the front room. As I swung around the corner, I looked at Josh, who was laying still on the floor. It was a cursory look. I really didn't think he was getting up to offer refreshments.

The upper floor search must have taken about three minutes after killing the boy. From the time I pulled up on the street, the whole operation to that point would have been about five minutes. I knew that was just about enough time. Any longer, and I wouldn't be leaving the house safe and undetected.

A quick scan of the downstairs recreation room yielded a door lit at the end of the room. She was in the bathroom.

The woman wasn't hiding, crouching behind a door, bubbling with fear like her son. She hadn't heard anything from my activities upstairs. I could hear the soft sounds of water splashing around. She was just having a bath. Her husband and kid had just been killed, sliced open like the pair of cows they were, and she was making her body all wrinkly. How nice for her.

So, what is she doing? Cradling her dead husband's head, or swooning over the dead meat in the van? Nope. She's soaking away the troubles of her very superficial world, such as it is, in a nice hot bubble bath. I could hear small bubbling sounds of a bathtub mingling with a human body moving around in it. A small voice, singing quietly to some song I didn't recognize. I could only grab a small bit here and there.

Her husband didn't make a sound. He went down only letting out a little faint whisper — more of an exhale than anything recognizable. The boy made some wet sounds, but little else. As I pressed my ear against the door, I was listening to the last sounds this chick was ever going to make.

"... be watching you..."

"... breath you take..."

I have no clue what song it was. Whatever it was, she wasn't doing it any credit at all.

I tried the closed door and found it wasn't locked. The knob didn't make any noise as I turned it and slipped very quickly into the room. Then I stopped dead. The room was very dark, the only light from two candles. One was on the vanity while the other was on the lip of the bathtub. My eyes were totally useless in the darkened room. I slipped the door closed, held my breath and pressed myself quietly against the wall trying to get my body to absorb itself into the paint and wallpaper.

From the tub, the sounds were soft, and unalarming.

Water was gurgling around the woman, as she laid down in the tub, a facecloth over her face. Once in a while I could hear her breath, as she mouthed the words to the music. I could see her feet, sticking above the waterline at the far end of the tub. It was on my right in the room, the taps at the near end. There were light remnants of bubbles floating in the water, stuck to bits of her legs. For a moment, now just a moment, I thought about the fact this was a woman, naked not four feet from where I stood. In the old days …

By my estimation, it was nearly 20 seconds since I had slipped into the room, and she was onto a new song. By then my eyes fully adjusted to the room. During that time, I was scanning quickly from corner to corner, acclimating myself to the room, and the obstacles I was facing. It was small, no more than 12 feet square. A large mirror was to my left, above a vanity, cluttered with cosmetics that ran the entire length of the room. Opposite to that was the bathtub. At the end of the tub was the toilet. A large bath towel sat crumpled on the seat.

I took a tentative step forward and peeked around the corner and into the tub. She was laying back, up to her neck in the water, her body completely hidden by the soapy bubbles that filled the tub three quarters of the way to the rim. Just her head was visible, her hair pulled up, and held in a towel on top of her. Her eyes were covered by a matching facecloth, and she was listening to a radio with a set of headphones. Her head would rock a little one way or another, as the music pounded away in the dim quiet of the room. I could just hear the music that was playing very loudly through the headphones.

The machete in my right hand was transferred to my left one again as I moved across the room, no longer concerned about the noise I was making. I grabbed the radio from the floor and held it up. It was a big ghetto blaster, with speakers built into the unit. Because it was so dark in the room I had no clue about the colour. I suppose it doesn't matter.

It was heavier than I expected. In retrospect I know why ... now.

I slipped it in the water and jumped back a little as she jerked violently below me.

"What the fuck?" she yelled. Her eyes immediately darted to me after tossing the cloth into the tub. "What the fuck? You could have electrocuted me, you fucking moron. If you hadn't lost the power cord ..."

It dawned on me like a hammer. Batteries! The fucking thing was probably running on a dozen giant 'D' batteries. Great!! It weighed a ton because of them.

Then her eyes dialed into focus, and she saw that I wasn't her husband. Her face changed in a heartbeat, from that of a woman startled half to death out of a bath, to shock and terror. "Who the..."

She immediately lunged at me, pushing herself out of the water at a speed I wasn't prepared for. Her rapid escape from the bathtub set me back a couple of steps and my ass came to a jarring stop on the vanity cupboard, knocking a candle into the sink with a very loud tinkling sound. Her body quickly cleared the side of the bathtub, and she was on the bath matt, standing buck naked facing me. She was reaching for a towel to cover up her privates, mistakenly thinking I was after her body. When she located the towel, her eyes quickly moved to it and when they sought me out again, they got very big.

"Sorry dear, this is not what you think."

Shhhhkkkkkk!!

She fell hard back into the tub, propelled by the weight of the first impact of the machete. The water splashed and gurgled for a moment, then quietly settled around the body that had crashed into it. The red stain that centered from the large, angled impact to her head, quickly diffused throughout the bathwater. The second strike was out of habit and in this case not at all necessary.

I stood just staring at her for, Christ, I don't know how long, watching the stain slowly even out in the tub and calming my breath. Both of her feet were dangling over the side with small puddles of water growing under each heel. There was no twitching or any residual effects of the attack. She had just died after one strike to the head with the machete.

Shaking my head in amazement, doesn't it make sense that the most interesting was saved for last? It turned out it would be her who gave me the most grief. But at least now it was over.

"Kenny, that was all for you."

I shoved myself away from the vanity top. It was then that I noticed the floor under my feet.

11
JUNE 2002

"You're shittin' me."

"I'm not shitting you sir, it's urine."

"Urine?" Jim McKinnon repeated. He had long ago learned to repeat the question so as not to get screwed later on. "You're sure?"

The identification unit officer looked up at him, with one of those, 'I've had a very long day, don't be obtuse' looks.

"I'm sure Inspector. It's pee. Piss. Urine, whatever." He motioned down on the floor next to where he was kneeling. "You want to have a whiff?"

"No," McKinnon said, taking an involuntary step back from the gummy mess on the floor and shaking his head, "that's okay."

Under his breath, the officer smiled, "Yeah, I thought so."

McKinnon looked over at the woman, lying in the bathtub. Then he moved his gaze back over to the yellow, drying spot on the floor. He shook his head and moved closer to the tub. The bubbles that had once filled the tub were long gone, with just the small outlines of the individual bubbles traced in small circles of red scattered around the enameled surface.

The officer pointed at the victim, "So, how does a woman, killed over there, lose control of her bladder and piss, three feet away on a linoleum floor over here," he flicked his finger back to the vanity base, "without any blood, of which there is admittedly quite a bit, getting spilled?" He looked down at the perplexed identification officer, who was still busy collecting samples. "How does that happen d'ya think?"

"My guess is that she didn't. When we get the samples sent out to the lab in Vancouver, I'll bet this," he said looking down at the floor, "will turn out to be male piss. Or at the very least, someone other than our victim's or her husband or the child." Now looking back up at the detective, he smiled. "The real question is, why would our buddy, who had just finished three uniquely horrible murders, left nothing in the way of easy forensic evidence for us to find, not take the time to walk three steps to the pooper, and piss right there? Flushed and gone." He pointed at the toilet at the end of the room.

"Yeah, that is the question. Why would he not do that? I mean who would've thought to look into a toilet for forensic evidence, when there is nothing else around it? Would you have any reason to suspect there was something going on that would involve the inside of the toilet. No." He answered his own question for the ident unit officer. "I don't get it." He shook his head, and McKinnon looked over at the man on the floor patiently putting samples into small evidence bags. "You?"

"I don't know. I would have run screens on the toilet, just a matter of course. If he did take a leak in the toilet, we would have shown his sample as an unknown."

McKinnon looked at the toilet, shaking his head. "But he didn't use the toilet or the sink, or probably the tub, he just pissed right there, on the floor."

"True."

"What the fuck?"

"Part of the profile." The ident officer pointed at the floor, "Maybe this is what gets our guy off. The killing is good, but pissing is oh, so relieving." He was smiling as he tucked more of the evidence bags into his kit.

"Maybe. I don't think so. It just doesn't feel that way."

The officer paused for a moment, shrugged and moved back to the procedure of collecting evidence, speaking as he worked the scene. "Normally, a suspect will leave something of himself at a crime scene, Locard's Theory." He paused long enough to see McKinnon nodding his head. Locard's Theory in a nutshell was that no matter how small, there was always something left when a victim and criminal interact. Some physical tidbit. It was a rule, there was always something. But usually, you have to look pretty hard. "And in cases like this, there is usually a greater challenge in finding that trace." He motioned at the woman, "But here we have a not unattractive woman, lying naked in the bathtub, with no sign of sexual trauma, but still very dead. So, our suspect didn't do all of this," he punctuated with a sweeping motion of his latex-gloved hands, "just to get to that." He pointed at the woman's exposed pubic area. "He didn't want to get a little. And to answer your forthcoming question, I did run a rape kit on her."

McKinnon was nodding, "I was wondering about that. He didn't do it for the sex. He did it because he likes to do it. Maybe he likes to kill. I don't know." McKinnon shrugged his shoulders. "Maybe the act of killing gets him off. Maybe that is the motive. He gets to replay it in his mind forever now. Kind of like really perverted home movies — but virtual. You know when he's at home, by himself with his thoughts, his right hand and some Kleenex."

The man below him nodded.

"But," the officer said to him, holding up a long,

wooden, cotton-tipped evidence swab to accentuate his point, "if this was our guy's first killing, maybe his emotions were running so far out of control, his body just let go. You know. He was so excited with it all. My dog used to do that when it was a puppy. Always pissed himself. Maybe he was just excited about all of this," he waved his arm in an exaggerated arch, "So, he pissed himself." He shrugged.

"Well, yeah, that could be it." McKinnon surveyed the room. Everything was where it was supposed to be, albeit a little disorganized. The soap dish was just an inch or so from the edge of the sink, the little ornaments were placed almost symmetrically around the countertop. A fat scented candle was laying on its side in the sink, an obvious victim to the struggle in the room. Towels, in shades of the main colours in the room, were still neatly hanging in a row, their bottoms level with one another. It looked like every bathroom on the planet, just enough to make it unique, but still contain all the fixings needed to function. Nothing was notably out of place. Nothing except the dead woman in the tub. But there was one thing that was amiss.

"Hey Tim, did you guys find the missing towel?"

The ident officer looked up at the towel rack and shook his head. "No, didn't notice one was missing." He checked the laundry basket that was near the tub and shook his head again. "It isn't in here. Which towel are we talking about?"

McKinnon looked at the younger officer with questioning eyes. "You aren't married, are you?" The man didn't look up from his work but shook his head in response. "I figured. The bath towel." He pointed at the neatly hung towel left on their rod above the toilet. "You have a hand towel there," then pointed at the tub, "the facecloth in the tub. But no bath towel."

"They aren't all the same?"

It was McKinnon's turn to shake his head.

"I bet he took it," McKinnon thought out loud. "I mean wouldn't this," he pointed at the floor, "leave a bit of a mess?"

The kneeling officer paused a moment then hunched his shoulders in a 'I don't know,' kind of shrug. "Unless he pissed here on purpose, kind of like marking his spot."

Now it was McKinnon's turn to shake his head once again, "No, it would make more sense that he would have pissed all over the counter, the drawers and such. Maybe on her, who knows. Or maybe he was a Schnauzer." He kneeled down to have a closer look at the white cupboard drawers. "They don't have any stains on them, so all of that just dribbled out, down his pantleg."

"I'll double check when I am done with her. You mean he just pissed his pants? I'm not buying it." He glanced down at the woman in the tub and shook his head again. "No, this kind of action, this violence is a guy in total control of the event. Very physical."

"Yeah, that could be it," he agreed. "But it would seem to me, that if our suspect was so in control, his emotions wouldn't be running completely amuck."

"Amuck?"

McKinnon explained, "Yeah, amuck. You know, without any semblance of order."

"Semblance?"

McKinnon stopped and looked at the man. "Forget it. It just doesn't feel like the guy got out of control on this one." He looked at the ceiling tiles, "The husband, two shots in the doorway. Split his head fucking near in half. He went down. Then the kid in the minivan. Two shots and his lights were out." He looked at the woman again, "and then this." He slapped his notebook shut and made for the door. "It doesn't feel like a rampage. Out of control. There are no multiple impacts on the victims, no splatter on the walls. There are two wounds on each body. Not dozens. Jesus, this guy just walked through the house killing everyone he came across. No emotion at all. He just killed them."

"Have you come up with any ideas on a weapon?"

The ident unit officer stood up and moved to the woman. "Weapons? I think the man and woman were done with one, the kid with another. I can give you a hint of a response, but nothing definitive. For her and hubby it was thick, heavy, sharp and straight." He held his hand straight out, his fingers pointing at the inspector, like a knife. "What I mean is, the blade is flat, like a chef's knife, but longer and a lot heavier with a longer sharp edge."

"Why do you say that?"

"His head was impacted by something heavy that drove in, through the skull plate and into the brain. It was a clean wound, from the nose all the way to the back of the head. It wasn't a jab, it was a long, hard vertical movement, straight down. That would take a long sharp cutting surface."

"Meat cleaver?"

"I don't think so. Not that heavy and I think longer. Somewhere in between a cleaver and a chef's knife would be my guess. Machete?" Everyone was familiar with the Rwandan genocide eight years before, where the weapon of choice, primarily because of availability, was a weighted, large machete. He moved to the tub and looked down at the woman. "But the guy was strong, no matter what kind of weapon we talk about. He goddamn near split both heads in half with a single blow. Dad was done with a right-left movement. Her, the opposite. Both pretty powerful strokes, so he didn't favour one arm over the other for this." He shrugged his shoulders, "But you'll know more after the autopsy is done."

"The kid was killed with a knife though."

The ident officer looked up nodding, "Yeah, my guess is a filleting knife. Maybe a small hunting knife. Very sharp and pointy. That was a jab, and it went very deep. It must have driven to the hilt. Again, more details with the autopsy."

McKinnon looked down at the small stain on the floor. He knew that getting a DNA profile from urine is sometimes sketchy, at best. The body acid has a tendency to dissolve all that important stuff. But there was a chance they could pick something out. Maybe they'll get lucky.

"Tim, how long to get a DNA back from the lab these days?" He looked around the room, and added "Urgently?"

He was grabbing some swabs out of the little metallic case he always brought and replied, "Usually about two weeks. Maybe less if we put a rush on it."

McKinnon smiled softly, "Please ask them to put an extreme rush on it."

"What else are you looking for here?"

"I'm thinking all that urine will help us get a nice clean footprint somewhere in the house from our suspect." He shook his head. "It shouldn't be hard to find."

"Yeah, okay ... thanks," McKinnon said as he turned his back on the room.

"Hey Inspector."

McKinnon stopped. "Yeah."

"What about the piss? What do you think? Really."

The detective looked at the stain on the floor. He

paused for a moment. "Could be a couple of things. Maybe that," pointing at the drying stain, "is our guy's sexual release. But I don't think so. Again, there's no emotion anywhere else around here. It was ... surgical. With purpose. He came to this house to kill these people. Each stroke was very economical. He didn't need more effort than was delivered. He was able to kill all three with nothing more than what the job required. Nothing more." He backed out of the room to stand in the hallway to view the scene in an overall mental image. More to himself than anything, he mused, "This isn't his first time doing this either. The kill at the front door was clean, quick, debilitating. Without any hesitation. The door opened and bam! And it was quiet, he didn't want a fuss. The kid, who I think was second, was a mop-up. And her," he motioned at the figure in the tub. "Just like snuffing out one of her candles. This was a job to this guy and he is good."

McKinnon shook his head slowly. "No, this wasn't his first time. We have got a problem here. It isn't a robbery, at least from what I can see. It almost has all the hallmarks of a hit, but this woman doesn't seem like the drug kingpin type, does she?"

McKinnon started to back out of the room again, "So, to answer your question, to be honest I think our guy forgot to go potty before he left home."

12
JUNE 2002

So, how many times have you heard the words 'avenger of death' and 'incontinence' used in the same damn sentence? Not very fucking often.

I can't believe I did that. I can't believe I let it happen. I can't fucking believe I didn't know it was happening!

Then to just stand there, looking at the floor, listening to the life seep out of the woman a couple of feet away and feel the sickly, warm piss streaming down my leg. It was all surreal. But at the same time, it was all too real. I mean, come on!

I pissed my pants!

I have never pissed my pants! Not once. Not even during those long nights when I listened to that yutz across the room snore himself into oblivion and out again. Not once. I could always hold it. I could always count on my ability to hold my water. It was necessary. You just had to be able to do that. Babies or guys with slight mental deficiencies were unable to hold a little water. I mean, I have heard that after giving birth some women can't hold their water … or old women when they sneeze!

But not me. Not ever.

I mean, here I am, having just killed an entire family and killed them really well, thank you very much. Proud as peaches, yup. I was all of that. No one saw me come in. No one could trace how I got to Kamloops without really wanting to. I have no reason to want these people dead. At least as far as the authorities are concerned. I have become the master of disaster. A sleek, mean, killing machine.

Until I pissed my pants. Boy, what a pussy I am.

"Ooohh, big killer boy," I said to the shocked face in the rearview mirror. A surgical strike in and out, then like all amateur criminals I leave a little piece of me behind. Well, not even a little piece. I really thought I was better than the normal type of criminal. I do have some extensive experience in this field you know? I have some background. There is some maturity here. I am able to think things through with a little more clarity and due course than the average killer, simply because I have done this a time or two—actually dozens of times. My planning had nailed this. There was very little exposure, very, very little chance of getting caught. But I didn't take into account a requirement to hit the pharmacy on my way to kill a bunch of people and pick up some big boy diapers.

"I pissed myself," I said to that same dumb man in the mirror. "Dumbass! Unbelievable!"

The stop by the little roadside park out of town was simple enough. In my bag in the trunk, I had a complete change of clothes, some lighter fluid, the weapons, plus a small camping axe, a second fillet knife and a heavy, 16-ounce ripping hammer. Innocuous each and every one but used with the correct dose of targeted effort and talent, every one of them could be lethal and quiet. It is always nice to have a backup available.

Checking to ensure there was no one else in and around the little park, I pulled into one of the secluded picnic spots, stripped and changed my clothes — right down to skin. The clothes were tossed into a large fire pit, sprayed with a generous amount of lighter fluid, and set alight. The weapons then all went into the water. A long walk up and down the rocky beach, tossing each in at varying depths and locations, did the trick. I paused holding the hunting knife for a moment, considering hanging onto it for the trip home. But decided no one on the bus was going to be a danger to me. You could run into some genuinely weird people travelling the Trans Canada, especially on the bus, but rarely needed to defend yourself.

For a few moments I squatted near the clear water and washed my hands once again. I had already used cleaning wipes on my hands to get rid of the blood I could see. The rear-view mirror in the rental provided some assistance in cleaning my face. Luckily those folks weren't squirters. There was very little blood anywhere but my clothes — particularly on the long sleeves. I did, however, have to spend an inordinate amount of time cleaning my private bits and legs rights down to my big toe. I don't think I have to mention why that was necessary.

"Goddamn it!" I walked back over to the little sedan and whisked the towel I had taken from the bathroom and sat on for the trip here. A close inspection of the seat proved there was not a drop of piss on the light-coloured seats. Luckily, I had enough lighter fluid to ensure the towel went up in flames as well.

For twenty minutes or so, I sat on a picnic bench beside the fire pit and watched the flames slowly die off into a smouldering mess. I was upset with myself for the second time in an hour. I couldn't believe I'd forgotten the goddamn towel on the seat of the car. My focus was entirely on the disaster in the house. I would have to do some research on what forensic details could be gleaned from urine. I was pretty sure DNA wouldn't make it, but not one hundred percent. Jesus, what an idiot. What an *old* idiot.

A quick stir with a found stick, a bit more of the

fluid and the last of the material was gone. Unrecognizable. It did smoke to high heaven, though. The shoes I had worn were rubber soled, so it smelled like shit and really coloured the sky. I just hoped no one would notice as they sped by the park. I knew it was a weekday, so fewer people would be out and about travelling this lonely road. But again, not one hundred per cent sure.

I sat down again on the bench and pondered the day's events. I had to take a few minutes to center myself again, get my emotions under control. It riled me up almost instantaneously when I ran over the events in the bathroom. Pissed my pants! I knew in the 1990s that DNA was going to make my life hell as that science got better and better. I had read with interest the case of Colin Pitchfork in England and his conviction for the rape and strangling of two teens in 1986. The DNA in his seminal fluids was used to identify him the following year. He was still in prison. That was a place I didn't want to spend any time at all. No sirree. Pinetree wasn't far off being in jail, but I could walk out the door at any time I felt like it. It also had the added bonus of Mary. The food, however, was probably the same.

It was about that time — the mid 90s — I started to slow down my activities. Opportunities arose and I took them, but they were few and far between. I was also starting to age a little and it was physically getting more and more difficult to do what I had done well, accurately and without mishap. But that damn DNA, that was a big thing. That was a game changer for me.

It seemed after my little problem I wasn't in the mood to continue the bus trip west and sightsee in Vancouver. So I left the campground and after a quick stop at the little hotel to make sure the room was cleaned and clear, I returned the car to the rental agency and headed for the depot. I bought the first bus ticket I could get a seat on to head back east. I didn't care where it took me, as long as it was out of town and back towards Pinetree. The ticket clerk was very kind. She understood how hard it was for me and showed great sympathy for my loss. I had told her I had just buried my brother Stanley. What a wonderful man he was. Gave most of his money to the poor homeless people of Kamloops, the Humane Society, and Seniors for Seniors. He was a saint. Truly.

Stanley probably didn't piss his pants once in his life.

She could get me on an eastbound bus back home in about two hours. There was a coffee shop and bar at the end of the hall, and a magazine stand right across the main foyer. It would be no time, she said, until I was climbing on board the bus to take me back home.

She was right about that. But I did stay away from the coffee. No need to risk that for a second time.

I sat on the uncomfortable long benches while I waited for the bus's departure and shook my head in wonder at what had happened. That quiet time gave me some moments to collect my thoughts and truly analyze the situation. I considered my lack of immediate reaction to it. I should have cleaned it up. But after a few minutes of thought on that, I realized that would have lengthened my exposure in the house. Besides, I really wasn't that good of a housekeeper and probably would have left some of it behind. I really couldn't be sure I would have gotten it all. Frustrating, but realistic.

Everything else had gone pretty much on plan and on schedule. I was in there a little longer than I really wanted, because of the search for mom, but I could live with that. The only shortfall was the piss. 'More like a waterfall,' I mused.

I made it back home without any major incident (read that as I didn't wet the only other pair of pants I'd taken on the trip). Of course, I did wear thick padded underwear for more than half the trip. Every time I got up to use the washroom at the back of the bus, I felt the entire population of that long vehicle was checking out the very noticeable bulge around my bottom. And those looks were not in a good way. Nope, no smooth panty lines there. Just a big ol' man-diaper. When we got to Swift Current and pulled into that little city, I got off the bus to stretch my legs and took a moment to toss the unused diapers into the bathroom garbage and put on some actual underwear.

It felt so much better. For fun I spun around in the washroom and checked out my ass. "Nope, no unsightly absorbent pads to worry about there."

The last stretch of the ride to Brandon was a snooze. Lots of flat scenery to lull me to sleep. My old Cardinal watch showed it was a little after 10 when the cab dropped me off at the front doors of the Pinetree Retirement Center. Because of the late hour, I had to buzz the rent-a-cop at the front desk to get let in. The new security measures dictated that all exterior doors be locked at 9:30 p.m. All guests were gone by that time, and anyone left in the building could still get out through the panic hardware on the doors. I didn't even get a hearty welcome back when the security guard who was on the other end of the intercom found out who it was. There was just a grunt and then the buzzing of the lock. Real hero's welcome.

Of course, I had only been gone for a couple of days.

When I walked back into my room, there wasn't

even a hello from the bozo of a roommate across the room. I threw my bags on the neatly folded bed and went down the hall to the magazine stand. It was all locked up, but I could read the headlines from the afternoon paper. It seemed the mosquitoes were winning the war in Winnipeg, which shouldn't come as a big surprise to anyone. It was Manitoba after all — and the middle of summer.

There was nothing in the newspaper at all about the family in Kamloops. It was, after all, halfway across the country, so not really headline news here. It would be buried somewhere in the middle of the newspaper. Page 3 maybe. Anyhow, I wasn't too worried and didn't feel like spending a dollar to find out what I certainly already knew.

I meandered back to my room and not so quietly put away the few things I had left in the bag. Because I burned all of the stuff I wore for the murders in Kamloops, the putting away of my clothing didn't take really long — just a pair of socks and a couple of pair of clean underwear.

The very long hours on the noisy, droning bus, with children, drug addicts, grandmothers and vagrants heading home drove up my anxiety levels which meant I couldn't sleep well. Well, that and maybe the continual rolling around of the 'incident' in Kamloops. I still couldn't believe it happened.

"Truly am an old man."

So, in spite of the exhaustion I was feeling, the falling asleep part of my evening didn't happen for some time. Even with hundreds of miles of distance, and a day or two of time, I couldn't get past the piss part of the trip. The worrying part of my psyche was ramping up with "what ifs." But then after an hour or so, the logical part of my head kicked in.

They may be able to extract DNA, but would there be anything of 'me' that would directly bring them to my door? I doubted it very much. Maybe back to the past, who knew? During the heyday of my dark time in the late 60s and through to the 90s I did a lot of crazy shit. Sometimes almost weekly I was indulging. But then that damn DNA research overseas started to pop up in my research in the 80s and 90s and I got very nervous.

As I laid in bed, I ran through the days I spent, the nights and sometimes the glorious weekends I had enjoyed. They were fun, carefree times! All I had to do was stay isolated and smart. In and out, leaving nothing behind that could be tangibly connected to me. Have fun in a town and then, depending on the size of community, either hang around a while, or take off and head down the highway.

But time, in this particular case, was on my side. There would be very little linkage between my fun and any trace evidence I left behind. What I did in Kamloops in 1979 wouldn't be connected to Fort St. John in 1969. Nor to Thunder Bay in '71. All of the other dots on the map that were strung together through me would remain unconnected and isolated. Just fun, coloured, metal dots all over a map of Canada and some of the northern United States.

No, I was pretty confident that I was alone out there, and no one was running after me. They would be looking, no doubt, as so many had in the past. But I would be the faceless killer, unknown and so very dangerous because of that. I knew that there would be an incredible amount of investigative prowess brought to bear on what happened in Kamloops. You just didn't do what I did, and have everyone shrug their shoulders and go, 'Oh well.'

No, there were going to be a lot of people working this one. The only link between me and that family was Kenny, and he wasn't talking any more. It may be curious to some investigator if they looked hard enough and found out that the victim's late father rented a car in Kamloops the day they were killed. But I doubted anyone was going to get that creative or dedicated.

Then it struck me as I laid there in the dark, that I was still that same faceless killer from so long ago. No one had put together that I was the one behind all of those mysterious deaths through all of those years. I was still safe and protected. I felt my body relax, melt into the bed.

It was then I slept.

13
SEPTEMBER 1967

Chief James Mullins was not the nicest guy in town. A well-known stickler for details, Mullins wanted to see everything in a report, no omissions, no errors. Tick Smith knew full well the wrath that could befall any officer who dared to forget to dot the I's or cross the T's. It was often not fatal but could truly place you in a pile of shit. And God help you if you spelled anything wrong. Mullins felt that paperwork could make or break a case, so he dwelled on it incessantly. The previous chief of police wasn't so picky on the paperwork side of things, so Mullins made it his job to be thorough on every detail that crossed his desk.

Smith had been in that position twice. There was a traffic ticket he wrote when he was a rookie, a new cop mistake. It was a minor error on the time that allowed the driver to talk his way out of the ticket in court. And then when that break-in happened at the IGA, some evidence didn't get properly logged in. Neither was truly lethal to his career, but more to his peace of mind. Now with the city's fourth recorded murder in its long history on his plate, Smith really didn't feel he needed to fall out of grace with the old man again. He double checked the I's and T's before he walked down the hall to the chief's office.

The chief's secretary, Karen, was at the desk again, after a month off. She had broken her right ankle on a Friday afternoon when retrieving some luggage from the upstairs bedroom in her house. She had been packing to head off on a long-weekend holiday. It took the ambulance half an hour to get to her, and three days for the doctors to get back from their long weekend at the cabin to set her ankle. So instead of a holiday, Karen had enjoyed a month of allowing the bones in her ankle to heal. She wore a cast and was still very grumpy about the whole incident. The word at the office was, do not, under any circumstances, talk about holidays anywhere near Karen Yanick. She was still a little sensitive about it. One just didn't walk up to her and speak of your recent trip to the Rockies with the family, how relaxing and beautiful it was.

So, the combination of going to see Chief Mullins and his secretary was weighing heavy on Smith as he walked into the outer office. The detective wasn't sure which he was more afraid of, but if pressured for an answer, he probably would have told you it was Karen.

"Karen. How are you doing today?" he mustered with just enough joy to not seem overly compensating his caution.

The secretary looked up at the young detective and sneered. She pointed at the cast, "Can you guess how I'm doing detective?"

Tick Smith nodded his head quickly and cleared his throat, "Yeah, I can."

"The chief wants to see you right away." Always a stickler for small talk. She reached for the intercom. "Sir, Detective Smith is here … finally." She peered up at him over her horn-rimmed glasses, "Yes sir." The hint of a sardonic smile wasn't very subtle at all. "You should go right in Detective." With a smile she added, "If I was you."

Smith smiled his best cheery smile and walked past the cluttered oak desk. "Thank you." His hand didn't look like it was shaking as he grabbed the bronze-coloured doorknob. But Smith could sense the small vibration as the handle turned. He had made it halfway through the administrative gauntlet relatively unscathed, but a quick bark back. Not bad. Now came the chief.

The head of the police department was a career man in law enforcement in the City of Brandon. He had started off a rookie and worked his way up through the ranks. The chief was well respected by the men, because he had done just about everything there was to do in the force. He was gruff, and always smoking those huge cigars that everyone hated. No one could figure out how to get him to stop smoking the damn things indoors. But should the truth be known, no one had the guts to ask him to take it outside. Many had hinted, made faces or held up handkerchiefs over their faces, but they weren't seen or they were simply ignored. It was well known that if the man liked you or if he wasn't mad at you at that particular time, he wouldn't smoke near you. But if the cigar was lit when you walked into his office, it was a sign that some unpleasantness was on its way. So, before you entered his office you always paused outside the door and took in a deep whiff of the air.

Smith noticed the cigar was out, so breathed a small sigh of relief. For now.

Chief James Mullins wasn't a tall man. Five feet five inches tall if he was an inch. But he was as wide as he was tall. Freight train is the immediate mental image a lot of people got of him. His hair was a complex mixture of grey and black, with a long thick widow's peak. The blue eyes were hard, even on a good day, looking for weakness. The whole package just added to the locomotive look he personified. That posture wasn't just through the solid steel body, but the way he managed people and the department as a whole. For Mullins, whether it be a door that may be hiding a suspect, or a small personnel problem that required a gentle human touch, the shortest distance to the solution according to the mantra of Chief Mullins is whoosh—straight through the heart of it. But the city didn't have a crime problem. At least until recently. Mullins simply wouldn't allow it.

"So, what have you got on this one Tyrone? Where are you?"

The detective hated his Christian name. Tick was better than anything his parents could come up with. The nickname came from an unusually strong panicked reaction to having a wood tick lodged under his arm when he was a kid. Even now a couple of decades later, a wood tick was not something he relished having to deal with. Wrestling a suspect to the ground? Sure. Wood tick crawling up his leg? Not so much.

Tick settled in, ready to start his report. Nothing like gently getting into the subject.

"Single male, dead, Carl Carrington. Wife, is, well, a little shaken up. To say the least. She was raped. She confirmed that much."

"Can we get anything out of the rape?"

"Not any more than usual sir. We'll be able to identify the blood group of the killer, but not much else."

"You're sure she was raped, Detective?"

Smith nodded, "Yeah, she was raped." He referred to his notes. "The attending doctor, uh …" he said, looking for his place, "Larsen, said there was tearing, and seminal fluids left in both canals." Tick looked up at the sour faced chief. "Brutal was the exact turn of the phrase from Larsen."

"Wasn't the husband?" Mullins queried. Smith knew he wouldn't be making small talk during their conversation.

"No sir," again referring to his notes. "There was no evidence of sexual intercourse on the man. Pants were done up, no wounds on the body other than the fatal ones. Clothes all intact and done up."

Chief Mullin's face had wrinkled up. His inability to stomach details of sexual assaults was also legendary. "Whatever. All we can get is blood typing out of it? Towards a suspect?"

"Yeah. She can't remember the face of the guy. He had a balaclava on. Thought it might have been one of those army issue ones. You know, green with cloth cap on the back and sides."

Mullins nodded. "You thinking someone from the base?" his head twitched to the northwest in the direction of the Canadian Forces Air Force Base.

"Maybe sir. But you can buy those balaclavas anywhere in town. Second-hand shops, army surplus. They cost like, a quarter. So, anyone could have bought one. They aren't exactly unique." Mullins looked up, but Detective Tick Smith headed him off, "I've got a couple of uniformed officers out looking into that. But it's a long shot."

"But it's a shot. Right?"

"Yes sir." Smith flipped his notebook over, "but it's a long one. The base was on alert yesterday. No one allowed off the grounds for the entire day. Second day of training for base staff for some mock disaster or other. Only those personnel scheduled for medical or other emergency reasons were allowed off base. There aren't a lot of those, so we're running them down as well. But it doesn't look like anything is going to come of it."

"What about civilians who work at the base?"

"That could be," Smith admitted. "But they weren't

allowed off base either. Seems it was a high alert from early morning until end of the workday. Well passed the time of the attack."

The chief nodded his head and picked up his fountain pen. "It seems with our military friends, it's always a 'high alert' for something or other."

"Yes sir."

"What else?"

Smith quickly checked his notes. "We did a door-to-door in the building, and neighbouring ones as well. Not a lot of people home in the apartment block at that time of day. It would appear most of the people who live there work for a living. There was a total of 15 people home at the time. It was about the same for the neighbouring buildings. Nobody saw or heard anything unusual."

"That is great."

"Yeah."

"How do you think it went down?" Mullins picked up the pen to jots some notes, thought better of it and placed it neatly in the middle of the blotter.

"Carrington was sliced nearly in half. One wound extended from his left to right, completely across the neck. It was powerful enough that it nicked the backbone on the way through. It was a deep, strong, single cut. Immediately fatal. It is my guess that as soon as Carrington opened the door he was attacked. No time to react or defend. It is a secure building with intercom needed to gain access. So, he wasn't expecting anyone — like that — at the door," the detective stated. Smith waited a moment while the details filtered into the chief.

Mullins paused for a moment, considering what he had just heard from his young detective. He did like how thorough the man was but couldn't let him know it. "You said the one wound."

"Yes sir," Tick Smith checked his notes. "The second was a near identical repeat of the first stroke, but higher. It caught him on the cheek, causing severe damage to the bone and eye."

"But the first was fatal?" Smith nodded in agreement. Mullins looked confused, "So, why the second?"

"My guess, sir, is that he was in an immediate panic mode finding the guy there and just reacted, no thought at all. He was just disarming the threat." He watched the chief nod his head in agreement.

"How did he get into the building then if it is so secure?"

"Again, a guess, he just buzzed a few different suites until someone just let him in."

"Really puts your faith in those new security systems, doesn't it?" Mullins shook his head slightly, then looked back up at the detective.

"So, both cuts were the same? Same direction? Angle of attack?"

"Yeah. The coroner thinks it was a left-right motion."

"So, our guy is right-handed."

Mullins again consulted the blank piece of paper in front of him. "What about the weapon? Anything on that?"

"The wound is slow at giving up secrets' sir. It's flat, big, almost like it was a long blade, run across the throat. But had enough mass to it to be able to inflict significant damage in a single hard motion."

"Long blade. Like what?"

"I'm not sure. Something big, and heavy." Smith looked down the page in his notebook. "The coroners not sure what it is."

"Could he match it? If we found it?"

"He says maybe."

"Maybe?"

"Uh, well, his best guess," again referring to the notes, "is a 75-per-cent match. If he had the weapon to test against the wound. He has taken casts and extensive photos of the wounds should we find the weapon."

"Seventy-five per cent? Christ that's damn near a perfect match."

"Well, it's close sir. But it's not absolute."

"What would be absolute? A confession?"

"If it was forthcoming, yes. But with a pile of circumstantial evidence like the blood typing, the knife or weapon, seminal fluid," Mullins cringed again, "maybe some other trace evidence we can dig up. All of that might be enough to coerce a confession out of our suspect if we catch him." Smith looked down at his notes, and hesitated. He slowly closed the notebook and looked up to the chief. He was waiting for the next question. It wasn't long in coming.

"Well? Is it?"

Smith looked down at his notebook, hoping it would magically levitate more answers his way. But it sat still and silent on his knee. Hiding everything tightly inside.

"It looks like the same guy, yes sir."

14
SEPTEMBER 1967

"You're sure? You are sure it's our guy?"

Mullins didn't look happy. Smith wondered if he had inadvertently crossed the chief for the third time. After all, the third time's the charm. The detective scanned the desk but saw no cigar. He looked for the words.

"Yeah, I'm pretty sure. Methodology, the blitz attack at the doorway, the victim was sodomized," Mullins involuntarily made another face. He could listen all day about murder and property crime but didn't have the stomach for anything to do with rape. Smith kind of thought he was a prude. Probably still had two beds in his house for him and his wife like those television couples. Smith's bet was the two didn't even sleep in the same room. He was a good cop, a good chief, but not the most hip of people. "It all tracks that it was the same guy. Too many coincidences to be anyone else."

Smith continued, after quickly picking up his notepad again, "She had the scratching down the middle of her back that has been our suspect's signature. Several clumps of hair were pulled out during the attack. They were found on the floor. She was kicked around a little by our guy. She was bent over something in the house." Mullins' face went another shade of sick. "We're not sure what yet, we really haven't had a chance to talk with her. But my guess is a dining room chair. They are about the right height, and left bruising on her hips, upper thighs, and waist."

Mullins managed to pull a question out of his pallid

face. "When is the seminal fluid going to typed? When are we going to know if it is the same guy?"

"We should have it done later today, sir. Once we know the blood type on this latest attack, we'll know if it's the same guy. But my bet is, that it is."

"But he's never killed before."

Smith was happy to change topics, a little. "Well, that's true. But, in the other three attacks, there hasn't been anyone else home. Just the victim. Carrington had called in sick. So, he wasn't supposed to be there. It was an accident. A mishap of fate."

"Some accident. Where did Carrington work?"

"Salesman at the furniture store on Fifth."

"Morris Appliances?"

"Yeah."

"Do we need to look at anyone at the store, or anyone he may have screwed in some sales deal?"

Smith looked down at the linoleum floor and noticed how ugly it was up close. "I don't think that would be a solid application of personnel sir. But I suppose it couldn't hurt."

"It couldn't hurt, Detective?" Mullins looked incredulous. He leaned forward, like a football front line getting ready to pounce. Smith knew he didn't have a chance. Tick Smith almost said 'oops' out loud.

"It couldn't hurt? That's what you said, right? It couldn't hurt?"

"Sir," Smith began, "this whole thing isn't normal. What happened to Mrs. Carrington wasn't normal at all. It wasn't some horny teenager looking to get his rocks off. Or a customer that was pissed off about a broken fridge. This was a planned, deliberate attack. I mean, we know there are a few deviants around the city here, but no one has even come close to this level of consistent violence. We got pervs, drunken attacks, that sort of thing. But nothing like this. This is new."

The chief leaned back in his wood and leather chair. It creaked very loudly, straining under the load. "I have spent nearly an hour on the phone with the mayor this morning, Detective. Can you guess what we were talking about?" Mullins sneered as he answered his own question. "No, it wasn't how the town was growing so well, or the state of the federal political arena. It was how the fuck I was going about my job. The mayor and I chatted about how effective I was as police chief if we, and I do mean 'we,' Detective," motioning to both of them, "couldn't catch one fucking rapist in a city of 26,000 people!" Smith noticed his colour was coming back. Actually, the chief's forehead was turning red with a large vein popping out right in the middle.

"So, now you and I are now going to have that very same conversation." He took a couple of deep breaths and leaned back again. The colour on his face was changing again. Smith wondered how many shades of pissed off the guy had. So far in this meeting he had seen at least four. But he'd only been in the office for a few minutes.

"Yes sir."

Chief James Mullins laced his fingers together in front of him. He seemed to be trying to regain some of his calm. For the first time he looked hard at the young detective in front of him. He was not what a typical person expects from a police detective. He wasn't neatly dressed, though he wasn't unkept. Mullins noticed the man just wasn't current in his attire. He wore a white shirt and narrow tie, which was required, but his shoes were old wingtips, nearly a generation out of style. His hair was closely cropped, a requirement of the job, though he did sport the slight pompadour that was all the rage at the moment. The chief of police had let that go, as long as the hair was off the officer's collar and above the ears, what was on top didn't matter. At least he didn't look like some San Francisco hippy.

Then he noticed that the young man was very uncomfortable sitting across the desk from him. This was a position he had seen many a young police officer take in this office. Typically, if you were called to the chief's office, it wasn't to chew the fat, talk baseball and such. You were here because something was up. Something was happening that required a bit of a conversation. Normally, Mullins enjoyed putting these young bucks in their place, making them feel they have overstepped or under-stepped as it were. He knew what the uncomfortable look was like for people who sat in the chair across from him. But what he saw in Smith was a different kind of uncomfortable.

There was something else he hadn't been told yet.

"What is it?"

"Sir?"

"Detective Smith. Please tell me the very last thing that you want to share with me about this case. And tell me now."

"Yes sir." Smith straightened up in the chair and looked dead even into his chief's eyes. "I believe he's going to do it again."

Mullins was surprised. "The rape, you mean? Of course, he is."

"No sir," said the young man, "the murder."

15
SEPTEMBER 1967

Chief James Mullins leaned back into his leather chair once again, and once again it protested loudly at the strain. He laced his fingers in front of the hairy wall he called his chest. "How the hell do you know that, Detective?"

"It's a feeling sir."

"Like having the flu ... that type of feeling? Should I buzz Karen and have her call the department doctor for you? If it's that type of feeling, 'cause it's no problem at all." The chief leaned over the black telephone positioned to the right of the green blotter, his hand hovering over the handle. "We don't move forward with feelings Detective Smith, we work on facts, evidence around here."

Smith suddenly thought he could have presented this part of the analysis better. He smiled but quit very quickly when he saw the face of the chief hadn't reflected that effort at humour. "Sir."

"No, I'm interested in how you have managed to get ESP or something and pulled that sort of deduction out of your tunic. Please, tell me. Help me to understand this." The sarcastic side of the chief was fully exposed now to Smith. The detective wasn't sure he liked it, though he was definitely leaning towards not liking it at all.

"Sir, there's a couple of reasons for that deduction." He looked down at his polished shoes, and noticed a couple of scuffs he should have taken care of before he came into the meeting. "I just didn't pull them out of my ass, sir."

"I didn't say that, Tyrone."

"You were thinking it."

"Maybe so," Mullins relinquished. "But I didn't say it. But now that you have brought that up, what the hell are you talking about?" The chief shook his head slowly. He was trying to wrap his head around the concept, while at the same time trying to anticipate the storm of pressure that would be brought to bear through the mayor and city fathers. "I don't get it. That's a real jump for you. You have always been a logical solid detective, not given to these flights of fancy. But now. You *feel* this is going to escalate. How? This isn't like you. This just doesn't make sense to me."

"Nothing has changed with me sir." The chief nodded his head, but didn't look his detective in the eye. "Just hear me out, then you can decide if I'm crazy. Okay?"

"All right Tick. Help me ... feel." The heavy sarcasm hung in the air for a moment, while Tick formulated the words.

Tick Smith opened his notebook again, bookmarked to the page with a small paper clip. It didn't have his regular thorough annotated notes on it. This page was different. It held just point form thoughts. No order, just as they came to him while walking around the Carrington apartment. Smith quickly scanned down the memorized list once more, took a deep breath and prayed it all came out like he had rehearsed. He knew going into the meeting that Mullins was not given to speculation. He was a believer in fact. Put your hand on it and it's fact. Will it fit into a report? Fact. If you are just thinking about it, speculating, then you'd better look for work at the university. As Mullins put it, flights of fancy weren't welcome in his department.

But the pieces of the puzzle were right there in his hand, written down. He didn't see a random bunch of observations and thoughts scribbled in his nearly indecipherable handwriting. He saw a series of pieces that did fit together like one of those Japanese puzzle boxes he had seen somewhere. It looked impossible until you broke the pieces down and looked for the connectivity. The best part, and what he hoped would convince Mullins, was that everything on this list was fact. It all led to a conclusion he hoped couldn't be denied.

"I'll start with the sexual assault," Smith began.

Mullins squirmed in his chair. "If you must."

"It was pretty much the same as the rest. Buggery, vicious scratching on the lower back and pulling out of clumps of the victim's hair. It's what we've seen before. It's the same as the other three —nothing new. In fact, nearly identical in all the details. Except this time, there was a little more. The whole thing was more … intense. Heated. The lacerations were a little bit deeper, and there were more of them." Smith paused and looked to the doorway. "I can get the forensic photographs if you want sir, they are just down in my office."

Mullins held up his shaking hand. "No, that's okay I'll take your word for it."

"All right. Well, the first three victims had wounds that extended from roughly the mid back region through to the buttocks. I think we averaged it out to about eighteen and a half inches total length. Average, some were longer, some shorter." Smith looked at his boss and answered the unasked question, "I thought there might have been a significance to that measurement."

The chief nodded his head again. "Did the injuries

get longer from the first case to the third?"

"No, they were all within an inch or two — on average. Probably the length of his reach in the position he was." The chief nodded but stayed quiet. Though Smith couldn't see it, he was confident that Mullins had pictured the act in his mind and the sour taste flowed through his entire body.

"Anyways, there wasn't any increase in the violence or the injuries through the first three. But what happened with the Carrington woman? The lacerations start at the shoulders, almost a foot above the normal and extend through to the buttocks. The average number of scratches has been 11 on the previous three attacks. On the Carrington woman, that number increased to 26. More than double. It was just …," he paused for the correct police phraseology, but couldn't find it handy, "just fucking awful. The pain that woman was in, and yet, she never left her husband. All this was happening to her, while she was looking at his body." He tilted his head at the thought, "Unbelievable. She stayed with him, on the floor after our suspect left, holding her husband's head, feeling his body get colder. Fucking awful just about sums up my feelings sir."

"You and I can agree on that."

"Okay, so that's one point. The lacerations show an increased fever pitch to the rape. This one was different, because there was a death involved. None of the others had a death. When the apartment door opened yesterday afternoon, both men must have been shocked to see the other guy standing there. Carrington was there just because he was home sick. Our guy was standing there with a big knife in his right hand ready to take on Mrs. Carrington. The weapon was used to kill, just because he was surprised to see a man. A threat."

The chief and Smith looked at one another for a moment. "Our guy wasn't expecting to need the weapon for anything more than show. But after the first reactionary strike across the throat, he hit him again, this time just above the left eye, with a down-and-in trajectory." Smith made the motion with his right hand, "Diagonally."

"Another point is the intercourse itself." Smith glanced up at the chief, who was looking up at the ceiling, his fingers still laced together over his chest, and the expression of 'here we go,' look on his face.

Smith quickly checked his notes, but really didn't have to. "It was repeated."

Mullins came out of his shell for a moment. "What was that?"

"The attack on Mrs. Carrington wasn't a one timer. In, out and done. He went after her a couple of times. Maybe as many as four separate penetrations with ejaculation. Both vaginally and anally."

Smith leaned back in his chair and let that piece of information gel a little in Chief Mullins' mind. The older officer's fingers weren't just laced together now, they were rhythmically tapping in front of him as he sifted through what he had just heard. Smith had the thought that maybe the chief, too, would be having a feeling.

"How many times did our suspect penetrate the previous victims?" Mullins thought for a moment, "The other three?"

"Once each, sir. But in the previous three, there wasn't a death. I'd be willing to bet my paycheque that the next one will involve a homicide as well." Tick Smith looked at his notebook, and back up at the chief. "It was like the murder somehow released the monster in our suspect. Opened a door. Something he has had tucked away for a long time. Suppressed. Our suspect killed and then he went into a frenzy of excitement that the act of taking a life released."

The two men looked at one another, Smith patiently waiting for Mullins to give him a sign to keep moving on with the details. Mullins sifting.

Mullins was visibly shaken now. His eyes were firmly planted on the paper in front of him, the fingers clasping and unclasping quickly. "Did he take a souvenir again?"

Tick checked his notes for accuracy then said, "It looks as though her bra was missing. The previous three were all missing their panties. All in all, sir, things have rapidly changed for our suspect with this one. He has gone from a multiple rapist, to a killer-rapist. The killing came first, then the rape. It will be that way from this point on. It will be violent, and it will be totally invasive."

"What do you mean," Mullins asked? "Invasive?"

"There will be more of what we saw here, maybe a little more. It was the murder that took the restraints off this guy. He just let himself go — no constraints, no decorum, just rage."

Mullins was leaning forward, his elbows on the desk, interested in a thought that was in his mind. "Do you think we have two suspects now? Maybe someone imitating the original? What are they calling them, a copycat?"

"I don't think so, sir. There were no details released to the newspaper or radio station about the three rapes, so how could someone imitating the rapist know to scratch their back, have anal intercourse and grab out clumps of hair?" The chief winced like he had been shot. "Sorry sir." Smith was waved off.

"But we'll know for sure when the semen blood typing comes back from the lab?"

"Right," Smith acknowledged. He glanced at his watch, it was just after nine in the morning. "If we are lucky, we will have them back to us by lunch."

Mullins placed both hands on the desk, and looked at him, "You don't think that by not going after a second suspect, you are wasting some valuable time?" He looked down at his hands, "If there is a second suspect, that is?"

"The blood typing will be done today," Smith affirmed. "But no, I don't think we are wasting any time. All available clues are being pursued on this guy. That's all we can do."

"So, we wait?" Mullins asked.

"We wait. But I don't think we will be made to wait long."

16
JULY 2002

The Serious Crimes Unit or SCU at the Kamloops detachment of the Royal Canadian Mounted Police is a small, cramped space that is overutilized and understaffed. It is contained in a rather large and magnificently austere building in the core of the city. Originally the room was the steno pool. But as that technology was slowly replaced with white computers with green screens placed on all the desks, it was handed over to this new investigative arm. Nationally the unit, SCU, was created to help deal with gang-related activities which included biker gangs, organized crime, and other serious crime situations. That scope was broadened, over time, to include any crime that posed an ongoing threat to society on the whole.

The SCU often liaised with municipal police departments on break-and-enter strings, serial smash and grabs, narcotics or homicides.

Over time, SCU became the catch-all section. It was where administrative officers, who weren't quite sure where crimes that defied an accurate description and therefore eluded accurate allocation of resources, put things. In other words, it was the garbage can for crime.

It was where Inspector Jim McKinnon worked every day. Literally, every day. His dedication to the unit had been personally expensive. He had developed a wide butt from sitting in front of computers or mounds of file folders for hours on end ... his beltline had gone from a thin motorcycle tire to something that would better fit a semi, and the hair on his head had turned grey, and then invisible. Not a rugged looking handsome man, McKinnon was just a cop. He wore his hair (what was left of it) a little longer than regulation. But the people he typically talked with, and interviewed each day, wore their hair a lot longer than that. He could never be on par with them, but he could look a little less cop.

His wife Angela, who stuck with him through it all, was as dedicated to the unit as he was. She understood the value of it, and respected McKinnon for the work he accomplished. A large picture of her hung above his desk, and a smaller candid snapshot sat to the right of his phone. When he was in the office, nary an hour sped by where he didn't ground himself with his wife, and gaze longingly into her eyes.

He was a romantic, often called his wife half a dozen times during the day, regardless of what he was working on, to tell her that he loved her.

It was just his way. Though some of the other officers in the detachment may have thought that was a little less than machismo, he didn't care. He wasn't changing.

He was drawn to the picture of her face as he wound his mind through the already thick file laying before him. Her eyes were calm, in a sudden world of violence, where no man could hide, and no human could have survived.

"Ang, this one is bad. Really nasty. It just doesn't feel ... normal."

"It is going to feel a lot less normal in a couple of minutes."

McKinnon looked up from his messy desk, passed the sheaves of papers and into the stomach of his identification unit officer Russell Jenkins. The young, good looking career officer was standing stiffly at the threshold of the door, holding yet another pile of papers. But there was something in his eyes.

"What is it?"

"The DNA we grabbed from the floor. The lab turned up the heat and managed to get some results from it. And pretty quickly too."

"The piss?"

Russell came in and sat down heavily in the old chair. The chair was a leftover from his first marriage, one of the first things he ever bought as a rookie constable. It still made him look when someone sat down in it a little too hard or was holding something liquid and very spillable above it. Well-used as it was over the years, there were no creaks or groans above what he had learned to expect from it. It had lasted far longer than the short-lived first marriage had.

"Actually sir, we in the ident business like to call it freshly relieved biological fluid." McKinnon just stared at him and waited. He had an entire family in the fridge, he didn't need gallows humour today. "Well, it didn't match the woman, or the husband or the kid."

"So, it's an unknown?" He nodded his head, "So at least we have something to work from. If it ever comes to court."

"I wouldn't say, exactly, that it is an unknown."

McKinnon sat forward. He was now interested in what the officer had to say. "So, we know who it is?"

"No."

"Russell, you just told me the sample wasn't an unknown. That means, normally that we know who it is. That is a logical deductive process. We have identified the person who volunteered the sample." Fucking kids and their fucking games McKinnon thought.

"I didn't say, sir, that we know the name of the person who gave the sample, I said that it isn't an unknown."

McKinnon sat back in his chair, reached to his right, and slid the top drawer open. "Russell, I have just opened the top drawer of my desk. In it, is a wide variety of everyday items, like pens and pencils, small sticky notes, erasers. In fact, in it is a whole range of stationery items that are valuable in the day-to-day operations of a small department like this. What you should be concerned with, however, is the standard issue Glock nine-millimetre handgun which is safely stowed there. Well, not exactly safely stowed. The safety is currently in the off position."

"It's an interesting story, sir," the young officer said, ignoring the threat. "This sample."

"I'm all ears," McKinnon said as he closed the drawer.

"It starts with a string of murders in the Brandon, Manitoba area in 1967. They have remained unsolved. The first," he paused while referring to his casebook, "was a young man by the name of Carl Carrington. Full throat slit, right to left. Died on the hallway floor, while the assailant raped his wife."

"You said right to left. So, the guy was right-handed?"

"Yes sir, the same." McKinnon nodded, now his head was swimming.

"That is a pretty strong first attack. Were there a series of rapes, or assaults of any kind that were precursors to the murder?"

Jenkins smiled and nodded. The old man was sharp. "Three women reported being raped. Don't forget, that times were different back then. There wasn't the support for women to report sexual assaults like there is now. The rapes, though, escalated in personal violence, when the murder happened. The suspect didn't really progress in his violence through the attacks, until the murder. It was a game changer for him. The case file indicates that the murder was just an accident, husband was home when he shouldn't have been. You know how it works, the thrill of the attack increased as the level of violence intensified. It was going to end in a murder if the guy wasn't caught. It was just a matter of time sir."

"You said a series of murders."

Jenkins checked his papers and continued. "The second victim was a young lady, named Colleen Mishenko. Twenty-two." The sergeant held up a picture of a very attractive blonde, with hair styled for the time. "Coffee shop cashier and waitress. Found by her landlord, after her boss reported she hadn't been to work for a couple of days. She was raped repeatedly, and her throat slit, left to right."

"Was she bound?" Then McKinnon added as an afterthought, "gagged?"

Jenkins scanned a couple of pages, flipping back and forth. "There is no mention of it, and from the crime scene photos you can't really tell." He held up an eight-by-ten glossy picture that showed just the face of Colleen Mishenko. It wasn't the same girl he had just seen. The head and shoulders shot indicated she was lying on a bloody bed, with sheets tossed casually over her. But not covering the face.

"Jesus."

"Yeah. All the crime scene photos from that time, at least the ones in this file, are like out of one of those supermarket detective magazines. Gruesome, but not helpful."

"It was the way it was done back then Russell. No

fault, no blame."

"Anyway," Jenkins continued, "she was victim two." Sergeant Russell Jenkins checked a page under one of the photos. "No cause of death listed by the coroner."

"Ya think?"

The ident officer normally wasn't caught off guard by his boss's humour, but this time, it did cause him to falter a little. "Uh, okay," he struggled to find the next section within the thick file. "Victim three was a housewife, Wilma Carnegie, aged 46." He held up yet another large photo, this time of Harriet from Ozzie and Harriet. It was the common face of murder victims. There was the before, and then the sad after. "Not unattractive."

"What did her husband do?"

"Was a driver for a car parts company."

"So, he wasn't home a lot, travelled around the area on overnight trips?"

"I would assume." Jenkins flipped more papers. Another vivid photo. McKinnon noticed again that the body was covered, but not the head. One of Wilma's eyes were open, staring blankly into the camera lens. "Same cut pattern, same multiple sexual attacks."

"How many more?" The pattern was easy to follow.

"Just one. The last one," Jenkins said, as he held up the before picture of a singularly beautiful woman, with large dark eyes, and very modern hair, for the time. "Her name was Melinda McGregor. Legal assistant in one of the city's biggest firms. She was the last one. And the most brutal." The sergeant paled a little and stared at the folder on his lap, "They uh, didn't find all of her." He held up a picture, again a head-and-shoulders shot, with the head laying at a particularly odd angle to the torso. McKinnon couldn't see the eyes.

"What was missing?"

"Right breast," Russell said as he read, then corrected himself, "no, actually, just the right nipple." He looked up at the officer and paled even more. "He uh, took a section about the size of a golf ball."

"That was his first physical souvenir?"

Russell nodded. "Yeah, as far as I can tell. He had taken bras and panties prior to that, nothing consistently, and nothing of any of the victims."

McKinnon held out his hand for the crime scene photo. It was an original. Not a downloaded copy. But an original eight-by-ten glossy. "What's this?"

"It's the crime scene photo."

"It's an original."

"Yeah."

"How did we get an original here?"

A light visibly kicked on in Russell's face. "That was the really neat part about the 'known' DNA sample. Someone put a seminal sample from these unsolved rapes and murders in the CPIC* system. When our suspects went in ... the samples hit and voila." He held his arms out like a magician after popping a rabbit out of his hat. McKinnon thought that maybe linking murders from nearly 40 years before to his family here was a much better trick.

"So how did you get the originals?"

Russell smiled slightly. It was a 'I know something you don't't' sort of smile.

"They arrived this morning."

McKinnon feigned a concentrated look into his top drawer. "Yup Russell, the gun is still there."

"The detective in charge of that original murder investigation in Brandon has a buddy who put them in the system when it was created a decade ago and flagged them if they ever had a hit. We put the DNA markers in, they matched, and bingo." He repeated.

McKinnon was shaking his head, "This guy has to be 80-something. What the hell is he still doing chasing some fucking perp from half a century ago?"

"I guess he has a hurt on for this guy."

"Okay, but that hurt eventually goes away."

"Not if you made a promise."

The voice was strong, and even. And deep. It was an announcer's voice. It belonged to a man standing in his doorway, respectfully waiting to be ushered in. If he was 80, he was the best preserved 80-year-old McKinnon had ever seen. The hair on his head was greying but hadn't totally given itself to white. There was a slight paunch to his body, but not what you would call fat or even heavy. But it was his eyes that drew in McKinnon. They were cobalt blue. Amazing. There was no sign of any aging there.

"Sir?" McKinnon asked. "This is a private conversation ..."

"My name is Tick Smith. I was detective in charge of that, and the other three murders."

McKinnon looked at the man, studied him for a moment. He was still handsome, ruggedly. He wasn't smiling but the inspector knew that if he did smile, his whole face would light up. He would not be a man who could bury his feelings. His face would give them away. Right now, McKinnon could see worry. He could see panic. McKinnon knew it would take a lot right now to make this man smile.

"We appreciate your help here, sir, but really you didn't have to come all the way here. Sending the file would have been more than enough."

"I know, and to be honest with you," Tick admitted, "I wouldn't have wanted some old fart standing in my doorway either. But this is my case. Still."

"Sir, it was your case, what, 35 years ago? I'm not so sure how that is going to hold up now." McKinnon looked at the seated officer and questioned with his eyes. Then he looked back up at the man in the doorway. "How did you get in here anyway?"

Russell Jenkins coughed and held a hand up lamely. "I thought he may be able to give us some insight on this sir." McKinnon looked at him with something not far off distaste.

"Did you now?"

Smith stood stock still in the doorway, his hands flush by his side. "I let him get away 35 years ago. I have never, ever stopped looking. There have been times, to be honest with you, many times over the past couple of decades, that I hoped he was dead, or maybe locked up for another murder somewhere. I really hoped that was true. Because this guy is a fucking monster."

The silence in the room hung heavy. No one was sure what to say, or what to do from that point on. It was a stalemate. McKinnon considered the man in the doorway. He was aging well so must have kept up with some kind of physical regime. And, he had made the trip to see him about this. For a moment he softened.

"You said you made a promise?"

"Five years after the first murder, I married Martha Carrington. Every day of our life together, I looked into her eyes, and promised to never stop looking. Because every day I looked into my wife's eyes and saw the pain of the first day we met." He smiled a little, just the corners of his mouth. "I loved her, completely. I married her for no other reason than that love. But each day, I woke up to see that pain. Each day I renewed my vow to catch this guy."

"And now he has killed again," McKinnon completed the thought for Tick. "Now he has poked his head above ground. And he has done that in my town."

"Exactly."

McKinnon slid his desk drawer shut and walked around it, past Russell to the doorway. He extended his hand. "Jim."

Smith took the hand firmly, happy to see that the inspector didn't soften his grip just because it was a senior citizen involved. "Tick."

"Tick?"

"It's just Tick."

McKinnon nodded his head, "You've met Jenkins?"

"I have," Tick admitted. "By the way." Both Russell and McKinnon looked at him, "I'm 64."

*(Canadian Police Information Center)

17
JULY 2002

The two men sat quietly at the bright red and white checkered luncheon table in the neighbourhood café that was located right across the street from the station. The ebb and flow of people either arriving, ordering their meal or paying for the tab and leaving noisily, kept their attention diverted from the topic at hand. As uniformed staff entered the restaurant, they quickly looked at McKinnon, then took a seat at the far end of the large room, as distant as they could be without going to some other place to eat. Tick watched as the ritual was repeated several times during their meal. It was always curious to see the reaction of the populous to the people who deal with death every day. This was something he had been used to throughout his career. Some of the officers joked when they saw him socially, others just steered clear to avoid the awkward conversations.

He understood that both he and McKinnon weren't like funeral directors, who somehow comfort those who have lost a friend, or family member. They were the ones that asked the questions about how it happened and if anyone was involved in the death that maybe shouldn't have been. To get to the truth, police had to make everyone feel uncomfortable. They had to probe from all sides until the truth was exposed, naked and lying on the floor.

Then Tick caught himself. He wasn't like McKinnon anymore. He was done with the business and had been for a while. He was retired. He knew that McKinnon, sitting across the table looking deeply into a newspaper he wasn't reading, still wasn't satisfied with any explanation for what happened. Tick could relate. He was retired, but still the weight of that day in 1967 bore down on him.

"You can talk about it, Jim, if you want. No problem here."

"Talk about what?"

Tick Smith was a little disappointed at the poor effort to deflect the question. He had come to expect more from a Royal Canadian Mounted Police inspector. "When you were looking at the crime scene photos, what did you get? What did you think our guy was doing?"

"It wasn't the killing he went for ... that was for sure. Our guy always killed after he was done with the sexual assault. It wasn't an after-thought, but it wasn't the express purpose he was there. He didn't go there to kill. At least not at first."

Tick nodded, "We think he killed for the first time, when he did Carl Carrington. It wasn't premeditated, at least I don't think so. Carrington came home sick from work. It was normally something he didn't do but he wasn't feeling well. At least that was the original story she told us. But they had a fight the night before, so he was in heavy kiss-ass mode. It was the man's guilty conscience that ultimately killed him. Must have surprised our guy who was there for the wife we think, and bam, did the hubby. Twice. Right left motion. I assume like the killings the other day?"

McKinnon thought about not answering, but then nodded.

Tick Smith continued, "It was a dead even, strong stroke. So, we figured he must have been just a hair taller than Carrington. That would put him at about six to six-foot-two."

McKinnon pushed the newspaper out of the way. "I

appreciate what you have done for us Tick. Really. And don't take offence to this. Please." He rubbed his stubbly face, as he searched for the words.

"It's a young man's game ... murder?" Tick asked. "Is that what you were looking for in the newspaper? Or, pretending to."

"Well, yes," McKinnon admitted, "but I was really hoping to dress it up a little better than that, but yes. That was the general thought."

"I'm not going to beg Jim. I'll start with logic." He wiped his mouth with his paper napkin, more to control the sweat on his upper lip than clean up his meal. "But I'm not going to rule out begging. Not just yet anyway." Both men forced a smile.

"I appreciate logic." Then McKinnon added, "But not so much the begging."

"No one knows these files like I do. Every piece of evidence, every shitty little lead, is on paper in the file I brought to you this morning." Then he tapped his forehead, "and it's locked up here as well. I've disassembled, then reassembled the crime scenes in my head a hundred times. A thousand. Piece by piece, looking for that one little thing that would give me a direction. Just the smallest pointer." Tick leaned back deeper into his chair. "But there wasn't one. Not a single one."

"The photographs of the people he killed and raped are still burned into my mind. I don't even have to look at the 8x10s to see that room, those dead people, every nuance." Tick paused for a moment and pushed himself a little closer to the inspector. "I asked you a couple of minutes ago what you saw when you looked at the photos. You never answered me."

"Saw?"

"The victims and how they were left. What did you

think when you saw them?"

It took a moment for the RCMP officer to speak, not to put the thoughts together, but to consider if he was going to allow this old guy across the table from him into his head. 'What the hell,' he thought.

"The first thing I thought about was the fact that our guy didn't know the victims."

"True. Why?"

"Because the faces weren't covered up. There was no attempt to dehumanize them as people. The victims. And after he was done, he left them the way he finished. No attempt to cover their bodies, at least nothing in particular that I could see. The sheets were thrown across their bodies haphazardly. Kind of a casual, 'There, done with that' kind of thing."

Tick nodded, suddenly his mind swimming in the past. "Our photographer covered the bodies."

McKinnon was now at full attention. He shook his head, clearing the cobwebs of confusion. "He what?"

Tick hung his head, with admission, "When I arrived at the scene, after the uniforms, the female victims weren't covered. All of the blankets, quilts, and sheets were tossed into a corner of the room, or at least away from the bed itself. Most of the attacks were on beds by the way, except for his first. I don't think that was in the case notes either. Again, a different time." Tick shrugged his shoulders in an admission. "But it is what it is or was. So yes, all were naked and exposed when I got there."

McKinnon was still confused. Now nearly angry. Police science had advanced by leaps and bounds since the Sixties, but he was sure it wasn't the dark ages then. He shook his head in disbelief. "I don't get it. Why mess with the crime scene before you took the pictures? That doesn't make sense. You don't have anything that takes you to the moment the crimes took place. It's all corrupted."

"For the time, it was normal Jim. You have to remember, we didn't have the capabilities, or the understanding of the very nature of the crime scene like we do now. Hell, I remember our fingerprint guy using his wife's compact to dust for prints at a B and E. Our replacement order hadn't come in yet." He smiled a little, not apologetic, but self-deprecating, "I hate to say it, but it was the Sixties. And it was the Sixties, before the phrase was coined. As far as forensics is concerned, we were struggling to come out of the Spanish Inquisition."

"So why did your guy cover up the bodies for the crime scene photos?"

"He was an old man. Had a small photo studio just down from the police station, complete with developing capabilities. It was convenient." Once again, his shoulders shrugged. "But you had to suffer with his Christian sensibilities. Hated nudity. So, he would cover them up. We relied on the autopsy to verbally describe the injuries to the body, in the hope that would offset the lack of photographic evidence at the scene. I don't know. We learned to work around it."

"Amazing."

"You should have been there. Frustrating as it was. It was a blast."

McKinnon just stared in disbelief, and repeated, "Amazing."

"The fact is, you wouldn't have known that, if I hadn't have been there and now sitting with you here. Does that information now change the profiling you just did?"

"A little. He didn't know his victims, at least not

personally. We think he did know their routines."

"So," Smith said, "back then he wanted a clean slate to work on, on the bed. Nothing that could bind his pleasure, get it tangled. His mission back then was like yours now, very clear and purposeful." McKinnon was still reeling from the photos and wasn't thinking clearly.

"You see Jim, we didn't have the Behavioral Sciences section of the FBI to help give us a profile of our killer. That guy was still playing elementary school basketball at the time I was dealing with this thing," he said pointing at the opened file folder.

"I realize that, Tick. It's just that I'm not sure how much of this evidence you brought us is still valid. How much is pertinent to today?" He stared at Smith, realizing he had walked directly into the web.

"Normally, I would have said 'check and mate'. But this time, I'll let you go." Tick took a small drink of coffee, grimacing at the cold sludge on the bottom of his cup.

"I appreciate that."

"We can't use what we have in the files I brought to you. Most of it has been tainted, like the photos. Not deliberately, but just through ignorance. But we can use it. We can manipulate it to help find this guy."

Tick Smith pierced the air between them and told a small white lie. "I want to help bring this fucker in. I don't care if I make the arrest, I just want to know it's done." He held up his hands in a mock surrender, "So whatever I can do, please, let me do it."

McKinnon was in a position where refusing would put his investigation behind the eight ball. History was playing an integral part in his case, even if it was more than three decades ago. If the photo evidence was any indication, there was no way of knowing what good solid evidence was, and what was spoiled. The decision, he realized, had been made before Tick Smith had shown up in his doorway.

"You'll have to sign a waiver of liability. You know the drill."

"I realize that," Smith agreed. "I have no trouble with that."

"I want you to know that I am doing this under duress. You are a civilian now Tick."

"I know, and when this is over, I'll happily be a civilian again. Actually, be a happy civilian for the first time." He pushed the coffee cup away. "You know what I remember most about the Carrington murder scene? It wasn't Martha, tragic and beautiful all at the same time. It wasn't the pain she was suffering physically and mentally. It wasn't her husband lying cut open on the floor." He looked up at the inspector sitting across the table. He knew the investigator would understand that it was the little things that made you wake up in the night, thinking about some old case, some old body. "It was the smells."

"When I walked in, I was assaulted by the visuals of the rooms. The beige furniture, walls and carpet. It was all the rage of the time," he added unapologetically. "There was the biggest patch of blood you ever saw. At least to a kid on his first real murder investigation. It was just fucking huge. Huge. So red, and heavy. The body was surrounded by all the people that needed to be there, and of course some of the curious too." He stared into the distance, not seeing the people in the restaurant, but seeing a room 35 years away. "All the cops looked so big, so official. And on the floor was this little man, deflated, and white."

"When I have that image in my head, the thing I

remember is the smells. Not the household smells, like old cooking. But the human smells. You know, the thickness of blood that is congealing. His bowels let go, so that was mixed in. You could almost see it in the air. But I could smell her, I could smell the perfume Martha put on that day when she got up. I don't know what it was, but it's still here, in my nose somewhere. Some molecule of perfume, still stuck to the inside of my nose. That is what I remember."

"I know Tick. I wake up with the same sort of thing." He looked at the man sitting across from him, and realized there was something else that was coming. "But it wasn't the blood or the perfume, was it? That isn't what makes you wake up sweating?"

Smith nodded his head in silent agreement. "It was the third human that had been in the room, and what he left that I can't shake. No amount of cologne will mask the smell of his semen on her. It's the smell that shouldn't have been there. It was the ultimate invasion of her life, and it shouldn't have been in that room, ever."

Both men sat silent for a few minutes, lost in memories they couldn't shake. Lost in memories that made them human, in a subhuman business. It was always a memory that would wake them up, lost in their own bed, unsure of where they were. But it was also the memory that gave their lives some purpose and direction to follow. Making the memories go away is always high on a cop's priority list. Some drink it away, others beat it away. Still others take therapy to help deal with the nightmares. Sometimes the issues are dealt with, but until it is settled, it will never truly go away.

"Your wife?"

Another faint smile, "Died about seven months ago.

Cancer."

"Sorry."

"We had a very good life together. A very full life. There are no regrets."

"Children?"

"No. Neither of us wanted to bring a child into our life, into the world. Too much baggage, and I didn't want to have children. Not when I was a cop. Someone has to be the cop, and I always felt that being childless was the sacrifice you made. You?"

"Wife, yes, children, yes. Two boys. Both are grown up and gone to Vancouver to work. So, we are enjoying the pleasures of being empty nesters."

"Did they follow you into the family business?"

"Not a chance. I would've shot 'em."

"That is probably a good thought, Jim." Both men smiled, until Tick saw something different in his tablemate's eyes. He couldn't quite put his finger on it, but there was a definite hardening. He suddenly switched into 'bad cop' mode. The switch was sudden and totally unexpected. "What is it?"

"It's nothing you have to worry about Tick." McKinnon folded the napkin that had been on his lap and pushed his chair back from the table.

"What?"

The RCMP Inspector paused for a moment. "We have three television stations in town. Two are national affiliates and are okay, you can deal with them. But a couple of years ago, an independent sprung up. We call it 'ME TV', 'cause it's all about the reporters and anchors, fuck the story. They are kids and they are all idiots wanting to make their bones with every story. They have no idea of the balancing act we have to take on a case like this and they just come at you in your face."

"Don't you have a media relations officer they have to go through?"

"I think he's sleeping with one of the producers, so I have no doubt he told them where we would be."

"They're here?"

"Waiting outside, getting set up." He flipped his hand to the rear of the restaurant, "You go out the back door. I'll see you back at the stationhouse."

"Sure. But there is no need. I've dealt with these people, the media my whole life. It's no trouble."

"All right but don't tell me later that I didn't warn you."

"I think that having me on television just might work for us though."

"Work?" McKinnon asked as he got up from the table and headed for the cash register. "What do you mean, work?" He threw two tens at the cashier, then stole a quick look at the two people looking back into the eatery.

"He'll be watching. He'll want to know what's going on." Tick nodded his head in thought, "So he'll be watching."

"Right, but what did you mean 'work?'"

"He has a thing for me. Has since 1967 when he first killed. I get Christmas cards, birthday cards, all kinds of shit."

"You've had contact?" McKinnon was standing still in the middle of the room, staring at the retired law enforcement officer. His mouth was hanging open.

"Contact? I don't know if I would go that far, as to say I've had contact." Tick Smith wore a simple, but disarmingly effective smile. "I've only talked to him twice."

18
JULY 2002

"Are you okay, Ivan? You look a little green behind the gills. Under the weather."

Mary and I were waiting for the second cup of lukewarm coffee to be served to us in the Pinetree dining room. At least that is what the staff call it ... the dining room. Has a nice connotation to it, doesn't it? We poor residents of the home prefer to call it the cattle car. We are all herded in, have food pushed on us, then herded out again.

Now, I know for a fact that a few of us do have teeth left in our mouths. Out of the hundred or so that eat with us, probably, oh ... all. So why the hell they give us the mushed-up crap they cook to within an inch of its life, is beyond me. Quite often, a couple of us will slip out of Pinetree and hit a fast-food restaurant for a burger and fries. Holy cow, I mean how 'out on a limb' is that?

"I'm fine, just a little tired from the trip is all."

Mary looked into my eyes, and waited for more, but that was all I was ready to pass along. She reached for my hand and asked, "I thought you were going to be gone for a few days? You were just gone for a couple."

"True," I admitted. "Then I slept for another day — all the way round the clock."

Mary looked over at me with questioning eyes. "But it still wasn't a long trip."

"I changed my mind." I tried to give her half a smile, "I just wanted to see Keegan's face when I told her that I was leaving."

"Ivan..." Mary pleaded. Her hand hadn't moved

from mine but still the eyes questioned. This was an entirely new situation for me. In the 'old days' I would have just made up a lie to get me out of the moment I was in, knowing I wouldn't be hanging around long enough to have the truth, should it get out, impact me. But I really did like Mary, loved her company and couldn't figure out how to wordsmith around a lie. It really did bother me.

"Really, I'm okay. Just tired. Been a while since I had a day spent like that. You know, on the road all day. All that good food and coffee..." That thought left a bitter taste in my mouth. "I just needed a chance to get away from this hole for a while. It's driving me crazy here. No freedom and of course Kenny." My hand reached out and held hers tightly. "At least the company is great. I wouldn't be here if it weren't for you and Kenny. Well, I guess, just you now. If something were to happen to you, that would be it. I'd be out of here like a shot."

"Where would you go?"

"No clue. But it would be away. Far away from this shithole."

"Ivan!"

"Sorry." I leaned back heavily in my chair and looked out the windows of the cattle car. "It's been a tough few days, sweetheart. I feel like I am all tied up in knots, my legs wrapped up around my neck, and my fingers clutching tightly to the soles of my feet." My eyes were searching hers for compassion, "I really didn't sleep all that well last night. My neck feels like a corkscrew." I involuntarily rubbed my neck in the spot I felt would be appropriate.

"You sound like you need a massage, young man."

"She doesn't come until Saturday."

Mary blew a little smile towards my side of the

table and gave my hand a little squeeze. "I didn't mean from the staff, you dufus."

"Oh."

We got up and Mary held my hand and walked directly to the elevators. "Don't want to waste any energy on something so trivial as walking up the stairs, do we Ivan?" she smiled.

"No dear," was my feigned subservient answer. But I felt I had responded with a bit less enthusiasm than would be expected for such an occasion.

In a way I still feel like shit for that lie. I slept like a baby the night before. The only pain I felt when I woke up was the re-oxygenating of my muscles as I awoke. I was operating at one hundred per cent. Well, a septuagenarian 100 per cent.

We held hands like a couple of teenagers in love. And that was okay. We were in love, or at least in my case, a bad case of the likes. The concept of love was still a bit foreign to me. Though we were a couple of days past the teenager stage, we both knew that teenagers didn't know how to make love the way we did or could. There was an intimacy that youth simply didn't know how to share or give. An abandon that could only come with time, and experience.

As we stood at the elevator, waiting for it to come up from the basement, my eyes wandered down the hallway looking for any pairs of eyes that were lingering a little too long on the two of us. Again, an old habit come back to play. The newspaper stand just to the left of the elevator doors was full. The current paper was always placed on the top with the previous day still lingering beneath. If you were so inclined, you could probably read the last two weeks of newspapers that were lying underneath.

It wasn't the headline that caught my eye. That had

something to do with unemployment in the city or something. Really didn't give a shit about that. But next to it, was the secondary headline that did catch my eye.

"Family Slaughtered in B.C."

There were plenty of newspapers on the pile, so my initial desire to reach over and grab the top one was curtailed somewhat. I knew there would always be one around to read later. But the desire to glean what I could from it was nearly overpowering. My damned eyes weren't strong enough to read the fine print without my reading glasses. So, I couldn't make out much more than the name of the city, "Kamloops".

"Ivan, could you pick up a paper for me?" I broke out into a very toothy grin. Mary really was an amazing woman. I just hope she wasn't reading my mind because she probably wouldn't like what she saw.

"Sure sweetheart." I could see my fingers shake a little as they wrapped around the thin paper and tucked it under my arm. "Sure glad we don't pay for this thin rag. A buck, can you imagine?" I tapped it where it was securely held. "I mean, not even 24 pages." I shook my head. Again, the remainder of the paper wasn't really of interest to me. But that story on Kamloops would be.

"Ivan, we pay for the newspaper in this place, even if we don't read it. Don't you worry about that. It comes with the room, you know that." I nodded quietly to her chatter. My mind was beginning to wander back to Kamloops.

The bell chimed the arrival of the elevator at the main floor, pulling me back from my revelry and the grey doors slid back into the cold cement wall. There was nothing but the medicinal smell of the basement in the car.

"Our carriage madame."

She allowed my arm to guide her into the square car. As the doors quietly clamped together, my arms slid around her waist, and caressed underneath her breast.

"You seem to be in a bit of a hurry fella. How're your muscles doing?" she mused.

"They're okay. But will be better soon."

Both of us smiled. "Yeah, very soon."

As the car meandered up the shaft to Mary's floor, I glanced at the newspaper. Flipping it over, I involuntarily sucked in my breath. It must have been loud, because Mary looked at me with concerned eyes for a moment.

"You, okay?"

"Fine, yup," I lied for the second time that afternoon.

"You can't die until we're done buddy." She gave my hand a little squeeze.

"No one is dying today. I think it was a hiccup."

"Okay." She looked up at the floor indicator above the door and sighed. "Jesus this thing takes forever. Next time we take the stairs."

"Okay dear. Patience."

I guess I really wasn't taking advantage of her. Not really. If she didn't want to do the horizontal polka, I couldn't have coaxed her up to her room for anything. No force on earth could move Mary when she put her mind against something. She was very headstrong.

So, I wouldn't be taking advantage of her. We were going to take privileges with each other's bodies. But that didn't make me feel any less dirty.

It goes back a long time. Longer than I care to admit that I've been alive. I recall a day when I thought that being able to remember 20 years into the past was incredible. How old was I then? Thirty? All that history and world events and I was around to see and document it. Now, far more than half a century of happenings are locked in my mind. It's still incredible to me when I have time to think about it. In all that time people on the planet have gone through a world war, a number of police actions and armed conflicts, seen the moon now as much more than just a big cheese ball hanging in the sky, the rise and fall of the Beatles, and the death of a president.

And I remember all of it. Most importantly I remember everything I did. Everything. Some events are a little loose on the details, but I remember everything, every person. Every place I was. I had given it up long ago, all the habits and all the darkness.

But with Mary, I fell back naturally into something. It was a habit that pushed my mind back decades.

I was still a little off. It was just age. Being unable to stop the hands of time and all that crap. But I was thankful for Mary. Thankful for her wanting to be with and being able to give herself freely to me.

There was an integral need for my body to have a sexual release after I let the blackness out for a play. The Kamloops adventure really pushed that need to the top of the heap. I didn't dwell on it, even though I had a lot of time on that bus from British Columbia to Manitoba to think it over and analyze it. But it was there, bubbling in the background, never far from the surface.

Again, all things on the table. I knew exactly when it started for me, this desire for sex after a killing. It was purely accidental all those years ago, when *he* opened the door instead of his wife. She was supposed to have been home alone. I had no time to think when I saw him standing there, I just reacted. It was a moment of religious clarity for me. I was already a little excited at the thought of her, but the moments after he went down, the desire for release exploded in a logarithmic scale. I had never felt that powerful, that much in control. He had been my first, but certainly not my last. Far from it. His wife, though, still holds a special spot for me.

I suppose if I had half a desire, I could analyze why this happened, the roots of it in my childhood. But through my formative years, when I was especially active — I really liked it and didn't want to question it. I suppose I was an addict, the sex being the drug and the killing the small capsule it was wrapped within. I don't know why I needed to have sex afterwards. It was just what seemed to be an appropriate way to finish off the whole experience. It was just ... right. Or at least felt right. It worked for years and years. I couldn't see any reason to change that now. Just because I had reached well beyond what is officially considered senior citizen mode, certainly didn't take away any physical feelings I had. They were still there. Simmering.

And age didn't seem to have taken away any of the abilities I had possessed in my previous lifetime.

I was sure that Mary would be horrified if she knew what I had done. It was just her way. It was that pureness I liked about her, respected in her. It wasn't lost on me that I was the complete opposite of her as a person. It is what initially drew me to her. So, I wanted to share what only she and I would allow us to share. I suppose that is why the guilty feelings will always haunt me.

But I needed release after Kamloops. I needed someone to hold me close, feel what it was like to be close. So close that no other person could slip in between. With Mary it was gentle, almost loving. Though I really had no idea what loving was like, I knew what it looked like, but not how it felt to actually experience it. For me, it was like looking at a picture of a lamb, knowing it was soft, but never having a conception of that because I could never touch it.

Afterwards, I laid beside her, listening to her soft breathing, our fingers intertwined under the covers. Her body emanated warmth, yet her skin was slightly cool to the touch. The activity in my mind wouldn't let me sleep, even really rest.

With her eyes closed and her breathing soft and rhythmic, my mind slipped back to the newspaper. Underneath and to the left of the main article, was a photograph. The photo wasn't of anything too interesting, just a grainy, black and white of the front of the Kamloops Police Station. It looked like a hundred other old brick buildings that serve the same purpose no matter where they are located. Three stories high, like a school built in the same era, of brick and mortar.

But it wasn't the building that caught my attention. It was the people in front. I don't know what the caption was. I didn't bother to read it and it really wouldn't have mattered.

But, I'll be a son of a bitch if he didn't go to Kamloops!

19
JULY 2002

Royal Canadian Mounted Police Logger Tape. #2002070152

"Good evening, Kamloops Serious Crimes Unit. How may I direct your call?"

"Good evening. I'm looking for Inspector James McKinnon please."

"I'm sorry sir, Inspector McKinnon is unavailable at this time, is there someone else who could help you? <pause 11 seconds> Is there somewhere else I could direct you to, sir?"

"I would like to talk with Inspector McKinnon please. Now."

"As I said, sir, the inspector is unavailable right now. I could put you through to one of his staff members. <pause four seconds> Would that be all right, sir?"

"Please pass along this message to the Inspector for me, will you?"

"Of course, sir."

"I'll wait on the line while you pass the message along. Do you understand?"

"If you wish sir. But as I said, the inspector is busy right now."

"As you say. Please let him know that the man Tick Smith has been chasing for 40 years is waiting on the phone and will only wait 40 seconds."

"Sir?"

"Did you get that. Tick. Forty seconds. <three second pause> Beginning now."

"Sir?"

"Thirty-eight."

<phone line put on hold>

20
JULY 2002

"Who is this?"

"And I ... am talking to who?" The question slammed back at McKinnon. It was the beginning of a tense standoff. Two wills, opposed, staunchly on hostile footing, with no quarter for taking a step back, or sideways. Neither side willing to move. It was not where the inspector wanted to be after two short, adversarial questions.

"This is Inspector James McKinnon, Kamloops Serious Crimes Unit." He looked over at Tick Smith, who was standing by McKinnon's neat desk, listening in on another line. The two men stared at one another, waiting patiently. The pair had spent the previous day going over the historic and current files of the cases looking for commonalities.

After three successive murders in Brandon, the killer had simply quit. Or so it appeared. Both Smith and McKinnon felt he had moved on, left the area completely for greener pastures somewhere else. Somewhere that didn't have a police force that was gathering evidence and data on him, somewhere new. Smith said that at the time of the original investigation in '67, he felt that the suspect had moved to Brandon and resumed activities he had already practised elsewhere. It was well-developed pattern but seemed to evolve in Brandon. That was a problem for law enforcement.

In the late '60s there was no real coherent way of putting crime together into a single online file like they do now. It was hundreds of small, individual police forces working alone —some municipal or provincial, some federal. They had no real knowledge of what went on in the next city, let alone the neighboring province. Forget across the country. And by the 60's, the TransCanada Highway gave anyone the ability to move from province to province quickly and invisibly.

It was not lost on the two of them as they had said goodbye that night, that this was probably the first time an interjurisdictional review had ever been undertaken of the case. It made the two of them smile.

The next morning it was a visit to the crime scene, left much the way it was on the day of the murders. That visit, along with a detailed review, took the vast majority of the day. In the end, the two men agreed this was an entirely different kind of murder from what their suspect had committed in the 1960s. There was no sexual component, no real violence other than the actual murders. Something had definitely changed with this one. The question the two of them had was, what would this mean for the days ahead? They agreed that a guy like this doesn't go quiet for years, then pop up for a one-off event like this. But this guy had to be an age, probably older than Tick. So, did he just have an overwhelming desire to just randomly kill an entire family? Was he after the woman and the other two were just damage control? Or was this the beginning of a new methodology?

"I don't think so, Tick," McKinnon said of a renewal in the killer's operations. "There was a reason for this one. He went through the house very cleanly, killing everything in his path. He even went so far as to track the kid down in the garage and do him. No, this is not a slight change from his old self, this is an entirely different MO."

Tick mulled over the words of the senior officer then said, "I don't think it's someone new because of the DNA left at the scene. It just doesn't make a lot of sense, I agree." The two men were talking in the living room of the very quiet house. Smith shook his head slowly. "No, this is the same guy. Something with this one has changed, though. I don't know what that is, wouldn't have a clue. But something isn't tracking from 1967 to today." Tick looked down at the darkened blood stain near the front door and shook his head.

"But some things haven't changed so much."

"Very impressive," the response came from the phone line after what seemed to be a very long time. "Let me talk to Tick."

This time the pause was on the law enforcement end. Smith looked at McKinnon like he was a kid in the candy shop, just waiting for parental approval to jump into the gumball bin. McKinnon was going over all the options; he didn't even know if this was the guy they were after. In his mind, he capitalized, THE GUY. If it was, he wasn't sure he wanted to involve an officer from outside his unit. Hell, a retired officer from outside the unit.

"One minute."

The mechanical response came quickly. "You don't have a minute."

Both men covered the phone mouthpieces and looked at one another. "What do you think?" McKinnon asked.

"He knows I'm here." Then to McKinnon's questioning look, he added, "The front page of the Globe," Tick explained simply. The inspector nodded his head, remembering his wife walking up to him, asking him who the older gentleman was that he lunched with. Both he and Tick were clear in the photograph. Though Smith was behind McKinnon in the shot, he was still distinctive and easy to identify if you knew him.

Jim McKinnon nodded his head. "Damn the torpedoes." He removed his hand from the mouthpiece and said, "I am putting you on speakerphone." He pressed the button, set the handset down on the receiver and both men leaned forward closer to the telephone. "Who is this? How do I know who you are?"

"If Tick is listening, he doesn't know me. But he does have an intimate knowledge of what I do. Probably recognizes my voice, though it's been a while. Something evil's afoot, hey Tick?" The prompt pierced the retired officer through his chest, and made him suck in a huge breath, trying to catch what he lost. For a moment his eyes watered. He felt as though he had been kicked hard in the stomach. Recovery, though, took very little time. Tick Smith took in a deep breath and spoke.

"It's been a while." He looked again at McKinnon and quietly nodded his head to let him know this was the Guy.

"Hasn't it though," came the killer's voice. Tick listened hard, trying to find more in the voice than just the words. But they escaped him, the words were so choppy, restrictive. What did jump out at him was the cold, almost edgy feel of the man on the other end of the phone line. That hadn't changed. Not in the decades since they had actually exchanged words.

"How's institutional life these days? For a man your age?" Tick inquired. He looked at McKinnon, who was nodding his head. The inspector liked the way this guy could think on his feet.

"Oh ... let's just say, it has had its wet, soppy

moments."

"I'm sure," Tick agreed, looking at McKinnon with questioning eyes. McKinnon silently mouthed the word 'jail?' Smith hunched his shoulders, not entirely positive that was the case.

"Why have you called me here in . . . ?"

"Sorry to cut you off, but the batteries on this damn cellular phone are almost dead."

"Charge it up and call back."

"Yeah, I'll get right on that. Maybe I should send you a letter, let you have my home address at the same time. It would seem that is what it's going to take, hey Tick? By the way, sorry about Martha. She was . . ."

"You fuck . . ." Tick spat towards the phone.

McKinnon held up his finger, to show Smith he was back in the call. He didn't need his one contact person blowing a gasket after so little egging. But Smith shook his head and his mouth formed the word "No." Both men stared at one another, for a moment, waiting for a crack. McKinnon finally gave him approval to continue.

"Tick, you there?"

"Yup, I'm here. Why are you doing this? Again?"

"I can't figure out society Tick. I mean really. They keep bringing back the old songs, adding a wacky overproduced drumbeat, and presto! It's a new song. Movies are being redone. So, like you and me, they just keep bringing back the good stuff. The original stuff."

"Cause we're better? I don't think so."

"Nah. I don't think so either Tick. I think it's just because we are the real deal."

"Ya think so? The real deal?" Smith was looking directly into the eyes of McKinnon as he spoke and asked the unasked question. "Why did you call?"

"What?"

"Why did you call me? After all these years."

"Just to let you know that I think that I'll come back into the game for a while."

"Into the game? At our age, we should be sitting on a veranda, sipping iced tea, and watching the traffic go by."

"Never cared for iced tea Tick. Anyway, I gotta go. Better luck this time, hey."

"Why now?"

The killer seemed to ponder the question for a moment. "They say Tick, that seniors don't have the ability to contribute to society in a meaningful way. We are best utilized for telling stories to children, about the way it was. The good old days. You know what I mean, memories. I guess I just want everyone to know that not all seniors are ready for pudding and diapers."

Smith smiled at the opening. "It seems some of us are ready for diapers."

The immediate silence on the line was consuming. McKinnon looked at the former officer seated across the table from him. He mouthed the word 'ouch.' Both men smiled.

But there was nothing, not even noise from the line itself. Finally, a single sentence landed in the office.

"Be thinkin' about ya buddy." And the phone went dead.

Tick Smith and Inspector Jim McKinnon sat silently for a moment. Tick looked over at the inspector and shrugged his shoulders to McKinnon's question.

"What do you think he meant by that?"

"Not sure. But I would say he is getting ready to kill again. And very soon."

"You antagonized him a little with that comment." Both men had big 'I just ate the whole thing' smiles on their faces.

Smith nodded and laughed, "Ya think?"

"Well, what do you think?"

Tick wondered aloud, "About what?"

"Why did he call? Why did he give us a heads up with the 'be thinking about ya'?" McKinnon popped open the file folder and looked at the crime scene photographs laid out in graphic detail. "I don't get it."

"He knew," Tick observed, "we would connect him with the murders back in Brandon. Leaving his piss on the floor pretty much assured that."

McKinnon thought out loud. "That was a risk though. Getting DNA from urine is tough." He looked at Smith, who was nodding. "So, there was as much of a chance that we wouldn't pick up anything from it, as we would. It was a risk to call."

"But then, he probably saw my picture in the newspaper. So, he had to call."

"You think he wanted us to put that together? Do you think he knew that it could be done?"

"He knew I was here, so that told him the obvious. We connected 1967 and the current killings. This is a person who has gotten away with murder in five decades. He knows enough to cover up the details. Confuse the evidence. He knows enough to have stayed out of my line of sight for all those years." The retired detective tapped the phone lightly, wishing it to ring, "Yeah, he knew there was a real chance that we could connect him through the DNA sampling of his urine back to 67."

"Plus," McKinnon added pointing at the newspaper, "you are famous. Put all of that together and he just had to call. Maybe one of those, 'I know you know I know' things."

Tick followed his gaze, "I'm not so sure about that. Do you honestly think he pissed on the floor on purpose?"

"Maybe. No." But as McKinnon said the words, doubt crept into his mind. "I don't know. Maybe he tried to get it up with the woman and just couldn't do it. He is a hell of an age now. Probably 70 to 75. Unless he thought ahead enough to have popped a handful of Viagra, he might have had a less than hard time with her," McKinnon smirked. "I don't know Tick; it just doesn't feel like that."

"What do you mean?"

"I don't think he wanted to get laid." McKinnon shuffled through the papers as he talked, "There's no trace evidence anywhere in the house, except the urine in the downstairs bathroom. There was no indication that the woman was sexually traumatized in any way. I mean none. Following your theory, if he found that he couldn't pull it out of his pants on fire, he'd be a little bitter about that, and get a little more excited in the killing side of the thing. There would have been a lot more intensive physical violence to the victims, especially to her. He has a thing for women. But like the others, two potentially fatal wounds. The first was to disable and kill. The other was simply insurance."

McKinnon flipped a file folder open and tossed a couple of photographs at Tick. On the top was the kid, sprawled in the mini-van, a deep wound to his neck, just slightly off the horizontal access of his windpipe. His eyes were closed, and a dark pool was staining his shirt, the seat, and the carpet beneath him. His hands were clasped together, almost as in prayer.

"See, just two wounds. Deep, powerful. Directed with just enough energy to kill both times." McKinnon thought about the new report on his desk, "Actually according to the coroner, either were more than enough to be fatal. The boy died from blood loss. Quickly." The inspector flipped through the other plain manila folders and correlated the printed word to the photographs.

"The husband, the same way, as was the wife, in that the wounds were very economical in nature." He looked up at Tick, who had that questioning look on his face. "He expended no more energy than required to kill and kill effectively." He read further down on the female victim's file, "And again, no sign of sexual trauma. Nothing. She was nude Tick but was nude because she had just got out of the bathtub or was still in the tub when he found her. So, the question still stands, why did this guy lose it on the floor?"

"Truth?"

"Yeah, the truth." There was no need to be evasive, McKinnon pondered.

"I think the guy is just fucking old. No one's fault. Muscle tone goes after a while and he was unable to hold it, especially with all the excitement that was going on at the time. It happens." Tick looked up from the pictures and found the inspector staring at him. "Not to me you understand, but for some."

"Oh yeah, totally, I'm with ya Tick."

21
JULY 2002

Cellular phones really are amazing little devices. From basically anywhere on the planet you can call any person, on any particular patch of ground.

Of course, a diligent member of the law enforcement community could trace your call within a small area. Say 50 square feet or so. But the neat trick is to be out of the area before the boys in blue arrive to spoil your fun. It's not like the old days, when on television and in the movies, the police would need 90 seconds or something to trace a call. Hell, even in the days before caller ID, once you made that call, from wherever you made it ... you were cooked. The police could freeze the line, and they knew exactly where the call came from. Somehow an entire generation of criminals actually believed what they saw on TV. Such bullshit.

But with cellular phones, it's a little different. They can grab your number right away, whose phone it is, and hell, they can even triangulate to within a few feet where you were. The key phrase there is where you *were*. It's amazing how far you can be from "where you were" with a five-to-seven-minute head start. And that is when the police are prepped, excited and ready for the call. When a random call comes in, with no warning or anticipation, the response time turns to half an hour — easy. Especially in the countryside.

I didn't really deserve any huge credit for the performance on the telephone. Actually, I was a little disappointed in my work. I let that stupid shit Tick get the best of me. I got mad. I was still winning the game, but he took that particular match. For a few moments, I stood stock still, staring at the small phone I held in my hand. The little stubby rubber antenna sticking out of its extremely thin body pointing out my particular downfall. In the small rectangular window, an antenna signal meter was showing full strength. Though just below that the battery indicator was flashing silently. I focused on the flashing battery, shaking my head in wonder.

Through my entire life I have honestly not done very well at controlling my temper. Never have. Not since I can remember anyway. It's one of those little things that I never was able to get a real solid grip on. It wasn't for lack of trying though. Hell, I even went to some anger management classes a long time ago. They were interesting and led me to trying to find creative ways to divert my energy when things didn't go quite the way I wanted them to. They taught me any number of ways to learn to control the red, searing anger that would swell inside my chest and head. Breathing exercises, counting, going for a walk. Shit, there was a pile of ways they figured you should try to get a temper under control.

They didn't work. At least not all the time. And, it turns out, I had other avenues to de-stress my life that were guaranteed to work. For a bit anyhow.

When I really blew a gasket I would lose time, lost in a black temper tantrum that could last for a couple of minutes, sometimes even hours. That was the only time I scared myself. When that happened, when I lost my temper. It's interesting to note that as I've aged, the incidents of my temper getting out of my control have decreased significantly. Those lost episodes are far less frequent now. I'm not sure if it's because I'm not as critical of my work or performance as I used to be, or if I just don't give a shit. I'm not sure. I just know that it's rare that I have a hissy fit. Very rare. Especially since my retirement.

But not today.

I grabbed the roll of duct tape from my coat pocket, peeled back about two feet of it, and threw the remainder in the trunk of the car. The long strip I attached to my forearm. They would know within a couple of hours of finding it what type of tape it was, who manufactured it and hell, even the chain of stores that carried it. I had purchased the tape 10 years ago at Kennedy's, so was fairly confident that I wasn't leaving anything of significance forensically behind. No one remembers anything that far back. So, all in all, the tape was good. But still, I slipped it back into the small bag in the trunk beside Catherine. Every movement provoked a jerky reaction from her in the opposite direction. Each reaction prompted a crinkle of the large industrial plastic bag I had lined the trunk with. There was no point in trying to calm her down. She would continue to be in full panic mode. I could tell from the wild look in her eyes that she was fearful of her future — and rightly so. She definitely had fewer moments ahead of her than behind.

As I thought briefly of that 'little problem' in Kamloops, I could feel the bulk of the diaper under my pants, and suddenly they felt very uncomfortable, very big and very obvious to any casual observer. I turned my eyes to the heavens above and asked, "Why me Lord?" Kris Kristofferson was always good for that sort of line. I let the tape dangle from my arm, as I discretely checked the condition of my protective undergarments.

It was with a considerable sigh of relief I found they were still as dry as a bone. I had taken to wearing some whenever I was out of the building and far from a washroom. I didn't want another accident to fuck my day up.

I felt the 'little problem' in Kamloops was due to a number of unrelated factors that culminated with the incident. A little too much coffee, a little too warm outside, a little too much stress because of what I was doing there. Far too little time during my movements to head to a washroom, then wrap that up with a little too much exertion in the killings themselves. All together, that spells a gigantic 'whoops'.

Of course, all that knowledge didn't help when I walked down the aisles of the grocery store trying to find the damn things. Now, as a logically thinking person, I would have thought the goddamn things would have been in the same section as diapers for babies. I mean, it makes sense, right? But once I asked the question to some pimply faced boy in white and red, with the name tag Aaron on his pathetic hollow chest, it became painfully obvious that I was looking in the wrong section of the store. Aaron gave me the 'deer in the headlights' look, and I think a little smirk, and then pointed towards the back of the store.

"The adult protective diapers are in Aisle 3 sir, near the adult supplements display." He said it a little too loudly. Stupid shit. Just another young asshole.

"Excuse me," I said out loud to Catherine, suddenly aware of two eyes staring in abject horror at where my hand was probing, shifting my overstuffed package to make things a little more comfortable. Defensively I held up both hands and said "There is no problem here, I was just checking to see if ... well." The wind wrapped the tape around my arm, gluing itself to the greying hair on my arm. "Forget it. Sorry."

That didn't seem to placate the eyes at all. They stared into mine, darting quickly to the phone in my right hand, the tape wrapped around my left, then over my shoulder to the grassy plain behind us. I suppose she was looking for one of those knights in shining armour to come bounding over the knoll, sword in hand, riding on a great white steed that pounded the rich grass with each yard it advanced.

I knew there wouldn't be a knight. Or a cop. Hell, not even a kid playing hooky.

This spot was chosen for its isolation. So, there was nothing here. No buildings, no people, no river, no road. Hell, there wasn't even cattle or horses grazing. Simply put, there was nothing. It was just a huge grassy field. Some badger bush smattered about, a few wildflowers and dandelions as well. But nothing moving. Nothing alive. Nothing that could even be closely construed as a witness or a saviour.

I guess I should have taped over her eyes. She couldn't speak, of course, with the tape wrapped around her mouth and a balled-up sock gagging her inside. So, all her pleading, her desperation had to be done silently, just an occasional sob. A gurgle for air. Soft, long tears gliding down her smooth cheeks.

"Catherine, that was a tough conversation. Tick can be such a dink sometimes."

She looked up at me, a clarity sweeping over her. Her breathing seemed to relax some, then like a switch had been thrown, her intake of air, seemed to get choppy, staccato. Her body seemed to try to burrow through the trunk and into the ground below. Her ankles started to show raw skin, and sinew, as she vainly tried to run. The look in her eyes was clear horror, fear and confusion.

For me, she was here for a simple reason. Like so many in her age range, she discounted seniors outright. In her case, we were in a lineup at the flower shop, four in total waiting our turn. I thought something nice for Mary would be in order. So, I had a sleeve of daisies in my hand, ready to pay at the till. I wasn't really fond of flowers, but I know the daisy is her favourite. I felt a strange desire to purchase the flowers even though I really didn't understand why. Sometimes those little moments of connectivity and the reasons behind them elude me.

So, up comes Catherine, making shallow excuses about wanting to get going as she had to work, and it was getting late. The first two people moved aside, but I turned and stared at her.

"Excuse me," she pasted on a smile as she spoke. "But I have to get to work right away, so could you let me go ahead of you?"

I did try my best smile. I am sure it wasn't good enough. "I am kind of in a hurry as well. Sorry."

Then came the fatal mistake on her part. It was probably her temper coming through. Not really her fault, but the fruit of her raising. Maybe it is just the way she is in general; I am not sure. The explanation really doesn't matter. What did matter, what dictated her future, is what she said next.

"What could you possibly be in a hurry for?"

Oops.

It wasn't just the words she uttered, it was the so easily pronounced sneer that went along with it. In her mind, she really couldn't see any value in the old guy ahead of her blocking her way, for all that young person life she had to live that day. I knew that she honestly felt that there was nothing that could have possibly been more important for me than what she had going on in her life.

Oops.

She didn't look so good now. As much as she

struggled with the tape that was binding her, it wasn't going to let go.

It was all happenstance. The ready kit in my car contained everything I would need for just this sort of opportunity. Even in full retirement, the little kit always stayed in the car, for what reason I have no clue, just habit. The car wasn't complete if it wasn't tucked into the driver's side wheel well. Tape, a couple of knives of varying shapes, sizes and purposes. All purchased years ago from big department stores or pawn shops — all untraceable and without any value. There was a couple of very large plastic bags, a large cover sheet of polypropylene, and a small foldable survival saw. I really liked that particular bit of kit but had never had the opportunity to use it. Hmmm?

When she walked out of the shop, little bouquet of flowers in her well manicured hands and turned the corner, I was waiting for her, trunk open and tape in hand. It was a 50-50 shot if she turned left when coming out of the flower shop, or right. I was parked to the right. Prophetic.

When she turned around the corner of the block and started down the side street towards me, I quickly surveyed the area immediately around me. It was very quiet in the downtown core of the city, no traffic or people walking, not even a dog. This was a place I had been many times before. She saw me standing ahead of her and suddenly a very exasperated look swept over her face. I could imagine she was thinking, 'Oh great, an argument with some old prick when I am so busy and in a rush.' But there was no argument, just a knowing smile on my part as my muscles tensed.

As she approached, a quick sidestep in front of her caught her off guard and she paused in a bit of shock.

Despite my aging muscle tone, my slow strike with a balled-up fist into her throat was far quicker than the absolute lack of reaction on her part. She exhaled sharply, doubling over. I utilized that motion to twist her slightly, and she toppled into the trunk of the car. Bewildered as she was, she still tried to claw her way out, arms and legs thrashing crazily both in the trunk and outside. My fist slammed into her nose hard, blood almost immediately spraying outward. But the impact stunned her, and she immediately stopped moving. Quickly, with the deftness of decades of practice, her mouth, hands and then legs were bound with a couple of quick wraps. I looked up above the trunk lid, then to my rear and saw no one once again. I looked down at her in the trunk, her eyes not quite in focus, smiled and slammed the lid shut. Her purse must have fallen when I first hit her, so I quickly picked it up along with the cheap bouquet of flowers and brought them into the front seat with me, tossing it all onto the floor. The car started immediately. I put on my seat belt, slipped it into gear, which it landed with a clunk as all Chryslers do, and pulled away from the curb.

I chose the Chrysler product because it was fairly roomy inside the passenger compartment, easily hosting four people. While it was fairly dependable, it is a domestic car that any corner garage could repair should something ever go wrong. Plus, the parts for it were cheap and the used parts market was fairly robust. But the large, square trunk, relative to the size of the vehicle was what really sold me on it. The trunk of my little Chrysler is just big enough for two people if folded properly, or a single small-boned lady with a bit of an attitude. Unfortunately, the damn car had a high trunk threshold, which meant she was really heavy to toss in. I also thought she was going be a lot heavier on the way out.

She was hog tied pretty well, so she wasn't going anywhere. The more she struggled, the more twisted the tape became around her legs and arms. If nothing else, I had a lot of experience tying folks up in my life.

Peeling the tape from my arm, I reached down, and placed the phone on her forehead, then wrapped the grey tape around her head. After making sure it wasn't going to slip off, I stood up, and took a last look around the spot I had chosen. It was still completely isolated and empty. I reached into the trunk, grabbed her by the shoulders and man-handled her onto the ground. She landed on her face and upper chest with a thunk that knocked the breath out of her. She sort of reminded me of a fish hitting the deck after being caught. I kneeled over her, looking at her face, with dirt, grass, sweat and blood mingling together to form a wonderful, horrid mask.

"I chose this spot for a reason Catherine. It's very remote, no one will come here by accident. No one will help you. So, don't waste any energy on that." Something caught my eye to the north. I stopped short, stood and stared for two minutes. But nothing remerged so I resumed my monologue. "But there is an upside to this location." Finding the recall button on the phone with my right hand, I pushed it all the while trying to not look down at the eyes, that were watching my hand's every movement. The misdirection worked perfectly. She didn't see the knife being withdrawn from my pocket. The knife cut cleanly through her throat, I watched her eyes roll up as the knife slipped through her skin, then look up to me pleadingly, small tears starting to form in the corners.

"The upside is two-fold. First that it has great cellular reception, and secondly, because of that, you will be found very quickly." Through the harsh wet sounds of Catherine's body trying to compensate for the blood and air loss, I pressed redial and almost immediately could hear the operator at the Kamloops Serious Crimes Unit saying, "Kamloops Serious Crimes, hello?"

This time she saw the second stroke coming.

22
JULY 2002

"She's not posed?"

It was a rhetorical question.

Both McKinnon and Tick were standing in the middle of the once barren field, now filled with all sorts of police and emergency vehicles. Their lights like beacons to the spot where a human life lay, ebbed away and empty. They were assembled in a great circle, some with headlights pointed in the general direction of the crime scene, others were parked sideways, with flood or spotlights forcing daylight to the early morning twilight of the field.

The RCMP officer glanced at the retired man standing next to him shivering in a thin cardigan sweater, Styrofoam coffee cup steaming in his shaking hand, not sure where he was going with the comment. But the senior citizen didn't offer any more other than a slight bobbing motion with his head, so he looked back down at the sheet-covered form laying on the ground. She had been on the ground for less than 24 hours, but already the gases generated by the breakdown of her body were oozing into the air around her.

McKinnon didn't like the smell of dead bodies — actually he was pretty sure no one did. He had dealt with enough in the valley, either in Kamloops Lake itself, or the many smaller tributaries that bled into it. People falling out of boats, tripping and falling off docks, or human beings tossed into the water like biodegradable garbage. It didn't matter how they went in; they all came out the same ... white, eyeless, fetid. All of their individuality was washed away by any length of time in the water. Rivers and lakes in B.C. were cold, fast and deep. But there were enough currents that kept the bodies floating in a predictable cycle of discovery. If they went into the water, McKinnon knew they would eventually come out. It was just a matter of determining where and when. If they lay in the warmer water towards shore for any length of time, fish and biological organisms would get at them in very short order. What they left behind wasn't pretty and wasn't something that you would allow the family to view because it didn't accurately represent the loved one they had lost.

You really didn't want that image to be the last they had of their family member.

"He didn't pose the family in Kamloops, right?" Smith asked as he slowly walked around the girl laying in the field.

Again, a rhetorical question.

"No." McKinnon ran through the crime scene quickly in his head before answering. It was something he had done a hundred times before. He was looking for any small details, anything that would give him a clue about the guy they were dealing with. It still bothered him, that the only direction they had came from piss. And the piss was the link back to murders three provinces away, almost four decades before. But he couldn't see any pattern, at least nothing that jumped out at him. All he saw, as he rolled the photos over in his mind, were bodies, left crumpled where they fell.

"No," Tick agreed. "He didn't pose any of the others back then either. At least the ones we know about," Tick added. "Your forensic guys have been through the site, I assume?" A silent nod was the answer he got from McKinnon. "No fingerprints?" His answer this time was a shake of the head. Tick noticed he, too, was shaking his head. Only he was doing so in wonder.

"And there were none in Kamloops? Right? No prints other than the family, and friends?" Again, a nod from the RCMP officer.

"It's the same as before."

McKinnon turned to face him.

"What do you mean?" The inspector thought maybe the man next to him was going somewhere with this after all.

"In the murders I investigated, there was never any fingerprints. Now back then we could make a case against a person without them but catching them in the act was far more important. Fingerprints were more of a confirmation of their involvement. We could look through the files, and there were a lot of cards back then, but it was luck to find the match. In fact, fairly rare. It wasn't like it is now, where we can put a person in prison by being able to prove that buddy was in the room at the time the thefts occurred. Back then, no shit, a smoking gun was considered to be required evidence by the crown attorney."

"How did you catch anyone?"

Tick smiled quietly in remembrance, "When conducting interrogations, the laws concerning physical contact with the suspects were a lot more ... uh ... liberal, relaxed back then."

McKinnon smiled as well. He thought, 'Oh to have that latitude.'

"Yeah, so we had a very high confession rate." Tick's smile was erased when he looked back down on the amazingly small swath of cloth on the ground in front of him. "But the lack of fingerprints does bring up an interesting focus for the investigation, doesn't it?

I mean, hell, he leaves piss in Kamloops, but no fingerprints. We can place him at the crime scene there, but here ... all we have is a phone call."

"Two calls back-to-back." McKinnon reminded him. "You identified him as our guy, the killer. From the voice on the phone."

Smith was nodding his head in agreement as he motioned to the sheet, "Do you mind?"

McKinnon swivelled around to find the senior officer on site. "Bill, okay if Chief Smith has a look?" Tick smirked at being called his old title. It would carry some weight but not an abundance.

"Make sure he's suited up. But okay."

"Suited up?" Tick asked. "You have a suit for retired cops carrying about 25 extra pounds around in a thick tire around his waist?"

McKinnon had already swivelled and was walking towards the dusty Ford Explorer that housed the Ident Units wares but spoke over his shoulder. "Hell, we have suits in here that will fit an RCMP Inspector that is carrying 25 extra pounds of rubber." He pushed his head towards the back of the truck and said, "Just make sure you take a whiz before you hop into this thing. If you have to go, it takes too long to get out of it. And it's waterproof. Therefore, no water in, no water out. You piss in this suit," he said, smiling while he handed the suit to Tick Smith, "you drown. Simple."

Tick sat on the bumper beside the Inspector, slipping his shoes into the stitched in socks of the suit. He tugged at the massive amount of material left over in the sock and would have to agree with McKinnon. A monster could wear this thing, and still have room to spare. "Is the mid-section this generous?"

"Oh," McKinnon said, standing up, and shuffling

his body into the white fiberglass suit, "and then some." Tick noticed the sound of the zipper going up wasn't as loud as he thought it would have been. It was almost like Velcro being done up. "They wanted to make sure the officers could still wear their sidearms, so there is a lot of lateral movement in this thing along with slotted pockets with Velcro closers near their weapon locations. So, there is actually a lot of lateral movement."

Tick smiled, nodding his head in agreement. "I had a guy work for me one summer, college student. Said he had a glandular problem. Medical, you know."

"Uh-huh."

"Personally, I think he just ate all the time. We had to stop bringing donuts into the station, 'cause the fat son-of-a-bitch kept eating them all. I mean he denied it and all. But there was always this tell-tale halo of sugar on the floor around his desk. It was like a bullseye of sugar. And can you think of a worse place to try to lie about forensic evidence than a police station."

"No. Not really. What'd you do?"

"Oh, we let him keep on working, and all of us went out for coffee a lot more that summer. It was on the application form the next year; the successful candidate had to be in good physical condition." Tick laughed at the memory, then sobered up quickly. "He died of a coronary a couple years ago. He would have been only about 55 or so."

"Baggage. Never good to carry around. Especially too much of it."

"With you on that, Inspector."

As the two men continued to zip up, tie down, and slip on, McKinnon suddenly quieted down. A niggling thought in the back of his head kept pushing itself forward, crushing his brain in sheer electrical weight. Once he was finished dressing, he sat back down on the bumper, a little heavier than he planned on.

Tick stopped trying to tighten down the built-in hood of the suit and looked at him. “What is it?”

“I think you’re right. I think the key question here is the fingerprints. Or rather, the lack of fingerprints.” He turned to Smith, focusing on the man. “You said there were no fingerprints, in any of the crime scenes? Right?” Smith nodded his head. McKinnon looked over at the sheet on the ground, being held down with stones picked up around the site. “No smudges?”

Tick paused for a moment and then answered, “I don’t specifically recall, but that will be in my paperwork. I would guess there would be some. We had a bunch of crime scenes to go through, so there would be smudges, no doubt. I often wondered if he had burnt them off with acid or something.”

“That,” McKinnon observed, “is pretty dedicated to the job.” He shook his head, “But I tell you what, with this guy, it isn’t a shock. But damn, that must have hurt.”

“He never did anything that would lead me to believe that he was anything but a professional at this. And by that, I mean that is his entire focus, it is what he does for a living. So, I could believe that. But the inability for him to leave a single fingerprint, or partial, always bothered me. He would have needed several sessions with his fingers dipped in a bowl of acid to make sure they were all gone.”

McKinnon was shaking his head again, “Damn.”

“Right? Damn is right.”

McKinnon continued, “There were none in Kamloops and according to Bill, none here either. Not on the cell phone, anywhere on the duct tape, on the body. Nowhere. No fingerprints. So, once again it does beg the question, why did he leave his urine on the floor of a murder scene three provinces over? It just doesn't make sense."

"It does in a way."

"How's that?"

"He knows that DNA typing is more or less a passive forensic science. At least right now, and is a sketchy and very long process at best. It can link him to the crimes, if we catch him. If we have him in custody we can pull a sample from him, then link him to a crime. But only if we catch him, or in the very least, identify him. I agree with you, it's the fingerprints that interests me as well."

"Because he's on file?"

"I am betting he has to be. Somewhere, for something on file. It might be through prior convictions, maybe military service, or ... I don't know. But that would be why he removed them completely. Takes that bit of advantage away from us."

McKinnon was looking around the site, taking in the furor that always accompanies a person's untimely death. She may have died alone, but now, after death, was surrounded with people who wanted to find out why. More importantly, who.

White suited officers talked and had coffee with those still in uniform. A pair of ambulance personnel were waiting off to the east, leaning against their vehicle. Waiting for the teams to finish up. The Identification Unit was starting to wrap up its end of the site, piling all of their gear back into the rear of the Explorer.

It hit McKinnon then. "It could be a cop."

Tick stood and faced the man, very sombre. "I

always had that niggly feeling. That sense that our guy knew too much about what we were doing, and what we could do to catch him. He'd leave some small shit but never enough to catch him, or at the very least, link him to anything else. Just enough to let us know he was still going. Just enough to let us know we hadn't caught him yet. It was like little signposts he gifted to us. 'This way'."

"So, you did think there was a possibility he was a cop?"

"Oh, absolutely." Tick pulled on the rubber gloves and started towards the body, very slowly, watching where each foot fell on the dewy grass. "I did. But back in the Sixties, in small town Manitoba, shifting the investigation towards a fellow law enforcement officer just wasn't going to happen. The chief was old guard. He wouldn't even consider it ... at least until I had the smoking gun. He wouldn't even let me look for a gun. And our boy never used one, a side point. Besides, I knew all of our guys. Like you know your guys. They were a mixed bag, some good, some not so good, but all cops on the right side of the badge. Believe me, I went through each one in my mind, late at night. But just couldn't put a face to the crime. Especially from our department."

Tick kneeled down, looking at the mis-shaped form beneath the white covering. For the most part, it looked just like the bodies he had seen many times before. Except for the rectangular shape nobbing from the top of the head. He pulled the sheet back from the girl ... it always made him instantly think about his wife. He couldn't help it. For a moment, they were her eyes, probing his, uncomprehending. But wanting. But with this one, the cellular phone, taped to her forehead pulled all eyes away.

"They figure she died about the same time as the phone call came to us. She's already settled into rigor. Single fatal wound ... right to left. It's an old familiar story now. Second jab through the bottom of the jaw for insurance — but maybe more for theatrics on that second one. Truly redundant." McKinnon looked at the phone for a moment. "Why the phone on her head?"

"Hands were secured in front of her with tape. Basically, hog tied. Maybe it was just the most convenient place to put the phone. To tape it down so it wouldn't move." The tape ends were folded slightly. It happens often, when wrapping gifts with Scotch tape. You unstring the tape long enough to make it around the present, and inevitably, half of it gets wound together in an unforgiving knot.

He turned one end over, and the white backing was tangled into the girl's black hair. Back in the hospital when the autopsy is performed, they would have to cut away the hair to get the phone off. Something caught his eye on the backing side. It stood out brightly.

"Look at this," Tick said, motioning towards the girl's head. McKinnon moved towards him, crawling on his knees the last couple of steps.

"What is it?"

"The girl's hair is black. Pure black."

"Right."

"A friend of mine's son has this type of hair. No matter if it's on his head, arms, back, wherever. It's pure black." Tick pointed towards the tape end. "If you look close, you will see a few grey hairs ... there." He turned the tape to reflect more of the artificial light that illuminated the area. "See it?"

"Yeah, I see it." McKinnon swivelled around looking for the officer in charge. He spotted him, in the cab of the SUV, writing on an aluminum framed clipboard. "Bill." The officer in charge looked over at the two men, hulking over the body. "Something here for you," McKinnon said.

"What is it?" he asked, as he set the clipboard down, and started to exit the truck.

"Tick ... Chief Smith found some hair samples on the sticky side of the tape here. They are grey, the girl's hair is black. You might want to bag this right now." He looked back down at the tape end, getting closer to get a better look. "I think there are a couple of follicles too."

Tick smiled and pushed back from the body. "Okay, now we can positively link our guy to both murders. If the DNA from the follicle holds true."

"I think it will Tick."

"Yeah, me too."

"So, is he getting sloppy?"

Tick shook his head slowly. Still not comprehending. "I don't know, maybe he wanted us to see it. To know that he put it there. That it was him that pulled this masterful crime off and that there is nothing we can do."

He reached over and pushed the telephone's power button. But it was dead. Nothing showed up on the status screen. "It's not much of a masterful crime, though, is it?" He straightened up, overextending his back to stretch everything back into place. Bending over was not where he did his best work ... at least not for a long time. Too much desk work his last few years on the job and very little exercise since that part of his life ended.

"Naw," McKinnon agreed, "anyone can cut open the throat of an immobile woman. If that is something you want to do, that is."

Tick slid the sheet back over the victim's head. He felt like he was tucking a child in for the night. "Sorry," he whispered to her alone.

He stood up quickly and walked back towards the truck. A small tear had formed in the corner of his left eye. If asked, he would say it was the result of aging and he always developed a tear in his right eye when he was outside, especially if there was a slight breeze. Of course, with the tear in his left eye ... the story would have to change slightly.

He looked at McKinnon and shook his head slowly. "No, not just anyone."

23
JULY 2002

"You were certainly Mr. Romance." Mary rolled the sheets back exposing her upper chest. In the glow from the streetlight just outside the window Mary looked wonderfully young. The sweat glistened on her skin, taking decades off her age and somehow endearing her even more in my eyes. I couldn't tell her that, because it was hard to explain. Hard to put into words what she meant to me.

Well, it was hard to explain, without driving her away in abject horror. I couldn't let that happen.

"I missed you, Mary." Our hands found each other and intertwined beneath the sheets. It was neat, for lack of a better word, to feel the clamminess of the air trapped beneath the cotton sheets the home provided for us. I'm sure they wouldn't exactly have been shocked if they knew what was going on between their sheets. Fuck 'em.

"Ivan, you were only gone for a little while."

"It's not the length of time Mary, it's just the fact that I have been away from you. I like being around you." My hands squeezed hers a little more, and she tightened her grip in return. "I like being with you."

Mary rolled over on her side, to stare straight at me. "That was nice. Very," she paused to look for the words I suppose, "strong."

"You had an orgasm?"

"First one in ... good lord it has been many, many years, Ivan. Years." She smiled a foxy little smirk, the corners of her lips, fractionally arching upwards. "I think I would like to have another one." She saddled closer to me, her breasts pressed against my chest, her hand reached down to grab my package. "Actually, I think I would like to have one again, very soon."

"Mary, you are going to have to give me a couple of minutes to re-charge. I mean, I gave it all for the team." But I could already start to feel rumblings of desire between my legs.

The two of us laughed, giggling like a couple of school children. My hand had wrapped around her waist, and the two of us laid quietly on our sides, pressed tightly together. The intimacy of the moment wasn't lost on me. It had been years since I had been comfortable enough with a female partner to lay naked next to one for any length of time. I think I knew then, at that moment, that I had never found a partner that I enjoyed being with as much as I enjoyed being with Mary. Never had I been so openly honest and affectionate, intimate. Never had I allowed someone to be that close to me, for that duration. It was simply something I had never done. Never allowed myself to do. The opportunity was never given, and I never took.

At least until now.

"What are you thinking?" Mary whispered the question, her eyes locked on mine.

I pulled her a little closer, "I was thinking that if I had found you a very long time ago, things in our world would have been ... different. Better. Mary, I have never really allowed anyone to lay beside me for any length. It just didn't happen."

"No one?"

"There was no one I felt comfortable enough with, to let them into my personal space, like this. At least until I found you."

Mary smiled slightly, "No one, Ivan?" I shook my head in response. "Everyone said you were a loner when you came here."

"A loner?"

"Yeah."

"I'm not really ... a loner."

"I know that now, and I guess I knew that then, too. You and Kenny took to each other quickly. Loners don't usually grab onto anyone at all. I knew you weren't the loner you tried to make everyone think you were." Mary pushed gently at my ribs, "You just don't have the knack for being a loner, Ivan." She snuggled closer to me, "And that's okay, you can't be good at everything. No one can."

"I've just never had the opportunity to share like I do with you." The two of us shared a kiss, long and passionate. "I've never really wanted to be with anyone like the way I am now." My eyes filled with tears. They were tears I couldn't stop ... couldn't control. And for the first time, it felt okay to have them dampening the pillow underneath my head. It felt right.

"Why did it take us so long, Mary, to find one another? Why couldn't we have found each other decades ago..." I couldn't find the right way to express what I was feeling. To describe how different many people's lives would be, if I had found that kind of love when I was young, learning about the world and myself. "It would have changed so much of my life, of the lives and people around me."

"It would have changed mine too, Ivan." Her hand began to gently stroke me, getting all the blood circulating again. Her hand was so practised, so direct, the response was immediate, accurate. "But right now, we have to think about this moment, right now. Are you following what I am telling you sir?"

"Oh absolutely. Yes."

For a moment I believed it. That meeting Mary

years before would have changed my life. But just for a minute. I didn't really believe that. I was just feeling romantic about the situation we found ourselves in. Plus, I think age had softened some of the harsh edges that I always had. Through the years I had done enough research on my particular way of being in the world to know that nothing would be able to change me. It was pre-ordained. Inevitable.

I didn't have a bad childhood at first. My parents were both lovely people — hard working, salt-of-the-earth sort of folks. We were immigrants, having come from Poland, arriving just after my fourth birthday that we had celebrated on the ship. I don't remember much of the trip, but do remember the very meagre birthday cake that was miraculously manufactured in the bowels of that vessel.

We settled in a small town in southern Manitoba, and started working the land almost as soon as we arrived. It was a hard, simple life that held pleasure when appropriate, support and love when needed. My father seldom drank, and rarely laid a hand on me and never on my mother. I was just a regular kid, so once in a while a little correction was needed on my bad choices. But it was punishment, never violence. Eventually my little brother came along, shortly after we had arrived in Canada. I remember that my mom was just lovely, patient and kind through the pregnancy and that couldn't have been easy. A boy and man to look after, a house to keep and small patch of farmland to work. They were keen and loving, despite the rigors that making a new life in Canada required.

But once things began to change, it didn't take long for those changes to overrun us. Dad died of a heart attack when I was 10 years old. Fell over dead in the barn while feeding the calves in the early morning hours in mid-May. Walking into the barn with a pail of water, I found him in the stall with a newborn calf, face deep in the fresh straw he had just laid down. I remember staring at him a long while, calling his name. Just too afraid to move, for this to be real. I called out to my mother, screaming. She ran as quickly as she could the 50 yards from the house to the barn, panic in her eyes. My mother rushed past me with barely a look and crashed onto the floor beside my father. The pain I heard in her screaming on that early spring morning is something I can hear to this day. It was just a total release of pain, anguish. That very moment my mother was completely destroyed. My boots were rooted to the spot in the hallway of the barn. I just couldn't break free to console her. So that early morning, I wept quietly 10 feet away from my fallen father.

Mom went a couple of years later when her heart, broken that May morning, finally gave out. Afterwards, I tried to make a go of our little patch of land, but just didn't have the knowledge or skill needed. We lost the farm then, two little boys alone in a community that really didn't know what to do with us. That was when I first saw those fake, sympathetic smiles, or at least I started to pay attention to them. I still hate those smiles, even when it is me doing the smiling.

My brother was just 6 when we were left alone. I knew I couldn't look after him on my own, so I didn't object when the police showed up to take him away to foster care. While Birger was fairly easy to adopt at that age, Dawid Brezinski, me, not so much. For me they found a job at the local Co-op elevator cleaning the floors because I was too old for fostering. No one wanted an older kid, gangly, awkward and prone to having fits of anger.

Birger didn't last four months. By Christmas he was dead, the victim of a fall on the stairs of his foster family's house. The cop who came to my squalid boarding room to break the news was nice enough. He tried to explain that accidents like his happened on a regular basis. I didn't believe him, not for a heartbeat. But I also knew there was nothing I could do, at least not as a young teenager. It was at that point I started to drink a little, then a little more. It gave me a sense of being a little less alone in the world, half the planet away from any family or real friends. Or at least the pain of that isolation didn't seem as debilitating.

It was then I let the black out for the first time. I really don't remember much about it. It was a long time ago now, age playing havoc with my memory. I do remember she was the town bike: you know the type, for a few cents anyone could go for a ride. That particular day, I didn't pay, hell I didn't even ask. I just took what I wanted from her. That experience left me invigorated — strong. I felt empowered by what I had done. There was no fallout from it. She couldn't or rather wouldn't report it because our town cop just wouldn't have believed her. Like they say now in the news, "She was a person known to police." That was a great way to put it. Very well known. Probably intimately by the police as well — favours for favours.

But the feeling of power, of the control that I got, that time and the many times afterwards was new, potent and so easily recharged with just another visit, another releasing of the darkness. The days when she didn't want it and tried to fight me off were even better. Those were days I bounded from her shack off Main Street, whistling and happy. Again, memory what it is, I honestly don't remember what provoked me that last time with her, whether it was something she had said, or something she had done, but something snapped, and I struck her, hard. It was a moment unlike any other. That physical release of singular energy directed towards her left me euphoric, on a different plane of reality. It was literally the thunderbolt that changed my life. I had to leave town after that. This time she did report it to the police because of the mess I left her face in. When the town cop dropped by my boarding house to arrest me I was already on the road to Winnipeg, my worldly goods hung over my shoulder in a big carpet bag. That bag was the last bit of personal history from my family.

Mary and I had made love before, but there was something there this time that we didn't have before. No explanation. No words. I couldn't even begin to try to reason out what happened. It was just there. For some reason, that night the two of us dropped into a whole new realm in our relationship. It was a place that needed no tour books, because it was a place we had always been, but never opened our eyes to see. My feet hadn't felt that light in years.

Oh, the unbelieving eyes that quickly darted towards the two of us as we emerged, hand in hand, from Mary's room in the morning. I'm sure I heard the clacking of dentures, skittling across the slickly cleaned linoleum, as mouths in abject wonder fell open. I think a couple of the little plastic teeth even broke out of their mouldings. Terrible sight.

It felt kind of like one of those old movies, where the peasants tossed flower petals on the floor, as the loving couple walked down the aisle. There were no petals here, but there were a few napkins tossed into one corner by a disgruntled resident, who had obviously already been to breakfast, and was malcontented once again at the quality of the food. Of course, who wasn't disappointed with the cuisine on a regular basis?

That's why Mary and I aggressively turned to the left instead of the right when we got out of the elevator, still arm-in-arm and headed for the parking lot entrance. A short 10-minute drive from that point would put us at the Royal Hotel and their outstanding all-you-can-eat breakfast smorg. I mean at $8.99 per person, you could pig out, and really not give a shit. That is amazing. And that particular morning I was hungry enough to eat a horse. Well, perhaps one of those small little Shelties, but still, it's a horse.

As we bounced down the hall to the doors, even the old blind chick lulled over in her wheelchair in the corner, bathing in sunshine, could tell something kind of neat happened the night before. She raised her face up towards the two of us and I swear to God, looked right at us. Mary and I both stopped dead in our tracks to look at her looking up at us. The old woman's eyes were clouded, totally unfocussed on anything, but searching with all their might to see the couple that were clacking down the hallway, getting ready to walk past her and out into the world. Yeah, she knew something kind of earth shattering had happened the night before.

Kind of neat.

Yeah, I like that. Not earth shattering, I mean hell, there are women the same age as us in Italy who are still dropping kids like nobody's business. There are documented cases of men able to get it up towards the 100-year-old mark. Of course, with a hottie like Mary beside them, I don't care how old you are, things are going to happen. Oh yeah, they are going to happen.

The night was definitely kind of neat.

But it was an important night. Actually, as things turned out ... it was a pivotal few hours in my life.

24
JULY 2002

There are huge chunks of time that have eluded me to this day. Just a chunk of time that is completely blank, no colour, no sounds, no feelings. It was as if someone had just lifted portions of my life and spirited them away.

I don't remember what happened. I actually don't remember much after walking out of the home arm-in-arm with Mary.

I don't remember unlocking and opening Mary's door first. I just know I would have, as it was my habit.

I don't remember starting the car and pulling north onto Hargrave Street.

I don't remember holding hands with Mary all the way to the hotel restaurant, although I am sure we did. For at that moment, we were teenagers again, having just spent an uninhibited night in her room on the second floor of Pinetree. So naughty of us.

I don't remember what we ate, not that it's important now.

I don't remember who we talked to. Once again, I am sure Mary talked to several people, because she was just that kind of person. There was very seldom a place that we walked into that she didn't know at least half of the customers. At times, it was an annoying blessing, at least from my perspective. You couldn't go anywhere with Mary where you didn't have to build in at least half an hour for her to chat with people that she grew up with in some small town that doesn't even exist anymore. Or with students that were now grown with children and sometimes even grandchildren in tow. Where did all these people come from?

Anyway, I don't remember the conversations, but there must have been a few.

I don't remember paying for the meal. I would have used cash, that much is certain. But how much it was, what we got, that I haven't a clue. I can guess that we both had the smorg. We were both a little hungry after the night before. I probably ate way more of the dessert side of the long colourful table of food than I should have. Always do. Mary probably gravitated towards the salad and fruit side. She always did. Once taxes were figured in, along with coffee and a tip, it probably came to the better part of $25. Gotta love the seniors discount.

I don't remember crossing the parking lot back to the Chrysler, though we must have. We probably kissed a little, once back in the security of the cheap plastic interior. I may have even copped a little feel. Mary's breasts were really something. She may even have made a grab for my package ... I don't know. That morning, the two of us were definitely a couple — at least as much as I could be. It was going to be great day and later when the sun slid gently through the prairie sky, it was probably going to be another great night.

I have a fleeting memory of pulling back onto Hargrave, heading south to Pinetree. More flashes of images than a solid memory.

There are no details in my mind about the car. Not my car, or the kid's.

I don't remember seeing him heading towards us from an off avenue. They told me later it was Ottawa Avenue. I don't remember him missing the stop sign, nor do I remember seeing his bumper diving for the asphalt as the tires gripped with all their might, in a panicked last-minute effort to avoid hitting us.

I don't remember the impact on the passenger side of the car ... the front two feet of his Toyota crushing into the passenger side of my car. I have a sense of a physical shock running over me. It pops in, then as quickly, explodes out of my memory.

I do remember Mary looking up at me. A faint smile spreading on her lips.

I do remember seeing that look, a look of compassion, of love in her eyes.

I do remember her eyes, suddenly shocked, then quiet.

I do remember having seen that sort of thing many times before but nothing as soft and caring.

After that, I don't remember anything.

25
OCTOBER 2002

"What time is it?"

It seemed like a simple question ... really, it should have been. I was in a hospital. A place of healing. A place where, it turns out, it takes an act of God to actually get someone to answer one fucking question. I mean really, "What time is it?" should have been way too simple.

The nurse's aide looked very uncomfortable, as I asked the question. And she was a lot more uncomfortable as I demanded an answer. Her little white uniform nearly shivered as she looked for the door.

"Sir, I'm going to have to get the doctor."

"Listen, I'm just asking a question. I don't think a doctor is required. What time of the day is it?"

"I'll be right back with the doctor, sir. Just give me a minute."

"Nah-no, what fucking time is it?" She just stared at me, not sure if to look at the little watch hanging from her chest for the answer, or bolt for the door that was just a couple of precious feet away from her. "What time is it?" I repeated.

"Sir." Her droopy little eyes slid to an even lower level, almost slithering over her lips.

"All I want to know is what time is it? That's it." I held my arms out in surrender. "Please, that's all I want. What time is it?" I must have grimaced from the pain that shot through my upper body, because the nurse made a face, let out a little peep of sorts, then she wheeled around so quickly, her little watch pinned to her chest, stood stock straight at a 90-degree angle from her body. Just as suddenly she was out the door followed by a series of small squeaks as her rubber-soled shoes skipped down the hallway. I suppose to look for the doctor.

When her squeaking faded away, I noticed for the first time that it was dark outside, and the room I was in was lit by just a soft panel light above my head. Though it hurt to do so, I turned and looked out the large aluminum-framed window. The sky was cloudless, and the stars were shining in all their brilliance, almost crystalline along with the unseen moon illuminating the whole area. It was a surreal, dare I say heavenly, sight. I chuckled softly, knowing it certainly wouldn't be in heaven that I was resting, in a soft bed covered by warm blankets. In no future I could imagine would I be ending up in heaven.

But it was then I suddenly realized the vulnerability of the situation I faced there. Did they know who I was? Really know?

The private room was completely void of anything personal of mine. The table to my right didn't have any flowers, cards or anything showing that someone had dropped by. I wasn't too concerned about getting something, but really wanted to know if Ivan McDonald was in fact the name of the man they thought was laying there. I couldn't remember what happened to prompt me into this stiff bed, monitor tagged onto my finger, but the stiffness and pain that shrieked at me as I wiggled around slightly, told me it wasn't something like a stroke or heart attack. It was more physical. I settled back into the thin pillow again and quickly surmised my situation. In a hospital, it appeared at night, and I wasn't 100-per-cent sure that my identity was secure. The next conversation I would have would tell me a lot more.

I heard the two of them squeaking up the hall long before he poked his head in the doorway, and spoke in a soft, very doctor-like voice.

"It's Friday morning, a little after two."

"Thank you. Doctor?"

He nodded, walked to the foot of my bed and glanced at the chart that hung from it. It was a cursory look, more for effect I'm sure than an actual checking of my vital statistics. He pulled a chair to the side of my bed and sat down. He noticed the aide still standing in the corner and gave a quick nod. She must have understood the signal, because she slipped quietly out the door. She was a little more relaxed this time, because there were no squeaks as she pranced away from my room.

"Not a problem. I'm Doctor Quick."

"Yeah. Doctor Quick?"

He looked very patient for a moment, waiting for little joke to come from me on his name. But I remained quiet. "You remember your name?" he asked.

"Sure. You know my name?"

"Yes." We both waited for a moment, then the doctor asked the question again. He was obviously not going to play the game for much longer. "What is your name?"

"It's Ivan Norman McDonald. So, doc, what is your first name?"

"Harry."

"All right," I said. "Harry."

"Date of birth."

"February 10, 1927. Here in town."

He wasn't writing any of this down, so he must have had all of the information already. It dawned on me, after a second short period of naked panic, that my wallet probably supplied a lot of the information he was looking for. He didn't take his eyes off me, though, looking for what, I didn't have a clue.

"Do you know why you're here Ivan?" He leaned back in the chair, crossing his legs, obviously satisfied I wasn't going to pass out or suffer a stroke or something. "Do you remember what happened?"

"No." I searched my memory, but the last thing I remembered was walking out of the home, past the blind lady, into the sunshine. I looked from him to the window, and the night beyond it. "What time is it, Harry?" He provided thc answer to the question that seemed to have been determined to elude me.

The doctor checked his watch again, then looked up at me. "Like I said, a little after 2 in the morning. You should be sleeping right now Ivan."

"Can't. Feel like I've slept for a couple of days."

Harry nodded quietly in the twilight of the room, his eyes still firmly on me. "Do you remember anything at all?"

An image of Mary on my lap, with something red, spreading on her forehead pounded into my brain. The image sent a jolt of pain careening through my mind. "Mary," I managed to whisper. "Where is Mary?"

Dr. Harry Quick shifted in his seat slightly. Not a lot. Just enough to let me know that he was about to tell me what I already knew. Deep in my heart, I already knew.

Now confusion was starting to creep into my mind. What happened to me? What happened to Mary? I had clear memories of our night together, walking out of Pinetree to go for a Sunday brunch, past the blind lady at the doorway … then…

"You were in an accident Ivan. A 16-year-old kid ran through a stop sign. He hit your car on the passenger door. A full-on, square impact." This was the type of news that he didn't look forward to telling me. Even in the dim light of my room, I could see a flash of pain in his eyes. "It wasn't your fault."

I paused everything. I tried to stop myself from thinking, but my brain had kicked in the adrenalin and was churning wildly. "I don't remember."

The knowledge took the breath out of my chest. I closed my eyes and waited for the inevitable statement. It seemed to take an hour for the doctor to wring up his courage and speak the words.

"She died at the scene. She ... there was no pain. Mary died almost instantly."

Without opening my eyes, I asked him to let me sleep for a while. She was gone. Dead. What the hell was going on? Accident?

The doctor took another breath, cleared his throat and continued. "He was 16," he repeated, "didn't really have a grasp of the danger of the speed he was going, how long it would take a vehicle to stop or to change directions. He tried to brake but was still going pretty fast when he hit you. Just an accident, missed the stop sign."

Again, a moment flashed. Then froze. Mary was lying on my lap, her hand on my thigh, shattered glass covering everything in the front seat. The little shards looked like small diamonds that reflected the bright sunshine. She was caressing my leg softly with almost microscopic movements of her finger. It was just enough to feel that connection to my life. Just to feel me there. A small trickle of blood was seeping from her nose, and another larger cut was flowing across her face, soaking my pantleg and through to the seat cover. Mary was looking up at me. There wasn't any emotion on her face, but her eyes spoke volumes.

I could see the reaction to the violence that had just been exacted on her. There were small tears sitting, resting really, on the very edges of her eyes. I originally thought they were in reaction to the pain, but as I stared at the mental picture, I see other, more personal expressions there.

The tears were more out of the love the two of us shared.

Then a jolt charged my body. I saw something in her eyes I had observed, hell I had caused many times before. I saw that faint glaze fall across her face, her eyes reflecting the cognitive loss that was happening inside her brain. The skin pallor softly changing to a lighter, less lively shade, then suddenly sweat oozed out of it as the body fought desperately to cling onto the life that was packing up to leave. The more the skin turned grey, the more change was reflected in her blue eyes. There was no longer a piercing, inquisitive look to them ... they were flat, unexcited. But they still held that look I had seen so many times. Bewilderment, shock, horror, pain and ultimately sadness. I had watched that exact moment that life had left a body so many times, but now for the first time with an actual emotional attachment. I didn't watch it leave as a killer who relished in that precise moment, but as a person emotionally tied to the victim. I experienced the pain firsthand, and it tore my chest apart.

I moved my hand gently to hers, and squeezed as tightly as I could, letting Mary know she wasn't alone. There was someone here who really cared for her. Her only reaction was a faint, almost undiscernible upturn of her lips into a feeble squalid smile. And it was then my heart broke.

"She didn't die instantly."

"Sorry?" he asked, as he looked up at me.

I ignored the man sitting by my bed. Each time a flashcard of Mary was exposed in my head, it sparked a small muscle contraction and I involuntarily jumped. Each small muscle movement sent a shiver of pain through my entire body, but was especially focused on my right side. It was as if I was experiencing in some small way the pain that Mary must have felt. I pray she didn't. I pray she was just numb, unfeeling at the end. The brain overriding all other senses. I hope that's the way it happened.

"Ivan, I have to talk to you about your injuries."

"I'm not worried about that right now." I looked up at the doctor, who was still staring at me intently. "I just want to sleep. Okay doc, just let me go back to sleep."

"Okay Ivan, I'll let you sleep." He reached over and touched my arm, I suppose in a show of compassion. In a better frame of mind, I might have been touched by it, the gesture, but that night: No.

"Ivan, there is going to be someone popping into your room off and on all night tonight. Okay?"

"Whatever."

"It's nothing to worry about Ivan. It's just standard procedure when a patient wakes up after a prolonged period of an induced coma."

Another huge jolt. Coma?

The words seem to drag, pulled back by barbed fishhooks, in my throat. "I was in a coma?"

"Yes. Your injuries were pretty bad Ivan. Lots of internal damage. Right leg, hip, ribs and arm. Some reconstructive work on your cheek. But it was the internal stuff we were most concerned with. We'll talk about it tomorrow."

"How long?"

"Sorry?"

"How long was I out?"

He looked through the window. Maybe looking for the answer, maybe for an easy way to tell me. From the pained look on his face, I could see that the magic solution evaded him. He hung his head, nearly to his chest.

"Your injuries were pretty extensive, Ivan."

"I understand that. You've said that." Suddenly every nerve of my body awoke and burst into burning magnesium of white pain. My whole body was wracked with shudders. It was the answer though, that I needed.

"Are you all right, Ivan?"

"All those injuries you told me about, just woke up."

"I can get you something for that."

"I'm okay. How long, doc? How long was I out?"

"About three months." He recalculated, "A little more maybe. Your body needed some time to heal without putting anything else at risk, so we induced the coma."

"Holy shit." My eyes seemed to suddenly pick up a few hundred pounds of dead weight. They would hardly stay open. "Three months?"

He smiled at me with far more patience than I deserved. "Yeah."

"Holy shit."

The doctor looked at me suddenly, with a questioning but patient smile when I told him, his fucking drug induced coma, had put me way behind schedule.

26
OCTOBER 2002

The retired police chief walked across the linoleum floor of his kitchen, stretching the coiled phone cord behind him to its very limit. Tick reached into the five-year-old Maytag refrigerator and grabbed a half-gallon jug of milk, then with the telephone receiver still tucked firmly between his chin and shoulder, walked back to the oak kitchen table and his fresh cup of coffee. As he sat, Tick Smith poured the milk into his coffee and listened.

On the other end of the telephone was McKinnon, in Kamloops at his desk. The two had communicated almost daily, each other's phone numbers now at the top of their respective speed-dial. This morning, the RCMP inspector was giving an update on the search for their suspect. As Tick Smith listened, he could hear there was nothing new, and a lot of what McKinnon was saying was becoming hauntingly familiar. Dead end here, no further avenue for investigation there. This piece of evidence could be purchased at any Kennedy's or any other mass market store for that matter in the continental United States or Canada, so no way to individuate them. No distinguishing marks, no identifying features or residual evidence. Nothing.

Tick sipped the steaming coffee, relishing its full flavour and hoping for its powerful jolt of high-test caffeine to kick in, and bring him back into the world of the living. Absently he looked up at the clock and watched the digital numbers flash over to "9:47."

"Fourteen minutes," he thought absently, "I've been awake for 14 minutes."

Tick was sleeping in with some regularity now. He

just couldn't help it. Each night he would crawl into bed just before 11, the quiet night waters of the nearby lake taunting him while he tried to fall asleep. The cabin was the place he and his wife loved to be, winter or summer. But the warm months of May through September were their favourite. The two had slept the sleep of the dead each and every night. The fresh air, coupled with the metronomic lapping of the waves in the lake put them out within 10 minutes every single night. And for a while, after her death, he could still sleep.

But not now.

The waves now jeered him. Coming over the sandy shoreline with an increasing irregularity, like the fictional Chinese Water Torture. He closed the two windows in their bedroom, but the waves managed to turn up their volume somehow and the noise filtered through the triple pane glass panels. After his return from Kamloops and the killing nearby, the calming lapping of the waves transformed into large body breakers, noisy almost to the point of being overwhelming. He turned on a fan, hoping that adding it would contribute a bit of white noise to the room. It hadn't worked. No matter what he did, the constant breaking of the waves a couple of hundred feet away, continued to seep into the room. For hours on end he would stare at the ceiling, with thoughts, ideas and memories washing over him until finally, with the sun peeking over the east end of the lake, he drifted off.

It seemed so cruel to him that the far side of the lake, with its impressive sunrise in a kaleidoscope of colours, were what drew the two of them to this cabin. Right on the lakeshore, just off the Provincial Trunk Highway with easy access to either Brandon to the left, or Winnipeg to the right. The cabin was small, though managed two bedrooms, large common room that held the kitchen and living room, a full bath off the kitchen, and a screened-in porch. Over the years, the two had pretty much rebuilt the cabin in totality. All the walls were torn open and filled with pink fiberglass insulation. Thermal windows installed, replacing the anemic single pane wooden frames, giving them a year-round retreat from the world. They slowly upgraded all the fixtures when they could afford them, and when Tick retired, the two pulled their nearly new appliances from the house in town and moved them to the lake.

Then she died and the cabin emptied of the life the two had settled into. Now all that was left was the mocking noises that kept him awake at night. His side of the bed had always been the left. He liked being near the door. But with Martha gone, he ended up bouncing from one side of the queen-sized bed to the other, balling, then fluffing his down-filled pillow in a vain effort to find the position that would eventually pull him into sleep. No matter the position or level of comfort, the thoughts and visions piled into his head, rolling like an old movie behind his tightly shut eyes.

It wasn't the murder of his wife's first husband that played on an endless loop. It was the last one. The girl. Not the horror of her death but the pure black fear she must have felt. Standing above her was a monster, using her own telephone, with whatever weapon he held in his hands threatening her. That much, that horror, he could imagine.

He thought of the victim's family. Of her parents, brothers and sisters, aunts and uncles, godparents and close family friends. It was their faces, their pained hearts that he couldn't shake loose. When he was a young officer, he saw the small creases of teary eyes of a family member as holding an almost Mona Lisa quality. The longer they tried to hold tight their emotions, the deeper the frozen lines became. Then, the hard fall at the inevitable tipping point where they needed to empty their emotions into teary puddles of humanity. It was hard to watch, hard not to reach out and hold them close to his tunic and tell them all would be okay. He knew that wasn't a total lie. Eventually the harshness of the pain would dull, slightly at first, then a little more each day. They just needed a little time. He could see that from his vantage point of emotional distance and isolation. Even as a rookie, he would never have dreamt of even suggesting that. Violent disbelief in the loss they had suffered was all part of the process of death.

In his years as a police officer, Tick was forced to tell parents the words they would never have believed they would hear. The death of their baby — whether that baby was a newborn, or one who had grown into adulthood, was an absolute, all-consuming pain that enveloped parents. It was immediate and absolute. There was no gradual slip into the pain. No one part of their body was monopolized by the hurt. Every shred of who they are shares the burden of loss that wraps itself around them.

As an officer, Tick knew of the classic seven stages of grief. He knew they were a defence mechanism the mind has against the numbing truth of the totality of the loss it was facing. Of all the horrible aspects of his job, it was starting the family down that path, into the seven stages, that was the worst.

As the needs came up, he would sometimes have to go back to the families, to talk, to inform, to explain. He saw the brave faces, the carefully measured movements as they offered, then retrieved coffee from the kitchen. He looked around the living rooms or kitchens of victims' homes, and saw the pictures cleaned, carefully placed in a shrine of flowers and toys. He had been in other rooms left exactly the same way the child had walked away from them. Days, weeks, sometimes months before. Dirty underwear and socks strewn about, with other less intimate reminders of the person who would no longer be asked to pick them up. The pain he could see was there, rippling just below the surface, inching its way around their bodies, looking for a way out. Looking for a way to wrap them up in a cocoon of pain and memories.

Tick Smith listened almost reluctantly, as parents told him about the things they missed the most about their children. It never ceased to surprise him what it was they smiled about, in that soft faraway look of a medicated memory. They all missed the birthdays, holidays, family-oriented occasions. Those were without a doubt the tough days. The days they feared. Those heart-wrenching days pounced on them like a vicious tiger from elephant grass. But still they wished it all to be a dream.

They missed the trials and tribulations of getting their children into bed at night. Missed the standard textbook of excuses the kids used to explain why they shouldn't have to hop into the sack so early. Those gentle bantering's back and forth preyed upon their minds once the sun went down and they waited for the valium to kick in. It seemed hours would pass before the prescribed drugs allowed them to drift off to the numbing, refreshing world of sleep. Until then, small, memorized scenes, a seamless collage of typical nights at home would flash through their heads. They saw the efforts the kids brought to the table, in vain attempts to somehow get another friend to stay for a sleepover. It was the arguments parents laid out in trying to convince their children that brussels sprouts were really good for them. The baths were never a problem, neither were the nightly reading of the story. Those moments brought genuine smiles.

But it was the closing of their heavy tired eyes that seemed to always haunt the parents as they tried to sleep after the loss. Even worse, the mental image of their child, sleeping, scattered about their bed, in total REM. Each parent he knew, each parent that had lost a child, hoped that is how their child looked now ... totally at peace, sleeping.

Tick was at the scene of the car crashes, hangings, gunshot wounds, hit-and-runs and any number of ways people found to die. He knew what the parents hoped for just didn't happen. Their loved ones ended their lives or had them ended, twisted in pure agony, lips curled in a painted jeer of horror and pain, and eyes hanging from their sockets. That is, of course, if all the parts could be found, which often wasn't the case.

It was horrid to Tick, the pain he was somehow responsible for bringing into their lives. He hated it, that part of the job. But he never ever shirked it off to a subordinate or partner. He knew the parents deserved to hear it from the man who was investigating the death of their little boy or girl. So, he would pluck up his courage, slowly walk up to the front door with his hat in his hand, and gently knock.

He owed it to them.

"So, what do you think?" It was all he could think of saying, not sure when the RCMP officer had ended his monologue. He sipped his coffee and waited for the reply.

"Oh Tick, I haven't got a clue. What do you think?

Dead, in jail, hospitalized, bored or tired of the killing already. Maybe he found out it doesn't do anything for him anymore. I mean is there a sexual element to this once you reach a certain age? I don't know. There are any number of explanations for what happened to this guy, why he stopped killing or at least contacting us. Contacting you."

It was a frustrating point in the investigation for McKinnon. It had been more than three months since the killer had taken a life that they knew of or made any sort of contact. A quarter of a year of going over and over each piece of evidence, hoping that the next microscopic surveillance of it would bring a revelation they had missed all those times before. Some previously undiscovered small, individuated fragment that would point the long arm of the law in the right direction.

But that fragment escaped their invasive investigative operation. It was nestled safe in its secretive location far away from his team of investigators. No matter the test, the procedure, the hope of the innovative investigative techniques, all ended up on the floor. Each one, empty and kicked aside while his team searched frantically for another avenue for their mission to take them. But none appeared under their microscopes.

Every law enforcement rookie has the 24-hour rule drilled into them. That is the optimum length of time to solve a murder. As each successive hour pounds past, the chances of a successful investigation are reduced by an almost logarithmic scale of one to 10. Most murders are solved within the first frantic hours of the examination of the scene and victim. Most are killed by someone they know; most are the result of a domestic situation that most media outlets will simply add as a passing note in their newscasts. Some are accidental, with the perpetrator aggressively wishing to reveal their participation in it. Accidental killings also include fights where both parties consented to the fisticuffs, but neither planned on death being the determiner of the victor. With all of those, the matter is resolved with the appropriate person incarcerated within one day, case solved and closed. But there are deaths that remain unsolved. The case open for days, months, and eventually years.

McKinnon knew it was usually the family that continued to push for more man-hours to be invested into their child's death. Monthly calls to the lead investigator, or the one who inherited the file after the lead retired, got transferred into another role, moved or just quit. McKinnon had heard of one mother calling the officer in charge of her daughter's murder investigation, every week, Monday morning, 8:30 a.m. for five years. No amount of time could placate the heartache.

Though each investigator will explain to the relatives of victims the importance of the first few hours following a murder, and how the forensic and human trail thins out after that period, none seem to hear. They can't. As a father, McKinnon understood that stand, that mindset. He would make the same calls, hoping upon hope, that his urgings would force a new clue to be gleaned from the wreckage of the case. He would hire a private detective to look into places law enforcement was barred from entering. He would launch a personal attack on whomever he felt was guilty of the crime. There would be no mercy, no quarter. There would be justice only. No matter the legal consequences. There would only be a conclusion.

For the families, McKinnon knew justice fades

away into bitter heartbreak after years of searching for truth. Hope is only rekindled when there is a break, and the case begins to move again. But those cases rely more on pure luck or advances in forensic technologies than detective diligence. A seemingly innocent discussion, or happenstance piece of evidence that jumps to the attention of the inspector, and then falls into place with a resounding clunk. A lot of accidental events, conspiring to bring an investigation back to the active sheet.

On his desk were the files of the murders in Kamloops and rural Manitoba. Four people dead, with family members crying for a murderer. For justice. They cried for the cameras of the major television networks and local stations, they cried for the newspaper reporters and their photographer, they cried for the families of other victims and the injustice of leaving their murderers free among the innocent.

McKinnon cried for them. For their loss.

But he cried for his team members as well. It was upon their shoulders the full pressure of upper management was falling. It was his team that bore all of the weight of the unyielding sheaves of official memorandums that fell upon them with unerring precision. Each one was bearing the strain well, or at least as well as could be expected. There wasn't a single person among his team that didn't want this investigation to wrap up with an arrest. There wasn't one who was wanting to walk away from it. It was more than just the professional challenge, although that helped motivate them somewhat. It was just a matter of they didn't like anything beating them.

No matter the hundreds of hours, the best investigative team the force had to offer, no matter the creative techniques and new procedures, the result was desperately the same. It left a cold empty feeling hanging on the case. McKinnon knew that unless something broke very quickly, he was going to lose the focus of his team. It wasn't their fault. They had just exhausted each valuable piece of evidence, every single shred of life. Something new was going to have to come along, he knew that.

But the man on the other end of the phone halfway across the country would never let go, never relinquish the case. It simply wouldn't be the way he worked. McKinnon knew that. He respected it, but saw the flaw as well. Never letting go of one case meant you weren't capable of diverting your full attention to any other. In some deep recess, there was always a residual, a fragment of the unfinished. In 99 per cent of the cases, that wouldn't matter. But in that one percentile, it could mean the difference between solving, and leaving unresolved.

He didn't like the prospect.

"Tick ..."

"I know," he relinquished. "It's been three months without a lot of new evidence."

"Without *any* new evidence buddy. The only thing we have is the matched DNA out of the hair follicles from the last crime scene ... the gift he left us. Other than that, we are coming up donuts."

"You are going to make the call, aren't you? I can hear it in your voice." Tick leaned forward and stared at a picture of his Martha hanging on the wall. She seemed to scream obscenities at him. He understood where it was that McKinnon was standing, the position he was in. He knew about shrinking budgets and re-allocation of man-hours. He was on the ground floor of the movement that saw careful studies performed about peak performance ratios for investigators assigned to unsolved, so-called cold cases.

'Hell,' he resigned to himself, 'I am one of those cases.'

"Tick I'm sorry, but like you said it's been three months," McKinnon twiddled the cord of the telephone. It wasn't an answer he relished, but he knew as a team leader, a manager, his resources were better spent on more current cases, with a greater degree of solvability. "I hope you understand, I really have no choice in this."

"Has something been said?"

"No, nothing yet. I know what I would say, though. And I think Tick, I know what you would say." The RCMP inspector, half a country away, hoped he was reading the man on the other end of the telephone right. He had thought about the call for more than a week, knowing it was on its way. Just waiting for the right set of conditions to come to roost. "Or at least I hope you would say the same thing."

Smith was staring into his coffee cup. He had absently picked up the spoon, and was stirring the hot brown liquid quickly, trying to bring his mind to grapple with the problem he faced. It was a cold case for him, and now, it would remain an open case for the officers in Kamloops.

"I had just hoped something would have come out of this investigation. I never had access to the sheer volume of forensic tools you guys do now. I thought with the DNA typing, we would have gotten that little piece we needed." Tick watched the coffee swirl in his porcelain cup, focusing on the little bubbles left in the wake of the spoon. "I really thought we had him this time. I really did. I thought this whole fucking mess was over. Well, at least I hoped so."

"Sorry Tick. He was lucky. And even though he

left a shitpile of evidence this time, that positively linked him to the latest murders and the ones from the Sixties, there is nothing that can point a finger directly at one person out of the millions of eligible suspects in our country. I mean, there are a whole lot of seniors in Canada."

"You should come to a bingo in town, if you want to see a lot of blue-haired people. I know what you are going through, I know what has to happen. I just hoped ..." Tick stopped himself short of babbling, "It's okay. Make the call." He couldn't hope to ask for anything else. Tick knew that by forcing himself and his case on the inspector, impelling the case forward, it would create a horrid, wide rift that he didn't want to start.

"Tick I really am sorry. There is nothing here," McKinnon swept his hand above the small mountain of evidence scattered haphazardly over his desk, hoping the man in Manitoba could feel the movement, see it. "Nothing."

"Listen buddy, I know that. I would make the same decision. You know that. It's hard this time, that's all."

"Maybe he'll come back, poke his head above the waterline for a few minutes and let us get a bead on him." McKinnon hoped he wasn't sounding too condescending, but he knew the chances of the murderer coming up for air again were slim. If he was the murderer, he would stay firmly below the surface, not making a single ripple in the calm waters above. He would force himself into exile. The man was bright enough to know the ramifications of the DNA evidence he left at the scenes in British Columbia and Manitoba, so he knows enough to be very careful about where he leaves his bodily fluids.

"It took him almost 20 years to surface this last

time. He'll be at nearly a hundred if he holds true to form. I won't be around, and I don't think he will either." Tick sipped the coffee that was cooling down then said, "I think the case is getting colder by the minute there, buddy. I think we had our shot, and it was a good one. There is no shame here. No other way. The ball is back in his court, like it always has been."

"Tick, the case is going to stay open, and active. We're not shutting it down. All the markers, the M.O., DNA sequencing, profile, are all staying in the system. If he does poke his head up, we'll cut the fucker off at the knees. I promise you. We'll get on the trail again by either blind stupid luck, or if our guy wants us to chase his shirttails again."

"Thanks."

"Listen I got to go. I have to talk to the man about this, okay?"

"Yeah, you go ahead." Tick walked with his cold cup of coffee to the sink, and carefully poured it down the drain, careful not to catch any in the small stainless-steel crease around the hole. It would leave a brown stain that would be hard to get out, if you did.

"Tick."

"Yeah."

"I'm sorry about this."

"I know you are. It's okay." He said the words, but he really wasn't feeling like it was actually okay. His throat felt thick, and painful jabs of tears formed behind his eyelids. Tick felt like he was betraying everything he had worked for his whole life. His job, and wife. All had just had the doors slammed shut in their faces.

"Tick. You didn't break your promise."

"I feel like I have Jim. Like there was something

there, that I could have done, but didn't because I was either blind, or just too stupid to see it. This has nothing to do with you. It's just the way I feel. I'm sure I'll be on better ground about this later. It's just a little raw right now."

From the front of the cabin, a slight, hurried knock came from the solid oak door.

"Listen I have to go, there is someone at the front door."

"I know."

"What?"

"I had them call me, when they were 10 minutes away from your place. It's a gift for you Tick. Take care. I'll call if anything turns up. I promise."

"Thanks Jim. You be careful."

Tick hung up the phone and walked the length of the house to the front door. When he opened it, a very young Mountie was standing there, struggling with a large cardboard box balanced precariously in his hands.

"Mr. Smith? Tick Smith?"

"Yup."

"Constable Langner sir. I have a package for you." Langner shifted his weight, obviously not used to carrying such an awkward load.

"Would you like to come in?"

The young officer shifted the weight in his hands, and smiled, "Just far enough to put this on a very strong table sir."

Tick pointed him at the rustic coffee table he had built out of barn-board several years before. "What is it?"

"I don't know sir. I was asked by my CO to deliver it to you and call an Inspector McKinnon in Kamloops when I was a few minutes away." He turned to the door and headed out into the sunshine. He paused on the front step, and looked at the lake, quiet and ripple free. “It must be a beautiful place to live sir.”

Tick nodded in agreement. “It really is. Very calming.”

The young Mountie deliberately stood for a moment, staring at the lake. “Sir, are you Tick Smith, used to be the Chief of Police up in Brandon?”

“I am.”

He turned and walked back to Tick on the step, holding out his hand. Tick took it, and was surprised at the strength, and restraint in the grip. For the first time he could see the name on the broad chest. Constable M.W. Langner. “It’s a pleasure sir, to meet you. I’ve heard a lot about you.”

“Really? Why? I retired very quietly. I don’t even go back anymore. Let the kids handle the bad guys.”

“I get together once in a while with a couple of the guys from the Brandon Police Department, and they still talk about you. Some of the shit,” he coloured at the word, “uh sorry sir. Stuff, you used to do.”

Tick Smith looked down at his slippered feet, suddenly embarrassed by the condition of his ratty old home-made leather slippers. “It was a long time ago, that I did all that--shit.” Tick bowed his head slightly. “But it was a lot of fun.”

“Well, I gotta go.”

“Would you like a coffee before you turn around and head back to Brandon?”

“No thanks, but I appreciate the offer sir. I think from the feel of the weight of that case, you have a lot of reading you have to do.”

Tick had forgotten about the box and turned back to the house. “Anytime you are in the area constable, don’t hesitate to drop by. The coffee is always 10 minutes from being ready."

"I will sir, thanks again."

"Thanks for the delivery service." The young officer waved, and he walked back to his cruiser.

Tick smiled, "Guess I should have offered him a glass of herbal tea. The kid probably doesn't drink coffee."

The box was still sitting there, straining the poor workmanship of his coffee table when he walked back into the room. He reached into his left front pocket and pulled out a small Victorinox pocketknife, carefully slipped it open, and sliced down the taped seams of the huge file folder container. When he popped the lid off, there was a large note on the top, written in marker, clearly in McKinnon's handwriting. Tick smiled at the note and sat on the edge of the couch staring at it.

"Tick.

Thought you might like your original files back. Tossed in some extra photocopies of stuff lying around the office, in case you needed some late-night reading. Maybe your promise isn't as broken as you thought.

Good hunting.

Jim."

Tick sat on the couch, leaning deep into the comfortable back and let the single tear that had formed in his left eye, lead the way to a whole torrent onto his chest.

27
OCTOBER 2002

I missed Mary's funeral by three months.

And from what Doctor Sunshine — Doctor Quick — is telling me, I'll miss most of the fall as well. Fall, my favourite time of the year, and I am going to be spending it in a hospital, with my time split between the pain of physiotherapy and just plain healing. Either way, it sounds as if I'll be in a constant numbing ache. Not exactly the way I had planned to spend my fall. My injuries are going to take a lot of healing time, because once again, according to the doctor, I'm not as young as I used to be. That is the truth. I can feel each of my years pinging with pained nerve endings. He also told me life will be a little different for me once I manage to get out of here.

I was thinking that life will be a little different for that 16-year-old kid when I get out. Fucker. Then the anger subsides a little and I figure I will let him live. Nah. I don't want to draw attention to this area of the country. Let 'em live.

For now.

But that acne faced kid continues to pop up in my consciousness. As I edge off to sleep, he slams into me, pulling me wide awake. My memories of the accident are slowly coming back. I can see Mary's face now, in the moments before the crash, happy and absolutely lovely in the afternoon sunshine. Then the explosion of glass and the painful impact drives into me. I can feel the numbing pressure through my body. It is a wave of pain that begins with my arm that had somehow managed to reach up just a milli-second before the crash to try and protect us, through to my hip that was broken by the seat belt jarring into my pelvis.

Then I slide back to her face on my lap, dying, loving. That is when my anger returns, and I quietly resolve once again to look after this kid.

I had told Doctor Quick this was going to put me off my schedule, but in reality, all it did was add one more task to it. So, while the body recovered, the brain started to plan, to work out the future once I was out of here.

The physiotherapist said my mobility will be cut down dramatically because of the damage from the accident. He tried to show me how restricted the movement in my right leg will be, by holding it up in the air at some angle or other. The uncoordinated shit actually fell over onto the polished linoleum. I mean I could see he was going to fall from the moment he began to lift his leg into the disinfected air. He tottered on his shoes, immediately impersonating a skinny, half cooked strand of linguine. It was an interesting demonstration to say the least. Once he picked himself up off the floor, he said I got the sense of what he was trying to show me. I agreed. Though for a moment, I really wanted to ask him to show me again just to make sure.

He was telling me that I'm going to go through the rest of my life falling over like a Bowery Street bum. Actually, I didn't get the demonstration at all. Well, I got it, just didn't agree with what he was pushing at me — what he was saying my future was going to be like.

But for the moment, what laid ahead of me wasn't as important as what had occurred. It seemed to be yesterday for me. Everyone else had seen three months slowly go by.

Shit, it seemed like literally the last time I remembered my head hit a pillow I was sleeping with a beautiful woman, who really cared for me. We made love passionately and with all the exuberance of 25-year-olds. Well, maybe 40-year-olds. Hell, we did things that last night I have never done, and now that Mary is gone, will probably never do again. It's really too bad. We were really good together. Not just in bed, but in the life part of the relationship too. I'll miss the talks, and the walks around the garden. Mary would point out all the plants and vegetables that were growing. I would listen patiently, not really knowing what she was talking about, or to be honest really not giving a shit what kind of green, leafy thing we were looking at. It just wasn't my thing. But Mary was totally immersed in the fauna. She seemed to know everything about each plant: what kind of meal you could make from it, the kind of herbal medicine that could be produced from its leaves, roots or whatever. Mary had it covered. While I didn't really care for the plants, I did enjoy her passion and immersion for the greenery. That part was intoxicating.

Funny, now that she is gone, I'm starting to get a little teary thinking about her insistent nattering about the lives of garden plants and fauna in general. It was a little irritating at the time. All right, it was a lot irritating, but now has a sort of nostalgic feel to it. Weird. Maybe the next time I get out of this place, and get a real meal, I will eat all my vegetables like she always harped on me. It will be tribute to her, in a quiet, non-aggressive sort of way.

But now that I think about it, it wasn't a lack of vegetables that took Mary's life. She didn't die from a vitamin B deficiency or anything like that. Her nails didn't fall off, or her teeth fall out because she neglected the rutabaga at supper. She died because some young shit ran a stop sign and drove his bumper right through her. But this young kid, I may be able to handle, diminished capacity or not.

It is going to take a little doing though. My right arm was very messed up. Mobility above my shoulder wasn't the best. I could raise it to about even with my shoulders. That was going to mean a lot less power in my down stroke. My left arm was okay, but it wasn't my power arm. A new plan of attack will have to be worked out. Plans made and compensations anticipated for this change in my capabilities.

So, the doctors and nurses here have been saying that I need something to focus on. I need to have a goal, they tell me. That dot on the horizon has now shown itself to me. All of the repairs that have to be done to my body to get it back into shape.

According to the doctor, all of the painful physiotherapy will now be a little easier to swallow. In front of me, as I re-learn how to go about the everyday things of life, will be a mental picture of that bumper diving towards the pavement, just moments before it hit the passenger door of my Chrysler. I am not positive, but am pretty sure I can hear the howl as the brakes bit first, prompting me to spin my head and see his bumper barrelling towards us. Maybe it is my imagination. It will have to be the bumper because I don't know what the kid looks like. Haven't got a clue. But I can imagine; long hair, pimply complexion, with no body mass to speak of. Probably spends his days in front of the TV playing games, watching lame sitcoms or contrived cop shows. I read somewhere the influence of TV on the masses was purpose driven. They wanted the population controlled, easily fooled. I guess, for a lot of people, if it is on TV, it's real. Duh.

It's not like they are watching the news or anything, I mean that is about as real as it actually gets. And the news is just entertainment as well.

I am pretty sure the doctor wasn't thinking the thing that would drive me, would be some kid that I wanted to kill. While the therapists are coercing me to keep stretching and building muscle mass, they won't be thinking the same thing I am — that I need another foot of upper extension to be able to bring that knife down with enough energy to kill someone. Probably not.

I'll tell them I need to regain my mobility to get back to my hobby, whatever that is. An arborist maybe? Who knows, but they will have to hear something, so that is probably what I will need my upper body strength for. Arborist?

Plus, I have some unfinished work with Tick. I'll have to keep on that as well. But that is just part of the process, the flow. The goal will always be on this bumper in my mind and the faceless kid that it represents. It will always be him I am killing. Every jab of pain will see the bumper, black, covered in bug guts diving towards the woman I love. It would be a considerable understatement, that I have a hurt on for this kid. I don't care what it brings me in the way of exposure or conflict. That kid took the only bit of humanity I ever had and he killed it. Payback is coming his way. Not for a while, but is definitely on its way.

But first, healing.

Then Tick.

Then I'll take the kid.

Maybe not in that order. But all three for sure.

The teenager I may save until the end. Kind of like a pimply bit of dessert.

28
DECEMBER 2002

Doctor Quick said it was a Christmas present from him. Who-ha!

December 22, I was out of the hospital, hobbling slowly across the ramp in front of the main doors of the hospital to the Medi-Van from the home. Ol' Bruce was still driving the worn-out Chevy cube van that had been converted to help those requiring aid in getting to and from appointments around the city. The Rotary club donated the money for the conversion to Pinetree, so in return their logo was prominently displayed on all four sides of the rusting van. But that was 12 years before and it was beginning to show its age. Actually, it was an age.

I had often watched the less mobile being wheeled to the driveway outside the home, waiting for their ride to the doctor, dentist or whatever. They all seemed so frail, dependently waiting for assistance out there. Huddled beneath their little shawls, no matter the time of year or the temperature outside, they waited patiently for ol' Bruce to fire the Chevy up. There always seemed to be a cold wind blowing down that curled through the roadway. I would be standing beside them in my tank top and shorts, having a chat with sweat rolling down my forehead, back or any other flat surface on my body. On them ... goosebumps with layers of clothing and the inevitable blanket.

Now it's the 22nd of December, and I'm hoping Bruce has cranked up the heater and set it to high 'cause my nuts are shrivelled up smaller than I ever thought they would be. We're talking peas here. It is so frickin' cold.

I said good morning to a couple of people who passed by the hospital ramp, wishing them a Merry Christmas. They commented on how mild a winter we had been having so far, and I nodded, shivered, and said it looked good for the new year. Mild, what the fuck were they talking about? It's below zero Celsius . . . in fact below zero Fahrenheit . . . it was goddamn cold. But they were walking around with little sweaters on, undone.

But I stood outside, taking in all the fresh air I could. I had been allowed outside only a couple of times. Just short excursions to the little hospital store and back. And then I had to have a handler with me — a big, female orderly who never let me out of her sight. Like I could go anywhere. I was never able to stand outside, enjoy the smells and the absolute feel of just being outdoors. So today, my release day, I sat outside in a wheelchair, my nuts crawling up to my intestines to try and stay warm. It didn't work. Every fabric of me was freezing.

But I loved it and couldn't stop smiling. I was away from the hospital. I turned around, and looked up at the building, all glass and concrete, towering six floors above me, and thought for the first time, how cold and inhuman the place looked. In living in the city off and on for years, I had always managed to avoid looking at the place. After all, it was where sick people hung out. I was never sick. I tried very hard not to look at it. I knew it was there. I was aware of the manpower problems the hospital, like all others in the country were having, but I really never looked at it. At no point in my life did I need to walk through the power-operated doors to the hospital. At no point in my life did I want to. It just wasn't where I wanted or needed to be.

Now it is a place I desperately needed to be away from.

"Ready to go home, mister?" Bruce hadn't even bothered to get out and help. He just popped the big side door open and lowered the wheelchair ramp down to the ice-covered roadway. He yelled from the warm comfort of his sheepskin covered seat. There wasn't much more than a quick look, and certainly no swivel in the chair to see if I was going to be able to make it up the deck of the lift without assistance. He may have raised a bushy eyebrow to clear the droopy hairs that blocked his vision. But there was no way to be sure because his farm implement baseball hat shielded his eyes from me.

After getting slowly up from the chair, cane in hand, I headed onto the ramp with my little suitcase and waited while it lifted me to the floor level. It was cold out there in the air, standing on the metal plate waiting for the 15-second ride to end when it was level with the inside floor of the van.

"Yes." I answered him as I sat down in the front seat. "Let's go."

He pressed a couple of buttons, then looked up at me in the large surveillance mirror above him. "Just have to wait until the lift is securely back in the van, okay?"

"Absolutely, Bruce." I didn't bother to look but listened to the mechanical clicking and scraping of the dilapidated gear struggling to pull itself back into the van. Bruce slammed a couple of switches back and forth and swore a streak of colourful, what I assumed was bus-centric language at it. The old Chevy must have recognized the intent of the tirade, because the lift finally walloped into place, causing the whole van to shake and shimmy for a moment.

"It sometimes causes a little ruckus," he bellowed to the windshield, "but you just have to be gentle with it, caress it into place."

"Gentle eh, Bruce?"

". . . as a lamb sir."

"Uh-huh." He reminded me of those backwater people from the Burt Reynolds movie Deliverance. 'What do ya think pa, should we be gentle with 'em, like little piggies?'

What a redneck.

"We are going to make a little side trip on the way back home, Bruce. Okay?" It wasn't really a question.

The shake of his head was almost imperceptible. He went to say something, then finally turned back to me. "I don't know, I've got appointments all day. Shopping trips, you know. It's Christmas. A lot of the patients got some last-minute gifts to pick up. I got three trips to the mall by noon." He quickly glanced at, then tapped with a gloved finger, the sheet tacked to the dashboard in front of him. "Fourteen people to get around in the next couple of hours. Not all of them can get around like you can. I have to help some onto the lift and get them buckled in back there. I don't want none of 'em hurt when I drive. It takes time. Ya know?"

"I know." I nodded and looked out the window that was quickly frosting up. The exhaust from the eight cylinder, poorly maintained motor was blue in the morning light, crystallizing as soon as it hit the air. It swirled slowly past the side of the van, rising in a white, willowy spiral towards the glass tower of the hospital. I watched it for a moment, then turned back to the driver, looking at him squarely in the eyes as he was looking at me through the mirror. "We are going to be making a stop on the way back home."

Bruce picked up on the subtle change from a question to an order. I could see him thinking about the 14 people he was to be delivering this morning, and how that would just totally screw up his carefully orchestrated schedule. I mean, how long could three trips to the mall take? It was only three blocks from the home to the mall. I don't care if he had to dress each client personally before taking them over, it wasn't going to take two hours to deliver 14 people three blocks. That just wasn't happening.

Ol' Bruce was going to have to forego one of his trips to the coffeeshop this morning and take me where I wanted to go. The driver shuffled in his seat, adjusting the sheepskin cover, wheezing a little in the process. He repositioned his baseball cap over his thinning hair, then muttered into the dash, "It better not be too far out of my way." He turned sharply to me. "Where do you want to go?"

"Golden Sheaves Cemetery."

"You shittin' me? That's clear across town," then remembering something, he added, "Hell it's outside of town by at least three miles. It'll take at least 20 minutes to get there."

"Then I suppose you had better hurry, hey Bruce." I didn't take my eyes off him. I could see his eyes shift back and forth quickly, searching for a way to get out of this little side jaunt. But nothing arrived.

"Son of a bitch." He pulled the shift level towards him in a mock show of effort and slipped the Chevy into gear. Something under the front engine cover banged in response to the sudden move, but it lurched forward towards the street. Two people walking up the snow-free driveway had to lunge out of the way of the metal juggernaut that was heading to the street come hell or high water. I heard someone shout at us, at him, then it was lost in the busy sounds of a heavy Chevy crunching over ice covered streets. Bruce looked in the side mirror, catching a glimpse of the couple, struggling in the deep snow pushed from the street. "Get the hell off the streets if you don't want to get driven over, ya lazy couple of shits."

The van suddenly veered heavily to the left, running through a stop sign, and causing several different makes of vehicles to honk their horns in loud, righteous protest. "Out of my way," Bruce yelled, "I've got to go all the way to the goddamn graveyard." His dark eyes, darted to mine, then back to the road. His courage was picked up a little by my lack of response. He turned fully towards me, ignoring the traffic, "All the way to the graveyard?"

"Uh-huh. And I'll be getting out for a minute or two."

"Oh, come on! Really?"

"Really."

He turned around, shifting the van to the left to correct for the inattentive drift. "Fucking great! A little walk-about!" He looked up in the mirror, "At the graveyard! In December!"

He kept muttering through most of the trip, occasionally taking a little sip of coffee that steamed in its holder on his left side. Most of it I ignored. Some I just didn't hear. The trip was basically uneventful.

After 15 minutes, I saw the tall, majestic trees framing the cemetery, towering above the windshield of the van. It was suddenly a dark place I wasn't sure if I really wanted to visit.

"Listen Bruce. You can save us both a little time, if you can show me directly where Mary was buried."

"Mary?"

"Yeah, Mary." I shook my head in amazement.

"You know, Mary. Five-four, about a hundred and thirty pounds, grey hair, glasses."

"Listen buddy," he piled on the brakes and shoved the van into park. "That describes about every single woman that gets into this van on any given day. You are going to have to be a little more specific."

"How many did they bury here in July?" His attitude was beginning to get to me.

"I dunno … six?"

"Six?" Holy crap, I missed a lot while I was having my elongated nap.

He spun around in his seat, his right arm hanging over the back of the seat. His hat still prevented me from seeing his eyes, though. He did have a lot of hair for a 65-year-old man. "In July, yeah, about half a dozen."

"How many were killed in an accident? Car accident," I clarified.

A little light bulb went off in his head. "Oh her. Yeah, I remember." Then something else lit up and his eyes suddenly appeared through the shock of grey hair and under the brim of his hat. He suddenly was looking at me with a little harder edge. "Oh, you. I heard about you."

Suddenly I became focused. Any little pain that was left residing in my legs abruptly was replaced with tension. "What have you heard about me, Bruce? Do tell." If the man was perceptive, he should have picked up the subtle change in my demeanour. No longer just a pain in the ass old guy who wanted to visit a dead friend, he should have understood that his life was now hanging gently in the balance. He should have picked up that nuance that changed in my tone from directness to calm precision. It was a place few people in my experience have ever walked away from.

"What have you heard?" I repeated.

Bruce must have sensed something. I could imagine the hair on the back of his neck bristling. He must have pulled from defensive mechanism in his primal past, now sensing he was in some sort of danger. "Nothing really. Just things." He pushed the comments away from it, hoping nothing would stick.

"What things, Bruce? Talk to me." I asked the question loudly, unbuckling my seatbelt in silence.

"Just about you two. The time you two were," he coloured. Bruce shrugged. "You know. Doing it, carrying on in her room."

The tension ebbed from me, washed away with the exhaust outside the windows. I breathed a huge sigh of relief. Calming myself. "We were a couple, Bruce."

"Yeah, I guess."

"We were in love, Bruce," I repeated with a little more gusto than I actually felt. It was absurd. I was trying to justify making love with Mary to a bus driver. "I'd like to see her now, if it's okay with you."

"Yeah sure." He looked out at the cemetery, quickly getting his bearings. "It should be just over there somewhere, on the other side of the military part." He gently slipped the van into gear, and we idled through the mass of dead people. I didn't even look outside. A few quiet seconds later we were stopped, and the door began the noisy collage of opening. Bruce pointed to a section 50 feet over.

"Just there. The one without the marker between the two tall ones. That's where she is." He swivelled in the seat and pointed again to make sure I saw her. "Just there."

"Okay." I rubbed my chin and followed the direction his gloved finger indicated down the line of headstones. It was hard to believe that someone so unique could be here, hidden among the boring grey granite. "I'll be just a couple of minutes." I said, moving to the doorway, pausing long enough to ask, "Okay, Bruce?"

"Yeah, I'll wait." He nodded his head a couple of times, then turned for his cold cup of coffee. "Right here."

"Good."

It took a minute or two to get to the spot where Mary was buried. From the van I knew there was a gap, between two large upright headstones. As I got closer, and could read the name Murphy and Hanrahan, the thought ran through my head, that it was good, Mary was buried in the Irish section of the graveyard. Then I looked two over, and the name Schneider was spelled out in relief in the granite. Behind, was Sigvaldson. Okay, so maybe a little more international in scope.

The space between the two headstones was wider than it appeared from 50 feet away. The gap was largely covered in smooth, windswept snow. Only a few freeze-dried flowers poked above. They looked like daisies, curled and brown, barely breaking through the crust of the snow. I was glad it was a bouquet of daisies on her grave because they were her favourite flower. No doubt. Everything in her room was daisies, from the bedspread on her super single, to the hand towels folded and hanging neatly in the washroom. The sheer volume left little doubt where her floral loyalties laid.

"Hello sweetheart."

Even among the headstones, where the demand for intimacy is at its peak, the words seemed to ring empty, almost shallow.

"How are you."

My body screamed in pain as I knelt down to where the plastic temporary headstone, complete with a hand-written name tag firmly glued on, was sticking out of the frozen earth. Ignoring the pain for a moment, I cleared away the crusty snowbank, and stared at the black tag. 'Mary Celeste.'

"I didn't know your middle name was Celeste." A small tear formed, then froze on the inside of my right eye. It always waters when there is a cold wind blowing. "I guess there are a lot of things I didn't know about you. Celeste. I like that name, it has a simple, strong elegance sound to it. No one will mess with you if your name is Celeste, right?"

"Of course, there are a few things about me you didn't know. Even now, I don't know if I can tell you all there is to know about Ivan Norman McDonald. Now that is a middle name. Right, honey? Norman. It's an Anglicization of my mother's maiden name. Or at least a part of it." I sighed and looked at the flowers, frozen and wilted and thought this was a place to start.

"Actually, my name is Dawid Brezinski. My mother's maiden name was Norwicz. Norman." I shook my head in wonder at what I was saying. "I haven't told one person that. Not one. That is for you." I nodded in silence, thinking of the weight that knowledge would give to Tick and that other cop from Kamloops, McKinnon. Then I packed that away for later.

Across the row of graves, I grabbed a quick look up at Bruce. He was still looking at his coffee cup, and I assume praying for me to hurry, so not to ruin his entire day's schedule. He would have to wait.

The wind seemed to calm down a little. For a moment, it didn't seem as brutally cold, in the unprotected landscape of the dead. But that moment passed quickly when a small skiff of snow came funnelling at me. I had to dip my head into the folds of my jacket to allow some measure of protection.

"It's damn cold out here, honey." The wind and cold was held away when I pulled the collar of my coat up, and my fedora down. "I've missed you, Mary. It's unbelievable that I have, but . . . well, there it is. I have missed you very much. These past months I spent thinking about you almost every moment of every day. I thought about the laughs we had together, I thought about the love we made. I thought about the times we just spent together reading or watching TV. Simple, everyday things."

It seemed the words suddenly went missing. I was experiencing something I hadn't felt before. I think it was emotion. A foreign feeling that I wished I could bury deep with all the others I assumed were lurking somewhere in my mind. They were safer there, suppressed in the black recess of my mind.

But it stayed, boiling beneath my eyes.

"I've miss you so much Mary. More than anything else, anyone else. It's a strange feeling for me. It's like a friendly tiger that has been caged for its entire life, and now finally free, wants to reach out and cuddle everyone it sees. Hug them to death, never letting them go. I've never experienced this before. I don't know how to feel. God, I wish you were here to help me through this. I need you."

From the roadway, a single honk of the Chevy's horn announced that Bruce had waited about as long as he was going to. I thought for a moment, I would make him wait. But I had said all there was to say. I had said what I needed to. So there was no need to stay kneeling in the snow by the fresh grave of my friend.

"I have to go now. I'll come back. Soon. I promise,

Mary."

Using the cane to the fullest advantage, I struggled to get up, the cold having froze my joints. My right knee came close to buckling under the pressure, but it held and after a great deal of effort I stood above her marker. I took a moment to remember her face. Her touch. I wanted to tell her I loved her, but the words just wouldn't form.

"See ya soon, honey."

Bruce didn't say a word when I got back into the van, but didn't wait for me to buckle up my seatbelt before he was on his way. The ride back to the home was quiet. He didn't even take a sip from his coffee cup, which I assumed was probably empty now. He stared out the windshield, holding the van on a straight course back through the web of streets to where we needed to go. He didn't even sneak a peek up at me through the large mirror above his head. Ten and two, his hands gripped the wheel, white knuckles showing the tendons beneath the skin.

As we pulled up at Pinetree, he flipped the switches to lower the door and began the process of excising me from the interior of the van, all before we had even stopped. Some orderly came out of the warmth of the hallway and stared at the two of us. He reached in and grabbed my suitcase, tossing it on the cement.

"Bruce, you are a little early. You weren't supposed to be here for another 20 minutes. We don't have the ladies ready to go Christmas shopping yet. Do you want to wait out here, or would you like to head down to the cafeteria for a quick coffee?"

Bruce unbuckled his seatbelt, took a quick look at me to see if I was listening, then pushed past me out the door. "I'll just go downstairs for a few minutes then. No need to freeze my ass off in the van if I don't have to."

He left both the orderly and I standing there in the snippets of wind and snow blowing through the covered walkway. The orderly, whom I didn't recognize, looked at me and asked if I knew how to close the door to the van. I told him I had no idea.

"Well, shit," he said, and turned for the doors, half running to catch up with the retreating Bruce, who was just about at the elevators. He hadn't looked back at the two of us.

I took a moment to stare up at the building, decked out in its finest re-cycled Christmas decorations. It looked exactly the same as the year before, and the year before that. But it did rekindle some old memories of the season from my past. Some good, some not so.

It was then I noticed my suitcase was still on the ground. The orderly had forgot it, in his panic to get Bruce back to the van to close the doors. I reached over and picked it up, and hobbled slowly to the doors, pushing my way through the warmth inside. It smelled the same, antiseptic and old. But it was safe. Not so much a home, but a haven for the winter.

A couple of the staff recognized me, and asked how I was doing, and passed along their condolences about Mary. I nodded and thanked them for their concern and just kept going. I got to the elevators, set the case down and punched the button to Mary's floor. It was going to be a couple of minutes, because it was in the basement. The orderly was still looking for Bruce. With all the coffee he had drank, he was probably in the shitter. I didn't have to wait long.

Looking back to the common room, none of the patients even looked twice at me. I was just another old person arriving in the holding pen, to wait for death, like them. All of us were hanging on to life with as much gusto as we could muster. It seemed strange to me now, that all these individuals were waiting for a solitary, very private moment, among a group of a hundred people all waiting for the same thing.

Now I had joined them again. To wait. But for me there was something else my patience was being asked to hang on to.

Looking into the room, the daisies were now gone. Whoever was in there didn't enjoy the same passion for anything that might bring colour to life. It was the clinical beige that all rooms were but taken to the far extreme of boredom, blandness. Nothing stood out, nothing spoke of an individual. All that was there was a bed, some furnishings and little else. Some slippers were positioned squarely at the side of the bed. They were the only things that were visible that showed there might be someone in the room. Nothing on the dresser, nothing on the walls in the pre-approved picture locations. In short, nothing — vacant.

I thought I might have felt something, standing there. The last time I had stood here, Mary and I were just going out for breakfast, after having made love. That thought brought a small twinge to my eyes, but it passed quickly.

"This part is over." The room now was just that, a room. Without the influence of Mary, it just wasn't what it once was.

"Ivan?" It was a nurse whom I recognized, but couldn't think for the life of me, what her name was. "Ivan, this isn't your floor."

"I know."

"Then why..." Then the realization must have swept over her, and her eyes got really big. "Oh, it was Mary's room."

"Yes. It was." I looked at her for a moment, and caught a glimpse of the nametag, 'J. Spearman R.N.' Joselyn, now I remembered. One of the few good ones here. Didn't feel the R.N. after her name meant really neurotic. "Who's in there now?"

"Maybe you'll be friends, his name is Edward Collins. He arrived just after Mary . . ." I could see she was searching.

"Passed," I offered.

"Yes, passed." She seemed to notice me for the first time. "How are you doing? I heard you were pretty banged up too."

"I'm okay. A little stiff. Still a little sore. But okay."

"Great, let's get you back up to your own room. It'll do you good to get back home again, right?" I nodded in agreement. But wasn't really sure this would ever feel like home again. Kenny was gone, and now Mary.

My room, including my dufus roommate, was exactly the same as the day I left it. He acknowledged my return with little more than a grunt. Fucker.

I was shocked to see the 'go kit' from the car sitting at the foot of the bed. On it, an envelope from the insurance company. The contents of both were a surprise: nothing taken from my kit—no one must have looked inside. Plus, the dollar amount they gave me for the K-Car was a genuine surprise. It was nearly double what I paid for it. I was pretty confident I wouldn't be able to find anything similar but pushed that search back until spring and I was feeling better. I knew what I would be looking for, it would simply be a matter of finding the right car. Especially now with my right arm damaged. But that would wait.

It was funny, living in a place that was a basically a

holding room for the dead. I never really expected any of my friends to die. None of us would ever be gone. The others, who cares? But us. We were invincible. I suppose that is true now . . . we were invincible.

Now, I was the last immortal person in the building.

29
JANUARY 2003

"Merry Christmas, Tick.

Sorry to have just dropped out of sight like that. Unexpected travel plans. I hope you are enjoying the holidays this year. Last year was tough I know. Like this year for me. Talk to you in the spring."

The very anxious voice on the other end of the telephone asked, "When did you get that?"

"I picked it up yesterday but forgot about the mail until this morning when I opened it while having my coffee." Tick looked across the kitchen at the white cupboards and noticed a couple of small brown spots that he had missed while cleaning. "Made me spit my coffee all over the goddamn kitchen."

"No shit," McKinnon agreed.

"Listen, I have to get this out to you. I'll photocopy it this afternoon at the town office, then package it up. You still have my fingerprints on file?"

"Yeah. I'll pass them along to the forensic guys, to make sure they don't deduce you are the bad guy. Wear gloves from now on right?"

"Right, absolutely," said Tick, looking down at the thin blue rubber gloves that were laying on the table beside the torn envelope.

"Read it again, Tick." Tick picked up the envelope by the corner, slipped the card out, and carefully propped it open on the tabletop.

"It's a plain card, no poetry or factory message on the inside. Just a "Merry Christmas" on the front cover, surrounded by, it looked like holly and, you know, regular Christmas shit."

Tick turned his attention to the envelope. "The

envelope is the mate for the card. Fits it exactly. Cheap, with just enough glue to hold the seams together. But he used tape to close it, so no DNA. One seam had already let go by the time it arrived here.

"The handwriting on the envelope seems to be female. I suppose that is what threw me off. He always typed the address. Always typed it. This is another change for him."

"No return address?"

"No, not even a mark in top left, or on the back flap. Post marked in Saskatchewan though, I don't know where. It has the capital 'S' at the beginning. So, from the gap."

"The gap?"

"Yeah, you know, the gap between Manitoba and Alberta."

"Oh."

"You're not from Saskatchewan, are you?"

"No."

"Good." The sweat that had suddenly collected on his neck, cooled, and dissipated.

"Tick, what is the postal code?"

Tick bent over until the envelope was barely five inches from his eyes. "Looks like S-0-G-0-E-0, I think. The G could be an O. But I think it's a G. The ink is a little faded and hard to read. If it is a G, it is a town called Balgonie, just outside of Regina."

"Okay, I got the postal code and will follow-up on that from my end. How about the note?"

"It's typed. Looks like just a regular ribbon-type typewriter. Not an electric with a cartridge. There is a little smudging around some of the features of the E and M which are hard letters for a ribbon to deliver a clean outline."

"Impressive."

"Been through this a few times buddy. I know what to look for. Still have my official Sherlock Holmes magnifying glass handy. Easy to pick up. And again, I'm not sure, but it looks like the pressure on the T, particularly when it's capitalized, is a little off. Heavier at the top, than the bottom. Could be the signature we'll need to individuate the machine." Tick pulled the opened card closer to him and peered at it intently. "I don't remember there being anything unusual about the capital T before. I think it's a new typewriter. But I would have to check into my files to be sure."

"That doesn't really help us any, does it?"

"Not unless this new typewriter has been used in some nefarious activity before, and the signature is on file somewhere."

"I'll have it checked out just the same . . ."

Tick heard the uncertainty in the inspector's voice. "I don't think it'll go anywhere either. But we have to look right? At least we'll know what kind of typewriter was used, maybe even the model number if the stars align."

"No doubt, Tick. It just seems this guy is always covering his ass, giving us nothing to work with."

"That changed in this note though. Listen." Tick re-read the note slowly with a deliberate gait. He tried hard to keep his voice from inflecting anything but delivering the 42 words with a flat monotone. "Do you get it?"

"The trip?"

"Maybe, but more importantly. The reference to the tough season. Do you think he is sharing that he had a tough season?" Tick could hardly contain himself. "It's the break we have been looking for. Something has happened in the few months since we last heard from him. This is the break Jim. We just need to figure out what happened. That is the doorway to him. Maybe someone died."

"Okay?" McKinnon questioned. "How does that help? Do you know how many people died in December? Even just the week before Christmas?"

"No."

"Well, neither do I," McKinnon admitted after a short pause. "But I am willing to concede that the number will fall somewhere between a lot and a shit-pile. Tick, how is this the break we have been looking for? Sorry I just don't see it."

"You can use some sort of filter in the fed's computer system."

"Some sort of filter?"

"Yeah, a filter. It looks for just what you ask it to. Tosses out all the shit and keeps the good stuff."

"Tick, I know what a filter is. I still don't see the break. There could be hundreds of people here, thousands. We wouldn't just be talking about spouses, we are also looking for boyfriends, sons, daughters, parents. Christ, man. Hundreds."

"Actually, I was leaning more to thousands."

"Thousands?"

"Yeah, I don't think it was in December the loss occurred. I think it was earlier, somewhere between his last kill and December."

"You're shitting me. Tick, we may not even be looking for someone's death. Maybe his dog died? Or he lost a bundle on the Grey Cup. That is a six-month long window of absence you are looking at."

Tick smiled a little, but it was a soft smile. "I know, Jim, I know. But we have to start somewhere."

"Okay," McKinnon said over the phone. "I'll start getting someone to look into it. But I am telling you right now, it is a long shot."

Tick nodded softly, "I know." He kind of thought this would be the reaction he would get. "But I did think of a way to cut down on the search. Use a multi-layered filter. We are looking for a guy who is at least 65 years old. Who has travelled somewhere in the past four months. With the new security measures put in place since 9-11, that shouldn't be too hard."

"Tick, don't bank too much on what you see on television. Most of that is done for the politicians, who want it done for the media, the cameras. They don't really have a clue what it takes to ensure the security of this country. Hell, they aren't even sure how to lock their doors at night."

"A lot of what you are referring to right now is theoretical. Manpower, they have up the ying yang. It isn't hard to hire young men and women to man the borders, look under a few cars and trucks then pat themselves on the back, saying the country is safe now. Of course, the politicians reach around as only politicians can, and pat themselves on the back for helping to put all this in place."

Tick was all too familiar with the role of politicians and the law. The elected officials said they would like this law, or that one put into place, because some old lady that has always supported them wants it. Screw the law, the criminal code. Screw the lawmen, who have to interpret and enforce this new law. Just make it so that old lady McPhee can shoot anybody's cat if she wants to and can get away with it.

"Tick?"

"I'm here."

"I'll try." There was a long pause. "I'll try," McKinnon said with a huge sense of commitment. "I don't know what will happen, but we'll never know until we ask."

"It's all we can do."

"What kind of filters do you think we are going to need? Age, travel, loss of significant other?"

"Not in that order. Start with the loss. That should cut down on the volume by a hundred-fold. The age is next, again just cutting down the available pool of suspects. Finally go with the travel."

"You do know what kind of databases we are going to have to access for this? We are starting with the social security registry, followed by a cross reference with Census Canada, and all that is further compounded by logging on to the Canada Customs and Revenue Agency, to see who has been to Disneyland lately."

Tick wiped a little of the coffee stain from the cupboard door, then gave the whole panel one good swipe for good measure, smiling the whole time. "I would say that just about wraps it up. You think?"

A chuckle was transmitted through the telephone system to Tick Smith. "Yeah, buddy, I think so."

"Did you and the family have a good Christmas?" asked Smith. For a moment he was sad, melancholy over the solitude he endured on December 25. But, it passed quickly.

"Great," McKinnon said. Then added, "Everyone was home for the day. Free turkey meal," he tacked on the end as an explanation.

Tick looked across the smooth snow in his front yard to the lake and waited. The two had grown very comfortable with the silence of friendship. Neither really needed to talk, if there was something coming, that just hadn't got out yet.

"Tick, you know you are welcome to come out here for a holiday. It's really quite beautiful in this area of the country at this time of year. And I'll personally guarantee that it's a hell of a lot warmer too. None of that 35 below shit. Nice and even at zero is the way I like it."

"Zero?"

"Yeah, that's what it was on Christmas, and I think that's about what it is now."

Tick looked out the window over the sink and saw the mercury sitting at minus 26. "It's a little cooler than that here. About 25 or 26 actually."

"You are looking at your thermometer?"

"As we speak."

"As we speak, Tick my friend, the old trusty hardware thermometer is resting right at . . . oh, about minus two. It's still melting."

"Minus 26 here."

"Shit, that's cold. How about New Year's?"

"New Year's?" Ticked leaned against the counter and surveyed his little world. The thought of going someplace warmer, albeit a little warmer for the new year seemed very enticing. He could use a break. Maybe even get some sleep.

"Yeah, I've booked off the entire holiday period. Don't go back until the 6th of January. First real holiday we've had in five years. It's interesting Tick, a side benefit of this case."

"What's that?"

"Since we began on this, the team under me has pulled together, gelled into a really solid unit. They have found new and creative uses for their time and in so doing, our rate of success in the crimes faced is dramatically higher. Our backlog is down to less than half a dozen active, recent cases."

"Including mine?" Tick Smith asked.

"Yours is at the top of the list, Tick, not to worry.

We have a few old cases that just can't seem to find their way through to a conclusion. Some may never be, you know how it is. Cold cases."

"I watch the series on CTV. Not bad."

"Cold Squad, yeah, I like it. Typical television crime show where you can solve it in 60 minutes, but better than most. So anyways, we are, basically caught up. And, because of that, holiday here I am. And unless I am mistaken, your calendar is free these days, at least until golf season kicks off again in Manitoba. When is that? July?"

"You mean July spring golf? No, I usually don't get out there until the weather really warms up in August. God, you guys in B.C. think the whole weather world revolves around you. I have golfed in March you know. Once, about 10 years ago. First time ever."

"I was stationed in Portage and Winnipeg, Tick. I know the drill. So, what do you think? New Year's in Kamloops? Could be a good time. I'm a really good cook. And my wife is a lot better than I am. Plus, there will be no kids around. They are all heading out to whatever they call a party. The last thing they want is to spend any time with the adults that helped bring them into the world."

"I don't want to be a third wheel."

"No third wheel buddy, just three friends spending some quality time together helping to bring in the New Year. I'll even let you make breakfast. But you have to promise it'll be good. Otherwise, I'll make my wife cook."

"Oh, I wouldn't want to be responsible for that. It's an honour I'm sure to cook breakfast in the McKinnon household."

"So yes?"

"Sure, yes."

"Outstanding. Look forward to it. Call me back when you have the travel plans all worked out."

"I will," Tick said, smiling into his coffee cup. "Probably get back to you later today or early tomorrow. But don't forget, it's not all that far away. Just a couple of days. I'll see what I can do."

"If you run into any trouble, I may be able to pull some strings and get you into an official standby seat. That would work."

"Official standby?"

"Yeah, the RCMP have seats reserved on official standby in case one of our officers needs to get anywhere fast, and don't want to go through all the official horseshit of purchasing a ticket, going through departmental reimbursement, blah blah blah. You know the drill."

"Oh yes, very familiar with departmental bullshit. I actually invented some of it for our force. I'll call you back later today."

"Super."

"All right, talk to you." Tick pulled the phone away, and heard faintly his name being yelled at the other end. He pulled it back to his ear.

"Tick, you still there? Tick?"

"Yeah, I'm here."

"One thing. You said you didn't get the card from our buddy until today?"

"No, I didn't open it until today. I got it yesterday from the post office."

"What is the date stamped on it?"

Ticked pulled out the magnifying glass again, and angled it over the envelope careful not to touch the paper with his fingers. "Looks like the 24th."

"He knew you wouldn't get it on time. Not being mailed from Saskatchewan the day before Christmas.

You weren't going to get it on time. Hell, given the Canada Post issues, I'm surprised you have it already. Only been a week."

"No, you're right. There is no way he could have thought I would get it by Christmas."

"So, my question is, has he ever been late for an important day, like Christmas, before? Birthdays, anniversaries?"

Tick straightened up and looked down at the envelope. He scanned his mind through the years of receiving cards and letters from the killer. He shook his head in amazement.

"I don't know why I didn't pick up on that. No, he has never been late. In fact, there has always been a couple of day of grace, before Christmas, Easter, whatever." Tick glanced across the kitchen at the mounds of paper on his table. He had been living with the dead for months now. He ate in his chair in the living room because there was no room on the table.

"I've got photocopies of all the envelopes from over the years he has sent. I'll go through them. Some of the copies are poor quality from back when wet photocopiers were the only ones we could muster. Some are photographs if memory serves me. Still, you may need to make a call to have the originals looked at by departmental guys. Make it official."

"Let me know what you find out about the flights, and the dates when you call back."

"Funny, isn't it? I'm not sure what this is all about, this late card. But I agree, I think there is something to it. I think it may lead to something. What? Who knows? But it's interesting. Later."

Tick hung up the phone, and was already halfway to the table, before the phone finished its jingling and came to rest in the manila-coloured wall mount. He knew exactly where to look, to find what he was looking for. He had broken down the evidence, chronologically. Through the lean information years, there wasn't very much in the folders, so finding what he was looking for took no time.

Quickly he ran through a dozen paper thin folders, looking for one thing only. No matter if it was a photostat, photocopy, lithograph, or photograph. Those he could read, told the same story.

"I'll be a son of a bitch," he said to no one in particular, but to everyone all at once. Tick moved through all the folders, carefully checking the date on the postal stamp for each horrific card or letter he had received in the 30 years of searching. The handwritten date on the outside of the envelope indicated the date it was delivered. When he found one legible, he wrote it down, along with the corresponding holiday date and the date the card arrived. Though each of the mailing dates were different, they shared one commonality. One thread spun its way all through the decades.

Each letter had been mailed two weeks to the day before a holiday, or special occasion.

Tick was happy for the first time in ages. He looked at the list in front of him. The corresponding dates he considered to be the one break, as uneventful as it may seem, that could break the case open. To him this one little variation in the modus operandi, might be the straw the camel was looking for to break its back.

Something kept the murderer away from the post office in the two weeks before Christmas. It was that something that Tick knew McKinnon and he would have to spend the rest of the investigation pursuing. He didn't have a clue what they were looking for. But at least now they were looking for one thing.

The question would be, what happened around

December 11 this year to mess up what has been a very predicable schedule? Jail? He didn't think so. He was pretty confident the whole no-fingerprints things would have popped up in databases from all over. Out of the country? Again, Tick didn't think that would be it. Even out of the country, he was pretty sure that killer would have managed to get something tossed in the mail at about the right time, or he would have booked a holiday through different dates. That left illness. That couldn't be predicted. If incapacitated, he would have been unable to grab a cheap card and toss it in the mail. Or, if he could, where the card was posted would have given an indication of where he was located. So, it was better to hold off on the card until later. This really was interesting. He stared at the card and envelope again, wishing for something to pop off the page, that simply wasn't there.

Tick leaned back into the press back chair and was thrilled as his body let go a huge weight. For the first time in ages . . . years, he thought, they were finally on the right track to this guy. There was something to this delay. He was back on a killer's trail.

Tick looked at his watch. He had just gotten off the phone with McKinnon less than half an hour before. He had a couple of calls to make to arrange for a flight. He guessed that would take about half an hour. He could wait to tell McKinnon the good news.

"Yeah, that's long enough of a rest." Tick Smith stood up and headed for the phone.

30
APRIL 2003

It is absolutely rejuvenating!

Once the weather breaks, everything seems to change, evolve, lighten.

It's amazing how the first spring flower can renew a human battery. All winter I had been shut in, trapped in that home for seniors, waiting for that first spring flower. The potted plants that were delivered from the greenhouses around town just didn't do the trick. The flowers had to be grown outside, fresh from the black soil of Manitoba. There is a timing to everything. Potted flowers throw the natural rhythm of mother nature out of whack. There are certain times that specific flowers should bloom, and that is the only time they should. Having tulips bloom all year is just wrong. But poking through the last vestiges of snow, straining for the thinly dispensed heat of the sun, is perfect. Appropriate.

I tried like hell not to let the winter bring me down. I don't think I have that S.A.D. thing where you get irritable if you don't get enough sun. I'm not sure I believe in the seasonal affected disorder. In my day, and there I am sounding old again, we used to call it stir crazy. But I suppose science marches on and political correctness softens the language.

Through a lot of busy activities, I didn't let being cooped up for the winter force me to lose focus on what I was doing. What I was planning to do. As each storm passed by, spraying its tiny claws of ice at my windows, I recalled the plan and the way I was going to bring this whole thing to a close. I read somewhere that doing mundane things, like crafts, allowed your mind to focus on something other than a major problem in your life, freeing the subconscious to work through the dilemma. I certainly did take over the one-thousand-piece puzzle championship in Pinetree. That turd McKenzie up on the fifth didn't know what hit him. Loser. Of course, here I am boasting about kicking the shit out of an 88-year-old man, in a wheelchair, whose only claim to fame, ever, was his ability to put puzzles together faster than anyone else. Boy am I a big man these days.

But then the first tulip pushed through, against the weather, bringing one radiant dot of green and to a lesser degree, yellow. It was a stark contrast to the grey and white of early spring. Coming back from a morning walk, I noticed it, or more succinctly, its dash of colour jumped up at me. I stood outside for an hour just watching it being gently pushed about by a warm southerly spring breeze. Its head wasn't fully blooming yet, but just a smidge, a crack of yellow was visible above the green husk. Even the green was unmistakable in contrast with the rest of the area. Nothing else was even close to budding, yet this single tulip decided it was time to push through and move into the wakening spring world. I was fascinated.

A couple of staff had come out to see what it was that I was staring at, and when I told them, they looked at me a little funny, said "oh" and walked back into the building. I'm sure the story of Ivan and the tulip has now fallen old, but for a few minutes I was the craziest and most talked about man in the building. In this world of reality television shows and short attention spans, that notoriety would last until the next patient walked out of their room with no clothes on.

One or two patients did come out to see what I was looking at. Mrs. Roberts stood with me a few minutes and tried to make small talk about the spring, and some glorious springs she had seen. I didn't really pay attention to her, I'm sorry to say. Her stories were fascinating, I'm sure, it's just that at that moment, there were more important things floating around the inside of my head. Bigger issues were firing the synapses. She'd been trying to sweet-talk me since I got back here. Little treats of chocolate, or cookies dropped off at odd hours. Polite "May I join you at the dining room table." The usual courting dance of the senior citizen. I didn't have the heart to tell her that she was dancing alone.

There was no interest on my part to kindle a relationship. I couldn't even go down the hall past Mary's room. It brought too stark of a pain to my heart. Plainly, it just hurt to think about her being gone. I thought about the promise I made to her, about visiting her again at the cemetery. But I couldn't do it. Something prevented me from asking Bruce to load up the old Chevy and head back out of town to where she was. A couple of times I had dressed up and stood in the hallway in front of the main doors, waiting for him to come. But I neatly folded my coat, and walked slowly back to the room. It just wasn't going to happen. Not for a while.

Mrs. Roberts soon left, huddling back into the building after not getting anything out of me, other than the most uncommitted grunt I could muster when asked about supper plans.

A lot of stuff ran through my head in that hour watching the tulip. I thought about the accident. Of Mary's head on my lap. But I pushed that away quickly. I thought about the physiotherapy I underwent in the hospital, and then here at the center. The quick, cursory questions asked by the police. They checked out my driver's licence, as they should have. I wasn't too worried about it, because it was legitimate. Sort of. They asked me what I could remember about the accident. Then one came back to give me an update on the case. He told me the kid had been given a five-year driving prohibition, and three years probation.

I may have commented to him that it didn't seem like a fair punishment for the taking of a beautiful life. He shrugged his shoulders, and said the accident was just that. An accident. He didn't do it on purpose. He got the punishment the court felt he deserved. He hadn't been drinking or doing any drugs. He just missed the stop sign. Sorry.

I thought about the letter I received from the kid, Kelly Anderson, about a month after getting back to the home. I wasn't going to read it. But late one night, three weeks after receiving it, I finally opened the plain envelope and read the card inside. It was nice. For a kid. It was filled to overflowing with shallow words like sorry, or never do it again. Of course, also tossed in here and there was a couple of should'ves. I smiled when I read the, "please forgive me."

"Yes, all would be forgiven later son, don't you worry about that." I never replied to the card. Couldn't think of a single appropriate thing to say. There were a few inappropriate responses, but I thought better of sending them. My response to it, to him, would come later. Then he would know the depth to which he stabbed my heart. But not until then.

Not until the end.

Watching the tulip sway under the gentle nudging of the wind, I thought of Tick and the RCMP Inspector in Kamloops. They would have to be dealt with in time. The Christmas card would have kept the candle lit for Tick. He was so predictable. I made a note to thank the family of my roommate for dropping that in the mail for me back in Saskatchewan when they got there at Christmas. They were more than helpful to send it from there, so my friend would be able to collect the postmark for his collection.

Tricky? Yeah, I suppose. But still fun.

Of course, the whole travel angle would have been dug into by the best computer minds in the country. Probably the little aside I tossed in about the tough season would have got him looking down that avenue as well. I smiled at the thought of him chasing my tail exactly where I wanted him to follow.

I thought about this McKinnon fellow. He was a wild card. Career officer, head of the Kamloops Serious Crimes Unit. So probably had some solid investigating skills. You don't get promoted to that level without having some big results in your history. Probably had a good crew working under him. From a look at the video on the news I saw of Tick and this guy, plus with the newspaper article I read, there seemed to be a relationship building between the two men. Of course, I couldn't be sure, but that was the feeling I got. Tick would be looking for a sympathetic soul to commiserate with, to share his tale of woe. Plus, he would be looking for an inspector that could be of help to his own private investigation.

But this McKinnon fellow could really throw a wrench into the works if he was to be left to work unbridled. I would have to make sure he was looking down the alleys and backroads where I needed him to. And those side excursions would be as far away from me as possible. That would bring the game to a little higher level than playing with Tick. He I could predict. But McKinnon? I wasn't too sure about where he would go if I wagged my tail left. Tick would follow along like a little puppy. But this other guy, he could turn right to see how I would react.

A little extra care and attention are going to have to be taken from now on.

There was an interesting parallel I thought of, as the tulip danced for me in the spring breeze. It was indicative of nature's big plan. The natural progression of sleep, then rebirth. It was all part of the plan. Now standing there, staring at that flower struggling out of its slumber, I thought about my own plan. I thought about my emergence from the cocoon of hibernation. The thought made me stronger. Hopefully a little more cunning, in being able to survive in an environment much more dangerous than one the flower would have to face. The worst-case scenario for the tulip, a dog could pop along and decide it was time to take a targeted leak on its pretty yellow head. For me, the worst that could happen would be a quiet "John Doe" funeral in some out-of-the-way graveyard with no one there to mourn my passing. Not really too much of a different set of consequences, based on the premise.

I worked the entire winter at gaining back the mobility in my back and legs. The doctor was amazed that a man my age could have come so far in recovering from his injuries in so little time. There was some residual stiffness in my right leg, particularly in the early morning hours, or when the humidity was high. But once I got up, moved around a little and got the blood moving, all was back to normal. In fact, I felt I had a little more stamina, 'better lungs' we used to call it. The dedicated regimen was probably responsible for that. Walks at twice the pace and twice the distance weren't any effort for me now. Well, once I got the pain to die down in my leg, we were off to the races. No marathons or anything, but what the mall walkers did was a poor excuse for a cardio workout in my world. I could have taken them all.

My right arm was gaining each day as well. The exercises the therapists had me do every second day were great at increasing mobility in that arm. They looked at me with curiosity as I completed another totally different regime at the end of each session, with strong, chopping wood motions with both arms.

So, when I stood, looking at the flower after my morning walk, it symbolized a lot to me. It meant a lot to me. It was a small, poignant reminder of Mary and what she meant to me. It also marked the beginning of a really interesting spring of activity.

As the snow melted, I felt the only real stumbling block to any forward momentum was the lack of wheels. My precious K-Car was gone, written off by the insurance company. To be honest, I didn't think I could sit in that car again without seeing Mary dying on my lap every moment.

It turns out that a Chevy Celebrity would do the trick! It was a little bigger than I was used to, not by much, but enough that I noticed it. However, like the K-car it was front wheel drive, meaning a larger, deeper trunk. That would be handy. Plus, the threshold of the trunk was low. With the slightly diminished power in my right arm, it would be easier to toss what I needed to into it, plus pulling it out again wouldn't be so laborious. That probably wasn't what the engineers were thinking of when they built it.

In addition, it was beige. You just don't get a better, ignore me, kind of colour than beige. It literally would disappear into a parking lot.

The first thing I did was toss the 'go-kit' into the driver's side wheel well. I had checked it as soon as I discovered it in my room in December, ensuring that it was still complete. No one had touched it since then, but I quickly triple checked the contents as I placed it into the cavernous trunk. One had to be certain of these things.

What all of this really meant was, “Let’s go!”

31
MAY 2003

Cora Douglas didn't mind the errand at all. It gave her an opportunity to get out of the crowded office for a while. The fresh air revitalized Cora, cleansing off the staleness of the office air and the people that filled it. She always paused when she walked out the doors, took in a great breath, smiled at the sky, then set about the tasks assigned by her boss.

She knew the others in the office thought she was just ass-kissing. Never hearing the whole story, Cora would catch small fragments of gossip, quickly reigned in when they realized she was within earshot. She was aware of the whispers in neighbouring rooms, little glances towards her and the small verbal jabs thrown at her. But she didn't care.

Having worked there for three years, she had yet to really get to know anybody. A couple she would consider friends, but not enough to have a great desire to straighten them out as to her excursions for the office manager. They were work friends from 9-5 only. They didn't mix after hours. They didn't go to movies together, or the bar. Once a month, a small group would go out for lunch, but that was it.

So, what they thought about her, she didn't care because it made no impact on her life at all. They had no clue.

'Maybe it was jealousy,' she thought. Jealous at the thought of getting out of the office for a while a couple of times a week. But Cora couldn't understand what the big deal was. There was no other benefit for her, other than getting out of the air-conditioned room for a few precious moments. Away from the whiny voices around her, griping about the job, the boss, the hours, the pay, the benefits, blah blah blah. The work they accomplished at the corporate head office for the Walker Insurance Company was repetitive, and simple. They put in data from satellite offices around the country on new clients, changes to existing policies, and once in a while, claims on the policy.

It really wasn't mind-challenging work, but Cora enjoyed the regime of it, the dedication it took to make the right entries for each client. She took pride in what she was doing. She understood her place in the company — her role.

Usually on Fridays, Merv Canart would come up to her and ask her if she had time to skip out for a few minutes, to do a little running around for him. Cora would catch little smiles on the catty little mouths around the room when he walked across the carpeted floor. But she didn't care. There would be snickers when he handed her the cell phone, in case there was something that came up while she was out. Again, Cora Douglas didn't care. They were stuck in their chairs, and she was heading outside.

The trip was routine. To the bank for a deposit if there was one. Across town to the office supply box store if there was a need to fill, downtown to the accountants, and sometimes, if she was lucky, over to the WestPark Mall for something or other.

Cora smiled, because today was one of those lucky days. The trunk of her little Toyota was crammed with supplies from the stationery store. So much paper and a cache of pens, paper clips, pencils, re-writeable CD-ROMs were crammed in the tiny trunk, the rear bumper looked as though it might drag on the pavement if she hit any kind of pothole. When she looked in the rear-view mirror on the way to the mall, instead of the vehicle behind her, Cora saw an awful lot of pavement.

At a stoplight, she adjusted the mirror, and checked her makeup. Her hair was just starting to grey. It always amazed her that her mother, at her age, had gone completely grey. But her few strands of grey hair were just poking through in sporadic places around her full dark brown mane.

'I'll have to have that fixed,' she thought. 'That and the wrinkles under my eyes.' It was another family curse, this time from her father's side. He called them smile lines. She thought they were just a little less funny. In two weeks, she had an appointment with a plastic surgeon to talk about this new treatment called Botox injections, to smooth out the wrinkles. It scared her, but so did the thought of going through life alone. She knew the injections wouldn't help her in a relationship, but it might help her get to the relationship part. Maybe.

She quickly ran over the rest of her face. Not bad for 35, she thought. Clean, straight teeth, high cheekbones, cornered by the damn wrinkles, dark eyes. "Captivating" was the way one of her many dates had described her eyes. When she was a teenager, her little brother had said her eyes were the sign of the devil. She beat the crap out of him. End of argument.

No extra chins, though she knew if she let herself dive into the donut aisle, they would quickly multiply. The rest of her body was the same. She was big boned but had less than 25 per cent body fat thanks to the twice-a-week workout. Cora sometimes looked at her body when she was alone in the house. Standing in front of the full-length mirror, she would imagine herself pregnant, her relatively flat abdomen pushed far out in front. She thought about the fat that would naturally accumulate, and the tremendous amount of work that would be required to pull herself back into the form she started out with. The whole ordeal scared the shit out of her. And at 35 years old, the clock was definitely ticking on the child thing. Definitely.

The pregnancy part, not the giving birth, not the raising children, scared her. She was looking forward to ballooning like her mother. Pictures of her mom when she was a single teen were amazing. Beautiful, dark, thin. Now, she was three inches shorter than Cora, at five-foot-two. But she probably weighed half again as much, tipping the scales at 250 pounds or so.

That was the part that petrified Cora.

Behind her, a horn honked, and Cora jumped on the gas pedal, jackrabbiting the Tercel through the last set of lights into the mall parking lot. Just as she turned left off the main road into the vast lot and started to look for a spot big enough to wedge in her car, the cell phone rang.

"Hello?" Cora answered the phone, then held it between her chin and shoulder and she wheeled the car into a spot that was only 150 yards from the entrance.

"Cora, it's Merv, where are you?"

"Just got into the mall parking lot." She switched off the ignition and sat back to relax.

"Damn."

"Why?"

"I had hoped to catch you before you left the office supply store. I was just asked to get some labels for the shipping envelopes."

"That's all right. There's a stationery store here in the mall. I don't think there is any great saving to me going all the way back across town, at least not enough to pay for my time and gas. I'll just pick them up here.

"Okay, great. You have enough money?"

"Oh, lots. Got all the supplies we wanted, and I still have about $75 left over. So, yes, lots of room."

"Good, listen, why don't you pick up coffee and donuts for everyone to end the day. After all it's Friday, why not relax a little."

This was unexpected. "Sure, great, I'll do that. Just have to grab a couple of things here, and I'll be on my way back. Say, 30 minutes." She looked at the dash clock, clicked on the ignition, and saw it said '4:21'. Yeah, that should work out.

"Good. I won't tell anyone; it'll be a surprise."

'You bet it will,' Cora thought.

"Bye."

"Bah-bye." She loved saying that. It was irreverent but linked her somehow to her childhood. Bah-bye. Bah-bye. Hysterical.

"Excuse me."

"JESUS CHRIST!!" Cora nearly jumped out of her seat. The cell phone got thrown on the floor.

"I'm sorry. But I can't seem to find my car."

Cora held the steering wheel in a death grip. The knuckles of her hands were white, and she could feel the sweat of the adrenalin rush beginning to form on her palms. Her heart pounded in her chest, and she could feel the veins in her neck echo rhythmically. She looked slowly to her left and saw a quiet plaid shirt and fortrel pants standing by the driver's window. She leaned over and looked up to see a grey-haired gentleman looking down at her with a gentle smile, and what she considered to be real, appropriate smile lines.

"I'm sorry, did I startle you?" He leaned over and appeared fully in the window. "I didn't mean to. I've just misplaced my car. I haven't a clue where it went."

"You . . . what?" It was taking Cora a moment to

catch up to the conversation. Her hands were still firmly wrapped around the steering wheel cover. She could just make out Winnie the Pooh's head on the rubber wrap around the cover. It was a gift from her father.

"I really did scare you." He was still smiling. "I am sorry. I didn't mean to do that. I thought you saw me walk up to your car."

Cora relaxed a little, her hands slid off the steering wheel, and she wiped the sweat off on her pant legs. "You really did scare me. I didn't see you coming at all." She thought back to what he had said before, about being lost. She looked at him closer, and saw a man, in his early 70s with the neatest blue eyes she had ever seen. In a way, she was captivated by this older man, staring down at her. He was attractive in a grandfatherly sort of way. Immediately the nurturing instinct in her took over.

"You said you were lost?"

"No, no. I'm not lost, I know where I am. I just don't know where my car is." He smiled, and Cora thought dentures, for sure dentures. No guy that age could have his own teeth. "I came to the mall this morning to have lunch with my daughter Catherine, then I looked around for a bit, and now, my car isn't where I thought I left it."

"How did you come to the mall? Which street?"

"From the west, off Portage Avenue."

"Did you park by the grocery store, or the liquor store."

"Uhm," he looked up, and around for a moment, taking in a very slow and methodical 360-degree view of the parking lot around him. "I think . . . neither."

"All right, that means you were probably on a side lot." Cora reached for her door pull, and a gentle hand, with light brown age spots on its back, rested on her doorsill. The man leaned a little further towards her. Cora reached up and patted him on his hand reassuringly. "It just means that you have parked somewhere other than here. It won't take long to find your car. What colour is it?"

"I'm sure it won't take long. The car is light brown. Old Chevy Celebrity."

His eyes turned down from Cora's face, and for a moment she thought he was checking out her boobs, or maybe her legs. The top she wore left no skin visible on her cleavage, but the skirt always rode up a little when she was driving. "Funny thought," she mused. But she didn't think this guy was a perv. He didn't start out looking at her body. Just her eyes.

"Is the cell phone still working?"

The question threw her off. "I'm sorry?"

"The cell phone, you threw it when I scared you." The man pointed at the phone lying on its back on the carpeted floor. "Again, I apologize for doing that."

"It's no problem." The phone was on, and everything appeared to be okay. "I think it's okay. The little lights are all on."

"Good." He nodded his head, then the eyes quickly darted up to the parking lot. For a moment Cora caught a definitive change in demeanor of the man. He didn't move but shifted somehow. Tensed. "You might want to turn it off. Save the battery. For later."

Now something set off alarm bells. She couldn't pin it down. It wasn't one big thing but rather the accumulation of a bunch of little things. The way the man had crept up to the car while she was on the cell phone. Unseen. His eyes never settled on one thing, but rather continued to rush around, scanning the entire area. He was leaning on the door, and even though she hadn't tried to open it, she knew he was holding it closed. Keeping her in the car. The question about the cell phone.

'The cell phone,' she suddenly thought. 'It's the cell phone!'

Her world suddenly felt as if she were experiencing it through a suit of cotton candy after a monstrous pressure impacted her left side. Then, it was gone. But far away Cora Douglas did hear one word.

"Surprise."

Her first sensation as she came out of her unconscious state was an absolute inability to move. Her next sensation was blind panic. She struggled against the bindings that held her, but soon found there was no quarter given in the fastenings. All her gyrations managed to accomplish was piercing pain lancing through her arms and legs and burning sensations erupting on her neck. Cora realized she wouldn't be able to wiggle her way out of the predicament, so she forced herself to calm down. To take stock.

Her eyes and mouth were covered. No light penetrated the blindfold, and when she squinted, small hairs were pulled out, sending miniature electric jolts down her face, making her eyes tear up. The same thing happened when she tried to move her lips. The tape was on so tight, she couldn't even get her tongue between her lips.

She was totally trussed up. No way to move anything more than slight jiggling of her fingers and toes, and some mobility in her head. But not much room for latitude there. Her arms and legs were immobile. As she struggled, in a measured careful effort, she found a tingling sensation feather up both her arms and from the knees down. The knots were so tight they were cutting off the circulation to the extremities of her body.

For a moment, another wave of panic swept through her. She could lose her hands, her feet! Then she remembered how she got into the situation and Cora realized losing a hand or a foot might not be the worst thing that could happen to her. Just losing a limb might be a blessing in this situation. Cora thought the man was an old guy, so rape probably wasn't on the agenda. So why all of this shit?

Panic bathed her again, but she pounded it back down. She listened to the sound of her breathing, focusing on that. She thought that no matter what, she would focus on the breathing. It was what was keeping her alive right now. In . . . out.

'Just breathe, Cora,' she screamed silently to herself. 'We'll get through this. If you just breathe and don't panic.' In a few minutes, Cora could feel herself starting to come down from the terror of her situation and begin to grapple with possible options to get herself out of it.

She was in a car. In the trunk. She thought it was hers, but she couldn't be sure. Then realized it wasn't unless all of the supplies she bought were taken out. Plus, she realized she wouldn't fit in the trunk of her small Toyota. So, it was another car.

From the sound of it, they weren't in the city any longer, but on a highway. The steady metronomic clump beneath her, she knew were expansion lines in the asphalt. They were coming too quickly together to be in town.

The country. Away from civilization! Away from help. Cora beat down another wave of panic and focused on her breathing again. She had read somewhere, that focusing on breathing for pregnant women during the labour of childbirth is a little self-hypnotism technique developed over the eons of motherhood. She hoped it would work now.

The car suddenly braked, small protesting screams from the tires penetrated into the trunk space. Cora was thrown forward against the boxes that were in the trunk, one hard edge pinching her back. Then she was thrown hard to the left, as the car dived into a stiff right-hand turn, then clunked as it jumped from pavement to gravel.

'Oh shit, a gravel road.' Cora thought, 'The middle of nowhere. The end,' she screamed silently. 'We are near the end of the road.' The sound of her breathing was no match for the strange mixture of engine noise, wheel hum against the gravel road, and small stones being spit up, pinging against the metal body of the vehicle that was holding her captive. Cora couldn't hear the ragged noise the air made as it pushed out of her. Her panic was returning now, overwhelming all other senses. She struggled passionately, a death struggle against her bindings. From within her, Cora suddenly tasted the bitter bile of vomit edging its way up her throat. It filled her mouth with the harsh, warm fluid that she couldn't swallow back to its proper place.

She felt it force its way down her windpipe. Burning. Stinging all the way to her lungs.

Her panic was totally out of control. Her gyrations produced excruciating pain, but she didn't, couldn't notice. The logical portion of her brain shut down. All that remained was pure animal desire to escape, to live.

Then she began to fall into total blackness. No one she loved was there to catch her. No long-lost family member, like her nana, to welcome her. It was black, empty.

Cora's final thought was how cheated she felt, in not seeing her life pass before her eyes. There was so much she would have liked to have seen again. One last time.

A half an hour later, Cora couldn't have seen the trunk lid open, and a dark shadow, backlit by the sun over his shoulder, peek in. Cora didn't feel the man's hands roughly probe her neck and find nothing. Then grope for her wrists, searching for confirmation of the vacancy of her pulse.

Cora didn't feel the tape, being roughly pulled from her eyes, her mouth. She didn't feel the wad of hair that was pulled with it. Nor did she feel the small bit of skin that was pulled away from her lips.

Cora Douglas didn't hear the man swear quietly, standing above her, looking down on her lifeless body.

"9-1-1."

"You're recording this call?"

"Sir?"

"You are recording this telephone conversation. Right?"

"Yessir. 9-1- . . ."

"Shut the fuck up. Tick, McKinnon, I didn't do this one. Okay? The stupid bitch went and died on her own."

- soft thump of phone hitting something-

"9-1-1. Sir, are you there? 9-1-1."

(faint) "Stupid bitch."

32
MAY 2003

Within 35 minutes of opening his eyes, Tick Smith was drinking coffee out of a silver-coloured insulated mug Martha had given him on their last anniversary together and was on the road to a small town southwest of the Manitoba provincial capital of Winnipeg. In that time, he had made a pot of coffee, showered, shaved, and had a quick breakfast of two thick slices of whole grain toast, with a single poached egg on the top. Not his usual breakfast of just coffee, but he felt he would need a little extra get-up-and-go today.

In that 35-minute period, Tick Smith had scrambled into a relatively clean and pressed set of clothes. "Not as neatly done as Martha," he mused. But Tick knew he didn't have the time to be as fastidious as his wife had been. Not today.

In that abbreviated period, Tick Smith had learned he was back on the trail of the killer. Tick Smith was now back in the hunt. To no one else he was truthful, but he muttered, "It does feel fucking good!"

In the car, swivelling through the slower traffic on Highway 3, he wondered how people could get anywhere travelling at 100 kilometres per hour. The legal speed limit, he had determined while still a beat cop in Brandon, was the most dangerous speed a person could travel on a public roadway. He quickly checked where the red needle was pointing on his speedometer. Steady at 140 kilometres an hour. Even his status as an ex-law enforcement member didn't protect him from speeding tickets, and he had been stopped his fair share over the years. But surprisingly few tickets . . . only three. He knew that Highway 3 had the fewest Mounties on it of any paved roadway in the province. The nearest detachments were miles off the road in larger neighbouring towns, but they were not anywhere near where he was going. It is probably because of that very same light police presence that he is off to a small community just a stone's throw from the United States border in the very southern portion of the province.

This was a great road to go fast. Of course, because the highway also boasted the smallest population of any paved roadway in the province, the maintenance of it was relatively light. Tick Smith carefully weaved his car around the potholes and breaks in the pavement, never turning off the cruise control. He sped up to get around another slow driver before he got bogged down in more mid-morning traffic.

To the spot where they had found the girl, Tick figured he would make it in less than 60 minutes, at his current speed.

The driving gave him an opportunity to mull over the frantic conversation earlier in the morning that caused him to bounce out of bed.

"How far are you from a town called Kaleida?"

"Sorry, where?"

"It's called Kaleida, I think." There was a short pause, then McKinnon came back on the phone, "Yeah, called Kaleida. It's about 90 minutes south and west of Winnipeg. I've got it on the map here. It's off of Highway 3. Says on the map it's about eight kilometers east of the town of Manitou, on Highway 3. Then south." The question was asked again, "How long until you can get there?"

"Just past Manitou," Tick had done some quick calculations in his head, which was still pushing the gauze of sleep out. "I can be there in about an hour and a half. That is the end of the earth, you know?"

"All right, good." McKinnon heard Tick breathing heavy, stifling a yawn on the line. "Sorry to call so early Tick. It's got to be what, 7:30 there?"

"Yeah, but that means it's 5:30 in the morning where you are. It must be a positive hit?"

"It is. Our guy has poked his head up out of whatever hole he was in." Halfway across the country, the retired chief could hear papers being shuffled quickly, some mumbling, then the phone being repositioned. "A 911 operator took the call from him at 7:46 last night."

"Well, he's holding true, and making the phone calls."

"True, but this one was a little different. The officer in charge had a hell of time tracking me down. You, I don't think he gets the connection to you at all yet. Through the departmental grapevine though, that young officer that dropped off the files last fall," McKinnon and Smith had paused to try and remember his name. "What the hell was his name, Tick?"

"One minute, I'm thinking." Tick had pictured the case file material that was lying on every possible flat surface around his house. He was hoping to see the young constable's face again, wishing his name would jump out of the printed words and pictures. When he remembered how overburdened the man was at his front door, the name came to him. "It was Langner."

"Right. Anyway, this Constable Langner remembered the two of us. He called me last night. I've been on the phone since then trying to nail it down."

There had been more shuffling of papers, then a mechanical sound near the mouthpiece. "Here, let me play you the conversation with the 911 operator. Like I said, the call came in about 11 hours ago."

Smith listened with absolute fascination to the voice on the phone. It was twice removed from original now . . . over the cell phone to the 911 operator and again relayed back to him from Kamloops. The man's voice had held the same inflections, the same tones and pacing. It was eerie with foreboding, especially how it ended. But everything was the same. Tick listened to the short conversation, then had asked McKinnon to replay it.

For a couple of minutes neither man had said anything. It was Tick who broke the silence. "Okay, so what's the situation on the ground?"

"I don't know a whole lot buddy, except we have a deceased woman in her early 30s. She was found in a rural area by a passing farmer. She was dropped off the side of a road, well away from prying eyes and ears. That's about it for now. When you get there, you can get filled in. But it's interesting the phone call to 911 though."

"It sounds as though he was pissed at this woman. Ya think?" asked Tick Smith.

One thousand kilometers away, McKinnon had shrugged his shoulders, "My guess, he must have been planning this killing for a while and the woman, uh, what's her name, Cora Douglas, spoiled his fun. She died on him in the trunk of the car before he could do his thing." McKinnon paused again, while he shuffled some more papers in front of him. "From early reports, her mouth and nose were full of vomit. So, she died enroute to the isolated spot he was going to do her at."

"Well, that was rude of her, wasn't it?"

"Yeah. Long before he had the opportunity to sink his teeth into her, which was in all probability a mercy.

So, all winter he's been getting ready to get started again in the spring; waiting for the snow to melt; the warmth of the sun to heat up the earth, and then pow!! All of that patience, that planning is for nothing. Kind of like a dropped egg. She's taken the thrill away by having the poor taste to die before he managed to take that last breath out of her mouth." He had paused for a moment, then picked up on the last thought, "I suppose I would have been pissed as well."

Tick pondered all the information he had been given then asked, "How did you guys identify her so fast? ID with her at the site?"

More shuffling of papers across three provinces. "She was reported missing from work at about supper time last night. They were expecting her back for a Friday donut party and she was bringing the donuts. Her car was found by the Winnipeg Police Service shortly afterwards in the parking lot of a mall. All of her ID was inside it, along with her purse, money, goods. When she was found, we confirmed her photo ID."

"We are lucky you know," Tick had mused over the telephone.

"How's that?"

"We have another shot at him and very soon after his killing this time." Tick shook his head as he thought more about the situation, they now found themselves in. "Again, something is off on this one. Jim, you are a professional, right?"

"Right?" McKinnon had answered but wasn't quite sure where the man on the telephone was going with the question.

"Our guy is a serial killer. This is his job. His whole vocation. Everything else that he does is to support that one single job. In his mind, everything else is just fluff next to it. Everything else is filler. He doesn't care about anything or anyone else in his life, except the killing. He's a professional, make no mistake about that. Like you and like me." Tick had thought about that for a moment, "Okay more like you now, but he is very good at what he does. And like you, he can't afford to get pissed at every little setback that confronts him. You and I know how difficult it is to do the job, when emotion clouds the vision, masks the goal."

"Tick."

"I just don't get this."

"What do you mean?" asked McKinnon.

"Up until now, this guy has never shown any emotion. Professional. Right from the beginning last year with that family out your way. He has been an emotionally dead fish, like a carcass washed up on the beach. Except for the little notes he has passed along, there has been nothing. But I've always thought that those notes were more contrived than filled with emotions that were genuine. This guy is cold. He just thought that this was the sort of thing a serial killer should do. Taunt his pursuer. Egging him on. But the notes were flat, there was no . . ." he couldn't put his finger on it. Now, for the first time he realized what was wrong with all of those notes. The one little thing that stood out as being different. "It was like he was reading a book on how to apply pressure but didn't really have the emotional capability to pull it off. He really didn't care if I caught him or not. Or he really didn't think I could ever catch him. Either way, he just didn't care, so he kept poking at us with the notes."

"So how did you feel about the notes, these cold fish papers?"

"Nothing. They irritated me, that's all. I suppose

you could say my lack of emotion was in response to his emotional vagrancy." Smith was amazed that all that came out of his mouth. He had thought to himself, 'It really does pay to read all those psychological books.'

"Well, he has found some emotions now Tick. That was one pissed off serial killer on the phone last night."

"I would agree with you." Tick had noted that his travel bag, packed near the foot of the bed as it always was, was ready to go at a moment's notice. He contemplated grabbing the hollow point ammunition for his gun from the locker in the root cellar, but felt he wouldn't need it.

"Can you get to the crime scene near Kaleida? Can you get there right now?"

"I can leave as soon as I shit, shower and shave."

"Cool," McKinnon had nodded his head, suddenly realizing he had said 'cool' and wondering if his kids would be happy with that. They often mused about the fact that he was a little rigid when it came to picking up new things. Stuck in the rigid mentality of the force. Tough place to be. "I'm flying out in a couple of hours. I should be able to join you by about coffee time this afternoon."

"Cool." Tick had smiled. It did sound rather cool. "Are you bringing anyone else with you, anybody from your team?"

"No. They can do a lot of work sitting at their desks here. They have a first-class major crimes unit in Winnipeg. For now, we will piggyback on their investigation. There will be no trouble."

Tick had thought for a moment, then questioned McKinnon. "They don't know me. How will I gain access to the crime scene. I'm going to need them to allow me in."

"There is a guy, the sergeant in charge. His name is Pete Martin. Ask for him, I'll clear it from this end. You'll be okay. It doesn't hurt that you are ex-police. You may want to remember your old badge. Just to help the cause."

Tick knew exactly where his old shield was. He glanced across the living room to the north wall, directly across from the large picture window. It was still housed in large oak frame, that also contained his ID wallet and a brass plaque bearing the years he had been on the job. He said, "I'll have to figure out how to get it out of the frame, Jim."

"I was kidding Tick."

"Jesus man, don't you know how old I am. You could have caused a stroke by making me think that much, this early."

"Sorry." McKinnon had paused for a moment. Tick heard the pause. It was deliberate. It was the reason for the call. One of many. "There is one more thing buddy."

"What's that?"

"He's close now, to you. He's really close."

"So?"

"Take care, that's all Tick, just watch your ass. We're entering a new game here with this guy. A new phase. You said so yourself, there was emotion in this one. This sudden filling of the vacant emotional pool, to paraphrase you. That scares me. Overtaxed emotions often lend themselves to unpredictability. And unpredictable behaviour can be very violent and reactionary."

"I've been closer to him before. At the beginning. So now, after everything else, this doesn't bother me much. I'll be all right."

"I'll see you later."

"Back to the bodies." Tick mused, not really expecting an answer, and getting none. He placed the handset back into the cradle when heard McKinnon hang up the phone. Then he turned for the bedroom and his travel bag.

His car accelerated slightly as he thought about the conversation with McKinnon. The adrenalin somehow managed to force his right leg a little bit forward. His speed was edging on 160. He allowed a breath and backed off the throttle, allowing the car to settle back at 140. He had a small smile as he sped through the countryside.

"We *are* closer."

The white Royal Canadian Mounted Police cruisers blocked the gravel road, about a kilometer from the village of Kaleida. There were two, with the new age recruits standing with their flashlights in one hand, and the other resting on their firearms. The one that ambled up to Tick was at least 250 pounds, with two or three chins folding away from his lower lip. He seemed to be pouting about being stuck this far from the action. The second officer, a woman, with an attractive way of filling out her uniform, stayed back near the vehicles, and the protection of the shotgun. Tick couldn't get a good look at her.

"Good morning, sir, this road is closed today. Where are you off to?"

Tick pointed his fingers down the road, beyond the cruisers, and looked up as innocently as he could. "Down there."

"Sorry sir, road is closed today. This is an official crime scene, so I'm going to have to ask you to turn around and take another route."

"They are expecting me," Tick squinted at the brass badge on the man's tunic, "Constable Ayote. My name is Smith, Tick."

"Tick?"

"Old nickname."

"What's your real name?"

Tick told him, and the fat officer toddled off back to the cars and his radio. He leaned into the cruiser, grunting loudly as he wedged himself behind the wheel. He yanked the handset out of its holder and said something into the radio. He waited for a moment or two, then looked up at Tick. He nodded again, then hung up the handset. His partner leaned into the car, and obviously asked what the hell was going on. She shrugged, and headed back to her car, got in, fired it up, and backed it far enough off the roadway to allow Tick's car through.

"Sir," Constable Ayote wheezed, having run back to the car, "Sergeant Martin is waiting for you down the road. The crime scene is about three quarters of a click straight ahead. You can't miss it. Really."

Tick pointed to the large area just out of sight, a halo of emergency lights flashing in the daylight. "There?"

"Yes sir."

"Thanks constable."

"It's a pleasure to meet you sir." He smiled, and the sweat could be seen blotting the collar of his uniform.

"It's been a pleasure to be stopped by you, Constable." Tick smiled, as he rolled up his window, and started down the road. He waved at the female officer, who did no more than continue to stare straight through him and raise a single finger from the trigger guard in salute. Smith thought, 'At least it wasn't the . . . what did the neighbourhood kids call it? Oh yeah, the swear finger.'

Tick Smith actually stopped the car, about 200 yards from the crime scene. Constable Ayote was right; you definitely couldn't miss this one. In his career, Smith had been to many crime scenes, many more than he could definitively remember. He didn't have to search his memory for anything like this, because he knew there wouldn't be anything like it. Often investigators, when first on a scene, would compare it to crime scenes in their past. It gave them a grounding of sorts with what actions to take first to preserve and analyze what was laid before them. It was a step saver.

But not this time. There would be no steps saved.

"Real life," Tick said out loud. "It's way fucking weirder than fiction."

Ahead of him on the road, were at least a dozen vehicles of one shape or another, cruisers, sport utility vehicles, mini-vans, and cube vans. The lights on the top of the cruisers, and dashes of SUVs were pushing through the remaining morning mist that speckled the scene. The haphazardly parked vehicles, were spewing exhaust from their idling engines, adding to the surreal scene. From this far away, Smith could see the dew resting on the vehicles, softening their shine. 'Been here all night,' he thought.

Dozens of people were milling about with either officers in uniform or those in clean white forensic jumpers. Almost all had clip boards, with pencils and pens hanging from them. Several were standing together, huddled in little groups, talking about who knows what. Some of the conversations were animated with laughter and wild hand and arm motions. Others were centered around one man and his clipboard.

But behind, haphazardly illuminated by the

emergency lights that were blanketing the area, was the most unlikely scene he had come across in nearly 40 years in the business.

A giant John Deere four-wheel-drive tractor was parked at a funny angle on the roadway. Its front wheels turned slightly to the left and overhead lights pointing north. It looked like a giant David, standing off against a whole group of tiny Goliaths.

Behind the behemoth, was the largest cultivator Tick Smith had ever seen. Even at 200 yards, the size of it was astounding to the firmly 'non-agriculturally friendly' retired cop. The tractor he knew would tower over him, but the cultivator behind the tractor dwarfed it. The spider-legged cultivator arms were resting at an odd angle and the one extension piece, from the center section had a large, grey sheet draped over sharp talons. The sheet was lightly flapping in the cool morning breeze, suspended several feet in the air. It was obvious she had been picked up by it.

Tick shook his head, thinking she would have been no match. No contest. The John Deere and the massive equipment in tow, had won.

Away from the crowd was one man in uniform, and though Tick couldn't see if there were any stripes on the epaulets, he knew that would be Sergeant Martin. He had the air of being the guy in charge. Others, just in their body language, were deferring to him for direction and thought.

"Mr. Smith?"

It was a formal greeting. It was one that Tick hoped wouldn't be indicative of the way he would be treated here. A formality, not really having been invited into the scene, but allowed to peer over the shoulders of the 'real' officers who were doing the work. Tick knew he had treated crime scene hangers-on like that, and for a moment wished he had treated them a little kinder in the past. Maybe that would have given him leeway into the way he was going to be treated here. Kind of a pay-it-forward situation.

"Tick." He extended his hand, and gave his best 'thank God, you've let me into this sacred site' smile.

"Tick," it almost made the older man blush, the sergeant actually bowed slightly, "Pete Martin. Good to meet you, sir."

They shook hands for a moment, sizing each other up. Tick broke the grip, and the silence. "No one calls me sir, except the kids that come around the house asking for money for some charity. It's just Tick."

"Okay, Tick." Martin pointed his head at the site and asked if Tick wanted to get a closer look. "You'll have to put a suit on Tick. But you are welcome to observe."

"Thanks, Pete. I appreciate that."

The two men were quiet while the older man slipped into the reinforced paper suit, as dignifiedly as possible. There were a number of people looking at him, wondering no doubt, what the hell the old guy was doing at a major crime scene. Martin had no such questions. He had heard about Tick. He had heard about McKinnon. He had heard about the killer. He was very happy to have a little experienced help in the investigation. Urban legend has it that the killer had taken apart the old man's wife's first husband. That's how they met. He had also heard that the old man still gets Christmas and birthday cards from the killer. Unofficial scuttlebutt has it the killer and Tick Smith have some sort of thing going. Who knows?

"You've been after this guy for a long time, Tick?" It was stating the obvious.

Tick answered with an obvious answer. "I've been

after this guy nearly my whole working career." He looked up at the sergeant, standing above him, waiting patiently for Tick to finish the final adjustments of the suit. "I'm ready to finish this, though. I am really tired of chasing this prick."

"No doubt. When did he first kill?"

"That I am aware of, in 1967."

"Wow!" Martin did the math. "That's nearly 40 years. That has to be some kind of record." He caught Tick watching him, assessing his reaction. Pete Martin was suddenly embarrassed. "Sorry. That's a long time to be after one ghost."

"You're telling me." Tick laughed, then put his hand reassuringly on the RCMP officer's shoulder. "Like I said, I am ready to excise this ghost. So, let's have look and get started. Okay?"

"Absolutely." Martin held his hand out almost in a formal manner, to guide Tick to the site.

"What happened? Anything jump out at you?" Tick asked.

Martin pointed at a man, in a plaid shirt and jeans, huddled outside one cruiser, with a jean jacket on to keep warm. "That's Walter Kowalski. He was just finishing some field work last night when he had a problem with the left set of shovels. The hydraulics got jammed somehow, so he decided to take an alternate route home. This way, according to Kowalski, would take a little longer, but had no fences near the roadway to get everything caught up on.

"So, he comes tripping down here, raising and lowering the outside arms to try and get it working properly and snags on something. Kind of like trolling at fifteen miles an hour."

"He said he was going fifteen miles an hour? That is pretty quick."

"He's got nothing to hide and it appears was in a rush to get home. Who knew there was a body in the long grass?" Martin breathed heavily, arranging his thoughts. "So, he snags her and pulls his tractor, cultivator and everything into that little arrangement you see there." He pointed at the scrambled metal in the ditch.

"How did he know he had picked her up? Her body mass wouldn't affect the equipment or his tractor that much."

Martin shrugged his shoulders. "Said he was just lifting the outer shovels to see if he could force a section that was giving him grief, when he saw something stuck in it."

Both men looked up at the equipment and the flapping cover sheet that was suspended in mid-air. Martin continued the explanation.

"So, he climbed down from the cab of the tractor and then monkeyed up that set of cultivators. It was about then he saw what was caught up there. Mr. Kowalski shit himself understandably and pretty much fell back down."

Both men turned to the dazed farmer in the back seat of the cruiser. He wasn't paying attention to them, but staring at his hands that were kneaded together on the lap of his dirty overalls.

"I mean, those shovels really did their job on our victim. He wasn't sure what it was at first, but the closer he got to it, he realized it was a person. Well, most of her. According to his statement, and you can read it later, he sat down on the ground and just allowed the tremors in his body to subside a little. Then he called 911."

Martin shook his head. "Would've scared the shit out of me, too. I mean, that piece of equipment did a nice job of tearing her up."

"Yeah," Smith replied, but wasn't really listening anymore — he was looking at the scene in front of him.

"When are you planning to get the girl out?"

"The medical examiner was here last night, so maybe a bit later this morning they hope. Once the ident guys are done. Or maybe when the Kamloops guy gets here." Martin looked up at the police tape that was hanging eight feet above their heads, and said, "You want to have a look? We were kind of waiting on you guys."

"I do."

"Come around this way," Martin said, "there is a ladder set up against the side of the unit." He pointed up, "We have secured her upper torso where it was lodged. The rest of her was back there," Martin turned and pointed to a second corral of tape 30 yards away directly behind the tractor and cultivator. The tape was blowing lightly in the breeze, with a now extinguished perimeter of lights set up around it. Somewhere nearby were the unmistakable sounds of portable generators idling away, providing power for any equipment that was still necessary for the investigators.

"You didn't say, how did Kowalski know there was something caught? He couldn't have gotten up here?" Tick climbed as he talked, inching up the silver ladder.

"No," Martin said. "When he climbed up as much as he could on the equipment to look at what was caught there, he noticed that it was her arms hanging from one of the front row shovels. Both were connected still to one another, like a daisy chain, joined at the wrist. It was, well, you best have a look yourself."

"Sorry, Pete, this has been a long night for you."

Tick said quietly.

"Tough day for all of us Tick. Yours has just lasted for a few more years than ours. No harm, no foul." Martin looked embarrassed at the situation. But at the same time, was glad this wasn't one of those old two-by-four up-the-ass kind of cops. He had seen a bushel of them. They weren't any fun and couldn't find their own ass at a crime scene, despite the handy piece of lumber protruding from the butt. It would make things a lot easier on down the investigative road that this was a good guy caught up in a bad situation. It would work better for everyone.

"It's not pretty Tick." Smith looked down at him. Martin wasn't looking up at him, but rather appeared to be focusing on anything other than the body. "On the shovels, it isn't pretty."

"Thanks Pete." Then Tick turned quickly away, and up the last couple of steps to where the ladder was securely tied to the cultivator arm. There must have been at least a half a dozen ropes hanging off it. And as he moved up, there was no wobbling or jiggling that is normally associated with climbing a ladder. At the top he jostled a couple of times to get comfortable, then reached for the blanket.

Under the sheet, Cora was firmly wedged between the shovels of the cultivator. Her eyes, open and glazed. Her left arm hanging loosely straight down from the shoulder. The duct tape was still holding her hands together and the right was severed at the shoulder. Actually, severed isn't the right term, it was just pulled clean out. The arm was dangling straight towards the ground, tissue and bone exposed. But the most prominent feature was the yellow handled screwdriver driven between her eyes, right up to the hilt. She looked like a unicorn. He hated himself for allowing that thought, but there was no escaping it. Someone had wrapped some white gauze around the handle, then around her head, ensuring it stayed as she had been found.

That same old sadness that always overcame Tick, swept down now from afar, and enveloped him in despair. To see what a human being can do to another human being, always disturbed him greatly. Though the killer hadn't done most of the carnage he was looking at, his actions caused it to happen.

"The fucker will pay."

"What's that?"

Tick smiled down at the sergeant standing on the grass below him. "I said 'the fucker will pay.' The guy that brought Cora Douglas to this spot will pay. I didn't realize I had said it out loud."

"What about the screwdriver?" he yelled down.

Martin thought for a moment. Tick could see the pain of the memory seep into his mind. The RCMP officer looked back up, "I assumed it was driven there by him." He looked up at Smith, who was still examining the body. "You heard the 911 call?" Smith nodded. "You know, we may have actually heard the moment he did that."

Tick was nodding. That certainly was in the realm of possibility.

He spread his arms outwards in an arc. "There were no other tools anywhere around here?" Martin shook his head as he looked back up at the retired officer on the ladder, peering around the shovels that were individually tagged for photo-identification.

"So, he drove that thing into her head?" Tick asked.

"That is the general thought. There are smudged prints on the hilt, but I am unconvinced they will lead anywhere. I will have the Winnipeg guys look into that pretty quick."

He looked back at the secondary scene. He angled his head towards it, "The cell phone was beside the rest of the body back there. Was a little hard to find at first, because the cultivator churned up the soil pretty well. The phone was damaged fairly severely, so that made it even harder to find."

Tick looked at the tire tracks that were leading back to the second site. "The equipment couldn't have broken it?"

"I don't think so Tick," Martin explained. "The tracks are close, but don't pass right over it. Besides we lost the signal before we could really get a good read on it. We knew it was near the Kaleida cell tower, but that is about it. We had a member out here driving the roads. He was about 10 miles east when we got the call from our farmer."

"No one has touched it?"

"Guaranteed."

Smith looked down at him, "I meant the screwdriver."

Martin smiled. "That's what I meant. I can say that with a very high degree of confidence no one has touched it." Martin knew it would have taken a big man to pull that thing out. And he wasn't talking about strength. Plus, it was to stay exactly where it was until the autopsy. "Guaranteed," the RCMP officer added. "The only thing we did was secure it for the trip."

Martin looked introspective, then asked. "Has this guy ever done something like that?"

"No. He prefers a knife or similar sharp object of some sort. That was probably going to be her fate. I think he was just a little emotional about his plans going wrong. All the months of planning, and suddenly, poof! Gone!" He looked back at the agricultural equipment, then the second scene a few yards away. Tick Smith leaned back into the equipment, distancing himself a little from the dead girl. He said, “I think he was just pissed at her for having died before he planned. I think Pete, our boy had a temper tantrum.”

33
MAY 2003

I spent the trip home trying to re-think my strategy for the next killing. There had to be a better way to get around the problem of quieting down the victim without causing her to die from asphyxiation. But I couldn't come up with it offhand, though you think I would have by now. I do have some experience in these matters. But, now I have to consider the age factor and how to adjust for the injuries. There were too many caustic emotions floating around in my head, all fighting for the right to be in the forefront and consuming all of my valuable attention. The clearest of all emotions was anger.

In the car, on the dark road home, was the first time that I had a moment to think clearly. Before that, emotion consumed and steered my every thought.

I couldn't get over how quickly it got dark. That took me completely by surprise. Once the girl was dead, I had returned to the front seat of the Celebrity, mulling things over and reflecting on the position that I was in. The only sounds I could hear were the ticking of the motor, as it cooled down, the wind sucking through the hedgerows, and small sounds of crickets, far away. It was so quiet.

"Fucking bitch!"

I slammed my fist into the steering wheel and heard the cheap plastic crack, as it strained under the impact. Looking over my shoulder, I turned slightly and yelled towards the trunk, "The perfect plan, you bitch, and you completely fucked it up!"

Once I cooled down a little, I went to the back of the car, and looked in on her. Her skin was very white, pale against the blue dress that was tangled around her and the grey of the cheap garbage bags that lined the trunk. Both her eyes were open, staring towards the back of the car.

I can't describe the frustration I felt at how this whole event changed. I shook my head in dejection.

"Fuck!"

The disappointment I felt swept through me with the sensation of a coiled up, black snake. For a moment, I stepped back from the open trunk and the dead girl inside. Once again, I could feel my muscles tensing, ready to spring into action. But all that adrenalin wasn't needed, and it would take some time to bleed the hormone off. A shadow began to push into my vision as the darkness started to make its presence known.

The planning worked well — but was completely wasted now. The discipline — wasted as well. I couldn't form the right word to how I was feeling, but disappointed just didn't seem full enough. Angry enough.

I walked away from the car, about 10 feet, forcing myself not to look at the car, or the trunk. A few more feet away and I found myself looking at the farmland that spread away from me on all sides. It was familiar, the aroma of farmland. I smelled the fresh dark hint of black, rich earth being worked, ready for the spring planting. As I watched the sun stretching down for its final run into the land, it suddenly dawned on me how long I had been walking.

7:38.

"Holy shit! It's nearly eight," I yelled and turned on my heel, looking back at the car. It was small, and a long way away. "Ah, shit." I yelled again. Immediately I picked up my pace into an aggressive gate, metronomically getting closer to the car with each step. All that walking in the winter and spring seemed to pay dividends as my arms and legs chugged in perfect synchronization. But with every step I took back towards the car, I was coming up with new ways to humiliate her. It was a three-minute walk, so I had plenty of opportunity and an ever-increasing motive to hate her.

When I got to the car, I grabbed my go kit. Inside it, I selected the first thing I saw, a heavy flat-tipped screwdriver. It had a rubberized yellow acrylic handle and was about eight inches long. It looked new, shiny and bright in the bag. I had bought it specifically for this day at a grocery store. It was in a bin of a hundred other generic brand tools. I have to say I smiled when I felt it in my gloved hand. "Let Tick try to find out where that one came from."

With a sharp movement, I rammed the zipper closed and tossed the bag back onto the floor behind the driver's seat. After a short pause, to vainly try and calm down, I turned and headed for the back of the car. Looking down on the dead woman, the screwdriver bouncing, vibrating in hand, I yelled, "Un-fucking-believable!"

For a moment I tried again to will my temper below the point of boiling. I knew there was still a lot to do and so needed to keep my wits about me. I didn't need to be falling off the deep end just yet. Pinetree was still two hours from where I stood, and it was getting dark quickly. I knew I had to finish up here right away. I couldn't take a chance on my exposure and really didn't want to drive a long distance in the dark. Another acceptance of the limits of my aging body.

I picked up the woman's cell phone and dialed. The police operator came on after three rings and I began to speak. But as I spoke the anger again welled up inside me, finally bursting through the thin plastic veneer of calm. As I finished the call to 9-1-1, I whirled around, took three small rapid adrenalized steps towards the trunk of the car and in a single fluid movement, brought the screwdriver down cleanly into the girl's forehead. It made a small sound, like a mallet hitting a steak on the cutting board.

Ok, I have to tell you, it was kind of an incredible strike. For a moment, I stood at the back of the car amused at the sight. It really quite amazed me, the accuracy I was able to deliver in the blind rage that consumed me. I had been aiming for and had hit, the center of her forehead. The vent of anger had accomplished what it was designed to do. Immediately, I felt purged, lighter, more in control again. As I stared down at the woman, the emotions began to drain away slowly, pouring onto the gravel. The violent explosion helped in relieving the pressure inside me, but I still felt empty. Wanting. I knew that I needed to kill her and was angry that she took that away from me.

She was heavier coming out of the trunk, having to lift her over the threshold with the necessity of being careful to not re-injure myself. All of those repetitive lifting exercises every morning for months allowed the entire movement to be done without aggravating any of my still healing injuries. She landed heavily on her back. Her light brown hair bouncing slightly with the head when it came to rest. After double checking the contents of the trunk, I slammed the lid down, then thought of the screwdriver. Looking down at the prone figure I muttered, "Fuck it," to no one in particular. The screwdriver was traceable to about 200 grocery stores across the country, and probably in the U.S. as well. I was pretty confident it couldn't be traced back to me. It was innocuous. So would be about as trackable as a single white piece of paper. I looked down at the girl and the perpendicular projectile pointing out of her forehead.

"That ought to keep Tick and the guys busy."

Pausing again I thought about how easy it had been to grab her. Through years of doing so, I had found that the entrances at shopping malls near the grocery store, were the best bet at finding and taking a person. And the best times are either right around supper when there are a million people milling about, or mid-afternoon when the exact opposite was true. People came bursting into the parking lot, because they forgot some little thing for the big meal they planned. They are so focused on getting into the store to grab their brussels sprouts that they focus on the door ahead of them. Never on what was around them.

It was simply a matter of waiting on the bench near the entrance doorway, waiting for a frazzled person to come streaking by, then following them to their car. For me, procuring a victim usually took about half a hour. My personal record was four minutes. But that was at Christmas, and it was in the Seventies. People back then didn't really get the whole personal security thing. Now, it usually took a little longer. Even though I was older, a grandpa, and to them a little more trustworthy.

But I also knew that once I had them, they were lost, usually never to be found. At least until recently. Now I enjoyed playing with Tick and McKinnon.

I knew it was risky using my own vehicle, but there was one thing that I had going for me. The police would never be able to link this old Chevy to any of the killings. No one noticed a mid-80's beige, four-door with a nice-looking older man in the driver's seat, funny little hat jauntingly tilted to one side. If I may say so, a pretty good looking older man. I kept up with the traffic flow on the road, always used my signals and never exceeded the speed limit. So, for all the police knew, I was just another old guy out for a coffee or grocery run.

They wouldn't have suspected in a million years what I was up to. And a fringe benefit of my age was the older I got, the further away from their radar I became. I still smile because it presented itself as almost the perfect scenario. Who would think that the man behind the wheel of the Chevrolet Celebrity would be a monster who had been hunted for decades across the country? Since initially walking away from the business, I had pondered the question of why I stopped. Other than the technology law enforcement was using would have made the work increasingly harder to get away with.

The key advantage for me, was the lack of any tangible links between the crimes. Everyone was chosen at random with fate playing a heavy hand in determining the eventual outcome. But discipline also was critical to managing to stay off the police radar, and in particular Tick Smith's radar, for so many years.

As I walked slowly back towards Pinetree from my parking spot, the day was once again mulling through my head. I was no longer upset with how things had turned out. Well, that may be a little too soft. I was still ticked off about it, but the blackness had bled off during the long quiet drive home. I was thoroughly frustrated, though, with the events and the way they turned out. Tired from the long day and the late hour, I was ready for a good cup of coffee and finally bed. As much work as I had invested into the recovery of my body over the previous few months, for some reason, each and every injury seemed to prick itself alive as I approached the building. I needed to give my healing body some time to recover from the exertions of the day.

A sweeping memory of Mary overcame me as I stepped into the outer entranceway. She would have been accommodating, even though I was walking back into Pinetree at nearly midnight. Her memory caused a small pierce in my heart and an involuntary jab of pain in my right hip. For some reason, I immediately started to favour it. I knew though, it was a shadow pain, not real. I wondered how the mind could trigger so many unconscious things to seem so real, including the pain of the accident. For a moment, a flood of memories came, of the times Mary and I had made love. Then, in a millisecond, they were gone. Wisps of smoke. Replaced with the black vacuum of an experienced kill.

"That day is done," I said aloud. Then I realized that a lot more than that had drawn to a conclusion. This wasn't a home any longer, it was just a place to hang my hat for the time being. It held no emotional attachment anymore, not that it held any real shakes before that. Other than Mary and Kenny. It was just four walls, a bed, three square meals a day and a noisy damn roommate. It was now just a day camp from which to run my operations.

After buzzing for security to let me in, I strolled by the brooding guard. No one stopped me from meandering down the quiet hallways. They would all be in the basement, watching TV or reading comics while relying on the call buttons to summon them back to work. And that was only if one of the residents had the guts to do so in the middle of the night. You never knew the reaction you would get at that time. Along with all the other residents, I knew it was better to wait until morning with an issue, rather than take the wrath of the uneducated moron who was paid $15 an hour.

Walking past Mrs. Robert's room on the way to mine, I noticed the light on over the bed. For some reason, I stopped and crept back to the edge of the steel doorframe. She was sitting up, reading a book of some sort. I couldn't make out the title but could see it was a hardcover. My eyes were too tired to read clearly, and the constant movement of her shaking hands compounded the problem. Again, I have no reason for this, but I stood staring at her for a few minutes, not moving, or daring to breathe. She read quietly for a moment, focused on each page. Then every couple of minutes she would flip a page in an elongated noisy shuffle. She would then adjust herself in the bed and settle in once again.

I have to say she was an attractive woman. Not in the way Mary was, but in her own fashion Mrs. Roberts was a fine-looking woman. A little skinnier than Mary, no more than skin and bones really. But she had high cheekbones, and her hair was down on her shoulders. It was something that I hadn't seen in her before. Every time she had approached me, I had blown her off, stayed somewhat aloof. The memory of Mary was just too raw, too present. I guess my grieving was continuing, but I was still unfamiliar with what that meant. I felt pain jab me sharply when the thought of her crept up on me. But it was like I was observing pain, not really experiencing it.

All these thoughts rolled about for a few seconds more and then I felt that it was still a matter of bad timing. As I turned to leave, she spoke.

"Are you going to stand there all night, Ivan McDonald, or are you going to come in for a visit?"

"Wha . . . ," I answered and turned quickly around, facing her. The book was now in her lap and she was staring directly at me. "Sorry, I was just passing by, and saw you reading."

"It didn't take two minutes to decide that I was reading, Ivan."

Given all the events of the days, her comment caught me off guard. I think I was embarrassed at how shallow and inadequate the comment was and felt my face flush. "Sorry, I suppose I was staring."

"That's okay Ivan. For some reason I couldn't sleep tonight. I am usually a good sleeper. Down at nine or 10 and out for the night." She shrugged her thin shoulders, "Tonight, I don't know. I just couldn't keep my eyes closed." Mrs. Roberts motioned to the chair beside the bed. "Why don't you come in and sit down for a few minutes. I don't think the two of us are going to be sleeping much the rest of the night, so we might as well keep each other company."

Again, Mrs. Roberts was catching me off my game. I waved my hand in front of me, "No, that's okay. I really should be going back to my room." I am sure that when I looked at her, I smiled slightly, "And besides, I am a little embarrassed I was staring at you. I just never saw you in . . . well . . ."

Mrs. Roberts smiled slightly, "How?"

"Well," I started, searching for the right words, "casual. You are usually all dressed up, ready for the charity ball without a hair out of place." I pointed at the bed. "This is nice."

"So, come in Ivan. Let's chat." Mrs. Roberts smoothed down the covers on the bed, then motioned at the doorway I was standing in. So many different emotions and thoughts were swimming around my head. I really didn't know what to do next. In or out.

Mrs. Roberts smiled demurely, "And close the door behind you."

For some reason, at that moment it dawned on me that I didn't know her first name. I think it was normal for us, because everyone was called by their last name only. An alien would be confused to find that in a seniors' home, everyone was named Mister or Missus.

"I don't know," I said, while my eyes quickly darted to the nametag on the door, "Beryl. When Mary died, a lot of things were put in the ground with her. It's been a long time."

Beryl Roberts stared at me a moment. A look of resolve could be seen on her face. "It's been 18 years for me, Ivan, the last time I made love," she explained. Her smooth face, with not a hint of embarrassment showing, smiled a little more. "Then, it really wasn't making love. It was just sex. Tom, my husband, had died a couple of years before. I was lonely. Joined a singles club, and what do you know, ended up in bed with a man who didn't love, or even respect me. It was just sex pure and simple." Beryl looked down at the sheets. "And it wasn't even all that good."

"I don't know what to say Beryl." Once again, I found myself struggling for a moment to find the right words. None came so I just shrugged my shoulders and stared at the woman. "I wasn't looking for anything, much less an explanation."

"Close the door, Ivan" she repeated. "Put your bag beside the washroom door." Beryl Roberts held out her hand to me, "Then join me in bed. If nothing else, just to sleep together for a while."

The small bag made very little noise as it slid across the polished linoleum to the washroom door.

The door quietly closed, hissing as the hydraulic cylinder smoothed its operation.

34
MAY 2003

McKinnon had arrived a little past three, with a rookie member at the wheel of the Crown Victoria. The nearly two-hour trip had left him feeling a little nauseous. It was an old affliction he couldn't explain but was omnipresent. He couldn't be a passenger in a vehicle . . . period. Just couldn't do it. Over years of looking at the problem with a sort of forced detachment, McKinnon had finally felt he came up with a reason; he just didn't feel in control. This trip he was in the front seat, which wasn't as bad, but if he got stuck in the back seat, real trouble.

Normally he would have asked to drive, explaining the problem diplomatically. He had done it before, emphasized that it wasn't a matter of lack of trust, but rather a matter of keeping the cookies down rather than having to stop the car to upchuck onto the shoulder of the road. But on this trip from the Winnipeg airport to the crime scene, he needed to get up to speed with the initial reports the young officer had brought with him from the Major Crimes Unit. It was understandably thin, but he still went over it several times, to memorize the details.

"She's gone?"

It was half a question but more, a simple fact.

Tick turned to see McKinnon asking the question as he got out of the cruiser, file folders spilling out with him. Smith answered, "Not all of her." The two men looked at one another for a moment, McKinnon trying to understand the response. But when they pulled up, two things jumped out at him. The girl was still stuck high atop the cultivator with a protective sheet covering her. Below her, Tick Smith was sitting at the bottom of the unit like a protective mother bear over her infant cubs. McKinnon could see the relief in the older man's eyes as they pulled up and stopped about 50 feet away.

"Is there anything left of the lunch?"

Smith paused with a puzzled expression, and looked at the inspector walking towards him, then up at the car. It seemed an out-of-character response from McKinnon. Crass and cold. "Sorry?"

"The lunch, is there anything left? Lunches on our national airlines aren't the best anymore, if you can get them at all. And we didn't get any other than some nuts and cookies the size of my pinkie. We didn't have time to stop on the way out of town, I wanted to get here as soon as possible."

The retired investigator smiled. "They do have drive throughs now, you know. Even out here on the prairie."

"Like I said Tick," McKinnon squared off to the man, "I wanted to get here in a hurry. So, no food?"

Tick shrugged his shoulders, "I don't know, maybe over by the I.D. truck, that's where the table was set up." Smith continued to look at the man who was now standing right in front of him. The pair reached out for a quick handshake, but it felt off to Tick. It was cursory. "Uh, what's going on Jim?"

"I'm fucking hungry Tick. I can't think, I'm so hungry." He motioned to the sheaf of papers inside a manila folder in his left hand, "I read everything the crew managed to get out of the scene on the way here. Actually, I read it about five times. So, I think I'm about up to speed on the general situation here. But I can't think Tick. I've been up for nearly 12 hours with nothing to eat." He started towards the I.D. truck, almost stalking it. He looked at his watch then up at Tick. “Sorry, but really, at this particular moment, eating is more important than the crime scene. I’m no good to it, to the victim, if I can’t think straight. And I need to think straight. Okay?”

“No argument here buddy.” Tick Smith followed the inspector around the back of the truck and found the table was nearly cleared off. Just a few dried-up sandwiches, what looked like chicken or turkey were left sitting exposed and crusty among the withered leaves of lettuce garnish. “Not surprisingly, all of the donuts are long gone,” Tick said, stating the obvious.

“Does no one here understand the concept of re-wrapping the plate after they have eaten?” McKinnon yelled to no one in particular. “Fucking gluttons.” In reaction to that outburst, many of those who were on scene seemed to discover something of particular interest either on the ground or in their notebooks. Guilty, but not really ashamed.

Tick stood nearby, looking for something that didn’t look like it had been in an oven for a couple of hours, with the moisture completely evaporated out of it. There was nothing that looked even remotely edible, but McKinnon managed to shove three or four remnants down his throat, peppering Smith with questions as he ate.

“The screwdriver?”

“I don’t think it was from around here. I think our guy brought it to the scene. It looks new, brand new. Nothing that has been jostling around the trunk of a car through the backroads in rural Manitoba or left outside in the elements for any length of time. It looks like a fairly hefty screwdriver, with, and this is my guess here, about six inches still imbedded in her head. It must have pounded the back of her skull when he drove it in. It won't be removed until the autopsy."

McKinnon nodded, taking in the response, then moved on. "What kind of condition was she in?"

"In what way?" Tick asked.

"Generally, when you got here."

Smith paused while he collected his thoughts. "The ident folks don't think she was sexually assaulted. All of her clothes were more or less intact. Well, at least as far as any fabric that covered a sexually vulnerable spot is concerned, her clothes were still mostly on."

"What was that?" McKinnon asked.

"The impact with the shovels on the cultivator did some pretty significant damage." Smith explained, "but the material and skin came off as a unit. In chunks." He searched his memory for the look of the woman, parts of which were hanging from the huge piece of equipment next to them or lying in the dirt 30 yards away. "Uh Jim, do you want to wait until Pete comes over to run through this?"

McKinnon stole a look over to the officer, who was leaning over a car hood, pen in hand, writing furiously. The two had exchanged a nod, but McKinnon understood that when you are in the middle of something this important, you finished things off. "It's okay Tick, I would like to get your opinions on this. Okay?"

Tick shrugged his shoulders and said, "Sure. The screwdriver, of course, you know about. Right between the eyes, up to the hilt. My personal feeling on that is that he was pissed off that she had died. Well, at least before he had the chance to kill her himself," Smith added.

"Emotional outburst? So, kind of what we talked about this morning."

"Yeah, kind of threw me off too. Up until now, like

I said, we haven't seen a lot of emotion out of this guy. So far, very clinical. The only one before today that was a bit emotional was his first. Other than that, he was honing what he did. Including what he was up to in Kamloops. Do the job and then get the hell out quietly. But this time, with this one, there is the personal message. It was a message he didn't even know he was giving us."

"What's that Tick?" McKinnon asked, still munching on a dried turkey sandwich.

"He's losing it. He may not know it, but he is losing it. There is a definite loss of his emotional control on this killing. How he nabbed her," Tick started to explain, "is still kind of a mystery. I mean how does a guy grab a young woman, broad daylight in the middle of a shopping mall parking lot? It has to be a blitz attack, incapacitate her, then shove her into a trunk and down the road you go. But that takes a certain amount of moxie, doesn't it?" he asked rhetorically. "A certain bravado and confidence. So, my guess here is that he has used that kind of attack before. That may be worth looking into. He has fallen back to an old habit that worked before. It is comfortable. It is practised. It is, however, a definite change in direction from his earlier stuff in the Sixties. Or at least," Tick finished up, "that is my best guess."

The RCMP officer was nodding his head in agreement. McKinnon said, "From what I read on the way out here, no one saw her inside the mall, after the phone conversation with her boss. She just disappeared. Poof?" McKinnon talked as he looked under scrap pieces of paper on the makeshift table, for any other scraps of food. After lifting up the last piece of paper, finding nothing and then tossing it aside, he looked up at Tick, exasperated. "That's all there is?"

"Well, that's all the food anyhow," the retired chief said with a small smile.

McKinnon looked at him plaintively, holding his arms up, palms out like Christ. "Is it too much to ask? Just a little food. Not much, just a couple of morsels? Too much?"

Tick shrugged, then leaned against the van. His arms crossed. "I was hungry when I got here. Remember, you woke me up this morning."

"Uh-huh. You'll remember buddy, that I was already awake, and according to my bedside clock it was about 5:30 in the morning."

"Right," Smith said, watching the inspector follow every possible crumb lead, looking for that one slender piece of food that would satiate his hunger. "Anyway, back to the reason we are all gathered here today, our guy." Tick Smith looked up at the girl still unceremoniously hanging in mid-air then added, "And Cora Douglas. We're here for Cora." The retired inspector reached into his pocket, and pulled out a pair of latex gloves and began the time-honoured process of slipping them on his slender hands. It was a process he could do in his sleep, completely autonomously. This morning, he watched his hands, as they laboured into the protective gloves.

"I don't know if I have told you this already Jim," Smith stopped putting on the gloves when he spoke, "but I think we've got the fucker on the run this time. I think we need to figure out a way to push him a little bit harder. I don't know how. But something else has to make him break discipline the way he has here. After this one, we need to push back. Until now, we have been reactionary to everything he has done. We've been looking at what he left us to work with, which as you know, was jack shit — at least for me it was." McKinnon nodded in agreement, now a little embarrassed for his hungry outbreak. "Now, I think we need to think about what we can do to draw this guy out. To make him make a mistake." Tick moved away from the impromptu food table and a couple of steps towards the car. "Now we need to push the buttons he has been so eager to play with all these years. Let's make him dance for us. I'm tired of the game buddy. Just tired."

"Sorry Tick. I'm with ya," McKinnon said, then shrugged his shoulders. "Long day," he added as a way of explaining.

Tick waved his hand, brushing away the obvious simplification of the situation. "There's no need for that, to make excuses to me. You and I are both standing here, in the middle of the fucking country. Okay? You and I wouldn't normally be here. We are here because this guy killed a young woman, just at the beginning of her life. So, there is no need to make any excuses for behaviour. That you are standing here is enough. It's enough to show there is a desire to get this fucking guy. So, let's just do that."

The two men stared at each other for a moment, the words dying away. Then McKinnon held out his right hand, which Smith shook with some hesitation.

McKinnon said, "That's nice Tick, a real Kodak moment. But I was actually looking for a pair of gloves from you. If you have a spare set."

Tick Smith shook his head, smiled, then threw a couple of gloves at the inspector. "Such an asshole." Tick started towards the car, the RCMP inspector at his heels, snapping the powdered gloves into place with a small burst of powder.

"Yeah, that's what my staff says. I don't pay it much mind though."

"Really? And here I thought maybe there was something special between us."

"Yeah, right. You are way too tall for me buddy. And of course, the age thing."

Both men stopped when they reached the cultivator and the tractor. It was truly a sight. Even though Smith had been on-scene for the better part of the day, he still couldn't get past the images.

"When are they planning on taking her off there?" McKinnon asked again.

"Yeah, about that." Tick looked at the officer, then back at the scene. "I was told they were waiting for you to get on scene. I suppose now is the moment." He waved at Martin, who was walking towards them. Because they were wearing gloves there was no hand shaking, just nods of hello.

"Jim McKinnon."

"Pete Martin." He looked at the tired Kamloops member of the force then added, "Thanks for coming out. Is much appreciated on this one." Now, Martin looked up at the girl, "Have you had a chance to have a look?" McKinnon shook his head and followed the inspector's gaze. Martin looked back down at him. "You'd better have a look now, they want to get her off and it is going to take some time."

McKinnon followed the same process that Smith had earlier in the morning and climbed the ladder. The officer propped himself against the ladder and equipment and gingerly lifted the blanket. McKinnon made a face and looked down at the two officers on the ground. "Fuck me."

"Very true," Martin added.

"Where is the rest of her?" McKinnon asked.

The Manitoba officer pointed to the other area about 30 yards from where they stood. "We already have her lower torso on the way to Winnipeg in the forensics unit. Our ident guys have taken a lot of photos for us." His head rose to the upper part of Cora, still tangled in the equipment. "We kind of thought this was more important for you."

McKinnon hung his head and shook it slowly. "That is great. Thanks Pete." He continued to examine the body and commented, "Not a lot of blood up here."

"Because she was already dead," Smith observed.

"Right."

"Son of a bitch." McKinnon shook his head and then said, "It looks bad from back there. But up close, it's remarkable." His funk lasted a couple of more seconds, then he snapped back. "What are we waiting for?"

Martin looked at him, then said the obvious. "You."

"How are we going to get her down from here Pete? We can't go over the body in any kind of detail 10 feet in the air."

"Before you got here, we were pondering that very situation," Martin commented. He looked as though he was going to add a bit more to that thought, when an officer yelled at Martin from one of the cruisers. Smith could see the young officer talking to the farmer who had returned to the site to find his tractor was piled up to its axles in evidence bags. Martin excused himself and walked over to the pair and was immediately assaulted by the farmer. Martin said something to him and he threw his arms in the air and stormed back to his half ton. The lead investigator was back at their side in one minute.

"Not a happy camper?" Smith asked, stating the obvious.

"He'd like to get his tractor and cultivator back, so he can get them repaired, then get into the field again."

Martin shrugged his shoulders, "Can't blame him. Though I'm not entirely sure I would use that piece of equipment for a while. Kind of has a darkness attached to it now."

Martin pointed behind them. "We've got a payloader standing by if it will help."

McKinnon climbed down the ladder then walked around the cultivator, looking up under it. He looked at Martin with a question. "What's holding her up there?"

Martin joined him near the ladder. "I think just a couple of shovels are jammed into her. At least that's all that I can see. I am hoping some tools will assist us in getting her down. It looks like just a couple of bolts hold each of the shovels on. Worst case, we cut the damn things off."

Smith looked at the farmer, his taillights receding in the distance. "He really won't be too happy with that."

"He'll get over it," Martin said.

McKinnon was nodding. "All right, let's do that. First though, let's grab the biggest tarp you can find and spread it out underneath her. Just in case there is anything that'll be jarred loose from getting her off that thing or the impact it will make with the ground." He looked at Smith, "You never know."

"No, you don't." Smith agreed.

Smith was surprised at how easily Cora came free of her bounds. Two men, dressed in clean respectful white jumpsuits managed to pry her free in just a couple of tense moments. The payloader provided a very solid platform for them to stand on. She was laid gently onto the bucket and the three of them were lowered to the ground. Still in the bucket, the two investigators paused the process and took photos, drew pictures and took notes, while small samples were taken from her by the ident team. It was a patient procedure that took about an hour. Smith watched over her while it happened, not really sure why. He supposed it was to make sure she was handled carefully.

When that work was completed, and Martin and McKinnon nodded in agreement and consent, Cora was laid on a waiting gurney, covered and walked towards the waiting ambulance. Gingerly they slipped the gurney into its locked spot, and the two men closed the rear door, hopped in the front and headed off toward Winnipeg.

McKinnon had watched in silence while the whole procedure took place. Once she was in the ambulance and the doors closed, he leaned into Tick. "Can't help but think of . . . "

"A unicorn?" Both men smirked. Gallows humour, they all knew, could never be shared with those who don't have to stand in the spot they now stood. The general public just wouldn't get it. "We are bad people," McKinnon said.

Martin was looking at his notes and either didn't hear the exchange or chose to ignore it. Smith thought it was probably the former. "Now this," Martin pointed up at the equipment, "is all after the woman was dead," he said to the two men who were both nodding in agreement. "Right now, I'm just talking about the accident between her and the cultivator." McKinnon and Smith both nodded once again. "A couple of shovels clipped her; I think from behind from the look of the wounds on her lower torso. It blew out quite a bit of her abdomen. The intestines ended up being dragged about 20 feet from the rest of her back there. It's really fucked up," Martin concluded. “I think she must have been jostled around a while before the teeth finally tore into her, serrating her, top from bottom.” He shook his head. “Nasty.”

Smith nodded, “No doubt.”

McKinnon looked around the scene, kneeling when he couldn’t see what he wanted. He poked and prodded at some brush or dirt. After five minutes of close examination, he looked at Pete Martin. He looked back at the tractor for a moment, then to the sergeant. “Anything else?”

“Not that I can see. But once we get her back to Winnipeg, we’ll go over everything with a fine-toothed comb. See what else we come up with.”

“Okay,” McKinnon said, “let’s do it this way. Pete, you and your team are on the accident itself, okay. Just the accident. Our investigations cross paths at that point. So, you keep on this,” he motioned at the tractor and huge piece of equipment attached to it, “and my team is on the girl and how she got here. Deal?”

“Only too happy to oblige. How far do you want this to go?”

“What do you mean?”

“You want the whole Magilla? Computer re-creation of the accident, the body, the cultivator?”

“Yeah, I want a full court press on this, okay? Everything. We can’t leave anything loose here. It all has to be sewn up tight. No questions when you are done. All I want out of your team are definitive answers. Okay Pete?”

“Done.”

“Okay.” McKinnon looked up at Smith who was standing by, waiting for procedure to be pushed out of the way. “Ready to get to work?”

“Waiting for you buddy.”

“You know, our vic . . . ,” he caught himself, “Cora

was probably hoping by the end of the trip that rape was all that was on the killer's mind. Two hours of bumping, sweating, being tossed around inside a tin can through the Manitoba countryside must have made her crazy. I kind of hope the blind panic she felt drove her past the point of sense. I hope she went insane at the end. So, she didn't feel her vomit forcing its way up her throat, killing her." He looked at the RCMP officer who in turn was staring at the dirt beneath where they had taken her down. He, too, could feel the terror that must have filled the mind to overflowing. The killer must have felt it, when he popped the trunk lid open.

"Our guy must have looked forward to popping the trunk. Wait for that first rush of fear and horror that would explode from her." He looked at Smith and asked, "Ya think?"

"Yeah, I would go with you on that. It could be the reason why he ties them up, binds and gags. They are basically immobile, trapped in a rolling coffin, which is exactly how it must have felt for Cora." Smith's eyes caught a small piece of flesh hanging from one shard of metal near the leading edge of the first row of shovels.

"Pete," he yelled. "Another little bit there." He pointed up, Martin followed his outstretched finger and nodded, with a thumbs up given back.

The retired cop's stomach churned slightly. It was in response to what he was looking at, not the stale meal he had consumed. Although the day-old bread and mock meat he had eaten was contributing to his general feeling of malaise.

"It's fucking awful to think about, isn't it? I mean there is shit like this happening all over the world, every day. But today, it's here literally in the middle of nowhere. It's here with us. I don't want to ever get used to this, Tick," he pointed at the flesh with bits of hair still stuck to it, "to seeing this." It was long and floating down from the metal and swaying slightly with the soft breeze. "I mean Jesus Christ, what the fuck is going on here?" McKinnon shook his head back and forth, staring at the flesh left from Cora. He had to make the change away from the personification of the evidence to just that . . . evidence. That is how he had to look at the stringy flesh and hair, that was slowly turning colour in the waning afternoon light. Not 24 hours before it was alive and a part of a young lady who was looking forward to life. Now McKinnon forced himself to think of it, not as a piece of a once beautiful girl ready to continue on through life, but as just a small cog in the evidentiary wheel that would bring the killer to justice. It helped a little to force himself to change the way he was thinking so he could look at the evidence with a little objectivity. But he knew that night, wherever it was that he would be putting his head, it would come back to sleep with him. Then it wouldn't be just the evidence, but the bits and pieces of flesh that were once a human being. Those were the night terrors that would revisit his mind in the small, dark hours. It would be those that would keep him awake at night. It would be those that he would have to eventually talk to his wife about. She was his confessor, his friend and gladly accepted all of his horror. Talking with her helped him sleep. But he was never sure if the horror he needed to share with her became the horror that kept her from getting a decent night's sleep. He supposed it was and felt guilty for it.

"Okay Tick let's go through the crime scene, bit by bit. All right? Left to right?"

"Done."

McKinnon gave the clipboard to Smith to hold and said with a light voice that belied the tension he was feeling, "You write, I'll dictate. You've seen my handwriting." Smith had. It looked like a cross between Russian, Japanese and the scratching of a chicken.

Tick Smith nodded in agreement. "Sounds fair, buddy."

"Good." McKinnon pulled out a small mini flashlight, clicked it on, checked the intensity by holding it to his palm and then aimed it towards the shovels where they were connected to the central portion of the unit. He forced himself to ignore the smells that enveloped him, a combination of flesh and fresh dirt. The two distinct aromas were now one common smell of death. From past investigations there were a number of smells McKinnon knew would haunt him. This was simply added to the list of things to try to avoid.

"I work with kids a lot, Tick. You have to make sure they understand how important the most seemingly insignificant piece of evidence can be in building a case. I don't mean any disrespect. So, I will be walking slowly through this, with lots of dictation."

"I know, buddy. It's all right."

"No really, I want you to understand. We are going to be here a while going through every blade of grass. I don't want to miss one thing." He looked back towards the other groups of evidence tape. "And all the way back there as well."

"I've been where you are, remember? I know what you are doing. And it's okay. I would probably do the same thing if I were in your shoes. Actually, I think I have done the same. Maybe not to this scale, but the same. So don't worry about hurting my feelings. Missing a piece of evidence that lets this fucker go would be a greater crime than denting my ego."

"Okay."

35
MAY 2003

I managed to slip out of the raised bed without waking up Beryl Roberts. The linoleum tiles were so cold I almost cried out when my feet hit the icy floor. For a moment, I stood in place, letting my body warm up the tiles underneath me and let my size 11's adjust to the surface temperature.

I was still dead tired. Exhausted.

The memory of the night rolled through my head, bounding back and forth. Our lovemaking had been tentative at first, but once done, Beryl had snuggled up to me. I could feel her skin was moist with spent effort, clammy and sticky. The narrow super single bed forced us to sleep almost as one. I really missed Mary's.

Slowly, I pulled myself out of the little sleep that I managed to have and looked at the small circular clock near the bed. It read about five o'clock. In trying to remember, I felt I had managed to get perhaps an hour of sleep, possibly almost two. But no more. The events of the day before kept spilling into my slumber and circulating around.

There was a great sense of something uncompleted with what had happened to the girl. Sitting on the edge of the bed, a small angry vibration spilled through my body. An outsider may have thought it was a shiver from the cold of the night, but I knew it was a burst of raw nerves telling me that the darkness inside was not satisfied. It was telling me that it still desperately needed to be fulfilled.

I shook my head to clear the thoughts, then looked to Beryl still asleep in the bed, tightly covered in blankets. I don't know how it happened, but I had whispered Mary's name while making love with Beryl Roberts. Though it sounded like a bad joke, I was glad it was hoarsely said into the ear that required the hearing aid. The small plastic gismo had been taken out and placed on the nightstand while I undressed. While watching Beryl put the hearing aid in its case and carefully close it, I thought, 'I suppose there will be nothing said worth hearing from this point on.' But I was wrong.

I had whispered Mary's name.

Quickly, I pushed her name and face out of my conscious mind, digging a dark hole and dropping it in while Beryl and I made love. This was different though, the time with Beryl. I knew I wasn't making love with her, I got that. I was just having sex with a woman whose first name was a mystery to me half an hour beforehand. I couldn't justify to myself why I was in this uncomfortable bed doing what we were doing. There was no explanation other than the darkness needed to feel complete and whole after the event the day before. It was a ritual that I knew had to run its natural course.

But still Mary's face rose to meet me once my eyes closed and the woman next to me snuggled in for the night. Even opening my eyes didn't force the entity into hiding, away from the unmistakable truth of seeing. She was still there, eating an ice cream cone like the last day we had made love. Smiling and laughing at my transparent attempts at cracking a joke.

It was then, lying down in a bed with a woman I barely knew, that I realized the love I had for Mary was more than I could have possibly understood while she was alive. Suddenly there were cascades of regrets coursing through all those late-night thoughts. They pulled in from places I hadn't visited in months, some in years. But they were there, vivid, real, and ready to let me know how badly I had screwed up by letting this one true love die. All of the killings, the rapes, all happened because I was looking for something to fulfill my life. Make it normal. What that could have been, I have no clue. All of it could have been prevented by the introduction of Mary so many years before. Maybe then I wouldn't have felt the compulsion to let loose the shadow inside. But that was so long ago, a lifetime. Now, looking down on Beryl, still naked beneath the covers, all those events, those directions, from so many years ago, suddenly were cast into the light. They were real and all too present.

Faces of people whose lives I had taken away, suddenly pushed themselves into my line of sight like ghostly spectres. Not the horror of their last minutes or seconds alive, but the happy, cheerful and optimistic looks they had when I had first stalked them. Faces that looked ready to face the world and all its challenges. But that look had changed so quickly when they realized the absolute power one man could have over their lives. I couldn't push their faces away and was forced to watch like a newsreel as the portraits rushed past me one after another after another.

I had tried to force myself to cry out, to relieve that pressure, but something was holding back my breath, choking the sound before it could burst into the room. For some reason, I had thought of them as friends, but that was wrong. They were just accomplices in my life. Each one helped me get to the point where I was now, each one a stepping stone along the way. Before this night, I could pull a face out of my memory and it would have comforted me, liked being wrapped in a warm blanket of remembrance. They really were like friends that had gone now, onto a better place. Though it was true that it was me who sent them to that better place, they were still friends, silent and supporting. It was their sacrifice that allowed me to go on, to breathe, to hunt.

Then a miracle happened in Mary coming into my sphere. Like all things in my life, a normal transition had happened and a short while later she had been taken. I always knew that nothing was ever permanent or static. Mary was no longer anything more than a memory, though a strong one. And now, it was Mary's face that pushed all of the rest out of my line of vision. Purging everything else out of my life. Her face, serene and quiet, floated over me. A halo of love.

Staring down at the floor in the darkness, this near stranger lying beside me purring quietly in her sleep, I knew I was deluding myself. Mary's presence in my life simply caused things to pause. I knew I would never have changed, no matter when I would have met Mary. This path I am on was always set, concrete and stretched out dark and absolute in front of me. Truth be told, I am a killer. It is what I do. What I am good at. It may have taken a few years to actually get to the point of taking a life, but then I knew, deep down, that it was what I was meant to do. And, when that accident happened with Carrington, it was a release like I had never experienced before. It was a literal game changer. It was an aspect that was now woven into me that I really didn't want to lose track of.

I may have looked for something 'normal' and for a while that may have been Mary. But I also knew that I would start lying, manipulating her the way I had learned how to do so many years before. It was something that I was just good at. It was how I had built my entire life. And now, at my age, there was no changing that. It just had to run its course to the end.

Mary believed our love was built on the same platform she had enjoyed through her previous relationships. She felt that what I had told her was the truth, with no hidden agenda. Everything as plain as the sleeve on my arm. But I knew that wasn't what I brought to the relationship. For that there were many regrets. Everything she had been told about my life was all a complete fabrication. It had dirtied everything I had shared with her—made each of the beautiful clear moments sullied with darkness and mud. I suppose there was sadness, disappointment, that I really would be nothing like normal—ever—and would have never been able to give that to Mary. All that I could offer to a woman, was a fabrication, an illusion that I felt she wanted to see. I molded myself to her wants and desires.

Once I got back into my room, I stood in front of the mirror in the bathroom, taking stock of the recent events. My eyes were dark, tired and unfocused. The stubble on my chin was a day old but seemed to carry more grey than it had previously. Even my shoulders, normally broad and powerful seem to fall a little more than they had the day before. The excitement of the previous day's activities, now evaporated and flat.

"You, my friend, have lost 'it.'"

I let out a long sigh, washed my body of the residue of sex, then slipped my pajama top on and buttoned it slowly. I am not a fatalist by any stretch, but I knew the time of judgment was nearly here. Despite all the best intentions or long-range goals, it began to fester in my mind that these were not going to come to fruition. Too much was accumulating around me, the detritus of failure. The bladder issue, though it hadn't dribbled down into my life again, was still there, idling behind the scenes. The long-term impacts of the accident. The temper blowout the day before.

Never had I seen two very close, back-to-back cracks in the long-established foundation of discipline. Sure, there had been small errors in the past. Everyone makes a mistake or two. It was always the management of them, to ensure they weren't repeated, that I was adept at. In the line of work that chose me, it was unacceptable to make the same mistake more than once. It would mean far more than exposure and ultimately failure. The lack of discipline is the difference between getting on with things or getting dead.

I turned again to face the mirror, resting my hands on the sink surround. There was a very old man staring back at me. A stranger. Seventy-four years old, mobility issues, aging brain and eyes.

"You are the real deal, Ivan," I mused laconically. Then slowly shook my head, repeating, "The real deal."

It was now evident that I should start winding this whole party down. I had retired years before, but it seemed that didn't take. So maybe it was time to finally put all of this to bed for the final time. Not putting a pin in it to hold it in place, but rather to burst the balloon.

But that was going to take a bit of planning. It was quietly disappointing to me that this point had finally come to visit me. Until the retirement, albeit short-lived, I was always on point, ready to find whatever was needed to keep going. The compulsion to kill was omnipresent. In the past, while I went more than a year sometimes between kills, the desire was never really gone or satiated. I knew that if given the ability to continually kill, like Vlad the Impaler, without anyone or anything dictating to me that I couldn't, the count would have been significantly higher.

At 55, including the most recent activity included, it was enough. Though it doesn't seem like much when you look at it over the period that I was active. When the first retirement began, I felt that more than one a year was enough to keep the darkness at bay, hidden from sight. Then the 50 milestone came along and that was a goal to be honoured. Respected.

Then years later, there was Mary. For whatever reason, that part of me stayed in the shadows — hidden but present. Her presence somehow filled the needs inside me, enough to keep from wanting to take another life. That was something I had never experienced before. It scared me a little. But at the same time, it was a relief that the fun with her was like a pressure valve letting go, keeping the darkness contained in that little locked case inside. Though late at night, I would turn the key, open that lid and have a peek inside. Not revelling at the contents but remembering some of the details of the events from decades of hunting and killing. Through the years I had been extremely careful and over time had gained a meticulous edge to ensure that capture was never on the agenda.

Late at night it was the ones who got away that haunted me most. Those innocent, ignorant folks had no idea that they had been marked, their fate decided. They had no idea of the gift they were going to give me. But providence intervened and they lived.

That young lady in PEI, whose family decided to come visit her at university as a surprise. I can still hear them yelling birthday wishes and hear her crying in joy. I was that close, not just in proximity but on schedule to being with her. Mom, dad and little sister were all present and accounted for, as was the birthday cake and gifts. You couldn't be mad at something like that. It just disappointed me. Kismet, karma, whatever, had allowed her to escape, blissful and ignorant of my intentions.

Or, the older woman I had befriended in Winnipeg was another cautious error. At that time in my career the attention to detail was such that it wouldn't allow me to take risks when unnecessary. Her house was in an older part of the city, with neighbours no more than six feet away. If things had gone badly and the blitz attack didn't work, then the risk of having her scream and running to the neighbours was far too great. Walking away was the best decision there as well. Of course, that prompted an angry reaction out of me, more out of frustration than actual anger. While I didn't normally kill men, that guy was the exception. Not a homophobe, just not my thing.

They never did find him. Never would.

There were more, but fewer withdrawals happened as I aged, and became more proficient at the work. The discipline of it suited my personality. I was able to decide quickly, identifying risk or opportunity in a triage type of mental math that determined whether the whole thing would come together without danger of capture or exposure. If anything wasn't exactly right, the pieces not falling neatly into place, I would simply walk away and began the hunt anew. It wasn't like there was a shortage of people to kill. Especially in the Sixties and Seventies. It was a veritable smorgasbord. Everybody trusted everybody. The memories make me smile.

But now that was at an end. Everything I did, all the actions were going to be clearly dictated by a need for justice and an end to this cat-and-mouse game I had played with Tick over the years. Decades, in all reality.

I needed to take this boy who killed Mary. Plus, I needed Tick Smith to be off the game, permanently. As the thoughts about it swirled around, the solution came to me as a revelation. Not a flash but like a warm handshake that evolved as it made itself known. I smiled and looked down at my toes pressing against the sheets.

"I'll be a son of a bitch."

I calmly closed my eyes. It was so nice to see the end ahead. It didn't wash away my dreams but did put them back into the box and allowed a welcome blanket of sleep.

36
JUNE 2003

To say that Kelly Anderson's life changed that day in July of 2002 would be an understatement of gargantuan proportions.

That accident coloured every single part of his life from that moment on.

He didn't care about the mark it was going to leave on his record. In fact, that mark was something he looked at each and every day. He had asked the lawyer that represented him to quietly get a copy for him so his parents wouldn't know he had it. He was certain they would want him to try to forget all about it. But it was under some books on his bedroom desk. He would slide it out and look at it, staring with repeated disbelief that it had actually happened to him and it wasn't just a broken memory. He had looked at it each and every night. It horrified and shamed him in a sweeping full motion.

He couldn't believe he had allowed it to happen. Further, that his lack of attention caused the death of a person, prompted the all-night sessions he now considered just a regular part of his life. Even with the sleeping pills prescribed by his family physician, a full night's sleep never materialized. It was now normal for him to have the heavy bags under his eyes and the zombie plodding through life, that the lack of sleep forced upon him.

The accident changed the dynamics of his household as well. His parents were overly supportive now, almost to the point of allowing him carte blanche in whatever he wanted to do. Couple that with a complete abandonment of discipline and Kelly was completely awash in a sea of despair. While he couldn't drive for another four and a half years, they allowed him to run his life in any way he felt compelled. What they didn't realize was that he wasn't really living a life at all. Time had frozen to a standstill that day when he missed the stop sign and hit that little square car square on the passenger door.

He had been fine, his seatbelt left him shaken up, but no injuries. His parents had told him that afterwards he had fallen into shock. He was a kid – only 16 when it happened. But he was a good driver. Passed his exams with only a couple of small errors. Never any speeding tickets, squealing of the tires or general mayhem. He loved the freedom that driving gave him and was careful with it. But that day he missed the stop sign. He may have been driving a bit fast, but that didn't matter. The sun may have been in his eyes, but that really had no relevance to him. He simply missed the stop sign.

Kelly Anderson took full responsibility for the accident. It was against his lawyer's advice, but he couldn't knowingly pass along any blame to anyone or anything else. It was his fault and his alone.

School was now a disaster for him as well. There were two clear factions that he could see. There was the group of cool kids who wanted nothing whatsoever to do with him, which was fine with him as he really didn't care. Then there were the kids who hung out in shop, who tried to get him to join in on their car mania. He tried it once, but all they wanted to talk about was the accident. Did he see blood? Were her brains all over the door like they said? It was all such insensitive horseshit.

So, of the two opposing factions, Kelly Anderson decided his best path was to be left to the third faction, his personal favourite — alone. Two options were discarded by omission and the other embraced by choice. He truly was alone in a school of 900 students. Doomed to walk the halls in solemn, brooding isolation. He knew his parents were worried about the way the accident had changed him but couldn't have cared less. His life was his to live. He had forced this on himself, no one else. The responsibility was clearly on his shoulders.

Kelly quit football immediately. He couldn't see the benefit of team sports when it was clear he wouldn't fit on any team. Then a chance encounter with an elderly gentleman exercising in the park struck a vibrant light through his veil. He watched as the old man moved with exaggerated deliberate motions. His actions were slow, yet tightly controlled. But it was his face that entranced the young man. It was serene, calm, absolutely vacant of emotion. After asking about the exercise regimen the man was showcasing, he made his first trip to ask about, then register for classes. So, he fell into the discipline of physical activity. His parents were relieved by it. He reveled in it, far more than he would have cared to admit.

The focus that karate demanded was what he missed that afternoon — that ultimately caused the accident. He had learned to focus on each movement, not for the outcome but for the act. Literally, it changed his life.

He had written to the man who was in the other car, pouring his heart out to him over the guilt and shame he felt at what had happened. He had promised never to let such a thing happen again. A promise he meant. The young man felt certain he would hear from him. That he would let Kelly know that his words had meaning or value. Whether to yell and hate or to cry with sadness, Kelly had hoped to hear. But he received silence.

Until now.

"Sit down, Kelly."

The young man fell quickly into the chair at the end of the dining room table. He had always been taught to be respectful of his elders, but the large machete being held in the older man's right hand spoke far louder than the order itself.

"I've been watching you," Ivan McDonald said. As he spoke, he was moving to the windows of the dining room to draw the curtains. He took a quick pair of steps towards the front door and slowly locked the deadbolt. His eyes had only darted quickly to each task but stayed focused on the young man facing him. "You know, now that I am here standing in front of you, I really am not so sure about all this," He swung the machete around the room. McDonald watched the boy's face give away all the emotions he had seen many times over the years: fear, horror, sadness and bewilderment. He knew that last one would change quickly. All were familiar, but each was unique.

"The newspapers really didn't do the accident justice, did they?" Ivan moved towards the boy, scraping the machete slowly down the table. He watched the realization come to Anderson, which quickly brushed away the bewilderment and replaced it with panic.

"There ya go," Ivan smiled. "Took a moment, didn't it? I knew you would get there. I guess since I wasn't in court for the hearing. Not that it mattered given the outcome, but you now know who I am."

"Sir, I . . ."

McDonald snapped, "Shut the fuck up!" The young

man sunk deeper into the chair, his hands gripping the arms so tightly they showed white on the knuckles. He opened his mouth to speak again. The apologies he had rehearsed over the months since the accident waiting just in the wings for release. But there they stayed, poised for opportunity.

The old man reached into the vest pocket of his jacket and pulled out an envelope, opening it and unfolding the paper within. The boy knew what it was the moment it emerged, as he could see his clumsy handwriting clearly written in blue pen. Anderson's eyes shifted slightly to the machete, laying on the table beside the man. The handle next to the senior citizen who had remained standing. Another movement caught his eyes, the shaking of the old man's head.

"Don't bother kid. I may be five times your age, but you are seated, and in an awkward position up there at the head of the table. So, you would have to get up, move all the way around the side of the table, reach for, and grab the machete then find a way to attack me." The killer's right hand tapped the side of the wood handle, riveted into place on the sharpened steel shank. "And all that is assuming that I haven't reacted by then. I mean I'm a little slower than I was, especially after the accident. But I am not that slow. That just isn't going to happen for you. So put that thought aside."

He flapped the letter in an exaggerated motion, prompting both of them to focus their eyes on it. The killer read out loud, "Mr. McDonald …" Ivan stopped, looked at the paper for a moment, then he set the letter down and looked up at the young man whose wide eyes were still focused on the letter. "Forget it. I really don't care what you wrote there. Guilty tripe," he spat as he pushed the papers widely across the table. He held up his hand when the boy opened his mouth to speak. "Don't, it just won't work. There is nothing you can say that is going to change the outcome of our little get together here today." After a short pause he added, "But what you do, may."

The older man's hand grabbed the machete, causing a sharp intake of breath from Anderson. He tapped the glistening tip on the paper, "You really shouldn't share your home address with a guy like me." He smiled slightly, "Really isn't the best idea for a long and happy life. But I guess you really couldn't know, could you? You thought it was an apology to just some harmless old fuck, a retired salesman or farmer or whatever." Ivan McDonald smiled at the thought for a moment then added, "You couldn't be further from the truth kid."

"Sir…"

McDonald held up the machete again, this time pointing at the young man's face. "Be quiet! I hate people that interrupt." McDonald walked back to the door, checked the lock again, then moved to the curtain to ensure it prevented anyone seeing inside the room. Old habits, the killer knew, were difficult to set aside. It was the discipline that kept him going, active and untraceable for so many years. So, he allowed himself the small luxury of double checking the door and curtains.

The student watched the movement with curiosity. It drew him in instantly. He knew this type of behaviour. He had seen it before, with the old man in the park last year. It was the same sort of discipline he was seeing again, but different. While the older man's face was stern, it was somehow calm and poised. It made him more curious, but also more fearful. Who could be calm in a situation like this? He certainly wasn't. But it did make him curious what it would take, as far as discipline is concerned, to be able to act like this, in this situation.

"But today," Ivan McDonald said, "let's take a slight deviation from normal, shall we? Let's chat."

Kelly was listening but this didn't make sense. 'What was this man going on about? Deviation from normal?' The confusion he felt must have been reflected by his facial expression because the old man paused for a moment, then smiled the most emotionless smile the young man had ever seen.

"I have been in this position, this exact place, a few times before kid. Just so you know. Actually, more than a few times." McDonald allowed a brief pause to remember, then snapped back to his focus. "This time we are going to do something different. We are going to talk first. And, I have to tell you this is weird for me." He stepped closer to the young man, who naturally leaned deeper into the hard wood chair, begging to somehow become one with it. "I'm not used to this, so bear with me."

McDonald paused for a moment, taking in the room, the glistening sunlight striking the furniture and walls, the thick carpet under foot, overstuffed pillows on a cheap loveseat, the long, oak coloured table at which the boy sat at attention. As his gaze moved throughout the room, his focus snapped back.

"You took everything from me. You have no idea. You fuck!" Ivan raised his voice and the machete rose with emphasis nearer to the shrinking boy, darting towards him to punctuate each weighted word. He shook his head again. "You have no idea about anything. Not a clue! And, I guess, you really don't need to know. I have hated you more than I have hated anyone or any single thing in my life. And it's a weird paradox, that of all the things I have done, and there have been a few, but they were through a desire, a need. Not because of a petty emotion like hatred. So… common." He shrugged his shoulders and looked into the confused eyes of the seated young man. McDonald took in a big breath, "But here we are."

"I could have done this at any time, you know." He tapped the machete tip back onto the paper. "You really shouldn't have given your home address." Once again, he shrugged, "I would have found you anyhow, really wouldn't have been that difficult. I am sure your name is on the paperwork from the cops somewhere. You mailing me a letter just shortened the entire process, made it easier for me. So, there you go. Lessons learned, a dollar short and a day late."

Ivan McDonald sighed, stretched his back and took in another deep cleansing breath. "But here we are," he emphasized. In the corner a Westminster grandfather clock struck the three-quarter hour chime.

4:45.

It was close now.

"Your parents carpool, don't they? Should be home in about 20 minutes or so?" Ivan observed a slight change in the stance of the kid and it brought him closer. He could see anger now gently nudging away fear, leaving just confusion as a houseguest in his mind.

"Yes, I have been observing your family for a bit, watching you, planning. The comings and goings of the Anderson home. Quaint and very, very predictable. You know, I never had a life like that, honestly didn't want it. It is too . . ." he stretched for the word, ". . . pedestrian."

"But here we are." McDonald repeated.

Kelly Anderson looked again at the machete. The

math in his head echoed what he had been told earlier by the man standing over him. He wouldn't be able to get there even with a six-decade age advantage. The weapon changed the dynamic of the situation, shifted the odds clearly away from him. And even if he could, would he be able to use it? That was an unanswered question. The older man seemed to read his thoughts and provided a clear answer.

"Yeah, it's a tough problem, isn't it?" He held up the machete and looked at it, as if he was seeing it for the first time. "It does take a certain kind of person to use one of these properly, with purpose. With conviction." He smashed the sharp edge of the weapon down on the back of the chair nearest him, causing a large wood shard to fly across the room, landing near a recliner. McDonald nodded with satisfaction at the damage it had done and noticed with amusement how the action had prompted the boy to literally jump out of his seat. It had done its job and scared the boy into submission. "Yeah, nice weapon." He held it sideways to the boy, so he could see the length and breadth of it. "Readily available, easy to sharpen and quite simple to use effectively." He tapped at the spot the machete had struck the chair. "Well, really doesn't take a lot of finesse now does it?" He lifted it again, "Just needs strength to make this thing really sing."

The blade hit the chair back again, this time with a stronger impact, cracking it clearly in half. The seated boy winced and stared at the damage it had caused.

The killer looked up at the clock and whistled quietly, "Well, time is a burning. As I said, your parents will be home soon."

The boy looked up at him. A gambit was created quickly in his scrambling mind. "No, they go shopping on Thursdays. Get groceries. They won't be home for a while." His hope faded as he watched the older man shake his head.

"No," he smiled. "They don't," McDonald said with certainty. "Groceries are a Friday after work ritual, followed by some takeout for pizza or Chinese." He looked at the slightly deflated young man. "It's okay," he added, "I would have tried the same thing, but please know that there is going to be no negotiation at this table." A small smirk erupted on the face, but Kelly once again saw there was no emotion in the smile. "Well, maybe not negotiation, but a bit of give and take. However, certainly nothing we talk about will change the outcome."

"At five minutes after the hour, your mom and dad are going to come in, worried about the day you had as always. I am guessing you are pretty much all they talk about now. Too bad. But understandable," he conceded. "Anyway, they won't see me until it is time for them to see." He again held up the weapon, "But by then it won't matter, will it?"

"Please," Anderson said softly. "No."

"Yup," the killer mused. He moved to the door, holding his machete high above his head. "It will be the old man first. He poses the greatest danger to me because of his physical strength." He shrugged, "But how much strength a bookkeeper can have is up for debate. But this," he said holding up the machete, "will effectively remove him from any further proceedings." McDonald brought the machete down in a swift, whishing motion. "Your mother will be shocked for a moment. Absolutely speechless. Gobsmacked. Frozen to the spot. She won't even be a challenge, as a stationary target." He pointed at the chair, its uprights now misshapen because of the damage, "as you can see."

McDonald walked back over to the table and looked down at the boy. "You won't be able to yell, because I will cut your throat just as they begin up the walkway. It will take you about 45 seconds to die, but that will be long enough for you to watch your parents open up like fucking shellfish. Even though you are bleeding out, you will know the pain of causing the death of those two folks. You will know the pain you caused me!"

McDonald walked a step closer to the seated boy and ran the edge of the blade along the outside of the kid's outer arm, opening up a three-inch long clear incision. It took a moment to begin to bleed, but once it started, the flow was rapid.

"The pain will come in a moment," McDonald observed. "It takes a second or two for the nerves to work around the cut." The boy cried out as the promised pain spooled up in his arm. "So that," he said, pointing at the slice, "is going to hurt like hell."

"Please," Anderson said in a loud stage whisper, giving away the helpless situation he felt he was in. "Please, don't."

"Oh, it's going to happen kid. Really is." He wiped the blood off the blade on the cloth placemat near the boy. "The good news for you is that you don't have to worry about your parents. They aren't going to feel a thing. Especially your dad. This thing," he said, holding up the now clean machete, "will cut nearly right through his head. It will just be over for him. Like turning off a light." He looked down at the kid, "Now your mom is a different story. I can pretty much predict what will happen with the old man. But the dynamics of the situation will change with your mom. She could start to run, a reaction that isn't unheard of. Then," he shrugged his shoulders, "who knows? May have to take a swipe at the knees to keep her from going too far. That is pretty painful." McDonald emulated a wince, but knew nothing of the pain he would inflict. "In the end though, she is going to be just as dead on the carpet as your dad. And, just like your old man, she will have no chance."

Kelly Anderson could only stare at the man, who seemed to be describing an event that is predicted, but just hasn't had the time to happen yet. 'How could he know this stuff? How could anyone?'

"Or, my friend," he tossed the machete up in the air half a rotation, catching it by the tip, and moving the handle closer to him, "you use this on me."

Anderson stopped breathing for a moment. The abrupt change in direction of the old man caught him totally off guard. 'What did he say?'

"I'm tired kid. That accident changed things for me. I'm tired of the hunt, the chase, being hunted and being chased." He held out the machete a little closer to the seated boy. "I saw that loss of Mary as a profound pillar toppled over on my life." He motioned again with the machete at the kid. But the boy wasn't looking at the machete now, but rather up into the clear eyes of the old man standing nearer to him than before. "I really don't want to keep going any more. It just doesn't make sense. I want you to have this, to take it, to use it. On me." McDonald said, nodding towards the weapon that was extended to him.

His head motioned to the door. "However, and here's the rub. Should your parents pull up before you make this decision, things will happen exactly the way I just said. Your dad first, then your mom. After that, all three of you will be dead and I will go and find someone else to kill or be killed by. Trust me when I say I won't stop."

McDonald didn't move, but just stared at the young man. "Just so you know, the sound this thing makes when slicing through skin and bone," again motioning with the machete, "is a 'hear-it-once-and- never-forget-it' kind of thing. It is unmistakeable. You will never be able to push it out of your mind ever again. Right now, I bet you hear the sound of that accident late at night, don't you? The loud bang, tinkling of glass?" The boy stared straight at him. But his thoughts were given away by the pain now in his eyes.

"That is what I thought. Well, the sound this thing makes will now replace that." In a fluid motion he tossed up the machete again, and then swung it with full force at the edge of the table next to the seated boy. Again, a large splinter sprung up, hitting the young man on the cheek, making him flinch.

"Make your choice boy," McDonald said, looking up at the clock as the hands edged passed 4:59. Almost on cue, the chimes began for 5. "They are headed home now as we speak." He again shifted the machete in his hand and held it out once again. The handle was so close to the chest of the boy, he would just have to raise his hand to take it. But his hand was frozen across his chest, his left hand holding the fresh wound on his right arm.

"I can't."

"Yes, you can. You have to. You have already killed, Kelly; the first time is the hardest. It creates the most baggage. It gets easier, trust me. Much easier." Ivan pushed the weapon closer, touching the chest of the kid who in turn shrunk away from it. "Take the fucking thing!"

Tears began to well up in the boy's eyes as they looked down at the dark handle pressed against him.

He shook his head slowly. “I can’t.”

Just then, he heard the unmistakable sound of the car pulling into the driveway. Ivan reacted as if the air had been let out of him. The machete dropped away from the boy’s chest and rested for a moment on the table. Anderson followed the movement with his eyes, staring at the glean of the sharpened edge.

“Well, that is disappointing,” McDonald sighed. “Your parents are home a little bit early.” He paused for a moment, hung his head, his chest deflated. Then McDonald withdrew the offered weapon, repositioned the handle into his right hand and looked down at the crying youth. “So disappointing. But, so be it. The rest of this is on you, kid. You had the opportunity, the golden ticket, and you wasted it.”

The killer moved over to the window and looked outside. Both parents were getting out of the car and starting up the walkway, talking animatedly to one another. He turned back to the kid and took two quick steps forward. The machete flashed forward towards the young man, catching him on the left side of his neck. It cut quickly, without any hesitation.

Anderson pulled back and reacted very quickly but felt the searing heat of the blade as it swung through his neck. He didn’t yell, couldn’t because the pain overwhelmed all his senses or abilities. He watched as the man headed for the door, but his hand quickly abandoned his arm for the fresher more significant wound on his neck. He could hear the soft metallic clicking of the lock being moved and could see the bright light stream into the room as the door opened. He could hear his dad asking if his son was home.

“He usually leaves the door open for us.”

The youth opened his mouth to scream but remained mute as his mother moved quickly through the threshold, completely unaware of the man behind the door. She stepped over to the corner table and put her purse down, then swung back and paused. Initially, she couldn't make out what was different, but a sound alerted her that something was off in her house. Her husband was just coming into the room when she saw her son seated at the table, eyes wide with horror, his chest covered in blood, silently screaming for her. As the door closed, a short swishing sound could be heard, followed by the sound of a machete driving fully into the skull of his father.

Shhhkkkkk!

In slow motion, his father stopped all movement, standing stock still. Then began to crumple without saying anything at all. His killer jiggled the blade back and forth to assist in getting it dislodged, making the father's head shake in an unnatural way as it hit the floor. True to McDonald's prediction, his mother wasn't able to put all of this together into something that made sense. The events were something that she simply couldn't comprehend or rationalize. The events that she was witnessing were so foreign to her, she froze in an immediate state of shock. So, she stood still, watching as the old man that had just driven a machete into her husband's head, refocused on her and began to move forward.

"Now you," McDonald said with finality as he raised the weapon.

McDonald turned quickly to the boy and said, "All of this was on y….." But the boy wasn't in the chair ten feet away but coming up behind him quickly. For one second the killer paused and that was all it took.

The machete he held above his head in preparation for the attack on the woman, was now ripped from his grip, dislocating his shoulder with a quick, sharp pain.

"No!" McDonald heard the boy yell. Then he heard in a faraway place the all too familiar sound of a machete hitting and then penetrating bone.

But in his quickly failing mind Ivan McDonald realized just how the sound must have been for all of those people. It was the real sound of death.

Intimate.

Personal.

Final.

37
JUNE 2003

"His name is Ivan McDonald. He's dead!"

Jim McKinnon sounded giddy with excitement. He hadn't even waited for a hello from his retired friend. The excitement literally burst through the phone lines.

Tick was shocked when he heard the name. It took a moment for him to bring his mind up to speed. "What the hell are you talking about? No, it's not."

McKinnon laughed slightly. Tick realized at that moment he had never actually heard him laugh. Chuckle perhaps but never a laugh. It was a weird laugh, almost a cackle. "Our guy Tick, our guy is Ivan McDonald, and he is on a slab at the morgue in Brandon."

"That can't be right. That can't be his name." Tick's mind was slowly catching up to the significance of the conversation. "I haven't heard anything about a hit on the DNA." Tick moved through the kitchen towards the coffee pot. He felt this might be a long call, needing something hot to smooth the way. As he reached for the pot, he noticed his hands were shaking. "I would have heard Jim."

"They didn't need to run anything. He had ID on him among other things. He was found earlier tonight. Fucking ID! Can you believe it?" There was some rustling of papers on the phone as Tick listened intently for more of an explanation.

"Come on," Tick expelled. It was meant as sarcasm, not just towards the inspector in British Columbia, but himself and the man he had been looking for, for decades. "No one makes that kind of mistake. Not after this many years of being so careful.

He had identification on him? That is just too simple, too dumb."

Tick heard the creaking of a chair and McKinnon spoke. It would be two minutes that would change the retired cop's life until the end.

"It's a weird story. There was an accident ten months or so back, and a Mary Carlton was killed. From what I was told it was a simple accident, kid ran a stop sign, T-boned the car and she didn't survive. We've seen this a hundred times before. Except, we've never seen an accident where one of the victims was a serial killer. So, skip forward from then and here we are. He went after the kid. According to the locals, and by the way your department is still pretty good..."

"So that," Tick said slowly catching up with the narrative, "would be about the time he went quiet?"

"Yup."

"Son of a bitch!"

"Yeah. I guess he broke a few bones, some other issues with his face along with some internal damage from the accident. Fairly messed up, I guess. So he was in a coma in hospital for a few months, then on to some physiotherapy."

"That is unreal," Tick said, shaking his head in wonder. "A car accident. A random accident?"

"So . . . according to the locals, our guy Ivan is waiting for this kid when he gets home this afternoon. He tells the kid he is going to kill his parents while he watches—a payback for killing his friend. But after our guy does the dad, the kid springs into action and kills our buddy instead."

"And?"

"And what Tick?" McKinnon sounded frustrated. "Lucky kid, lucky mom. Not so lucky dad. He killed the bad guy before he could do the mom. End of story."

"There is no way that is it." Tick was stirring his coffee as he thought. "What kind of weapon?"

More rustling on the other end of the phone. "It was a cheap machete, the kind you could buy at any store for 20 bucks. It had been sharpened, but nothing special or unique."

"Kind of sounds like the weapon in your town, hey?"

"Yes, sir, it does."

Tick was bewildered. It can't just end. It just didn't make sense. His mind was caught in a windmill motion wrestling with an entire career's worth of emotions, events and people. "It just can't be this simple Jim."

"It definitely is, Tick. That kid was so jacked up on adrenalin, he fucking near split this guy's head in half. I have seen the crime scene pics and they are amazing. That kid was pumped! I guess the injuries he sustained probably helped with increasing his adrenalin levels, along with seeing his old man get killed right in front of him."

"Did the boy have any injuries?"

"Oh yeah, our buddy had made an earlier cut on the kid's arm, then tried to cut his throat when the parents got home, but just did some superficial damage. Didn't hit any major arteries. So, the fight or flight response with this young man was pretty much on level 11. He was going to fight–hard. The local detective . . . Walker?"

"Chris, yeah," Tick clawed through his memories. "Good guy."

"Anyhow, Walker said the kid was into karate or something so … Oh I don't know, that may have helped, may not have. I think the adrenalin theory on this is way better than the idea of him going all Jackie Chan on this asshole." McKinnon chuckled.

There was a long pause, while Smith continued to swirl all of this around his head.

"So," McKinnon continued, "I guess McDonald made him an offer—either you kill me, or I kill you and your parents. Tough choice for a 17-year-old."

"What? That makes absolutely no sense," said Tick.

McKinnon paused for a moment, reading the report, then answered. "I would agree with you, but that is what this kid said. Maybe just the fog of battle screwed up his memory. Happens."

"Sorry Jim, I am just still not seeing this. You know him, he doesn't hesitate, he just kills. Bang! You are dead. He is a professional. We talked about this. This kid was alive long enough to have a chat, wait for the parents to get home and then watch dad get killed? Then, after that he springs into action to save the mom? It just doesn't track to the history we have on this guy. He never lets anyone live long enough to offer a counterattack." Tick Smith was staring out the window of his kitchen now, still in bewilderment. "He walked into the family's home in your town, does the dad immediately — that sounds familiar. He removes the biggest threat first. Then starts to go after the other two. He has never had a time lag or even evidence that would suggest he was into a chit-chat."

"True, but still," the excitement still building for the RCMP officer halfway across the country. "Wanna hear the note?"

"Oh, come on," he asked incredulously. "There is a note? Seriously? A confession?"

"Nothing like that. It is pretty short, buddy. They found it in his shirt pocket." More rustling. "Tell Tick I won." Pause. "That's it."

The words weighted down on the retired cop.

"That fucker."

"Yeah," McKinnon added. "That is how they got onto me so quickly. Your name popped up, along with mine on the case file. You are retired, so I got the call. Even though they know you, you are still retired."

"That fucker," Tick repeated to himself. He waited for decades to have *that* moment with him. It was all he wanted out of him, what he had promised his wife, and this son of a bitch had taken it away. It suddenly dawned on Tick that he had invested an awful lot of his mental energy to wanting *that* moment and now it was gone with no chance of retrieval.

"Take a moment Tick," Jim said, "it is done. We don't have to chase this ghost anymore. No one else is going to die because of him."

"I know, I know."

Tick was shaking his head now, "I know. I wanted this moment, me, I wanted this alone. I have been after him pretty much my entire career. That selfish old prick just took that away from me. Son of a bitch!" Tick was still staring out the window at the long shadows in his yard when he said, "Corny as it sounds, Jim, I wanted to put that prick into cuffs and lead him into the station. I wanted to do that. For my wife." In a flash he was back in that apartment, talking with Martha long before they were married, making the promise he had kept for more years than they had been married.

"Well, there are no need for restraints, Tick. Neither half of his now separated brain is going to escape on you. Our kid looked after that for you."

The retired cop stared down at his now cooling coffee and then up at the yard in front of him.

"I gotta go Jim, I need to think this through. I am

still struggling with it." He paused, turning back into the quiet kitchen. "What the hell?"

"I bet, buddy. No troubles. I will have everything sent over to you." There was a slight pause, "I am looking at this guy's picture now. I'll have it dropped off as soon as we can." McKinnon was staring at a man he knew thoroughly but had never met.

"You know Tick, he looks like anyone else you would see down at the coffee shop. Just an old guy, thinning grey hair and old-fashioned glasses. His picture actually has him smiling at the camera. Well, the lips are smiling, but the eyes are dark, lurking. He was just an old man."

"I gotta go."

"Okay, Tick. It's over. Done."

"The only thing now is the cleanup and background search on our guy right, Jim?"

There was a pause. "What?" It was a combination statement and question. It was the tone you gave when the person you were talking to knew something and wasn't cooperating.

When Tick Smith didn't respond McKinnon asked again. "What do you mean, Tick? They ran his background and nothing unusual showed up on this guy at all. Regular working type guy — a couple of speeding tickets. Not a long-term employee anywhere, moved around the city a lot but nothing weird. Local guy, now lives in a senior home — the — uh — Pinetree. There haven't been any local interviews done, but that will start right away. I don't think they will be in a rush. What's to search?"

"He lived in Brandon the entire time?"

More shuffling of papers 1,000 miles away.

"Mostly. But by and large yeah, in Brandon. There were short stints where there is no address — just blank spaces, but mostly he was in Brandon."

That news brought a small pang of sadness to the retired chief. "He had been under my nose the entire time I was on the force," he thought. His mind now raced, wishing he could see the photo that McKinnon had. He wanted an image of the killer. He needed to see if the two had crossed paths. At a restaurant, grocery store, getting gas. Brandon was a small city, the chances they had somehow been in close proximity were very good.

Again, Tick tried to remember someone who stared at him a little too long. Looked at him with familiarity. But he also knew, that when you have on the uniform, everyone looks at you a little longer than usual.

"You couldn't have known, Tick. Like you say, he was a professional. It was his job to stay off your radar. You couldn't have known," he repeated.

"Doesn't change anything, does it Jim? He was still a mile from me at any given time during my career. You are going to have to go back and interview any co-workers he had over the years. See if you can start identifying where he was all that time. Especially during those missing years. We need to find out who this guy was." The silence on the phone lasted about 15 seconds when Tick spoke again. "Because that isn't his real name Jim. It's an alias."

"What?" That tone again.

"Ivan McDonald was the name of my father-in-law. My wife's dad."

"That son of a bitch!" McKinnon yelled into the phone so loud that Smith held the phone away from his ear. "That son of a bitch!"

38
June 2005

Bitterness.

No, that isn't strong enough. Hate is closer to the mark.

If the actual truth was told, even hate wasn't a powerful enough word to describe how I was doing. It was close but didn't adequately communicate all of the emotions that were swirling around my head.

I didn't hate my mom. I know I love her. But she was just too tiring to be around. Since the attack she had entered a revolving door of emotions in the house. Horror and grief were first. The tears and deep, immersive sobbing could spontaneously burst out and the entire house would hold its collective breath while she cycled through the moment. Initially, I had joined her and the two of us would stand, hugging, crying in the kitchen until the wave had passed and settled in the dark cobweb of sorrow again. Or, we would just quietly hold hands as we sat on the couch watching anything to try and evade the despair that had waded into the house. It didn't take long, no more than a month, before I started to avoid her nearly all the time, fearing that she would need me to hold onto again. Her cloying hugs were to steel herself against the all-consuming pain she was enduring. I felt kind of guilty about the avoidance, but that soon passed as well. Eventually, an uncomfortable silence and isolation enveloped the home and the two of us inside it.

I was however, fairly pissed off at my dad. I couldn't figure out why he hadn't stepped up a little and been able to defend himself against the attack by McDonald. He should have been able to do something.

But all he did was die.

The sound the machete made as it arced through my dad's head delivered an intense reaction that still wracks my entire body. I wince visibly, like experiencing a small tremor. I can close my eyes and relive the moment my dad buckled on the entrance-way floor. A bloody sack of potatoes.

The first month or two, the sound it made woke me in the night, sweating and stuck to the sheets in my darkened room. Awake, analyzing the sounds the weapon made, I came to realize there was no difference between the noise it made as it moved through the outer skin of dad's skull, to the bone and brain beneath. It was all a synthesis of the various auditory elements woven together into a singular undefinable blanket of sound.

Ssshhhkkk!

After a time, I began to search out the resonations in my memory. It was weird, because parts of my subconscious endeavoured to hide it, bury them. Others though, were brushing aside the curtains and newly woven cobwebs of deceit to embrace the sound.

The old man was right. It was a sound unlike all others. It was connected, linked to a moment in an emotional history. A bookmark of horror. I really didn't understand how I had managed to hide my father's voice so quickly from my memory. I can still see his face, in the pictures strewn about the now abandoned dining room. On the credenza, on the walls, small tables, candid and posed images of my dad were placed so no matter where you looked, he was looking back at you. But his voice, his vocal mannerisms were gone. I really didn't mind that. In retrospect, I wasn't even sure what the last words the man had said to me. A small hope for a good day at school. A wish for safety perhaps. None of that mattered now.

Mom had taken me to a psychiatrist to help manage all of these emotions that lingered because of the traumatic incident we had been through. At the beginning of the bi-weekly sessions, the rage and tears had flown so easily, bubbling to the thin emotional surface of my psyche. By the end of the sessions, nearly a year later, I could no longer find the sadness or anger that had prompted my initial attendance to the dark, soft room of Dr. Truffyn.

School had become more of a tortuous environment for me. Luckily, the physical wounds required little more than the summer to heal. But, the scarring, white and dotted with a parallel signature of dots from the sutures, became a magnet for unwanted attention. Those who had avoided me after the accident, now were drawn like macabre flies to a rotting moment in time. I suddenly found myself asked to attend parties or events which I wouldn't have gone to before everything that happened. I learned quickly to beg off politely. "I can't," I would explain. "I have to look after my mom."

It was a lie. But it worked every time. Everyone thought I was such a good son. It was so much camouflage.

As time went by, I would just ignore them all together. Stare back into their curious faces with my emotionless, grey-slate eyes. The girls that had wanted to be near me or the boys who had wanted to hang out, all soon learned that my greatest desire was to be left alone. As isolated and cut-off as I was after the accident, the killings in my home propelled me even further to that quiet, dark environment of inaccessibility. Pretty soon, I walked the halls at school, a bubble of still, cadaver air surrounding me and repelling all others.

Then, eventually I found myself alone at Kennedy's, staring into a small display in the camping section.

Initially, the store management, once they found out from the media reports where the machete was purchased and its ultimate use, had removed the item from their store shelves. They felt it was ghoulish and didn't belong in their family-oriented business. But business is business, and their job is to sell items to the public that they need. So, as summer approached, they elected to restock the shelves with the long slender machete. No one made jokes about it, nor any untoward comments. The tentative restocking of the machete was undertaken, and it was put on a shelf for all to see. However, the only caveat was that they would never put it on sale, therefore making it more financially accessible.

So, $19.95 it remained.

I couldn't help it. I was a moth to a flickering light. I would pick up the machete when I was sure there was no one close to watch. The media had ensured my face was known to all, so anonymity wasn't something I had any longer. I couldn't be just a young man looking at camping equipment. If anyone watched me and knew what had happened, they would wonder why in God's name I was handling the steel and wood weapon gently, caressing and intimate. I couldn't help but look down the length of the blade, seeing the small imperfections in the cheap manufacturing process, thinking of how to work the metal to eliminate those little grooves and pits. Those were easily overcome issues. The school library had numerous books on how to sharpen knives and axes. I was also sure that in dad's poorly equipped workshop, there would be dusty sharpening stone I could use. No, that part was easy.

The issue that I could foresee was how to have it somehow find its way home and ultimately into my hand.

For me the greatest challenge had become how to retrieve that sound.

ABOUT THE AUTHOR

Gerald Brent Fitzpatrick is a former news reporter, publisher and news anchor.
This is his first published manuscript.

Made in the USA
Las Vegas, NV
22 December 2024

15128893R00222